a novel

# played
## for · a · fool

# STEPHANIE BLACK

Covenant Communications, Inc.

Cover image: *Dark Corridor* © Nico_Blue, courtesy iStockphoto.com

Cover design copyright © 2015 by Covenant Communications, Inc.

Published by Covenant Communications, Inc.
American Fork, Utah

This is a work of fiction. The characters, names, incidents, places, and dialogue are either prod-
ucts of the author's imagination, and are not to be construed as real, or are used fictitiously.

Printed in the United States of America
First Printing: September 2015

21 20 19 18 17 16 15     10 9 8 7 6 5 4 3 2 1

ISBN 978-1-68047-650-7

# played
## for·a·fool

OTHER BOOKS AND AUDIO BOOKS
BY STEPHANIE BLACK

*The Believer*

*The Witnesses*

*Methods of Madness*

*Rearview Mirror*

*Cold As Ice*

*Shadowed*

*Twisted Fate*

*Fool Me Twice*

To Samantha Millburn

with immense gratitude for her unfailing encouragement,
kindness, skill, patience, and all the other gifts she offers.

Sam, you are a treasure.

# Acknowledgments

My TEST READERS ARE A wonderful help in showing me what is or isn't working in a story, and I appreciate all who donated their time to read this manuscript. Special thanks to Sue McConkie for the thorough and super-speedy evaluation she provided when I was running far behind and needed quick input; thanks also to Rebecca Hall, Dianna Hall, and Bonnie Overly. For answering my questions and providing information, thank you to Anne Barlow, Amy Black, Jared Black, and Shauna Rasband.

Many thanks to my editor, Samantha Millburn, and to all the people at Covenant who pour their tremendous skill, talent, and dedication into the process of publishing and promoting my books.

As always, thank you to my husband, Brian, for his constant support. Even as an author, I don't have enough words to describe what a great man he is.

# Chapter 1

"HELLO, KRIS." MEGAN O'CONNOR looked steadily into her twin sister's eyes, confident, rooted, with no nervous urge to shift her gaze to the table between them or to the correctional officer sitting at the podium or to Kristen's prison jumpsuit or to other inmates visiting with family members. After three years, Megan had pruned away the last of her vulnerability to Kristen's manipulation. She was ready to reach out on her own controlled terms.

"Meg." Kristen raised one eyebrow, evaluating Megan. Kristen wouldn't see her growth. She'd still see Megan as a knock-off of herself: same strawberry-blonde hair, same pale skin, same blue-topaz eyes, but cheap and breakable. The traitor who'd thwarted her plans three years ago and sent her to prison for life.

That was fine. Let Kristen despise her. Megan's peace of mind was no longer in Kristen's power.

"Letters, huh?" Kristen said. "I figured eventually you'd feel bad and start writing me. I'm surprised it took you a couple of years."

"I'm not writing because I feel bad. I'm writing because you're my sister and I thought you might be bored enough to enjoy mail."

"I was bored for two years before you started writing."

"It took me a couple of years to want to write." Megan muzzled the sarcastic addendum that a delay in getting mail from the sister Kristen had tried to murder didn't meet the criteria for valid complaints.

"I'm glad you got to it," Kristen said. "It *is* nice to get mail in here."

"Thanks for writing back." After six months of unanswered letters, Kristen had startled her by replying to a letter, saying she was willing to see Megan and explaining the process for requesting permission to visit. "I'm glad to have the chance to talk to you."

"Congrats on being brave enough to visit me. Bet you thought I'd be chained up and you'd be talking to me through glass."

"I'm glad that's not the case."

"Oh, I know how to manage. How to get more and more privileges. How to . . . charm people."

Knowing Kristen was needling her, Megan held eye contact and stayed silent. Around them, conversations continued. A visitor jingling a plastic baggie of quarters walked toward the vending machines.

"I've forgiven you," Megan said. "I decided it was time to tell you that, face-to-face."

Kristen's expression went so distant that *face-to-face* suddenly seemed like the wrong term. Face to . . . nothing. Flailing to connect with someone who wasn't there. Was Kristen thinking about that rain-drenched night and the sensation of driving a knife into Megan's side?

Megan glanced around the room. Several of the inmates, visitors, and prison staff were eyeballing Kristen and her. Had Kristen noticed? She loved attention in general but hated any attention that resulted from being an identical twin. She'd be exponentially irritated that the spectacle of one twin as a prisoner and one as a visitor had made them even more interesting to rubberneckers. Megan kept surveying the room until the only people watching were the correctional officers, which was fine. Monitoring inmates was their job.

She looked back at Kristen. "How are you doing?"

"How do you think I'm doing?"

"I don't know. I'd like to know. You look good. Healthy."

"I know how *you're* doing." Kristen pointed at the diamond engagement ring on Megan's left hand. "You're welcome."

"You're . . . welcome?"

Kristen's lips flicked into a cocky smile so familiar that Megan imagined her slipping a twenty-dollar bill across the table and whispering, "Give that Shakespeare presentation for me. C'mon. You could probably recite *Hamlet* from memory. It won't take you any work to prepare, and my teacher won't know you took my place. We won't get busted."

"Look what I gave you," Kristen said. "I plucked you out of Mom's clutches. I got you the college education you wanted. Now I'm getting you a rich husband."

"You're getting me these things?"

"Be honest. If I hadn't come for you three years ago, you'd still be trapped at home, working jobs you hate, paying for Mom's designer shoes, and chasing off your slimy ex-boyfriend. I rescued you."

"*Rescued?* Kris, you lured me out of Morris Glen with lies so you could use me in a kidnapping. That wasn't a rescue."

"It still worked out for you. You owe me gratitude."

Should she laugh or call for the prison psychiatrist? "You fooled me, manipulated me, and tried to kill me. So . . . thank you?"

"You're fine. No long-term damage. Don't you think a few scars and your current life are a lot better deal than no scars and life as Mom's pitiful slave? You'd never have met your honey if it weren't for me."

Megan leaned forward, elbows on the table, then pulled back, unable to remember the rules about getting closer to a prisoner. "Have you been taking classes in spin doctoring?"

"This isn't spin. It's fact."

"You introduced me to Trevor Drake by duping me into pretending to be you and hanging out with Trevor and his friends so you'd have an alibi while you kidnapped his sister. I'm deeply grateful for Trevor, but I'm not thanking you for scheming to kidnap Rachel and blackmailing and murdering—"

"It wasn't *my* scheme, babe. Old Auntie Evelyn was the one ticked off because Rachel and Trevor's daddy liked to use his BMW to mow down people riding bicycles."

"That's ugly. It wasn't his fault. Evelyn's daughter was drunk and swerved directly in—"

"Oh, I know. Three cheers for the innocent, noble philanthropist, but Evelyn still thought her daughter's death was a legit excuse for saving up a quarter century of psycho-ness and then dumping it on the rest of us. Listen, that crazy hag tricked me too. I didn't know she wanted revenge, and I didn't know she planned to set things up so we couldn't let Rachel go. I didn't think anyone would get hurt. I thought Evelyn just wanted money."

"You could have let Rachel go." Discussing this with Kristen felt surreal but satisfying, the first time they'd talked about what had happened. "You made the choice to try to kill her to keep yourself out of prison. And you could have turned Evelyn over to the police when she initially suggested her kidnapping scheme."

"Ooh, good thing you were innocent of stupidity and greed. When I came and offered you big money, you told me to take a hike, right?"

Embarrassment hit, but the squall passed before Megan could even speak. "I wish I had." She spoke calmly, her voice only as loud as it needed to be for Kristen to hear it. "I'm perfectly willing to admit I was a fool."

"World-class, Meggie." Kristen kept her voice low, like Megan's, but colored it with a melodramatic campfire-ghost-story quality. "Guess what? I discovered a long-lost great-aunt who's dying of cancer and will leave me her money if I take care of her until she dies, but I'm tired of her picky ways, so if you'll spell me and pretend you're me so she doesn't freak out and think I abandoned her and rip up her will, I'll share her fortune—"

"Is there something else you'd like me to admit besides that I was a fool for believing your lies?"

"—and make sure you always pretend you're me, especially with super-rich Rachel and Trevor Drake—be *very, very* careful not to break character around anyone, especially the Drakes, and by the way, Rachel is your best friend, and make sure you go to that religion class with the Drakes on this specific night for no reason, and when they take an isolated back road home and get ambushed by kidnappers in masks, make sure you don't notice that the kidnapper tying you to a tree is your sister—"

"Before you have too much fun mocking me, remember that I did eventually realize what you were up to," Megan said. "And I stopped you. And now you're serving a life sentence."

Rage blasted all mercy from Kristen's face, leaving only the wrath Megan had witnessed as the police had pulled Kristen to her feet on the dock at Britteridge Pond. Megan thought of herself soaked with rain, dizzy from blood loss, exhausted from the fight to disarm Kristen, looking into her face and whispering, "I'm sorry, Kris."

She wasn't tempted to apologize now. "There's nothing we can do about the past. Let's move forward."

Kristen's demeanor mellowed into a superb imitation of cordiality. "You've definitely moved forward."

"Thank you. I'm grateful to be doing well."

"Want to help me do better?"

Should she make a joke about Kristen asking her to smuggle in a chisel or bribe a guard? Bad idea. Making comments about escape— even if the staff wasn't likely to overhear them—was idiotic. "What do you mean?"

"Money would make things better in here," Kristen said.

"Money!"

"We don't even get enough necessities, let alone extras, unless we buy them at the commissary, and we earn almost nothing for the jobs we do. You could help me be a lot more comfortable. Higher quality toothpaste, shampoo, edible food, books . . . I'm sure you can relate to the desire for books." She smiled a teasing, sister-bonding smile. "You're sitting pretty, or will be soon. Share the windfall."

Megan was speechless. Had Kristen finally responded to her letters because Megan had mentioned she was engaged to Trevor, and Kristen wanted a cut?

"I honestly did get your life moving," Kristen said. "If I hadn't brought you to Massachusetts, you never would have met your dream hunk or gotten your dream education. Your smartie brain knows that.

Forget everything that went wrong and pay attention to what I gave you."

*Forget everything that went wrong. Like your murdering Gail Ludlum.* Had Kristen heard that Gail's son was getting out of prison? Megan had planned to tell her, but this wasn't an opportune moment.

"I'm talking about tiny amounts of money," Kristen said. "It's not like I can buy a car in here. A couple hundred a month."

"The fact that I've forgiven you doesn't mean I feel it's appropriate to help you financially," Megan said. "Today, you've mocked me, dismissed what you did to me as a 'few scars,' and twisted history to try to make me feel indebted to you. This isn't a good time to ask for money. We need a positive relationship first. A genuinely positive relationship, not you buttering me up when you want something."

"I do want a positive relationship. I wrote back. I invited you to visit. I'm grateful you forgive me. You wrecked everything for me, but I'm trying to forgive you too."

"Forgive me for saving Rachel's life?"

"I didn't want to hurt Rachel. You know that. And I'll bet Rachel's doing great, right?"

"Yes," Megan admitted. "But—"

"Did she start that wedding planner business she was always chattering about?"

"Yes, she's having fun with it."

"I'll bet she married some sweet guy who adores her, right?"

"Her husband's name is Peter Hawthorne, and yes, he's a nice guy. My point is—"

"Think about it, Meg. It's almost Christmas. Can't you spare a little Santa joy? If a couple hundred is too much before you get married, no problem. Any amount would help. You were so generous with Mom. She's not still hassling you, is she? I could get her off your back." Kristen grinned. "I'll send her a letter telling her to never ask you for another penny. She'll be so appalled at receiving paper that was once inside a prison that she'll do whatever I say just to keep me from writing again."

"She's not hassling me."

"Good to hear. And trust me, I'm not asking for anything like her ridiculous luxuries. I'm talking about cheap, basic things like batteries and a sweatshirt—"

"No, Kris. We're not at that point. Let's talk about something else."

Still smiling, Kristen stared at her, but her eyes weren't holding the humor like her lips were. She was waffling between persisting with humorous persuasion and giving up and freeing her anger.

"Do you want to talk about something else?" Megan asked. "Or was this the only reason you wanted a visit?"

Kristen ditched her failing smile. "You selfish twit. Good luck with your life. I give you a year into your marriage before it falls apart."

"That won't—"

"You can't deal with anything on your own, and you'll never be strong enough to be a Drake. You always need someone to drag you along. I got sick of that by the time we were teenagers, and Trevor will too. He's a stuffed shirt, but with his money and his Superman biceps, he could still attract a much better woman than you, a woman who can handle life."

"All right." Careful to keep her demeanor composed, Megan rose to her feet. "Thanks for the closure. I won't be back, and I won't be writing."

"Oh no. I'm going to cry. Since you're not writing, do me one favor and find someone else who can update me when your life disintegrates. No worries, Mom will keep your bedroom ready for you."

"Good luck, Kris. You're still in my prayers."

"Get me out of them, then. Wimpy, annoying place to be."

After passing stoically through the process of exiting the prison, Megan sat in her car in the parking lot and watched occasional snowflakes waft from the December sky.

Facing Kristen after three years. Facing her for what seemed to be the last time. *Had* the visit been worth anything for closure? It hadn't felt like closure.

It had felt like jabbing at a wound she thought had healed and finding it was still raw, tender flesh she should have left alone.

# Chapter 2

Noah Sahlberg lifted a bottle of carbonated apple cider off the grocery store shelf and checked the label to verify that it didn't contain alcohol. Booze was the last thing—*almost* the last thing—he wanted to offer Bryce as a welcome-home-from-prison gift. The last thing he wanted to offer was friendship, but to honor Aunt Gail's memory, he'd give his cousin one hour. That was all.

Gripping the bottle, Noah made himself motionless, emotionless, impervious. He was Kalt, Gail's cast-iron, German shepherd statue—chilly, hard, dignified. He wouldn't kick Bryce with accusations that he'd caused his own mother's death. He wouldn't tell Bryce the thought of him spreading his ex-con grime all over her house made Noah sick. He wouldn't say he'd been a much better son to Gail Ludlum than Bryce had been, not that it needed to be said. That reality was so obvious that even drug-fried Bryce couldn't miss it.

The cider was cheap. Gail would expect him to offer more than that. Did the store have any type of gift basket or maybe boxes of dried fruits or nuts left over from the holidays?

He pushed his body into motion, taking heavy steps. He wished he could ignore Bryce's return, but every time he told himself he'd avoid his cousin, he heard Gail scolding him. *You're his closest family, and you can't even say hi? Kiddo, I'm ordering an MRI to find out what's beating in your chest in place of a heart. Don't you know how lonely he feels?*

Bryce *ought* to feel lonely. Why had he come back to Britteridge? If Noah had done things as horrible as Bryce had, he'd have never returned to where everyone knew and gossiped about him.

Horrible things. Nightmare things.

His legs stopped. His joints shook. What if there was a possibility—an infinitesimal possibility—that everything *had* been a nightmare, only imagination? Or that it *was* real but Noah had backpedaled through time and would have a second chance? He could go again to dinner on that Sunday in September three years ago. This time when Aunt Gail gave only absentminded thanks for the chrysanthemums he'd brought her and got cranky when she burned the rolls instead of laughing it off with an *I guess it's store-bought bread with our soup tonight*, he'd know these were serious warning signs. This time when he asked if anything was wrong and she said no, he wouldn't let it go; he'd press until she admitted she was being blackmailed. This time he'd go to the police and avert the kidnapping and save Gail's life. He could go to her house tonight and she'd swing the front door open, wrap her arm around him, and propel him into the kitchen to devour a piece of apricot crumb cake.

*Idiot.* It was insanity imagining he could rub the rust off his guard-dog eyes, remove the dents from the iron, polish his metal teeth, and stand sentinel so a killer wouldn't pass through Gail's door. Useless to think about it. Too late.

*Finish and get out of here.* Where would the store keep gift baskets? Produce? He didn't know this store; he didn't usually shop in Britteridge.

In the produce section, he found bins of shelled and unshelled nuts and small plastic tubs of candy but nothing with a bow on it. He picked up a container of chocolate-covered blueberries. Would this be good? No. Gail would want him to give a gift dressed like a gift, not something decorated with only a barcode.

He set the blueberries on the shelf and trudged past the bulk-foods area. A woman was pushing an empty cart in his direction, so he stepped to the side to give her more room to pass between him and the citrus display.

She smiled. "Thank you."

"Not a problem."

Her smile—superficially polite but still a smile—made him a little glad he'd wasted a couple of minutes hunting for gifts in the wrong area of the store. Had he met her before? Reddish-gold hair, light-blue eyes. Her knit hat was garish, too neon-green for anything besides flashing *Open* signs, but her face made him wish she hadn't already broken eye contact. Did he know her?

In his head, iron crashed into iron, clanging and cold. Impossible. She was in prison.

Her sister wasn't.

No. The twin wouldn't be here either. She'd have slithered away from Massachusetts to con new victims.

Noah walked past the woman, relieved she was focused on putting lemons in a bag and hadn't noticed his gawking. Bryce's return must have triggered old circuits in his brain, tricking him into thinking a strange woman was an O'Connor twin.

The floral section caught his attention; they'd sell gifts there. He wanted to hurry, but steeling his muscles so they wouldn't shake meant rigid limbs. He couldn't hurry, or he'd stagger.

She *had* looked like an O'Connor.

*You've lost your mind.* He grabbed a red-wrapped box from a shelf near pots of violets and checked the back label. Candied walnuts. The bottle of cider in his left hand struck something; the item clonked against the floor. He didn't know how his arm had twitched or what he'd knocked over; he didn't look.

Self-checkout lane. Out of the store. In the parking lot, his leather loafers skidded on a patch of ice. Arms noodling frantically, he regained his balance.

*Get to Bryce's. Get it over with.*

She'd really looked like Gail's murderer.

\* \* \*

Peeking between curtain panels, Bryce Ludlum watched the car's headlights switch on. Yeah, heirloom lace curtains were lousy camouflage, but his mother's study was dark, so he doubted Jessica could see him. He hoped she was assuming, despite the lights in the living room, that he wasn't home. Not that he'd glanced out the living room window, seen her car, and fled to the study so he could spy on her without confronting her.

Good thing the part of him that ached to open the front door had lost the vote. Lost it by about 0.5 percent.

Her car reversed out of the driveway, and Bryce spent a few seconds flouting his goal to quit swearing. The girl who'd played a big role in introducing him to drugs was not someone he could let into his post-prison life no matter how hot she was. Not if he wanted to stay clean. Not if he wanted to be a decent guy with a decent life, someone his mother could be proud of. He'd been stupid to let Jessica over the threshold when she'd stopped by last week.

What had she been carrying when she'd walked up to the house? A plate of treats? Cookies sounded good, but he wasn't hungry enough to risk opening the door until he was sure she'd left the neighborhood.

He pulled his phone out of his pocket and checked the time. Seven fifty-six. He'd have to open the door in four minutes anyway; Noah would be exactly on time.

Pretty defiant of Noah to visit a loser, a recovering addict, a felon involved in Britteridge's most infamous crime. If Noah's dad found out, his ranting would singe Noah's trimmed-every-three-weeks hair and roast his button-down shirt. Or had Noah finally told his father to shove off and try his tyrant act on the fish at the bottom of Boston Harbor?

Nah. Noah wouldn't do that. He felt obligated to Gail, so he'd risk one visit with his bozo cousin and hope his dad didn't find out. Then he'd retreat and hope again that everyone would forget he was related to a criminal.

Man, this house was quiet. Deep, dead quiet.

Bryce walked into the living room. It was clean—always clean; no way could he scorn his mother's memory by leaving Coke cans on the Hepplewhite end table, slopping guacamole on the french empire sofa, or spilling brownie crumbs between the keys of the upright player piano from nineteen-o-something. Bryce hadn't cared about his mother's antiques until he'd trashed his life to the point that he'd started researching how much they were worth so he could steal and sell them. Dumb plan. His mother had already secured small, valuable things like jewelry and first-edition books in a safe deposit box, and he'd been too whacked-out to figure out how to fence stained-glass lamps, mismatched Victorian chairs, or a Viennese enamel mantel clock.

The hands on the mantel clock pointed to the wrong time. He'd forgotten to wind it. He slid his tongue deep between his gums and his lips, trying to dampen his dry mouth.

The doorbell rang, and he looked at his phone. Either Jessica had returned, or Noah was two minutes early. He crept toward the front door, his sock-clad feet silent on the hardwood, and glanced through the peephole. Noah. He was safe. Safe-ish. At least Noah wasn't Jessica. And he was family. And company. Bryce opened the door.

"Good evening, Bryce." Noah held a glass bottle and a wrapped box and stood weirdly back from the door. He was probably scared that prison had transformed Bryce from apprentice demon to full-fledged steal-your-soul-on-contact demon. Valid worry. Prison didn't specialize in love-your-neighbor stuff.

"Hey," Bryce said. "Come in. Man, how cold is it out there?"

"Seventeen degrees. Someone left you cookies." Noah tipped his head toward the right side of the rope doormat.

"Thanks." Bryce stepped outside and picked up the plate. On top of the plastic wrap was a sticky note—*Sorry I missed you! Jessica.*

"Come in," Bryce repeated, backing through the doorway to get out of the January cold.

Noah edged forward, wiped his shoes on the doormat, then stepped inside.

Bryce shut the door. "Uh, thanks for coming."

"How are you doing?" Noah set the bottle and box on the hall table.

"Good." Bryce wanted to open the gift—he hadn't received any kind of present for three years, and the red wrapping paper made him little-kid antsy—but it wasn't good manners to rip it open without Noah's invitation. *Manners.* Uh . . . what was he supposed to do? *Coat. Take his coat. Offer him something to drink.* Bryce set the plate of cookies next to the wrapped box. "Can I—may I take your coat?" *Wow, grammar points. You're the man.*

"Thank you." Noah tucked his gloves in his pockets and removed his coat.

Did Noah look different? He still had a chin so clean he must shave twice a day and no wrinkles in his business-casual clothes, but he looked like he'd skipped the rest of his twenties, cancelled his thirties, and preordered his forties. Three years wasn't time for much real aging; he must just be tired. Or maybe he'd lost weight? Or been sick? Or spent the last three years locked in a cell getting prison pallor? *Good one. Maybe he got locked up for breaking federal law by scrubbing the inside of his neighbors' mailboxes and alphabetizing their junk mail.*

Bryce hung Noah's coat in the closet. "How's your life? Going good?"

No answer. Bryce shut the closet and eyed his cousin. Noah was staring at the cast-iron dog that had sat near the front door all Bryce's life. "Hey, I'll bet Kalt's missed you," Bryce said. "Old friend." As a kid, Noah had squeezed or patted the German shepherd statue every time he'd walked in or out of the Ludlums' house. Until his father had seen him do it. "You're still petting toy doggies? Do you suck your thumb too? You're twelve! Act your age!"

Noah brushed his palm across the statue's head. "You . . . uh . . . those cookies. Is that Jessica Barnett?"

"Yeah, but no worries. I'm not getting back with her."

"She's in Britteridge? I thought she moved to California."

"She was in LA for a few years. Just moved back to Massachusetts. She's in Lowell."

Noah stroked a knuckle up and down Kalt's iron ear. "Why'd she leave LA?"

"Ran out of money. Too hard to find good gigs. Her stepdad owns some junky apartments in Lowell and gives her a break on rent, so she can live here cheap while she decides what to do next."

"Why do you know so much about her if you're not dating her?"

"Will you quit with the judgy stare? She stopped by last week to say hi. We talked a little, but I wouldn't even give her my phone number. She tried to give me hers, and I said I wouldn't need it."

"If she's bringing you cookies, she didn't get the message."

"Trying a different tack, I guess. She's stubborn. I think she's after money."

"Your parents' money."

Not his parents' money anymore, but Noah must be hinting that he didn't think either Jessica or Bryce ought to have any of Gail and Charlie's wealth. *Bryce with money equals disaster.*

Noah ran his thumb along Kalt's jaw. "Did she ask for cash?"

"Not outright. She kept griping about how tight money is, how she works crazy morning hours at that donut shop. You remember that place in Lowell, how Mom used to go all the way out there to get those apple donuts with the caramel stuff on them, and you'd get all excited and say donuts gave you magic powers, but you'd only eat them with a fork because they were so sticky—"

"Yes," Noah said curtly.

"Anyway, she has to be to work at three or four a.m. or something. Crazy. She kept talking about how if she had some cash, she could move to . . . New York, I think? Wants to try her luck in another big music and theater place. Maybe you could pay her to wash your Lamborghini since you're such a successful, responsible guy."

"I don't drive a Lamborghini. The only thing I'd hire her for would be if I wanted to *steal* a Lamborghini."

Bryce grinned. "I'll bet she could do it. Hey, remember when she picked the lock on Mrs. Donelley's room, broke into her desk, and swiped that biology final?"

"Yes."

"Switched it for the test she'd written, except left the first page so Mrs. D. wouldn't notice. 'Show with diagrams what would happen to your body if your mitochondria sneaked beer into your nuclei, got smashed, and started singing a karaoke version of "Stayin' Alive."'"

Bryce laughed.

Noah didn't react. He looked about as alive as Kalt did.

"I'm *not* getting back with her," Bryce repeated. "I'm not completely brain dead. But at least she welcomed me home. Not many people are bringing me cookies. Come sit down. Do you want something to drink? Ginger ale, Coke, water, orange juice?"

Noah shook his head. Bryce picked up the cookies—ready-made dessert if Noah decided he wanted something to eat—and walked into the living room. He set the cookies on a lamp table and flopped into a green velvet chair that probably had a scrap of lettuce down the side of the cushion from Louis the Sixteenth's or Seventeenth's or Whateverteenth's lunch.

Noah inched into the room, inched past Bryce, past the couch, past the player piano. With his back toward Bryce, he stopped in front of the glass case filled with Gail's dog figurines.

Tempted to comment on how Noah as a kid had been obsessed with the dozens of dogs and puppies in Gail's collection, Bryce observed Noah's dead-still posture and kept his mouth closed.

Was this the first time Noah had been in this house since Gail's murder? Yeah, it must be. To get into the house while Bryce was in prison, Noah would've had to call Bryce's lawyer, and Noah wouldn't have wanted to deal with that. Had Noah wanted to come here, hang out in the place where he'd gotten more love at one dinner than he'd gotten in his entire childhood from his father?

Bryce's gaze collapsed to the Persian rug. Crazy how he'd been so glad at the thought of seeing family that, for a few hours, he'd ignored the friction inside him as his heart beat against the always-present grit of smoke, toxic chemicals, and mistakes.

"Hey . . . Noah . . . this . . . I know it's gotta be tough for you here. If you . . . want to leave, it's cool."

"I'm fine." Noah crossed the room and sat on the couch.

Bryce reached underneath the cookie plate and picked at the tape holding the plastic wrap. What should he say? Nothing about his mother. "I . . . started a job a couple of days ago. Grounds crew at—"

"Is this a transitional thing your lawyer set up? Part of your parole?"

"I'm not on parole. You didn't know that? I'm done."

"They wouldn't let you out on parole?"

"I didn't *want* it. I wanted to finish my sentence and be done, not have parole officers and cops pestering me. I did my time, and I'm starting over, clean."

Noah tapped his fingers on the carved mahogany arm of the couch and looked toward the picture of Bryce and his parents, which hung over the mantel.

Okay, he wasn't interested in an ex-felon's job blowing snow off sidewalks and clearing parking lots. Bryce removed the plastic wrap from the plate and wadded it up, his lungs chafing against his dirty soul each time he breathed. *Start over clean? What's clean about you?*

He'd ask about Noah's job. That would work better for conversation. "So are you still with that insurance company in Copley Square—"

"I was at the grocery store this evening," Noah interrupted, eyes still focused on the portrait. "I saw a woman there who resembled an O'Connor twin. I . . . assume it was coincidence, some random woman."

"Or it was Megan O'Connor. Definitely wasn't Kristen. She's got thirty years before they'll even think about paroling her."

Noah turned toward Bryce. His expression was sheet metal bolted over the crater of an active volcano. "Why would that girl be in Britteridge?"

"She lives here. Didn't you know that?"

"Lives *here?*"

"Yeah, you didn't know she stayed?" Bryce poked one of the cookies. Chocolate melted onto his fingertip. "She's been going to Britt."

"*What?* How did she get in there?"

He should try to soothe Noah by being calm and rational, but talking about Megan while Noah glared at him was raising blisters inside. "How'd you miss all this?"

"How would I know it?"

"Rumors? People talk about stuff like this. Might have gotten mentioned in the paper back when everything happened. I don't know; I haven't been here in three years, right? I thought it was common knowledge."

"I don't gossip with stupid people or read tabloid articles about subhuman murderers—"

"You know it was Kristen who killed my mother, right? Not Megan."

"Megan was involved."

"She got tricked."

"So you *defend* her? If she hadn't been involved, the kidnapping would have fallen apart . . . maybe never would have happened. Your mother would be *alive*."

Bryce averted his gaze and placed one sock-covered foot on top of the other. He switched the position of his feet, then switched back, focusing on the fidgety motion instead of his desire to punch his cousin. "I'm not defending her."

"She should have gone to prison with her sister."

"That wasn't up to me."

"The Drakes should have made sure she went to prison."

"Since when was it their decision?"

"You know the prosecutor would have found *something* to pin on her if big-shot gazillionaire Michael Drake had pushed for it."

"She saved his daughter's life."

"She was part of the reason his daughter nearly got killed in the first place. Why did she stay here after the kidnapping? People must hate her!"

"They don't. I haven't heard anyone say anything bad about her. And she stayed for school. I told you she's at Britt. President Drake paid for her education."

"*What?* You're messing with me."

"Seriously? You think this is a comedy routine? Catch up, Noah. Yeah, Megan's in Britteridge. Yeah, the Drakes paid for her education. Sorry to catch you by surprise. I didn't know you've been living in a cave of paper clips and business letterhead and have never seen the sun."

Noah didn't react. Good. Let him sit there wordlessly until he was old enough to qualify as an antique. Bryce could add him to the collection: *Statue of Scowling Man, Cast-Iron, Early Twenty-First Century.* He picked up a cookie and wondered if he could muster enough appetite to eat it when what he truly craved was everything that had wrecked his judgment, crushed his life, and killed his mother.

Noah finally spoke. "How big of a sucker *is* Michael Drake?"

"Not as big of a sucker as his son," Bryce said. "Trevor Drake and Megan are engaged."

"*You—*"

"I'm not messing around. They're getting married for real. Go ask someone else if you think I'm too filthy to tell the truth."

Noah jumped to his feet. "She's marrying Trevor Drake?"

Bryce nodded.

"The Drakes are all insane!"

"Not my circus, not my monkeys."

Noah's neck and jaw flushed scarlet. "He lets her into his school for free, and now she's marrying his son? Marrying a fortune? *That's* what she gets for helping set up the scheme to kidnap his daughter?"

If Noah wanted to yell, Bryce was on board with that. Bryce let his voice rise. "She didn't *know.*"

"She's an idiot. She's not innocent."

"What do you want? I can't control what the Drakes do."

"That girl needs to pay. You don't see that? You're okay that she helped kill your mom, and instead of going to prison, she wins—"

"It's not up to me."

"You can't even honor your mother's memory enough to care that Megan O'Connor is unpunished *and* hitting the jackpot?"

"I can't change that. Go shout at the Drakes."

"Does she think everyone's forgotten what she did and she'll never have to pay for it?"

"I don't know. I'll ask her on Friday. Trevor invited me to dinner, so I get to meet her."

"You selfish *bozo*." Noah stomped toward the hallway.

Bryce stayed slouched on the couch, staring at Gail's dog figurines as Noah grabbed his coat from the closet, stalked out of the house, and crashed the front door closed.

"Sorry," Bryce muttered.

# Chapter 3

MEGAN OPENED THE OVEN DOOR a couple of inches and scrutinized the lasagna. Sauce bubbled around the edges. The parmesan cheese on top appeared deliciously browned and the air had the tomato-garlic-sausage aroma she'd enjoyed whenever Rachel had cooked lasagna. She hoped it would taste right. Rachel and Trevor's grandmother had given the recipe to Rachel, and the vague instructions weren't aimed toward a rookie cook. "Chop a little fresh basil"—how many leaves was a "little"? "Salt to taste"—did that mean a sprinkle or a teaspoon? "Cook until done"—tricky to plan dinnertime around. Megan had had to text Rachel several times to ask for clarification.

She put on oven mitts and lifted the heavy pan from the rack.

Trevor stood at the island in his condo kitchen, slicing the baguettes he'd baked. "Smells better than Grandma's lasagna, Meg."

"Not possible." Megan made herself smile as she set the lasagna on the stovetop. She would not let on how rattled she felt about hosting Bryce Ludlum. When Trevor had suggested inviting Bryce to dinner, she'd pretended she thought it was a wonderful idea. It *was* a wonderful idea. Reaching out to him was the right thing to do, and she was determined to be friendly and gracious.

Secretly she wished she could avoid him forever. When she'd visited Kristen, she'd felt confident she was ready, but a month later, their debacle of a meeting was still agitating old nightmares and creating new ones. She felt no confidence that she was ready to face Bryce. How would this meeting turn out?

*You can handle this.* She wouldn't dwell on the fact that whenever Bryce looked at her, he'd be seeing the face of the woman who had blackmailed and killed his mother. She should have dyed her hair black and cut it short or worn glasses she didn't need or done anything to make herself look different from Kristen.

*You are not responsible for Kristen's crimes. Besides, changing your appearance doesn't change your mistakes. He can despise you just as much for what you did as he can Kristen for what she did.*

*Just as much? Kristen murdered his mother.*

*But if you hadn't been so clueless, you could have stopped her.*

Annoyed that instead of reassuring herself she was augmenting her stress, Megan mentally hunted for a new focus. *Stop thinking about yourself. Bryce has his own regrets; stop obsessing and assuming you're the center of his thoughts.*

*Stop thinking about yourself.* That included *not* ruminating about the letter she'd received this afternoon. She'd gotten hate mail right after Rachel's kidnapping; she thought she'd learned to cope with it, but it had been a long time since a vicious letter had arrived with the credit card offers and grocery store ads. Could she cope with it now? The letter, combined with her apprehension about meeting Gail Ludlum's son, had snapped a few twigs and a few branches off the strength and peace she'd spent the past three years nurturing.

At least she knew the letter wasn't from Kristen. All mail sent to or from the prison got checked, and Kristen wouldn't send anonymous insulting letters anyway. That tactic was too remote and far too passive for her.

*You'll be fine. After tonight, you can resume stressing about homework and battling Rachel's attempts to make your wedding reception an epic extravaganza.*

The letter would infuriate Trevor. She planned to tell him but hadn't felt like bringing it up while they were preparing dinner. Why hurry to show him a letter stained with insults and accusations?

*Do you think you can stick your bloodstained claws into the Drakes' money? Do you think Trevor can forget what a lying, greedy cheat you are? You won't be able to trick him for long. You should be locked up with your murderer sister, you grimy, wicked—*

"Thanks for all your help." Trevor arranged the bread on a stoneware platter. "I didn't mean to sign you up to cook for this."

"I'm happy to do it," Megan said. "I need the practice. A good change from my canned-soup-and-frozen-pizza college cuisine." What she truly needed to practice was emulating Trevor's charitable spirit. Instead of shunning Bryce for the drug use and thievery that had allowed Kristen to blackmail his mother, Trevor wanted to help him. Instead of despising Megan for the naïveté and neediness that had allowed Kristen to trick her, he'd forgiven her. Befriended her.

Fallen in love with her.

*Do you think Trevor can forget what a lying, greedy cheat you are? You won't be able to trick him . . .*

The peace inside Megan started shaking again, branches wobbling, leaves scattering. Marriage to the most amazing man she'd ever known—marriage for eternity, a love that grew forever stronger. Would it happen? What if Trevor changed his mind?

Trevor smiled at her, his autumn-brown eyes tender. "Megan . . . I appreciate your support on this. I know it's tough."

"It's not easy for you either." She grabbed the trivet off the counter and set it on the table, ready for the lasagna. "And it must be tough on Bryce."

"Yeah. Not easy for anyone. But good for all of us, I hope."

With no dinner prep left, Megan tried to think of another way to look busy. She opened the fridge. Her back to Trevor, she drew a huge, silent breath. While adjusting the box containing a blackberry pie, she pushed the air out of her lungs in tiny spurts, relaxing with each breath. *Trevor loves you. You know that.* She shut the fridge.

Trevor walked up behind her and curled his arms around her waist. "You okay?"

*Not okay at pretending I'm okay, I guess.* She leaned her head against his muscled shoulder. Trevor dealt with stress through weight training, and from the number of times in the past weeks that he'd mentioned heading for the gym, he was more stressed than usual. About Bryce's return? About work?

About their engagement?

"The ice cream is sitting in the bed of my truck," he said.

"Oops. At least it won't melt out there. I can run and get it."

"I left it there on purpose. During dinner, if you ever feel like you need a break, just say, 'Trev, did you get the ice cream for the pie?' *Then* you can volunteer to go get it and take all the time you want."

"You honestly left it out there to give me an excuse?"

"Yep." Trevor kissed her head. "If you need a break, take it. If we both need a break, I'll race you to the truck."

Megan laughed.

Trevor kissed her ear. "Will you let me win?" The doorbell rang. Trevor released her. "I love you," he said.

"I love you too."

Trevor headed for the door. Megan transferred the lasagna to the table and took the chilled pitcher of mint lemonade from the fridge. It was one of Gail Ludlum's recipes, something Trevor had drunk at her house as a kid. Megan hoped the taste would evoke happy memories for Bryce, not pain and guilt. Maybe she should have objected to the lemonade and suggested they choose a drink Bryce wouldn't associate with—

*Stop second-guessing everything. Calm down.*

She set the lemonade on the table and went to greet their guest. Bryce was lean and nearly as tall as Trevor, with a cleft in his chin and dark-brown hair cut very short. Sunburn reddened his nose and cheeks, probably from his work on the grounds crew at Britteridge College. He didn't look anything like his mother, with her messy blonde curls and round face.

"Bryce, this is Megan," Trevor said. "Megan, Bryce."

Hoping her face wasn't too nervous-pink, Megan smiled. Even though this was the first time she'd met Bryce in person, she felt odd at being introduced by name as though he didn't know who she was. But what would have felt less weird? *You two already know all about each other's train wrecks, so let's eat?* "It's good to meet you." She offered her hand.

Bryce gripped it and smiled back. "Congratulations. Great news about you and Trevor."

"Thank you," she said, relieved at his friendliness. "Let me hang up your coat." She took the jacket Trevor had already taken from Bryce and hung it in the closet next to her new leather coat. Every time she saw that leather coat—even now—it made her a fraction more cheery. It was the most gorgeous coat she'd ever owned. *Bargain hunting for the win.*

They sat at the table. "This looks great," Bryce said. "Haven't had homemade lasagna in ages."

"Megan made it," Trevor said. "My grandmother's recipe."

"Oh, nice. Hey, mint lemonade! In January, even!"

Trevor offered a blessing on the food. Bryce's comfortable *amen* surprised Megan; Trevor had told her Bryce wasn't religious. After his family's longtime friendship with Trevor's family, he was apparently at ease with the Drakes' ways.

Megan took a bite of lasagna. It tasted like the lasagna Rachel made. Thank goodness. Maybe the tough part of the evening was over—she hadn't wrecked the food; she'd met Bryce, and he was friendly. They should invite him over again, and she could try out her mother's chicken fajita recipe.

"This is delicious, Meg," Trevor said.

Bryce's piece was already mostly gone. "Seriously the best food I've had since I got home."

"Thank you," Megan said.

Bryce swallowed the last of his mint lemonade. "I love this stuff. Makes it seem like summer."

Grateful the lemonade had been a good choice, Megan refilled his glass. "You may need a barrel of it to keep things summery. There's a cold snap coming. It's supposed to get below zero."

Bryce helped himself to a second piece of lasagna. "I better find my thermal underwear. Or hurry and get a desk job. In Florida."

"Trevor's heading to San Diego next month," Megan said. "He tells me he'll take pictures of himself on the beach and send them to me so I can be vicariously warm."

"Nice guy. Why isn't he taking you?"

"It's business," Trevor said. "I invited Megan, but she doesn't want to miss any classes."

Bryce rolled his eyes at Megan. "So you're crazy."

Megan smiled. "It's an intense semester. I'd rather not flunk out, even for seventy-degree weather."

"A friend of mine is endowing a scholarship at Britt," Trevor said. "He's announcing it at a West Coast alumni conference, and he's invited me to speak and accept the endowment."

"He can't mail the check and save you a cross-country trip?"

"It's a significant amount of money." Trevor reached for the butter. "It would be polite to go shake his hand. It's not the best time for me to leave—I don't usually travel once admissions crunch time hits, but it'll work out."

"Rich friends, huh?"

"Tech start-up that went big and got acquired by a company with deep pockets. He came to Britt on a needs-based scholarship and wants to pay it forward to other kids interested in engineering."

"So he's the first rich guy in the family line." Bryce grinned at Trevor. "Sounds like a pain, having to succeed on your own."

Megan assumed Bryce was ribbing Trevor *and* himself, but Trevor's smile was a mediocre forgery; he didn't think Bryce's crack was funny.

"Trevor works at Britt because he's as dedicated to its mission as his father is, and he loves his work," she said. "Not because his dad was the only person who'd hire him."

"Just kidding around," Bryce said.

Trevor served himself another piece of lasagna. "How are things going for you?"

"Good, pretty much." Bryce squirted ranch dressing onto his salad. "Trying to keep busy. I . . . need to go through Mom's stuff at some point."

"That's not easy." Megan thought of sorting through her father's belongings and deciding what to throw away, what to keep as mementos, and what to donate to charity. She'd inherited the job when her mother had claimed to be too grief-stricken to cope with it. Megan had believed her until she'd learned her mother was digging into the boxes after Megan was in bed, rearranging things, and undoing most of Megan's painstaking work.

"It must be rough living at the house," Trevor said. "You sure you don't want to go somewhere else? The Mullinses have some vacancies in their rentals."

"Thanks, but I'll stay there for now. It's kinda good, actually. Feels like Mom, right?"

Trevor nodded. "True."

"It's a beautiful home," Megan said and realized she couldn't remember if the house *was* beautiful or how it looked at all. All she remembered was Gail on the hallway floor, blood spreading from her crushed skull. At least it hadn't been Bryce who'd found her. He'd been in Georgia at the time.

"Your mother was an incredible lady," Trevor said.

Megan took a bite of bread but had to add a sip of lemonade so her dry tongue could manage the food. Trevor spoke sincerely, but she didn't know how Bryce would react. Yes, Gail had been an incredible lady, but she'd also been so desperate to protect her son from prison that she'd buckled to blackmail and assisted Rachel's kidnappers.

"She loved your family." Gaze on his plate, Bryce stabbed a slice of cucumber with his fork. "I know it must have been torture for her . . . I wish she'd gone to the police . . . let me pay for the stupid things I did . . ."

"Terrible dilemma for her," Trevor said. "Kristen had convinced her you'd get locked up for life."

"Yeah . . . even *I* thought I'd killed that geezer."

Megan took another sip of lemonade. She couldn't believe the conversation had grown this candid this quickly, but she couldn't see a courteous way to change the subject. It would be ridiculous to ask Bryce about his job or movies he'd seen or babble about the new tires on Trevor's old truck while the elephant in the room squashed them against the walls. Better to be as frank as Bryce and Trevor. "You weren't the only person who did stupid things," Megan said.

Bryce's gaze swung toward her and struck harder than she'd expected. She tensed; his gaze swung to the side, back to her, to the side again. Was he wondering if she'd genuinely been dense enough to believe Kristen's lies when she'd lured Megan to Britteridge? "You stayed here after everything," he said. "Was it hard?"

Megan relaxed a little. "Yes and no. At first, I did feel notorious. Strangers would stare at me or ask questions, or say . . . painful things. But I had a lot of support as well. The Drakes have been amazing, my friends, church—"

"You joined Trevor's church, didn't you?"

"Yes, but I didn't join it *for* him, to make that clear. We didn't even start dating until over a year after I joined."

"Good for you." Bryce took another piece of bread. "He used to try to convert me, but I'm not a fan of five hours of church on Sunday."

"Three hours," Megan corrected.

"Yeah, three hours, plus all those extra meetings. I've watched you Mormons; I know how it works. You start with three hours. Then they put you in charge of something and it's five or eight hours plus weeknights."

Megan laughed and returned to Bryce's question. "Things *did* get better for me, living here. People are busy with their own lives; you don't stay the focus of attention. They even get bored of making tasteless jokes, thank heavens."

"Jokes?"

"Like 'How can we be sure you're Megan? Maybe you're Kristen escaped from prison!'"

"Cringe," Bryce said.

"Yes, it was awkward. But I love it here. I love New England. I love Massachusetts. I love Britteridge. This is the place where . . . where I finally moved on after stalling out at home."

"You're from Pennsylvania, right?"

"Yes, a small town called Morris Glen."

Trevor served himself a third piece of lasagna. "Has anyone given you a hard time since you got back, Bryce?"

"Ah . . . not too bad. Suspicious looks and silence, pretty much. No death threats or hate mail."

"You'll probably get garbage like that at some point," Trevor said. "There are a few trolls under the bridge."

Bryce looked at Megan. "Did you get stuff like that?"

"I . . . did get some hate mail." Megan used the salad tongs to pick a couple of lettuce leaves out of the bowl, even though she still had half a serving of salad on her plate. "Most of it stopped within . . . not too many months."

"So people treat you like a regular person now?"

"Mostly." Megan wished she'd told Trevor about the letter earlier. She didn't want to mention it now but felt deceitful giving cloudy answers when Bryce was asking direct questions. He sincerely wanted input on what to expect.

Trevor put down the butter knife. "Has anything happened recently?"

Her reddening face had apparently started confessing for her. "Just one letter," she said. "Not a big deal."

"Meg?" Trevor touched her hand. "When did you get it? What did it say?"

"Just . . . regular insults. No threats." Megan wove her fingers with his. "I got it this afternoon."

"Why didn't you tell me?"

"I was . . . going to tell you later."

Trevor nudged the ring on Megan's finger, centering the diamond. "Must be hate mail season. I got one too."

"You got a letter?" *Oh no.* Had the same person written to Trevor, repeating the same vicious insults about her?

No. Trevor wore a wry smile; that wasn't how he'd react to insults about her. "It happens when you work in admissions," he said. "A mother ranting about how I'd clearly become associate director via nepotism since I must be a blockhead with no qualifications or I wouldn't have refused to guarantee her child prodigy a place next fall."

"But acceptance letters haven't even gone out yet," Megan said, grateful for Trevor's detouring of the conversation to his work issues.

He'd recognized that she didn't want to give details about her letter in front of Bryce.

"Her genius son needs to make plans *now*." Trevor released Megan's hand. "He shouldn't have to slog through the applications process like the peasants."

In her peripheral vision, Megan noticed Bryce staring at her, not Trevor. "You got hate mail today?" he said, plainly addressing Megan. "About Rachel's kidnapping and . . . the rest of it?"

So much for shifting the focus of the conversation. "Someone just doesn't think I'm worth much. They . . . don't think Trevor should marry me."

"Oh. So jealousy. Not about the past?"

"Well . . . the writer made it clear that the past is why they think I'm a . . . tramp who doesn't deserve anything good."

Bryce toyed with his glass, tipping it so a mint leaf stuck to the inside, then swishing the remaining lemonade to wash the leaf free. "You did snag a lot of good out of this. No prison time, free college tuition, and now the kidnap victim's rich brother asks you to marry him. Commit more crimes and you'll get elected governor. People will name babies and cities after you."

Did Bryce agree with the hostile letter writer, or was he trying to joke? She thought of Kristen's faux-humorous gibe: "You're welcome."

"I'm not rich," Trevor said coolly. "That's my parents. And Megan never intended to commit a crime."

"Come on." The flicker of humor in Bryce's tone went dark. "She showed up three years ago pretending to be her sister—"

"She had no idea—"

"Yeah, she didn't know Kristen wanted her here as an alibi during a kidnapping, but she knew she was here to lie and swindle an old woman out of an inheritance."

Megan tried to keep her voice steady. "It was a foolish, selfish choice."

"The elderly aunt she was supposedly defrauding was the mastermind behind the whole scheme." Trevor sat straight in his chair, his shoulders squared. "Once Megan realized the truth, she nearly got killed saving Rachel's life."

"I know that." Bryce smashed a piece of sausage with his fork. "Sorry. I wasn't trying to insult her."

"I'm not insulted," Megan said. "I did come here hoping to get money. I did lie to everyone. I regret my mistakes."

Bryce kept poking at the sausage. After a moment of raw silence, he said, "Must be a strain, working to regret something that ended so great for you. Too bad your sister didn't let my mother live long enough to see what big rewards *she* could win for her mistakes."

*Time to go grab that ice cream*, Megan thought, but she held back from saying the lines that would give her a reason to exit. She didn't want to walk out; she wanted to handle this. She touched Trevor's knee under the table, knowing he was about to challenge Bryce's rudeness and hoping he'd take the tap as an *It's okay; keep your revolver holstered. Let him vent.* "I'm so sorry for what Kristen did to your mother. I can't tell you how much I wish I'd realized earlier what she was up to."

"Didn't know your sister too well, did you?" Bryce said.

"Apparently not." Megan cut another bite of lasagna but didn't put it in her mouth. Her stomach had an overfull, nauseated feeling, even though she'd only eaten part of her food.

"How's your uncle doing, Bryce?" The calmness in Trevor's tone didn't dilute the warning: they were finished discussing Megan and Kristen.

Tapping his fork against the knife next to his plate, Bryce said nothing for a moment. "Are you kidding?" he finally mumbled. "Haven't seen him. He'd never get near the scum of the family."

"What about Noah?" Trevor asked.

"He stopped by earlier this week."

"How's he doing? I haven't seen him in years."

"He's doing okay. Works in Boston at some insurance company. I can't remember what he does. Some hotshot math or statistics thing. Mom bragged for ages after he passed all his exams; I got sick of it . . . an actuary. He's an actuary."

Too troubled to care about this angle of the conversation, Megan took tiny swallows of lemonade and pretended she was listening as Trevor and Bryce discussed Bryce's cousin.

*Mistakes.* Multiple mistakes, huge mistakes, years' worth of mistakes. Letting her mother trap her into a dead-end life until she was so desperate to escape that she'd accepted Kristen's fairy tale about an estranged great-aunt and an inheritance and how vital it was for Megan to pretend to be Kristen to avoid upsetting the ailing, finicky old lady.

How could she have convinced herself this long-lost-relative story was credible—and that it wasn't wrong to lie to everyone as part of a plan to win Evelyn's money? Even after Rachel's abduction, she hadn't suspected why Kristen had really wanted her in Britteridge and why Kristen was always so adamant that Megan never drop her masquerade with anyone.

An alibi for a kidnapper. Being Kristen in Britteridge while Kristen was kidnapping Rachel, picking up the ransom, committing murder. Not until Gail Ludlum was dead had Megan started to discern how Kristen was manipulating her.

She touched her shoulder where Kristen's bullet had pierced her skin. A bullet scar. Knife scars. The mental scars of knowing her sister had used her and tried to kill her.

Souvenirs of her mistakes.

She'd healed—she'd thought she'd healed, that the Drakes had healed, that they were all moving forward. They *were* moving forward, but sitting here with Gail's son made her feel as though she was trying to flip to the next page on a calendar only to have the pages all flip backward, reversing into the past.

She hadn't received hate mail in a couple of years. Now, with Bryce only a few weeks out of prison, she had a new letter in her mailbox.

Had he sent it?

# Chapter 4

SWEARING UNDER HIS BREATH, BRYCE wanted to slam his front door behind him, but he closed it softly. A crash would alarm the neighbors. *Call the cops! The Ludlum kid is already out of control!*

He locked the door and stalked into the kitchen. Everything he wanted at the moment, he couldn't have, now or ever. Even a beer was too risky. He snatched a bottle of water out of the fridge and guzzled it, wishing he could dump it directly on the craving inside him.

What had happened to him at Trevor's? He'd been determined to show Trevor he was the good guy Trevor had hung out with until partway through high school when Bryce had started going to parties Trevor wouldn't attend. Until Bryce had gotten involved with the poisons that had shorted out his brain and started him lying to his mother and torturing her with worry.

She must have wanted to strangle him while she'd lied to Sandra Drake, her best friend, comforting her then sneaking information to the kidnappers who'd taken Sandra's daughter. Bryce's crimes had snared her between two horrible choices: put her friends through agony or lose her only son.

Bryce hadn't rallied the courage to face Sandra yet, though she'd invited him over. He'd thought it would be easier to start socially with Trevor. It had gone well for a while. At first, he'd been relieved they could talk openly and Trevor wasn't acting phony like they were ordinary old buddies. Then the discussion had turned to hate mail, and Bryce had let things zip out of his mouth that he shouldn't have said.

He'd sounded like Noah, railing on Megan. He was lucky Trevor hadn't torn his head off. Good thing the guy was too holy for that, controlling his fury, staying dedicated to his service project of helping the ex-con reintegrate into society. No decapitation allowed.

Bryce slumped into a kitchen chair and gulped more water. That hate mail . . . he'd received some letters when he was floundering in his addiction, messages attacking him for being worthless and an embarrassment. He'd figured they were from Noah. Gail had once confided that she suspected Noah of sending anonymous hate mail to his own father, and Bryce's letters had sounded like Noah: vicious words and proper grammar. Bryce had never confronted Noah; he'd been too far gone to care if his cousin loathed him.

New hate mail for Megan a few days after Noah threw a tantrum when Bryce told him about Megan's good luck. Coincidence?

Nah. Noah's work. Unsigned letters were probably his only tactic for striking out at people. Bryce could picture him cutting letters out of magazines to write "I hATe yoU" notes to stick on the windshields of people who beat him to his favorite parking spots.

*Yeah, make fun of him. You're a lot better guy than he is.*

Better than Noah? Better than anyone? Great joke. There was a career goal for him: comedian.

No way would Bryce tell Trevor he suspected Noah. Even if Noah was guilty, he was family. Bryce couldn't betray his cousin. His mother would be appalled . . . if she knew. He figured she still existed as a ghost or a spirit or whatever, but could she watch him? Yeah, she'd elbow past whatever angel guards were supposed to keep the living and the dead separated. *Get your wings out of my face. I need to keep an eye on my kid.*

Besides, Bryce didn't have proof Noah had sent the letter. Yeah, the timing was perfect, but Megan had other enemies. She'd received letters long before Noah had wigged out about how she needed to pay.

So what if Noah had sent it? Let him be proud that he'd hurt the only O'Connor twin he could reach, even though she wasn't the one who'd—

Bryce's gaze slipped through the kitchen doorway and plummeted to the unmarked hickory of the hall floor. He should scratch his mother's name into the wood, the date she'd died, an epitaph like "Healer and Mother" or "Died to Protect Her Useless Junkie Son." Why had she allowed a kidnapper and a blackmailer into her house? Hadn't she realized Kristen might get nervous about Gail's ability to keep lying to the Drakes and the police?

He'd thought about Kristen tonight as he'd watched Megan talking. He'd thought about Kristen tonight as he'd watched Megan talking. His mother had watched the movement of lips like those when Kristen had threatened to send Bryce to prison for life unless Gail betrayed the Drakes. Those light-blue eyes were like the eyes that had watched Gail walk along this hallway, her back to Kristen. A pale hand identical to the one that held a glass of mint lemonade tonight had clutched a hammer—

But this was Megan. Not Kristen. Megan, doing a lame job of pretending hate mail didn't bother her.

Why did he care? He'd stung Megan himself tonight.

*Should have left her alone. Think you can blame her? Act like it's not your fault? If you're going the no-responsibility route, go on and dope yourself, deaden the guilt.* Which of his old contacts was still around? He had plenty of money now. He could backslide . . . would *love* that relief. Wreck his mind and body, wreck his life.

Go back to prison.

He inhaled the biggest breath he could, forcing clean air into the crevices of lungs soiled with prison gunk. The sleepy buzz of the refrigerator and the tick of the butterfly clock were the only noises in the kitchen besides his breathing. No yelling, no cursing, no cell doors clanging shut. No worrying he'd get a shiv in the gut because he'd offended some gang member.

He'd deserved every minute he'd spent in prison, and he'd served every minute he'd earned. He would never do *anything* to put himself at risk of going back. It was too late to be a good son, but he'd be one anyway, a guy no one needed to lie for. He'd even be polite to Megan from now on. And he'd shut Noah down. He wouldn't rat on his cousin, but he didn't have to condone Noah's freaking out the Drakes. What if they complained to the police? What if the cops decided a lowlife felon might be the troublemaker? Bryce never wanted to speak to another police officer, let alone get investigated. No way did he want Noah churning up trouble.

Time to use the light-speed, one-step method of convincing Noah to back off: embarrassment.

After a few seconds of scheming, Bryce pulled his phone out of his pocket and texted Noah. *Had dinner with Trevor and Megan tonight. He's nuts about her. Never thought I'd see Trev so hooked. Megan said someone sent her hate mail telling her she's trash and Trevor should dump her. She laughed about it—as if she'd care about a loony letter written by someone who hates her but is too chicken to sign his name. Bet I get hate mail soon. Can't wait. Fun stuff. I hope you have a good weekend.*

Smirking, Bryce shoved his phone back in his pocket. Triple zap for Noah: that Trevor knew about the letter and still worshiped his "trashy" girlfriend, that Megan thought the letter was funny, and that Bryce suspected Noah. Yeah, one of those zaps was a fib, but he didn't want Noah knowing he'd hurt Megan. He needed to think he'd been busted *and* the whole deal had been a dud. He wouldn't write to her again.

*You're welcome, Megan.* Bryce had messed up at dinner, but he'd accomplished one good deed tonight.

* * *

His arm heavy, Noah lowered his phone to the kitchen table. Aunt Gail's sleek iron guard dog, corroding into flakes of rust.

Slowly, he picked up one of the Staffordshire spaniel figurines he'd been cleaning, a gift Gail had purchased on a trip to England four years ago—the last dog figurine she'd given him. With his cloth, he stroked the china, trying to prevent humiliation and anger from demolishing his ability to analyze Bryce's text.

Gail would be heartbroken to see Bryce still acting like a bratty kid, so indifferent toward her memory that he'd attended a dinner hosted by a woman who'd played a part in her murder. Then he'd taunted Noah about it.

Bryce knew he'd sent the letter. *Suspected* he'd sent it. Had he suspected Noah when Noah had sent him those letters years ago? He'd never said so, and he couldn't prove anything now. He didn't care about proof. He only wanted to jab Noah by rambling about Megan and Trevor's bliss.

Her bliss was phony. She wasn't in love with Trevor; she wanted his family money. That guy was a brainless clod. Noah remembered Trevor being smart in school, but acing calculus didn't mean he was shrewd enough to recognize that he'd put a diamond on the finger of a devil—a woman so hardened she thought descriptions of her cheating soul were hilarious.

How could people think there was this cartoonish dichotomy with all the evil gathered in her twin and all the good in Megan? She was on the same path as Kristen. In a few years, Trevor would "trip" and fall in front of a tanker truck. Megan would fake some tears, hug Trevor's money, and sail to Cancun with one of her lovers.

Noah set the spaniel on a towel and picked up the second of the pair.

His aunt was dead, and Megan was raking in rewards.

It sickened him that she'd progressed this far. She'd probably been plotting to capture Trevor since she'd met him. Noah should have paid attention to her machinations after Gail's murder, but his father's harangues about tainted relatives had been grueling enough; he hadn't wanted the additional torture of reading news articles that might mention Gail or Bryce. He *did* remember his father reporting that "the witch clone" wasn't going to prison, but Noah hadn't obsessed about it. Keeping his dignified façade welded together had taken all his strength, and he'd spent most of his time at work in Boston, where coworkers reading about the Ludlums and the Drake kidnapping had no idea he had any link to criminals. Megan's future had seemed so simple to forecast that he hadn't thought a lot about it; he'd assumed she would flee Britteridge, attempt to scam money out of people in a new location, then move on and try her scam again. Within a short time, she'd be in prison or she'd get murdered by someone she'd defrauded. Self-destruction.

Ignorant assumptions. All this time, she'd been in Britteridge, thriving and unpunished, and Noah hadn't bothered to seek out the data that would have changed his assessment of her future. His father hadn't mentioned she was still around; he probably hadn't known. Once he'd confirmed that his business hadn't been damaged by the offenses of his late wife's relatives, he'd stopped following the story. No one else had mentioned it to Noah either. Britteridge wasn't a big place, but he didn't socialize much with local acquaintances and rarely even shopped or went to the post office here. He'd been oblivious while Megan had manipulated everyone around her. If she'd known kidnapping and murder would win her this big of a prize, she'd have participated eagerly, even grabbing that hammer and murdering Gail herself.

Tears flowed into Noah's eyes. He set the spaniel down and rushed to close the blinds on his front window. If anyone saw him crying and told his dad, his dad would disown him. He was a failure, almost as pitiful as Bryce. Bryce didn't care that Gail's murderer was winning, but Noah had acted like he didn't care either.

And the Drakes were too naïve to recognize how she was using them.

He didn't care about the Drakes, but Gail had loved them. She'd be monitoring things from heaven, maddened that she couldn't warn Sandra Drake about Megan. Noah could contact Trevor or his parents, but they didn't know Noah well enough to trust him. If he accused and insulted Trevor's fiancée, they'd think he was a kook, *and* they'd suspect he'd written the letter to Megan. Michael Drake would pull strings and get Noah charged with harassment.

How could they believe it made sense for President Drake to admit Megan into his university *and* finance her education? Or for Trevor to fall in love with her? For people to *respect* her? She ought to be—at minimum—ostracized and hurled out of town. Yes, she'd intervened when her sister had tried to kill Rachel, but that didn't exonerate her. If she hadn't been so greedy, she wouldn't have participated in Kristen's plot at all, and she would have tipped off the police the instant Kristen had come to recruit her. She could have prevented Gail from getting blackmailed and Rachel from getting kidnapped in the first place. Why couldn't people see what filth she was? How could they act like the past didn't matter? He wanted to drag everyone back in time and batter them with the horror they'd felt during Rachel's kidnapping. That would jolt them into remembering who Megan was.

Maybe he should write an anonymous letter to Sandra and Michael . . .

No. A bigwig university president like Drake would receive a lot of crackpot mail. He'd think Noah's note was more of the same; he'd ignore it.

Noah returned to the table and picked up a spaniel. He wrapped it in one of the flannel pads he used to cushion fragile pieces and tucked it into the correct compartment of his wooden storage box. Did Michael and Sandra Drake honestly approve of Megan's marrying their son? Even if President Drake had helped Megan financially, that didn't mean he wanted her as a daughter-in-law. If he caught on to how dirty and sneaky she was, he'd pressure Trevor to break it off. Once stuffy-strict Trevor understood Megan's nature, he'd dump her gladly.

A defeated and humiliated Megan . . . Noah imagined Gail watching Megan flee Britteridge. *Whew! Good riddance, sister. It's about time.*

If he could come up with a way to expose Megan's character, show how rotten she was . . . still, that wouldn't be justice. Justice would be Megan on the floor in a puddle of blood.

He wouldn't—not a chance. But it was unsettling to think how easy it would be. He already knew her address. She hadn't even tried to hide it; it was online. Britteridge was a low-crime, friendly place. If he knocked on her door, the odds were high that she'd open it. He could hide a knife under his coat—

He picked up a crystal Basset hound and swathed it in flannel. *Get real. You wouldn't do that.* Gail wouldn't want Megan physically hurt, even if she deserved it. Humiliating her and exposing her trickery would be enough. *Thanks, kiddo*, Gail would say. *I'm glad someone finally paid that girl what she earned.*

Could he do it? Ruin her scheme for Gail's sake?

Why couldn't he? He was intelligent. Megan was clever, but she would be off guard. After three years of zero negative repercussions, she thought she was victorious. What if he could rip her spoils out of her hands?

Bryce didn't care what Megan was up to, and no one else knew. The only person who could thwart her was Noah.

He set the hound in the box, grabbed a notepad from the counter, and started jotting down ideas.

# Chapter 5

"Have a seat." Michael removed the reading glasses he'd been wearing when Trevor walked into his study. "Your mother wants you to take a couple of bags of cut fruit when you go. It's from the reception she helped host last night; she doesn't want it to go to waste. And take some to Megan."

"Thanks. If Mom has any cake left, I'd be happy to avert waste by taking that too."

Michael smiled. "I took care of the cake. How did your dinner go last night?"

Trevor settled into the leather chair across the desk from his father, contemplating how best to phrase his thoughts. His father always had astute counsel, and Trevor hoped his insights would settle the restlessness, shaded with anger, writhing inside of him. "It was . . . good and bad. At first, Bryce acted glad to be there, and things seemed comfortable. Then he started getting harsh with Megan."

"Harsh?"

"First, saying things in a joking way, like needling her over how she'd 'benefited' from the kidnapping. He got less jokey and more hostile until I called him on it and forced a change of subject. He backed down and was friendly, but after a while, he started with the zingers again."

"Considering the circumstances, it's not surprising he was awkward." Michael's brown eyes were remote, and from the melancholy in his face, Trevor knew he was thinking of something from three years ago. Gail's betrayal? His parents had forgiven Gail; they were sadder about her death than about her reluctant participation in Rachel's kidnapping, and now they were concerned about her son. But it had to hurt, dealing with the memories Bryce's return roused.

*Painful for everyone.* "I'll keep in touch with him," Trevor said. "Invite him to a Celtics game or something like that."

Michael nodded. "How is Megan doing?"

"Fine, I think. It bothered her, but she was very patient and kind with Bryce and says she doesn't blame him at all for resenting her." Trevor curled his shoulders inward, then arched them backward, working to release the tautness in his muscles. "I made a mistake inviting him to dinner with both of us. I should have met with him alone the first time."

"He needed to meet Megan at some point. I doubt waiting would have made it easier."

Trevor watched snowflakes hit the window behind his father. "It's got to be rough for him, being back. I thought he'd go somewhere else."

"Why did Megan choose to stay instead of going somewhere else?"

Excellent question. Like Bryce, she'd chosen to live in a place where she'd have to deal with notoriety, even hostility. Given nationwide news coverage, neither she nor Bryce would be completely anonymous no matter where they went, but things would be much more intense locally.

"I offered her the option of financing her education elsewhere if she didn't want to stay," Michael said. "But she stayed. Why?"

Trevor felt foolish at his ignorance of his own wife-to-be. He hadn't had a lot of interaction with Megan in the months following the kidnapping when she'd made the decision to stay in Britteridge. "I can tell you why she didn't go back to Pennsylvania. Her parasitic mother—"

Michael chuckled. "You might want to find a more diplomatic description for your future mother-in-law."

Trevor grimaced. Dealing with Pamela O'Connor was not something he looked forward to, but he wasn't too worried. Megan had made tremendous progress in handling Pamela's drama. "Besides breaking away from her mother's . . . dependency . . . I think Megan knew people here cared about her. Rachel really reached out and got her involved."

"Yes, that friendship has been a blessing to both of them."

"I hope it survives the wedding planning. Rachel's driving Megan a little crazy, urging her to do things bigger than we want."

"It's fortunate Rachel is more sensitive to the desires of her other clients, or she wouldn't have much of a business."

"True." Trevor thought of the stunned should-I-laugh-or-panic glance Megan had given him when Rachel had marched into her basement apartment and plunked such a giant stack of sample catalogs down that the rickety kitchen table had wobbled. "Anyway, I think Megan stayed because she felt she'd already started a new life here. You and Mom were great to her. She loved Britt, loved the environment. The positives outweighed the negatives, and her life in Pennsylvania after her father's death had been pretty negative. Grieving for her father, getting stuck catering to her mother, having to work jobs she hated, trying to save money for school only to have her mother siphon away her savings with so-called crises."

"I'd guess you're correct about her reasons for staying," Michael said. "As for Bryce, I'd guess his reasons are partly similar to Megan's and partly opposite."

"He wants a new start, but he doesn't want a new place," Trevor suggested. "He wants something familiar. Old, good memories from before his problems started." *Great analysis. Print yourself a Doctor of Psychology diploma off the Internet and hang it on your wall.* Why did he think he could read Bryce? He could guess what drove Megan, but he had no idea about Bryce.

"I think you're right," Michael said. "Home. Comfort. A deep foundation."

*Comfort.* Trevor had been a lot more comfortable before Bryce had returned. Enough time had passed that people rarely mentioned Rachel's abduction. He had reached a point where he didn't think about it every day and berate himself for failing to prevent it or for failing to prevent the attack that had nearly killed Megan. Now people were gossiping about the kidnapping again, and Trevor's brain kept pulling out memories he wanted archived and forgotten. Last night at dinner, he'd sunk to analyzing Megan's face, brooding about when she'd taken Kristen's place in Britteridge and neither he nor anyone else had noticed the switch. Why hadn't he recognized immediately that she was a different woman?

*Because you didn't know Kristen had an identical twin. Why would you have suspected that the woman who looked like Kristen suddenly wasn't Kristen? "Forgive me, but you seem nicer than you did before the kidnapping. By any chance, are you a completely different person?"*

"I hope Bryce is comfortable here," Trevor said. "I hope we all are, but it's going to take awhile." He reached into his pocket and took out the letter he'd persuaded Megan to give him. He stood and set it on his father's desk.

Michael picked up his glasses. As he read the letter, his demeanor went from pensive to flinty. He lifted the envelope and checked the postmark. "When did she receive this?"

"Yesterday."

"Has anything else happened? Has anyone given her a hard time lately?"

Trevor folded his arms. Every time he saw that letter, he wanted to shred it—and the sender. "She said she's gotten some teasing that's . . . tactless. Comments about . . ." He couldn't repeat it. It was ludicrous.

"Questions as to how someone like *her* managed to trap the most eligible man in Britteridge?" Michael finished.

From how hot and red Trevor felt, the sun had apparently shifted closer to the earth and aimed a solar flare straight at him. "It's ridiculous."

"Jealousy. Not surprising."

*Jealousy only because people think I'm a pathway to your wealth.*
"She said none of the comments have been vicious, and there isn't
anyone she suspects of sending the letter. We've already verified
that it couldn't have come from Kristen."

"Did she give you any names of people who've said unkind
things?"

"I asked, but she said she didn't want me thinking negatively
of people because of some off-the-cuff snarky comments."

"So setting aside her encounter with her sister, the most hostility
Megan has experienced face-to-face is from Bryce?"

Trevor hesitated. Before Rachel's kidnapping, he would have
made more of an effort to be fair, to fight suspicion when he had
no sound basis for it. Now his battle to be objective about Bryce
reminded him of how he'd instinctively disliked Kristen when she'd
first come to Britteridge and befriended Rachel. He'd seen hints
that she was manipulative, but when he'd tried to warn Rachel to
be careful of her, Rachel had been annoyed, and he'd felt petty and
judgmental. He'd told himself he was overreacting and Rachel's
friends weren't his business.

But he'd been catastrophically right about Kristen. If he'd
watched her more closely and done a better job of figuring out why
she unsettled him, he could have offered Rachel more convincing
evidence. Would that have changed things? Kristen's friendship
with Rachel had been an important part of her plan. If Trevor had
successfully coaxed Rachel away from her before—

"What are you rehashing?" Michael spoke gently.

Trevor slouched in his chair and looked down at the logo on his
new Britteridge College sweatshirt—a post-Christmas gift Rachel
had pressed on him when she'd decided his old Britt sweatshirt
was getting ratty and he wouldn't spend the money to replace it.
"Just thinking about getting fooled by Kristen. Not wanting to be
a sucker again. But I'm not accusing Bryce of sending the letter.
Given his attitude toward Megan and the timing of the letter, yes,
I'm asking myself the question. But at this point, I don't think it
would do any good to confront him. He'd deny it no matter what,

so why offend him and create a breach—more of a breach—when he's probably innocent?"

"I hope he is," Michael said. "For his sake."

Trevor nodded. They could reach out to Bryce, but whether or not he mended the wreck he'd made of his life was up to him. If he'd written that letter to Megan, he'd face-planted into the dirt on his first lap around the track.

Trevor breathed deeply, trying for the thousandth time to extinguish his urge to pin Bryce to the wall and interrogate him. *It won't help. Leave him alone.*

"Are you all right?" Michael asked.

"I'm more frustrated than I ought to be."

"Because it's not just the letter. It's the memories."

Trevor shifted his gaze back to the window and watched the snow falling from a silver-gray sky. Memories were the problem, the reason a nasty letter had angered him so intensely. He didn't know who had sent it, couldn't do anything to make the rat accountable, hadn't shielded Megan from abuse, just like he hadn't protected Rachel or Megan from Kristen.

*Talk about an exaggerated comparison. This is only a letter. A coward's letter. That's all.*

But he'd still failed Megan.

* * *

"Ugly place," Noah muttered as he drove slowly past the fourplex containing the unit Jessica Barnett occupied. Everything was ugly in January, but this shoddy house would be a blight year-round. Grimy snow crusted on what must be a weed patch instead of a lawn, cracked brick steps were a trip hazard, and the siding was a feeble shade of pink.

He hated turning to Jessica. He shouldn't go near her, but after a week of brainstorming and organizing his ideas, he'd realized he needed to hire out part of his plans, and unless Jessica had completely changed since high school—it didn't sound like she had—she'd be perfect. Her attempt to weasel money out of Bryce showed she was frantic for cash, frantic enough that Noah was sure she'd be home waiting for him, even though he'd set their appointment time in the note without asking if it worked for her. She would jump at his mention of a "lucrative job."

Noah continued down the street and parked half a mile away next to a mound of dirty snow topped with a wadded fast food bag and spilled french fries. After double-checking that he'd locked his car, he hurried toward Jessica's place, wanting to get off the street fast and hoping her neighbors would ignore him or think he was a drug dealer or some other dangerous criminal they didn't want to confront. His car wasn't anything interesting, and he'd compelled himself to let it get filthy with dirt and road salt. He wore an oversized hoodie and kept the hood up. A bulky thrift-store coat made him appear heavier; he'd loosened his belt a couple of notches so his faded, too-large jeans would droop, and he wore old combat boots. If his own dad walked past, he wouldn't recognize Noah. Not that Noah was worried about running into him; his dad would never come to this neighborhood.

He rapped on Jessica's door.

She opened it. It had been . . . Was it eight or nine years since he'd seen her? Not since she'd gotten kicked out of Britt. He tried not to notice how great she looked, but the only way to blot out that awareness was to go back in time and knock on the door with his eyes closed. She looked fantastic, better than she had when she was younger. With that heavy makeup she'd worn as a teenager, he'd never noticed her eyes were light green. They probably *weren't* that nice of a color. She might be wearing tinted contacts. Miraculously, she wasn't dressed like a prostitute. She was wearing jeans and a long-sleeved shirt—clingy shirt, yes, but it covered her.

"Hi," Noah said. Hadn't her hair been darker in high school— mud-brown, maybe? It was blonde now. Two shades of blonde, and a lot shorter.

"Come on in," she said.

He stepped inside and pushed back his hood. Jessica closed the door and scanned him from hair to boots. Embarrassed, he realized she was grading him the way he'd graded her.

"Still a dweeb," she said. "Pull your pants up. You look like a clown, not a gangster. Did you think you had to dress this way to enter my ghetto?"

He gave her a steely glare. He ought to walk out and leave her anguishing about how much money she'd lost, but acting offended would make her think he cared about her opinion. "Is anyone else here?" he asked.

"Uh, no. You told me you wanted a private meeting. Besides, I live alone. Roommates are a pain, and men are the plague."

"*Your* men. Your boyfriends probably make plague rats look decent."

"Still a stuck-up jerk. Wow, Noah, it's good to see you again."

"We weren't friends. We don't have to fake it. Are you interested in hearing what I have to say?"

"Sure. What was up with leaving me a note at work instead of calling or texting like a person who wasn't born in 1750?"

"I didn't have your number."

"You were too dumb to figure out how to find it?"

Noah shrugged. The truth was he hadn't wanted to leave an electronic trail. Police could check things like that, and if Jessica got caught, Noah wanted to be able to claim he had no idea what she'd been doing.

"And what was up with the 'I'll be at your place at eight on Thursday; if you're interested, be there' and not even leaving *your* number so I could call you if that didn't work?"

"What did you do with the note?" Noah asked.

"Threw it away. Why? Was I supposed to scrapbook it?" She strolled into a small living room with a hardwood floor and a braided rug. At least it was clean. *Very* clean. Noah had figured he'd be sitting in a pile of crumbs and dog hair. The couch and love seat were frayed on the arms but not stained, and the radiator under the window had no dust on it. The scratched floor needed to be refinished, but it was swept. Jessica knew how to clean? Astounding.

He sat on the couch. She took the love seat.

"What do you want?" she asked.

Noah had already decided he'd jump straight to the point. He didn't want to make small talk with Jessica Barnett. "You've been trying to squeeze money out of Bryce. You figure he must have inherited a vault of cash from his parents, and you want some of it."

Jessica laughed. "For real? Did Bryce go wimpy in prison and can't deal with me, so you're, like, his enforcer sent to bully me? I never asked him for money."

"Sure. Mentioning over and over how hard it is to find gigs that pay and how you hate your hours at the donut shop. Bringing him cookies? He knows what you want."

Jessica shrugged, still smiling, which irritated Noah. Wasn't she ashamed of the way she'd revealed herself as greedy and broke?

"Just being friendly," she said. "Better than you've done, I'll bet. You were always on his case in high school. Are you on a crusade to scare away any old friends who care about him?"

"Give me a break. You don't care about him."

"I do too."

"You care about his money."

"Have you been possessed by Gail Ludlum's ghost? Woooooh, stay awwwwayyy from my sooooon, you evvvvvil demon exxxxx . . ."

A blast of rage filled Noah. "Don't you dare mock—"

"Settle down. Look, I know Gail was pretty much your mommy. But she hated me; she split me and Bryce up, and I'm not going to pretend I mourn her. Do you really have a gig you want to hire me for, or was that note an excuse for you to come lecture me?"

Noah removed his parka and laid it on the cushion next to him. "I have a gig, but it's not a music thing. It's . . ." He hesitated. How should he say this? Jessica was feisty, and if he proposed the job in a way she found insulting, she might kick him out no matter how much she wanted his cash. Gail had excelled at praising people and inspiring them to do their best. How would she gain the cooperation of a girl like Jessica?

Jessica frowned. "If you think you can hire me for some scuzzy bachelor party—"

"Nothing like that. This is sensitive. Someone did terrible things but got away with them. I want to make trouble for her. Nothing big but enough to make her life difficult and show her fiancé what a monster she is."

Jessica raised her eyebrows. "Uh . . . why are you coming to me to whine about a girl?"

"In high school, you were . . . clever . . . at pulling pranks or getting revenge when people ticked you off. You never got caught."

"You want to hire me to play pranks on a girl who rejected you? Seriously? This is the most pathetic job ever. Maybe you should get over her."

"She's not an ex-girlfriend," Noah said icily. "She's a criminal, but one the law can't punish. She thinks she's won. I want her to lose. How about five hundred dollars for a couple hours of work?"

Jessica flicked her painted fingernail against one of the dangling pink earrings she wore. "Is this a prank on *me*? I didn't think you knew how to do funny stuff."

Concentrating on how Gail would have handled this, he said, "I know I'm lousy at it. You're the pro. That's why I want your help. I remember . . . uh . . . like the time that girl . . . Sophia Something . . . was hitting on Bryce, so you downloaded a research paper from one of those cheat websites and slipped Sophia's paper out of the basket and put the obviously plagiarized one there with her name on it."

Jessica snickered. "That was gold. Oh wow, I remember her totally losing it in the hall after Mr. Medina called her a cheater and told her she was flunking . . . *loved* that part. She didn't flunk though. Her mom printed out another copy of her real paper and brought it to the school, and Medina ended up believing her. Too bad it didn't last longer, but it was a good scare. She thought her chances at college scholarships had blown up."

"And you never got busted."

"Nope. Perfect timing. Sleight of hands. No witnesses."

"Your skills are what I need. The woman I'm talking about is the sister of the woman who kidnapped Rachel Drake and killed my aunt: Megan O'Connor."

"Megan O'Connor!"

"Yes. She was involved in her sister's scheme but never did prison time. Now she's marrying Trevor Drake."

"For real? How did she pull *that* off?"

"She's a master conniver. First she helped kidnap Trevor's sister and helped kill his mother's best friend. Then she manipulated President Drake into giving her a free ride at Britt. *Now* she's fooled the Drakes into welcoming her into the family. It's sickening. Who knows what she'll do next."

"*Wait*—President Drake let her go to Britt for free?"

"Yeah," Noah said. "He kicks you out and revokes your scholarship but gives his daughter's kidnapper a free ride. Told you, it's sickening."

Jessica scowled. Pleased that she was annoyed—if she had a personal reason for hating Megan, so much the better—Noah added, "She ought to be locked up. Instead, she gets everything she wants."

"I thought she wasn't involved in the kidnapping," Jessica snapped. "Not on purpose, I mean. Didn't she get tricked into it somehow?"

"That's what she says, but so what? Because she was gullible doesn't mean she's innocent."

"What do you want me to do? Burn down her house? You're crazy if you think I—"

"I'm not talking about anything big or risky. I only want to expose her character so everyone knows she's a lying leech."

"Embarrass her?"

"Yes. I want people to remember who she is, what she did, how much she hurt them. I want her unable to use or fool anyone here again."

"You want Trevor to end the engagement. And President Drake to throw her out of school."

"That would be excellent."

"You'd pay me to make her look bad."

"Yes. I know you need money."

"*Needing* money and *wanting* money aren't the same."

"You fry donuts for a living. You live in a dump neighborhood. You *need* money."

Jessica's shoulders tensed. "Maybe I don't want it bad enough to work for a mama's boy . . . *auntie's* boy."

Fury lunged inside of Noah, surpassing all his other emotions, making it difficult not to slap Jessica. He could hit her, and he wouldn't go to jail for assault because no one would believe her. Noah was respectable. Jessica was scum. He'd deny he was ever here, and she couldn't prove it.

*Hit Jessica and she'll never help you, no matter how much you pay her.* Noah interlaced his fingers in his lap. He wasn't violent. He would never hit a woman, even if she was obnoxious. "You interested or not?"

"What kinds of things are we talking about?"

Noah slipped a piece of paper from his pocket. He'd edited his brainstorming list and typed it up. "Ideas like this." He offered the paper to Jessica.

She read it. "What, did you copy this off some 'Ten Ways to Get Back at Your Ex' website?"

Noah gritted his teeth. "She's not my ex. And no. Why?"

"It's *generic*. Let me educate you, smarty-pants. I don't know much about Megan, but I do know about the Drakes, and they're extremely religious and strict. If Trevor wants to marry Megan, he must think she's the same way, right?"

"Yeah. That's why planting weed in her apartment—"

She shook her head. "Uh-uh. Trevor won't believe it. Megan will act horrified, claiming she was framed, and he'll believe her unless you set the stage. You've got to personalize this. Know your victim."

"You don't know her either, so quit acting like—"

"I can get to know her." She stood. "Want a beer? Coke?"

Noah bashed his anger down. "Coke's fine."

She exited. Noah swore under his breath. If he wanted to use Jessica's skills, he'd have to put up with her sass. She'd better make it worth it.

She returned with two cans of Coke and a bowl of pretzels. She set the pretzels on the coffee table.

"You interested in the job?" Noah said as she sat down.

"Maybe. Sounds kinda fun. But, ugh, I hate the Drakes. I should let this O'Connor chick exploit them. A couple of joints and a little wine in my dorm—what university even *cares* about that—and I'm *out*? Scholarship canceled? Thank you, Saint Michael Drake."

"Why'd you go to Britt if you couldn't live with their honor code?"

"I could have lived with it fine if a blabbermouth boy hadn't tricked me into showing him my stash, then turned fink."

Classic Jessica, thinking she could party without consequences. Unlike Bryce, she'd been able to skate through high school, indulging on weekends, trying most of the stuff Bryce had tried. But unlike him, she hadn't gotten addicted, and she'd still pulled off high grades. No wonder she hadn't thought she'd truly get kicked out of Britteridge College.

"Boyfriend?" Noah asked.

"Traitor I dated a couple of times. I got tasty revenge on him though."

"What did you do?"

"Not telling. But I did a better job on him than I did on Sophia. He didn't last long at Britt after that."

"Whatever. Well done. As to our business, you're not helping the Drakes. You're wrecking their son's engagement and showing 'Saint Michael' he was a fool for paying for Megan's education. Don't tell me you wouldn't enjoy showing them they're so dim they got sucked in by a con artist."

"Okay, maybe."

"You're on board?"

She picked up the list and flapped it. "Let me give you some better ideas of how to cause trouble. If you want to rattle people and stir up hostility for Megan, you need to start with something more dramatic than this."

"Fine."

"Plus, you talk about this like it's a one-shot thing. I'll tell you up front, that won't work no matter what I do. If the Drakes trust Megan this much, it'll take time to poison that."

"I understand that. But up front, I'm hiring you for *one* job. After that, I'll decide if I want more."

"You're going to have to pay extra if you want something good for starters. It will take a lot more than the couple hours' work you talked about. I want a thousand. For round one. Plus expenses."

Noah had assumed she'd demand more; that's why he'd started at five. "Seven fifty," he said.

"One thousand."

"I'm not going higher than seven fifty. If you want the job, that's what I'm paying."

"I'll do *something* for seven fifty," she said. "But I won't spend as much time on it, and it won't be as awesome. If you want the discount prank, fine."

"If you're threatening to do cruddy work—"

"Listen, pinhead. Want me to explain business to you? More labor costs more money. I'll do top-notch work no matter what, but less money gets you a smaller project, which gets you smaller results. If that's what you want, fine, but don't expect a thousand dollars of value for seven hundred fifty dollars."

He hadn't planned to go higher than seven fifty. She was trying to manipulate him. She didn't have skills worth a thousand dollars.

"You know I'm good at this," she said. "Let's talk ideas, and then we'll finalize the price."

He ought to state adamantly that seven fifty was his limit. But if he did, she might get spiteful and make worthless suggestions. "Fine," he said grumpily. "What are your ideas?"

\* \* \*

Jessica locked the front door, twisting the lock so violently the door jiggled like the rusty hinges were crumbling. She stomped to the window and pulled the curtains an inch apart so she could spy on Noah hurrying away from her apartment. *Waddling* away from her apartment, walking bow-legged in those sagging jeans. A guy with the creativity of a slug trying to pass for a hoodlum. She could have made herself look and sound exactly like an accountant or a computer geek or whatever it was he did for a living. Noah knew zip about disguising himself.

Gibson, the Maine Coon she'd adopted from the shelter a couple weeks ago, meandered into the room. Now that her cat was her audience, she released the insults about Noah and Bryce she'd held back while Noah was here, blitzing the cat with profanity but keeping her tone sweet. She didn't want to scare Gibson away.

Bryce had blabbed to his cousin that she was after money. He'd made her into a joke, a gold digger who thought her cleavage and a plate of cookies could win back her now-rich ex-boyfriend. So here came Noah, assuming he could buy her, that she'd sell any service for a few twenties or a hit of cocaine.

This started with Gail Ludlum. It was her fault, convincing Bryce and Noah that Jessica was worthless.

Why had she let Noah's note inflate fairy-tale bubbles in her head? She'd been so interested in the "lucrative job suited to your skills" that she'd ignored how arrogant the note was and had spent hours cleaning her apartment and fixing herself up, preparing for the appointment. Why had she been stupid and sappy enough to fantasize that a former classmate remembered her musical talent and wanted to hire her for a gig . . . maybe a company party . . . an event that would pay a lot and give her exposure, leading to more gigs. She'd get enough money to record her album—total professional production. The album would go viral. She'd quit the donut shop. She'd support herself as a musician and build her acting career as well. Give her five years, and she'd be a big-name star. Grammys and Tonys and Oscars would glitter on the shelves in her mansion.

Sure. Her break. Instead, she'd invited in a condescending pig who remembered her only as a troublemaker and thought her one marketable skill was pranking people. She should have told him to his face how much she hated him, but she'd locked the words up.

She needed this job.

Jessica wanted to punch her fist through the wall, but she was in enough hot water with her stepdad without ruining the flowery wallpaper from 1982. He'd already yelled at her for falling behind on her rent and said if she didn't pay up, he'd kick her out and rent to someone who'd pay double the cut rate he was giving her. She'd yelled back that she'd provided free live music at his work Christmas party and at his nephew's wedding, and he'd reminded her that was part of their deal—discount rent for her, and her voice and guitar at his disposal whenever he wanted free entertainment. "Sweet publicity for you, Jessie. I'll make you famous."

Sure. Sweet publicity. Events where every guy in the place was drunk and trying to paw her or giving her lewd compliments that had nothing to do with her music. She wouldn't get any additional gigs from those mobs, unless they were freebie gigs with her stepdad offering her services and claiming any tips she got. "If you don't like it, move out and go pay market rate for a new place."

That thousand dollars would help. Kiss the droopy seat of Noah's gangsta jeans or get evicted. At least she'd talked Noah into agreeing to the higher price.

Jessica lifted Gibson and sat on the couch to scratch behind his ears until he melted onto her lap in a warm pile of fur.

A thousand bucks to make Noah feel like a hero for skewering Gail's enemy—ugh, Gail Ludlum—using Jessica as the sword.

Someone to use. Not a real person. Same way her roommate had treated her in LA. Use her to meet the few connections Jessica had made in the LA music world, then skulk past Jessica and steal that plum series of gigs.

She'd gotten back at Zoe. That vintage Stratocaster hadn't been insured; it would take her a long time to replace what had been a great instrument before Jessica had broken into her car, stolen the guitar, and run over it. Sure, Zoe suspected her, but she couldn't prove it, and Jessica hadn't given her a chance to lash back. She'd left Los Angeles and returned to Massachusetts. Not like she had anything worthwhile going on in California.

Nobody got a pass on using Jessica. Not anymore.

Zoe had been a lot better at flattering her than Noah had been. Every time Noah had told her she was clever, he'd flinched like he'd whacked his toe on the leg of a chair. If anything went wrong, he'd deny hiring her and say this must be her revenge on the Drakes.

*I'm not going to make mistakes.* Jessica tugged her phone out of her hip pocket. With a tap, she stopped the recording function she'd activated when she'd gone into the kitchen to grab the sodas. She dropped the phone on the couch and slid her fingers under Gibson's collar to scratch where he couldn't reach.

She could control Noah. She was brilliant at pranks, and it did sound fun. She was bored, tired of the January cold—it didn't take long to get out of practice with New England winters—and needed something exciting to do. This would be a great adrenaline rush. She could make the Drakes despise Megan; she could get Megan to flee Britteridge and abandon the rotting remains of her reputation.

But . . . then what? Take whatever she'd wrung out of Noah and slink back to struggling to find gigs and acting jobs that would pay? Back to her greasy day job and her stepdad stealing her tips?

"Not happening." Jessica buried her fingers in Gibson's thick fur. If Noah wasn't offering her the break she wanted, she would make his offer into her big break.

She'd let him think he was in charge. She'd do this job so well that he'd be awed, and he'd hire her for round two and round three. When it was too late for him to shake her loose, she'd use *him*.

Use him to make the money she needed.

She could control him. She could control Megan.

The thought of Noah begging her to let him off the hook made her laugh. He'd be a whimpering baby.

Gibson twitched his ears and jumped off her lap. Jessica picked up her phone. With the evidence she'd have against Noah, she could make him do anything she wanted.

# Chapter 6

TEETH CHATTERING, RACHEL UNLOCKED THE door of her townhouse, rushed inside, and clicked the door shut to block the wind. At least it was February now. Two months until April, at which point it wouldn't be warm, but she could start hoping for spring. She flipped the light switch, but the living room remained dark.

"Oh, *perfect*." She played with the switch. Power outage? She hadn't noticed the neighborhood being dark. She glanced out the narrow window next to the door. The porch light shone. Something must have tripped the breaker for the living room.

She pulled out her phone to call her husband to report the problem but changed her mind. Did she expect Peter to rush home from his meeting to fix things for her? She knew where the circuit breaker panel was and how to reset a switch.

*Honestly. Don't be such a helpless airhead.*

Rachel stood in the dark living room, mustering her courage, annoyed that she needed to muster courage for such a trivial difficulty. If Peter were home, he'd joke about forgetting to pay the electric bill and jog into the basement to check the switch. It wouldn't cross his mind that a dark townhouse seemed ominous. It wasn't ominous, not at seven o'clock in the evening, with cars in the parking lot and people next door. Did she think a kidnapper had turned the power off so he could lunge out of the blackness and grab her?

She hated it when she treated silly things as signs of danger. She'd gotten better at not eyeing everything through fear fog—until Bryce had come home.

For the past month, little flashbacky memories had been bothering her. The grimy taste of dirt on her lower lip when she'd woken up blindfolded in that house on Britteridge Pond Road. The stale smell of the pillowcase, like it had been stored for years in the back of a linen closet. Jerking at the cable that chained her to a ring on the floor, straining to reach a door or a window. Pulling her sock up again and again to try to shield her chafed ankle from the shackle. Pain crashing into her heart when she saw Kristen walk into her cell and realized her friend had betrayed her.

Rachel sighed. She ought to be more compassionate, like her parents. While she wished Bryce would go away, her father had given him a job at Britt, and her mother kept trying to invite him to dinner.

*I have forgiven him*, Rachel told herself. *And his mother too. I want him to be happy.*

Why couldn't forgiveness erase bad memories? That would be awesome.

Rachel stepped farther into the living room. Maybe it wasn't even a tripped breaker. Moving cautiously so she wouldn't bang into furniture, she headed across the room and groped at a floor lamp until she found the switch. She twisted it. Soft light glowed.

*You birdbrain. It's not the breaker—just the overhead fixture that's linked to the wall switch. It's a burned-out bulb. Crisis! Call the SWAT team!* Smiling ruefully, she hung her purse and coat in the closet. There were extra lightbulbs in the basement utility room. *How many overimaginative chickens does it take to change a lightbulb?*

Bright, cheerful light illuminated the stairs to the basement. The stairs didn't creak under her feet, and no killers pounced on her. *No horror movies here.* In the utility room, she flipped the light switch, opened the cupboard, and scanned the boxes of lightbulbs. How many did she need? There must be at least two in the light fixture. What wattage? She should have checked before she'd come down here. *Another airhead move.* Well, she ought to be able to figure out which bulbs would work without checking; there were only a couple of reasonable choices—

The lights went off—the utility room, the stairs—the entire basement pitch black. Adrenaline jetted into her veins. Gasping, Rachel scrabbled through the bottom shelf of the cupboard, searching for a flashlight.

"Hey, Rach. It's me."

She shrieked, simultaneously panicking and recognizing the voice. "For heaven's sake, what are you doing here?" Her heartbeat thunderous, Rachel gave up hunting for the flashlight and stepped to the door of the utility room, one hand brushing the washer and dryer to guide her. "Are you trying to scare me to death?"

Megan's laughter and footsteps moved toward her.

"A scare *can* kill you, you know," Rachel said. "I read an article about it. Why did you break into my house?" Technically Megan hadn't broken in. Rachel had given her a key so she could water the plants and feed Peter's tropical fish when they'd gone to Disney World for Christmas. Megan had just texted her a few days ago saying she needed to return the key, but Rachel had told her to keep it for next time. She should have asked for it back.

"Do you know what happened to the lights?" Rachel asked. "I guess the wind must have—" A flashlight flicked on. "Thanks! I should have known you'd have a flashlight in your purse. You are the most prepared person ever. I have no idea what happened to mine. I thought it was in the cupboard here . . ."

Megan skimmed the flashlight beam over Rachel and settled it where it glared in her eyes. Rachel raised her hand to block the light.

"You're looking great," Megan said. "Your hair's longer."

"Uh . . . longer than when you saw me last week?" Absently, Rachel drew her fingers through shoulder-length curls, untangling wind snarls. "I'd tell you you look great too, but I can't see you."

"Nice sweater. That orange looks good on brown-eyed brunettes. I can't wear orange at all."

"Uh . . . thanks." Rachel lowered her hand and squinted at the shadow behind the flashlight. "Get that light out of my face, and tell me why you're haunting me. Did I forget you were coming over?"

"No, I didn't warn you. Didn't want to give you a chance to call the police."

Rachel laughed shakily. "You're strange tonight. Schoolwork getting to you? You should file a complaint with the associate director of admissions. Tell him—between kisses—that the work at Britt is *way* too hard, and when he's flying around the country telling everyone how awesome Britt is, he should stick a warning label on his brochures: 'Not to be confused with Disneyland or a resort in Maui.'"

"Actually I *am* here to file a complaint."

What was wrong with Megan tonight? Frustrated at the light still shining in her face, Rachel averted her eyes and took a step backward. "Okay, honestly, Meg, you don't have to do a sit-down dinner at your reception. I just wanted you to consider it. It's up to you and Trevor. I do want to show you pictures of these gorgeous fruit sculptures. The woman who makes them will give us a great price. But for heaven's sake, let's go upstairs and call the power company first."

"Don't call," Megan said. "I switched the breaker off. I got that idea from my creepy old aunt."

"*What?* You flipped the breaker to freak me out?"

"Yep."

Anger blazed, memory-fueled fury Rachel had never felt toward Megan. "That's not funny. You know that's not funny—"

"Oh, sorry." The flashlight clicked off. "After you people wrecked my plans and sent me to prison for life, I didn't know you expected me to be comic relief."

"What—" Understanding fired shocks along Rachel's nerves. "*Kristen?*"

"If you scream, I'll kill you."

This wasn't possible. It had to be Megan, but Megan would never tease her like this, would never think a cruel scare was funny.

Rachel strained to see the woman. Without the flashlight, it was so dark she couldn't even see her silhouette. "How could you . . . ? You couldn't escape—"

"Oh, please. Prison is designed to hold the dregs. I'm not the dregs. How hard do you think it was for me to charm a guard into helping me?"

*Not very hard*, Rachel thought, hyperventilating to try to keep herself from screaming. Beautiful, charismatic Kristen. When she'd come to Britteridge, she'd mesmerized Rachel, deceived her completely. Rachel should have guessed she'd charm and manipulate her way out of prison.

"What do you want?" Rachel's voice was a shredded whisper. "My family won't give you anything for me this time. They'll never pay a ransom again."

"I'm not trying that stunt again. I don't want anything from you. I stopped by to say hello. I hear my sister and your brother are getting married. I hope I'm on the invite list. Wouldn't want to miss it."

Rachel flailed mentally, wondering what weapon Kristen had. If a prison guard had helped her escape, she'd probably stolen his gun. Wait, did prison guards carry guns? Some of them did, right? Or maybe she had a knife, one of those makeshift weapons prisoners create out of toothbrushes. No, she must have a gun. She was smart enough to—

*Focus, you twit. Better assume she has a gun.* If Rachel tried to flee, Kristen would pull the trigger. Kristen couldn't possibly see her any better than she could see Kristen, but Rachel was cornered in a small utility room. If Kristen fired several bullets, she'd nail Rachel for sure. Dizzily, Rachel touched her thigh where a bumpy scar memorialized the bullet Kristen had fired three years ago.

"Meg is trouble though," Kristen said. "Does Trevor know that? She has issues. Are you sure you want her in your angelic family?"

*Don't pass out. Stop panting like that; you're making yourself lightheaded.* Rachel planted her hand on top of the washer and leaned her hip against it. "What are you going to do to Megan?"

"Did I say I was doing something to Megan?"

"If you hurt her, Trevor will break your neck."

"Oh, scary. As if he could catch me. Nice to see you again. Now back up until you hit the wall. I'm shutting the door. Wait for ten minutes before you come out, or you're dead."

"I . . . don't have a watch."

"*Count* ten minutes. Did you flunk second grade? That's sixty seconds times ten. Now back up."

Rachel retreated until her shoulders hit the wall. Kristen shut the door.

A flicker of light showed under the door. Kristen had switched her flashlight back on. Something rustled and bumped against the door. Afraid Kristen had changed her mind and was coming in, Rachel spun around and groped at the items on the shelves. What might work as a weapon? Cleaning supplies, laundry soap—

Quick footsteps moved away from the utility room. Gripping a wood-handled feather duster, Rachel stood motionless and listened. Footsteps traveling up the stairs. Muffled footsteps from the main floor . . . Rachel waited for the sound of an exterior door opening and closing. Faint noises . . . no discernible door clicks or thumps.

She kept waiting. No more footsteps. Kristen *must* have left.

What if she hadn't? What if she was playing with Rachel, warning her to stay down here for ten minutes, knowing Rachel would sprint upstairs the instant she thought Kristen was gone? "I told you ten minutes. You didn't listen." Then a bullet would—

She must be gone. Rachel needed to reach her phone, call the police, and alert Megan. Kristen was probably en route to her place; Rachel couldn't linger here, obediently counting seconds while Kristen caught Megan by surprise. If she intended to kill Rachel, she'd do it whether or not she counted to six hundred.

Holding the duster by the feathered end so she could use the long wooden handle as a bat, Rachel tiptoed to the door and rotated the knob as quietly as she could. With a cautious touch, she pushed on the door.

It didn't open. Surprised, she pushed with more force. The door didn't move. What was . . . ? The door wasn't locked; this knob didn't even have a lock.

Kristen had blocked the door with something. Abandoning her fear of making noise, Rachel slammed her shoulder into the door, wanting to scream at herself. If she hadn't asked Peter to reverse this door so it opened outward, it would have been trickier for Kristen to trap her. *That extra few feet of floor space for laundry hampers was worth this much to you, huh?*

She stepped back and kicked the door, then realized letting go of the handle had let the door re-latch itself, making it harder to force open. *Airhead.* She twisted the handle and bashed her hip against the door. It was only a five-minute drive to Megan's apartment. Kristen would get there—

*Focus. Kristen closed the door, then headed up the stairs a few seconds later. She didn't have time to do anything complex. You didn't hear her pushing anything heavy in front of the door or attaching any hardware. Maybe she stuffed something under the door? A doorstop?*

Could the neighbors hear her? "Help!" Rachel screeched. A deep breath. "Help!"

These townhouses had decent soundproofing. Her screaming from her basement *might* get noticed, but she'd better scream *and* work. If she had something flat, she could shove it under the door and try to push the barrier away. Too bad Peter's tools were in the garage. A screwdriver or file would have been useful.

A hanger. She batted at the clothes rod on the wall opposite the appliances until she found a hanger.

On her knees, she slipped the plastic hanger under the door near the doorjamb and swept it to the left. In the middle of the door, the hanger collided with something. She withdrew the hanger, inserted it at the opposite side of the door, and slid it toward the obstruction. It hit near the middle of the door. The obstruction was small. She whacked it with the hanger; the noise of the collision was muted. Not a hard metal item. Probably rubber. A wedge doorstop?

She withdrew the hanger, centered it on the obstruction, and shoved. The plastic hanger snapped.

"Help!" she screamed as she rose to search for a metal hanger.

# Chapter 7

At the sound of Randy Newman singing "You've Got a Friend in Me," Megan glanced away from her laptop screen and plucked her phone off the kitchen table. "Hey, Rach."

A hoarse yell blasted Megan's eardrum. "Kristen escaped! Lock your door!"

Megan sprang to her feet, jostling the table, knocking over her mug of reheated chicken soup. She snatched her laptop away from the spreading puddle. "*What?*"

"She escaped from prison. She was here threatening me, threatening you, then she left, probably coming for you. I called the police and sent them to your place, but she might get there first. *Lock your doors!*"

"She escaped—" Rachel had crammed so many words into a couple of seconds that Megan had to decode the warning before she comprehended it. "My door. I'll check—" She set her laptop on the counter. Even though she knew she'd locked up when she'd arrived home from campus, she still sprinted toward the door of her apartment. "How could she escape? She was in a maximum security—"

"I don't know! She said something about a guard helping her or about tricking a guard or something like that—"

Could Kristen be that clever? Yes. Could a guard—or guards—be that gullible? Apparently. Megan hurried to check the locks on her windows. They were small, high, basement windows, but big enough for Kristen to worm through.

Rachel was sobbing. "She's here for revenge, talked about how we wrecked her plans."

"Are you okay? Did she hurt you?"

"I'm . . . I'm fine . . . Just scared silly. I thought she was going to kill me, then she trapped me in the laundry room, and I needed to call and warn you, but it took me a few minutes to break out, and I kept screaming, and my neighbor finally heard me, but by the time he came running in, I'd gotten the door open, and I was terrified Kristen was already at your apartment."

Red and blue lights flashed through the window where Megan was adjusting the latch to see if it would lock more tightly. "The police are here."

"They're here too. Oh my goodness, how could this happen? This is a nightmare. I'm having a nightmare. Are you having a nightmare? Maybe it's just my nightmare, and I'm talking to myself—"

"Breathe, Rachel." A heavy feeling in her legs made Megan's steps wobbly as she returned to the front door. Boots thumped down the concrete stairs. Through the phone, she heard Rachel shrieking to someone else, "I *saw* her. She talked to me. I swear it was Kristen O'Connor. Call the prison. She escaped—"

Megan unlocked her door and pulled it open. Two guns pointed at her. She jumped backward and raised both hands. "I'm Megan. Come in. I haven't heard from Kristen. Rachel Hawthorne called to warn me."

The two officers stepped into the room. More red and blue lit the street as a second patrol car pulled up to the curb.

"I can show you my ID—" Megan stopped. What use was her ID when she and Kristen were identical? She could be Kristen with Megan's purse, and Megan could be dead or tied up in the closet.

She looked at the phone she held in her raised left hand. "I'm on the line with Rachel Hawthorne. I need to find out—" The screen showed Rachel had hung up. "Please, search me, search my apartment. Kristen isn't here."

While a female officer with a brown ponytail frisked her and the officers from the second car started searching the apartment, Megan tried to think how to prove her identity. She should be able to give bushels of evidence, but the only tidbits her panicky brain could locate were superficial things like reciting her class schedule, offering her e-mail password, telling what movie she and Trevor had seen last Friday—all facts the officers would have to verify, so none of them would exonerate her immediately and get the police to stop eying her like she was an escaped prisoner.

"Thank you for your cooperation, ma'am." The officer's name tag read *Hallstrom.* "Would you mind sitting there on the couch for a few minutes?"

Megan moved to the couch. The two officers who had searched the back of the apartment returned. Megan assumed they'd gone as a team so they could protect each other. It didn't take two people to search one bedroom, one bathroom, and a laundry room.

Was Rachel okay? She took her phone from the arm of the couch, fidgeted with it, and set it down. Rachel couldn't talk to her now; she was dealing with the police too.

A gray-mustached officer's phone rang, and he answered it, stepping outside through the still-open front door as he spoke. Megan wished they'd shut the door. The living room was freezing, and the open door wasted heat, but she didn't want to distract the police by griping about goose bumps and utility bills.

"Have you heard from Kristen at all?" Officer Hallstrom asked.

"No. I had no idea she'd escaped until Rachel called. Why didn't the police notify me?"

Hallstrom didn't answer. The mustached officer returned to the apartment and gestured to Hallstrom. They both stepped outside. Two officers remained in the apartment, neither of them talking, one watching Megan, the other watching the doorway.

Torturous minutes passed. Megan picked up her phone again. Neither officer protested, so she called Trevor. No answer, but that didn't surprise her. He was in San Diego, meeting with his scholarship-donor friend, and if he was face-to-face with someone, he silenced his phone and ignored it until his real-life conversation ended. She tried to text him, but her fingers kept misspelling things so atrociously that she gave up. She'd wait until she had steadier hands and more information.

The spilled soup dripped over the edge of the table. She squirmed on the couch and resisted panic. How long would it take the police to recapture Kristen? Would she hurt anyone? Didn't she have *any* conscience?

The dock on Britteridge Pond. Rain running down Megan's face. Kristen with a knife.

Gail Ludlum crumpled in a puddle of blood.

Blood soaking the leg of Rachel's jeans.

Why hadn't Kristen killed Rachel tonight? She'd caught her off guard, and Kristen must want revenge on everyone who'd thwarted her.

She must have been planning this escape long before Megan had come to visit her. Was that why she'd bragged about how she could charm people? If she'd been planning to escape, why had she pressured Megan to send money? As a diversion?

Megan reached for her phone again. Rachel had assuredly already called her parents, but Megan wanted to hear how Michael and Sandra were coping with the news that their daughter's kidnapper was free and had confronted her.

A tall man with wiry black hair and a gaunt face strode through the doorway. Megan remembered him well from three years ago. Detective Aaron Powell. She set her phone down.

"Hello, Megan," he said.

One piece of her anxiety disappeared. Powell already knew she wasn't Kristen.

He sat next to her. "We've checked with the Massachusetts Department of Correction. Your sister is locked in her cell."

This news jumbled the rest of Megan's anxiety. "But . . . Rachel . . . She said Kristen . . ."

"The guards checked on Kristen moments ago. She's in her cell."

"Maybe 'she' is a pile of wadded papers under a blanket and they need to check again. Rachel Hawthorne said Kristen confronted her."

"They didn't eyeball a lumpy blanket and assume she was under it," Powell said patiently. "They made certain. There has not been a prison break. Whoever confronted Mrs. Hawthorne was not your sister."

Baffled, Megan tried to recall everything Rachel had said on the phone. She'd sounded positive that Kristen . . . How could she have thought—

"It wasn't me. I don't know who Rachel saw, but it wasn't me. I've been here since . . . around five."

"Can anyone confirm that?" Despite his pragmatic tone, the words had to be an accusation. Rachel swore Kristen had confronted her, a confrontation that couldn't have happened, and Kristen's identical twin was right here. Open-and-shut case.

"I don't know if anyone saw me come home. Adrianne Mullins, the property manager who lives upstairs, isn't here. I went up earlier to ask her about getting a dripping sink fixed, and there was a note on her door saying she wouldn't be back until morning. There's only one other tenant, and I think he works late . . ." She tried to picture how the street had looked when she'd arrived home. "No, his car wasn't there." Wonderful. No witnesses.

"The other apartment?" Powell asked. "I believe there are four other units."

"Vacant. I did *not* go to Rachel's tonight. Check my car. It's cold. If I just got back here, the engine would be warm." *Not conclusive. You could bike home from Rachel's in ten minutes or run home in fifteen.* "What happened? What did 'Kristen' do to Rachel?"

"She didn't harm Mrs. Hawthorne. She surprised her, said things meant to frighten her, then fled."

After somehow trapping Rachel in her laundry room so she couldn't immediately call the police or Megan. Megan glanced at the puddle of chicken soup on the floor and wished she had a cup of something to dampen her dry mouth. "I . . . have no idea how Rachel . . . could have been fooled into . . ."

"Mrs. Hawthorne didn't see the woman's face. The intruder had flipped the breaker, and the basement was dark. She only heard her voice and saw a shadow."

"*Oh.* That makes more sense." Megan slumped against the cushions. "She didn't see her face at all?"

"No. She said it sounded like Kristen's voice, and the things the intruder said were meant to make her think it was Kristen."

Someone had mimicked Kristen's voice? Who would want to terrorize Rachel with memories of the kidnapping?

"Do you have a key to Mrs. Hawthorne's townhouse?" Powell asked.

Megan wished she didn't. "Yes. She gave it to me before Christmas so I could take care of their fish and plants while they were on vacation. I tried to return it, but she said keep it for next time."

"Where is the key?"

"On my key ring." Megan pointed to where she'd hung her keys on the wall hook over the microwave. "Do you want me to make sure it's still there?" She hoped it wasn't. If it was gone, someone had stolen it, and that would be evidence that Megan hadn't—

*Because you couldn't have taken the key off and hidden it?*

"Yes, please check," Powell said.

Her legs were too unstable for a quick pace; she plodded to the kitchen area and grabbed her keys. Rachel's key was there.

She brought the keys to Powell. "It's the one with the top painted green and *Hawthorne* in tiny silver calligraphy. Rachel likes making things pretty."

Powell took the keys. "Have you loaned your keys to anyone? Or ever noticed Mrs. Hawthorne's key missing?"

"No."

"Have you ever left her key in your apartment when you're gone?"

"I don't think so. That's my regular key ring, so if I'm out of the house, my keys are with me."

"I believe you recently became engaged to Mrs. Hawthorne's brother."

Megan nodded.

"Has there been any difficulty or conflict between you and Mrs. Hawthorne?"

"No. Rachel is thrilled over our engagement, and she's planning our reception for us. She's a wedding planner." Megan thought of a few recent discussions where Rachel had badgered her. "Low key doesn't mean 'totally blah,' Meg. For my brother and my best friend, I refuse to go so minimalist that it looks like the elders quorum got assigned to decorate." But those were differences of opinion, not real conflict. Good-humored disputes. Almost always good-humored.

"We're close friends," Megan said. "I would *never* pretend to be Kristen to scare her. That is outrageously cruel."

Powell studied her with that compassionate, empathetic expression that had encouraged her to confess the first time he'd interviewed her three years ago—when she'd admitted to masquerading as Kristen.

"How do you feel about Bryce Ludlum's return to Britteridge?" he asked.

"It's been . . . stressful. A lot of . . . remembering. Too much. But I'm glad he's doing well. Trevor and I had him over for dinner."

"How did that go?"

"It wasn't bad. Tense sometimes."

"Tense how?"

"Sometimes Bryce was . . . not very friendly toward me. I don't blame him. It was difficult for all of us."

"He was antagonistic?"

"A little. Meeting me must have been painful."

"I believe you received an insulting letter in the mail a few weeks ago."

"Yes." Trevor had asked her if he could share the letter with the police, wanting it on record in case anything else happened. "I have no idea who sent it." She would *not* smear Bryce by admitting she wondered about him. It wasn't necessary anyway; clearly he was already in Powell's notebook, and since Powell hadn't asked for details about Bryce's antagonism, she guessed Trevor had already told him about the dinner.

She couldn't imagine Bryce had been the intruder who'd scared Rachel tonight. Bryce, hiding in the dark and talking in a Kristen-sounding falsetto?

"Do you have any idea who might have wanted to scare Mrs. Hawthorne, either out of spite or as a practical joke?"

"I have no idea."

"Do you know anyone who would have the knowledge and skill to imitate your sister?"

Did she know anyone who was a skilled mimic? She couldn't remember any of their friends mimicking a celebrity or even attempting an Irish accent for St. Patrick's Day. "Rachel is nice to everyone. I can't think of anyone who doesn't like her. Her dad might have enemies though. Maybe someone is punishing her father by terrorizing her?"

"Has President Drake mentioned anyone who's angry with him?"

"I don't know of anyone by name. I just know that being an extremely successful businessman and the president of a university sometimes annoys jealous or unstable people."

"An angle to investigate. Are you feeling faint? You're pale." He looked from her collar to her forehead a couple of times as though using his X-ray vision to assess blood flow.

"I'm okay. I'd like to see Rachel as soon as you're done with me." Would Powell forbid her from going near Rachel, assuming she was the intruder? Could he do that, or were his only choices to arrest her or let her do what she wanted?

"Of course," Powell said. "We'll be done in a few minutes. Who else has a key to your apartment?"

"The property manager. I don't know who else might have one. I've never given one away, but it's an old apartment, and the lock is old. There could be keys out there." *And by a huge coincidence, a former tenant can mimic Kristen and has a vendetta against Rachel.*

"I'm sorry for the scare you had tonight," Powell said. "Don't worry about your sister. She won't escape. They're keeping a better eye on her than that."

Megan nodded, hoping she wouldn't find out how secure prisons were when *she* got sentenced for breaking into Rachel's apartment and threatening her.

\* \* \*

"Come in." Peter usually included down-to-earth Idaho warmth with his Boston Financial District mien, but tonight he didn't smile as he invited Megan into the townhouse.

"Thank you," Megan said. How could Rachel's husband not suspect her? Besides the obvious fact that she could pass for her sister, Powell had told her that no doors or windows showed damage from forced entry. Megan had the only extra key, and she'd known Rachel would be alone tonight. They'd exchanged texts about how they were both solo, with Peter at a bishopric meeting and Trevor in San Diego. If Peter typed the evidence into his mental spreadsheet and calculated the odds that Megan was guilty, the answer would be arrest-her-immediately high.

And though she didn't think she'd been in conflict with Rachel, Rachel might be taking Megan's objections to her wedding suggestions more seriously than Megan knew, worrying she'd offended Megan, worrying Megan was irritated with her. If Rachel had shared concerns like that with Peter, he'd add them to the motive column.

"Oh, Meg!" Rachel sprinted into the room and clamped her arms around Megan. "How crazy is this?"

Peter rested his hands on Rachel's shoulders as though he wanted to tug her away from Megan. Was he afraid she might morph into Kristen and try to stab Rachel?

"Are you all right?" Megan asked.

Rachel released Megan. Her eyes were bloodshot and her eyelids swollen. "I feel like I did ten rounds on one of those upside-down roller coasters. All dazed and icky, and I keep walking into things. How about you? You must be totally freaked out."

"I'm shaken up." Megan removed her coat. Peter took it and walked toward the closet, his head angled slightly toward her to keep her in his peripheral vision. She wondered if he would surreptitiously check the pockets of her coat for weapons.

Rachel clutched Megan's arm and escorted her toward the couch. "We're making hot chocolate."

On the coffee table sat a tray complete with teapot, hot-chocolate fixings, and three mugs. Peter approached.

"Do one for Megan first." Rachel pulled Megan onto the couch. "She likes marshmallows and whipped cream, and grate some fresh nutmeg on it. Meg, I don't think you've tried it this way yet, but you'll totally love it."

"It sounds delicious." *Delicious any other time. Tolerable tonight if she took small sips and tried not to think about Kristen.*

"I feel like the biggest dork in the galaxy," Rachel said as Peter scooped homemade hot-chocolate mix out of a Mason jar. "I should have known Kristen couldn't have escaped. It was the dark and the shock . . . What do I know about how prisons work? Maybe she *could* trick someone into slipping her out of there."

"Prisoners do escape sometimes. When you told me she'd escaped, *I* believed it."

"I'm so sorry." Rachel squeezed her hand. "Detective Powell questioned you, didn't he? That's my fault. I should have realized the Kristen-person cut the lights because she didn't want me to see she wasn't Kristen. Or you."

"It's not your fault, Rachel." Peter picked up the marble-sized nutmeg and grated a dusting of it onto Megan's drink. "Detective Powell might think she cut the lights because she was afraid you know Megan so well you could instantly distinguish Megan from Kristen. That would have ruined the Kristen scare." He walked over to Megan and held out the drink. "I'm not accusing you. I'm examining facts, trying to understand what happened."

"I understand." She took the hot chocolate. "Thank you."

"Oh gosh." Rachel grimaced. "I know you'd never do this to me—*never*. Are you kidding? I did tell Powell that, like four hundred times. I thought it sounded like Kristen, but I was so scared. First those burned-out lightbulbs—actually they'd been unscrewed, which was totally freaky-sneaky because the Kristen-person knew I'd go down to the basement to get new bulbs and she could ambush me there, so it was all prepped, which totally seems like a clever Kristen move, but it's not something you'd ever do, not that you're not as smart as Kristen, but you'd never do something so cruel. You're the best person ever, and I adore you, and you saved my life and nearly got killed doing it, and Peter was gone, and then the lights went off in the basement . . . Before she even said anything, I was freaking out. I don't truly know how good her imitation was. She could have sounded like Darth Vader, and my whack-o-rama brain would have said, 'It's Kristen! With a cold!'"

Megan made herself smile, but she couldn't feign amusement any more creatively than that. Rachel was a bubbly person, but she wasn't usually prone to rambling and exaggerating and repeating herself. How many times had she said she knew Megan wasn't guilty? She was talking to herself, not Megan, trying to squash her doubts, upset that she could have even a crumb of uncertainty about the woman who'd saved her life.

Peter finished mixing another hot chocolate. "How do you want yours, Rachel?"

"Nutmeg and like a pound of whipped cream. Thanks, sweetie." Her reddened eyes looked back at Megan. "I keep trying to remember details, but I never saw her face. It was *so* dark, and when she switched on her flashlight, she aimed the beam in my eyes most of the time. I got glimpses of her, but she was an outline, a phantom. I think her hair was light. I mean, I couldn't tell the color, if it was strawberry-blonde like yours, but I think it was light and about the right length."

*The right length.* The length of Megan's hair, not Kristen's. Rachel didn't know how long Kristen's hair was; she was assuming it still matched Megan's shoulder-length hair. Megan couldn't see any point in telling her Kristen's hair was actually shorter now.

"Was she the right size?" Megan asked. "Not a lot taller or shorter or skinnier or heavier?"

"Not a *lot* different . . . my impressions weren't very Sherlock Holmesy; I was petrified, but I did think she was Kristen, so she must have been about her shape. I have *no* idea who she was."

"Neither do I," Megan said.

Peter handed a mug of hot chocolate to Rachel. This conversation must seem absurd to him, Megan and Rachel speculating on who could have imitated Kristen. *Who do you think it was, Rach? I can't think of a single person who looks like her!*

"The way she was talking, she knew about everything that had happened." Rachel stuck her thumb in a drizzle of whipped cream melting over the rim of her mug. "But she could get that information from news reports."

"The information but not the voice," Megan said. "I tried to avoid being interviewed. Neither Kristen nor I said more than a few words on camera."

"Which means whoever did this probably knows you," Rachel said. "Knows us. Who would want to . . . I mean . . . What was the point? Does someone hate me? Hate you? Do you think this has anything to do with that ugly letter you got?"

"I don't know. It's such a . . . different tactic."

"How is this even happening to us again?" Tears made a glassy layer over Rachel's eyes. "*More* scary, freaky stuff?"

"I have no idea." Was she missing something obvious the way she'd missed Kristen's true motives when she'd coaxed Megan to adopt her identity? Megan would not blunder around this time as a clueless patsy while a spiteful schemer fooled everyone.

She wished Trevor were here. He'd returned her call before she'd come to Rachel's. Though furious, he'd been calm and comforting on the phone. Right now, she ached for calm and comforting and her head on his shoulder.

Carrying a mug of plain hot chocolate, Peter sat next to Rachel. "Are you all right?"

"Sort of." Rachel wiped her cheeks on her sleeve.

"Megan, did you tell Detective Powell about Bryce?" Peter asked.

"He mentioned Bryce himself," Megan said.

Rachel rested her mug on her knee and kept it steady with one hand while her free hand reached for Peter's free hand. "It wasn't Bryce in our basement tonight. He couldn't trick me into thinking he was Kristen. I'm not *that* big of a doofus."

"Detective Powell will talk to him," Peter said. "Do you think Bryce could be involved behind the scenes? That he recruited a female friend to help?"

"I have zero clue," Rachel said. "I didn't know Bryce very well. He's Trev's age, four years older than I am."

Megan tasted the rich, spiced chocolate from her mug. "Trevor said he doesn't think what happened tonight is Bryce's style."

"Why not?" Peter asked.

"It's been years since they hung out, but he said Bryce has always . . . leaned toward taking the easy way. He might have sent the letter, but Trevor can't see him planning something elaborate like what happened tonight."

"Too lazy to commit the crime," Rachel said. "I never knew you could make an insult out of defending someone's innocence. But Dad said Bryce is working super hard in his groundskeeping job."

"That's another reason to think he wouldn't make trouble like this." Peter put his arm around Rachel. "He just got out of prison. He's trying to put his life together. Why would he risk getting locked up again?"

"True. Breaking into our house and scaring me . . . It's sure not as big as trying to rob an old man for drug money and knocking him down the stairs, but it's still a crime."

Megan swallowed a disintegrating marshmallow. She had no idea what Bryce would or wouldn't do, but Trevor was probably right about him.

She knew Bryce resented her. He'd made that obvious. She wanted to talk to him about it in a setting where they could be completely candid, which meant when Trevor wasn't there. No matter how patient Trevor was, he wouldn't put up with Bryce saying anything too offensive. He wouldn't be home until late Saturday night anyway. He'd wanted to catch the first available flight, but Megan had, with considerable internal stomping on her personal preferences, convinced him to stay. Nothing was happening here now, and it was better to fulfill his commitments at the alumni conference than to bail out, disappoint his friend, and come home to the frustration of not being able to do anything to help.

Megan wrapped determination around swaying courage. She'd try to talk to Bryce tomorrow and ask him bluntly if he'd sent the letter. And even though it was doubtful he was involved in Kristen's faux escape, he was a Britteridge native with longtime friends here and might have heard gossip. Even if he didn't know anything or admit anything, Megan still wanted to make every effort to . . . No, clearing the air was an impossible goal. That could only come with time, if Bryce was willing to forgive her, but at least she could make it plain there was no enmity on her side.

Talking to him might be useless, but she wasn't going to passively stand by and hope everything would work out while Rachel struggled to pretend to herself that she was positive Megan hadn't cracked up and put a fresh, vicious spin on the Kristen masquerade she'd excelled at three years ago.

# Chapter 8

"AM I BRILLIANT? AM I *brilliant?*" Song lyrics kept springing into Jessica's thoughts, lines about victory, hidden genius, shocking your enemies with your power. Tonight she'd start composing a catchy tune.

Beaming at Noah, she tapped the button to turn off the last of the three digital recorders she'd used at Rachel's house. One on Jessica's person while she'd confronted Rachel, one hidden on the top of the kitchen cupboards, and one on top of the entertainment center in the living room.

Noah picked at a tiny stain on the sleeve of his Boston Bruins sweatshirt. Another thrift store "disguise"—this guy wasn't a hockey fan. She'd bet he watched golf tournaments.

"Didn't I sound like an O'Connor?" Jessica prodded.

"I haven't heard Megan say much," he muttered.

"From how Rachel reacted, you can tell I nailed it. Besides the thousand dollars, you owe me for the digital recorders and the Megan wig. You gotta cover my expenses."

"Costs come out of what I'm paying you. We already talked about this." Noah scanned Jessica's living room floor. Doing a cleaning inspection? Hoping he could call her a slob?

"You sure Rachel wasn't hurt?" he said. "You weren't supposed to hurt anyone."

"You heard her yourself. Didn't you listen? I didn't touch her. Her blabbering to the detective about a weapon is her imagination. I didn't have any weapon at all, and I didn't tell her I did. Admit I nailed this. *Admit it.* This was *so* much better than you'd hoped. I deserve to have my expenses covered."

"Yeah, you did the work. But we agreed on a thousand."

"Did the work? That's your only feedback? I owned this prank!"

"Shh!" Noah reached to grab her shoulder, but she smacked his hand back.

"Don't touch me!"

"Don't yell." He rubbed his hand against the couch cushion like he needed to soothe the two skin cells she'd damaged.

"I read everything I could about the kidnapping so I'd have the background." She lowered her volume but didn't lower her anger; her own voice reminded her of Gibson's hissing. "I even watched talk show interviews with some of Kristen's old friends and teachers to get a feel for her personality. I broke into Megan's apartment and planted a recorder there, then broke in again to get it so I'd have good samples of her voice. I also watched every news video I could find that showed Megan or Kristen so I could pick up any mannerisms. I practiced for hours."

"I paid you for those hours."

"I checked Megan's texts on the iPad she left in her apartment and found out she had a key to Rachel's apartment—Megan was saying she needed to return it, and Rachel said keep it. I also found out there's been bickering between Rachel and Megan about the wedding, which was good news—a reason for Megan to be annoyed with her. I checked Megan's calendar, found out about her four-times-a-week trip to the Britt track and broke into her locker so I could swipe her keys, copy them, and return them. I did that so perfectly that she never knew they were missing. With Rachel's key, I could check Rachel's calendar on her home computer, so between her calendar and Megan's, I could pick the right night to play Kristen when neither of them had anything scheduled, Trevor would be gone, and Rachel's husband would be gone. Do you know how tricky it was to find the perfect time? This involved a *lot* of prep. And I had to sneak in today to get the recorders back from Rachel's place."

"What if the police had found them?"

"Why would they search the place? Rachel never said Kristen robbed her. But even if they did, so what? These are generic. I was disguised when I bought them, and I paid cash. You owe me extra."

"I don't owe you extra," Noah said. "But if it will shut up your griping, I'll make it . . . thirteen hundred. That's the limit."

"Fine." She'd won. "Admit you're impressed."

"Fine. You shook them up. But I doubt Megan's going to prison. You heard Rachel apologizing for causing the police to suspect her. She won't testify against her. If it goes to court, she'll deny everything."

"*Wow.* You're criticizing me for not doing something you didn't hire me to do? Getting her arrested wasn't the goal. You wanted people to remember how awful it was when Rachel got kidnapped. I reminded them brilliantly. This is step one in making Megan look bad, busting up her relationship with Trevor, and making her life miserable. I'm off to a fabulous start. You heard the way Rachel's husband was talking before Megan came over—he suspects her. Even if Rachel pretends that no way would she do this, deep down, she knows it's the only sensible explanation, and Trevor knows that too. They'll worry she's more Kristen-ish than they thought or that she's losing her marbles. I did big-time plowing and seed-planting. Give me some credit."

"What do you want? A promotion?"

He viewed her as a servant, not even worth his thanks. She wanted to swear at him, but he'd ignore the message and judge her for being foul-mouthed. Insults weren't revenge. She'd get real revenge soon. He wouldn't have a clue how to fight her.

Not that she'd leave him any escape.

"It's time to get more subtle and do some watering and fertilizing." She played with the strands of glass beads she wore and shrugged. "Unless you're done. Unless you're satisfied and don't want my help anymore."

Noah picked up a digital recorder. "No . . . let's proceed."

* * *

Sitting at a table near the back wall, Megan kept rereading the list of wood-fired pizzas while she waited for Bryce, but her nervous brain absorbed about as much as it had when she'd tried to read *Beowulf* in Old English. Trevor had urged her to arrange this meeting after his return, but he'd finally given her Bryce's number. She'd texted Bryce this morning, asking him to meet her at Ricci's, explaining she would be alone. He'd texted back with a flat *Ok. Time?* No questions about why she wanted to meet him, no commentary at all. He must have known it was about what had happened to Rachel; Detective Powell must have talked to him.

Did Powell suspect him of being involved in the "Kristen" visit? Or of writing the letter? He'd spent his late teens and early twenties consumed by his addictions, refusing treatment, relying on his mother to rescue him and clean up after him. Would he try to avoid his guilt over his role in Gail's death by blaming and striking out at Megan or Rachel? Or did he have any idea who would want to strike out?

She lifted her gaze from the menu to check again if Bryce had arrived. He was walking toward the table, hands in the pockets of his jacket. He caught Megan's eye but turned his head and continued scanning the restaurant. Was he concerned someone here would recognize him? She'd chosen a public place to make sure she stayed safe but had tried to choose a spot in the restaurant where no one would be likely to overhear their conversation.

Bryce reached the table and sat.

"Hi," Megan said. "Thank you for meeting me."

Bryce opened his mouth but closed it as the server approached their table. Megan requested water; Bryce asked for Dr. Pepper. Megan touched the menu in a random spot and ordered the pizza listed next to her fingernail: pear and prosciutto. Bryce, without looking at his menu, ordered a sausage and mushroom.

When the server had delivered their drinks and walked away, Bryce said quietly, "You are a warped, ruthless woman."

Startled, Megan set her glass of water down. Without Trevor's muscly presence, Bryce clearly would have no trouble detailing how much he hated her.

"I understand why you feel that way," she said. "My role in your mother's death—"

Bryce yanked the napkin from around his silverware. "Bag the sappy penitent routine. What do you want? I'm staying out of your way, and you're siccing the police on me."

"I didn't sic the police on you. Detective Powell brought up your name."

Bryce gulped his Dr. Pepper. "And you made up garbage about how I wanted revenge on you."

Megan kept her tone pleasant. "I gave him plain facts: Trevor and I had dinner with you, it went okay, but it got tense at times, and you weren't always friendly, for which I didn't blame you. That's it."

The server returned and set a basket of bread and a small plate on the table. She popped the cork out of a bottle of olive oil. Megan tightened both hands around her water glass, keeping her expression polite, wishing the server would leave.

The server added a puddle of balsamic vinegar to the oil. "Your pizza will be out in a few minutes."

"Thank you," Megan said. The server walked away. When she was out of earshot, Megan met Bryce's gaze. "I never accused you of anything."

"Right. Do you think I blew every circuit in my brain and I'm too stupid to know what you're doing?"

*Maybe this meeting was a bad idea.* She hadn't expected Bryce to be so aggressive. "What do you think I'm doing?"

"Is it a power trip? Is that why you want me gone?"

"Power over what?"

Bryce leaned across the table. "Control-freak stuff. Don't want the druggie thief back in Britteridge, friends with Trev again."

"I never—"

"You're afraid Brother 'Service Project' Drake will feel obligated to be my buddy and take me to Red Sox games. You don't want him seen with an ex-con. It'll hurt his reputation. What's your plan for him? You think you can get him into politics?"

"If he wanted to go into politics, marrying me would hurt him more than hanging out with you," Megan said coldly. "I have no plan for him. He's free to—"

"Yeah." Bryce moved his fingers as though controlling a marionette. "You think you can yank his strings. A guy with access to a fortune, who drives an old Ford pickup and thinks nothing beats a hike in the Berkshires. You think you can get a villa in Spain, a Ferrari, and a penthouse in Manhattan. Good luck on changing him. Trevor's dull to the core. Why do you think he isn't married yet?"

So scorched with anger that she could have cooked the pizzas in her bare hands, she said, "I don't want to change Trevor. Are you done ranting?"

"I guess the guy's naïve enough to take you at face value. Kristen's the evil twin; you're the good one. What happened last night? Did Rachel tick you off? You hit her where it hurts, and when the cops come, you point them at the ex-con. Double win for you. Payback for Rachel, and the druggie goes to prison."

"I am *not* the one who confronted Rachel last night."

"Yeah. Someone who looked and sounded so much like you that Rachel thought Kristen had escaped from prison. But, no, it was me in a wig."

"I didn't say it was you. It wasn't me. If you have any idea who might have it in for Rachel or me—"

"Whoa, could there be someone in town who doesn't worship you? You're such a talented actor that even the cops buy it."

Megan ripped a piece of bread off the loaf, hoping Bryce would do the same and they could eat in silence and calm down for a few minutes.

Bryce didn't reach for the bread. Megan set her piece down. She didn't want to eat alone while he glowered. Not eating, not speaking, they sat there.

"I love Rachel." Megan broke the silence. "I would never—" She stopped. The server was approaching with two plates in hand.

With their pizza in front of them and the server gone again, Megan finished, "I would never hurt Rachel in any way."

"I don't care if you confess. Just leave me alone. I'm not going back to prison. I did my time, *all* my time, and if you try to blame your shenanigans on me, it'll boomerang around and whack you in the face. Maybe it already has. Trevor may be crazy with lust for you, but his father isn't."

"Excuse me?"

"What was tonight's plan? Flirt and giggle and say how handsome I am to get me to spill more information to help you blame everything on me? Trevor's not here to see you cheating—"

"I'm done." Megan stood. She took a twenty out of her purse, set it on the table, and picked up her untouched platter of pizza. She wasn't abandoning what could provide two meals for her; she'd ask the hostess at the front to put it in a box. "Thanks for insulting me to my face this time instead of writing an anonymous letter."

"That wasn't me!"

"Yeah." Megan mimicked his earlier sarcasm. "Someone who hates me like you do and wants me to know it but who isn't you." She walked away.

# Chapter 9

"I'M SABRINA ERICKSON." JESSICA OFFERED her fake name and held out her hand to the woman in the apartment upstairs from Megan's place. In the comment trail on a news article, she'd learned that "friends of the Drakes" had offered Megan a place to live in one of their properties; with minor research, she'd identified the Mullins family. She hoped the link between families was strong enough that the Mullinses' daughter managing the property would know personal information about Megan.

"I'm Adrianne Mullins," the woman said.

Adrianne was pretty. Her face was too long, but she had super-model cheekbones, and that platinum hair must cost her hundreds of bucks a month at a salon. She appeared to be about Megan and Jessica's age—late twenties. If she and Megan were friends, there was a healthy chance she knew something valuable. Jessica would mine every flake of gold. The discovery that one of the apartments above Megan's was vacant had delighted Jessica. It was an ideal cover for investigating.

Carefully, Jessica removed her hat, not mussing her brown wig. The wig, colored contacts that turned her eyes hazel, glasses, and platform boots that made her over six feet tall made Jessica confident that Adrianne wouldn't be able to give a description that could lead the police to Jessica—if anyone ever asked her about the prospective tenant who had been nosy about Megan, which they probably wouldn't.

"Thanks for giving me an appointment on short notice," Jessica said.

"No problem at all." Adrianne opened a cupboard and lifted a key off a rack. "Let's go see it." She led the way out of her apartment and up the stairs to the second level. "This house has four units and a basement unit, so five total." She unlocked the apartment to the left of the stairs. "Here it is."

Unzipping her coat as she walked, Jessica strolled into the apartment.

"Newly painted," Adrianne said. "The floors were refinished two years ago."

"Nice." Jessica leaned over and pretended to evaluate the polished and slightly warped wood parquet tiles in the living room.

"You can rent it furnished or unfurnished," Adrianne said. "I can show you an online slideshow of the furniture that's available."

"Yeah, I'll need furniture." There wasn't a lot to explore in the empty living room, but Jessica walked around, surveyed the baseboards and ceiling, and counted electrical outlets.

"The electrical system isn't original to the house, thank goodness," Adrianne said. "It's only about ten years old, and you can see we've added a lot of new outlets."

"That's fabulous. Old houses are a pain when there's nowhere to plug your stuff in." Jessica flicked the overhead light off, then back on. "Overhead fixtures."

"Yes, in the bedroom too. More practical than a bunch of lamps. Of course, you can use lamps if you feel the ceiling light is too bright."

"Let's see the kitchen," Jessica said.

Adrianne escorted her into a kitchen that had a white vinyl floor and gray laminate countertops.

"Gas stove." Adrianne opened the oven door as though trying to impress Jessica with shiny oven racks.

"Not much counter space." Actually, there was a lot more counter space than Jessica had in her shabby apartment.

"It's enough though." Adrianne patted the laminate. "My kitchen is the same layout. The fridge is included, unless you have your own you'd rather use."

"I don't." Jessica opened the fridge and jiggled an empty shelf. "What's the neighborhood like?"

"It's great. I just moved here after Christmas. My younger sister was managing the place, but she has a new job teaching art, so I came up from Boston to take over property management. Do you live in Britteridge now?"

"No, I'm in Salem, but I'm tired of the drive to school."

"You at Britt?"

"Yes. Grad school."

"What are you studying?"

Jessica had picked a field far from her interests and Googled it in case she needed to pretend to know something about it. "It's a master's program in math."

"That's awesome! You must know Mark Jenkins."

*I am the bomb*, Jessica thought smugly. If she hadn't read through the faculty list for the department, she would have thought Adrianne was talking about a student and flubbed her answer. "Oh yeah! He's a great teacher."

"Awesome. I met him through church when he was a student. Top-notch guy. Well, you'll love living in Britteridge. There are a lot of students in this neighborhood."

Still feigning interest in the fridge, Jessica opened a vegetable bin. "I'll be studying a lot, so I need a quiet place."

"It's *so* quiet here. The other tenants are always courteous. No parties or fights or anything."

"Hey, uh . . ." Jessica closed the fridge and eyed Adrianne. "I don't mean to sound nosy, but the friend who told me this place was for rent mentioned that . . . there's, like, some notorious ex-con living in the basement?"

Wrinkles appeared and almost instantly disappeared between Adrianne's blonde eyebrows. She smiled. "No, nothing like that. Your friend probably heard about . . . it's a weird story, but our tenant is not a criminal."

Jessica opened a cupboard. "What story?"

"Well . . . you might have heard about it on the news. She got tricked into getting involved with a . . . kidnapping . . . but she was innocent. She's just a student, very quiet, never causes problems. She's on campus a lot."

"Wait. She got tricked into *kidnapping* someone?"

"Her sister and her aunt set her up to . . . it's a long story."

Jessica prodded the slats of the blinds on the kitchen window. "My mom was way nervous when I told her what my friend said."

"Who is your friend?"

"Chelsea Anthony. I don't think she's met you. I think she knows one of your tenants or someone who used to live here. We talked about so many apartments that I can't remember the connection. Anyway, she said something about a . . . murder?" Jessica pivoted back toward Adrianne. Adrianne would explain; she wouldn't want to lose the chance to rent the unit because "Sabrina" was skittish about an alleged murderer in the basement. That new apartment complex a few blocks away was drawing a lot of renters. Adrianne must be having trouble filling this old unit; it had been listed for five months.

"Someone did get killed." Adrianne did a so-so job of sounding matter-of-fact. "But Megan—our tenant—did not kill or kidnap anyone."

"Like, wasn't it President Drake's daughter who got killed?"

"No, Rachel is fine. She was the one who got kidnapped. You didn't hear about this? It was huge news."

"Um . . . I'm not sure. I don't usually follow crime stories. When did it happen?"

"Three years ago. A little over three years ago."

"Oh, I wasn't here. It must have made the news at home, but I didn't notice." Jessica twisted the rod that opened the blinds and gazed at the snowy backyard. A shoveled sidewalk crossed the yard, leading to a gate in a chain-link fence woven with privacy strips. Tacky cut-through to the next street. "I'm . . . kinda squeamish about things. My mom will go ballistic if she thinks I'm living near . . . you know, trouble."

"You're not in any danger! When you're done looking around, why don't you come to my apartment and have a Coke or hot chocolate? I can explain what happened, and I promise, there's no danger. Please tell your friend that."

"Okay, sure." Adrianne was afraid that not only would Jessica not rent the place because of Megan, but she would also spread rumors that would damage Adrianne's chances of renting to anyone.

Was this a waste of time? Adrianne might not know anything Jessica hadn't already learned. But any tiny new nugget might give her an idea.

She followed Adrianne into the bedroom, stuck her fingertips into the carpet to feel how thick it was, opened and closed the window, and checked the latch. In the bathroom, she tested taps and flushed the toilet. Done with the tour, she followed Adrianne to her apartment.

Because she never drank Sprite, she chose it from the drinks Adrianne offered—not that she thought someone would realize Sabrina was Jessica because they both drank Diet Coke, but better to be careful of details.

"Pretty painting." She pointed at an oil painting of downtown Britteridge. "Didn't you say your sister teaches art? Did she paint that?"

"Yes."

"She's talented." Jessica sat on the couch and sipped her Sprite.

Adrianne settled in an overstuffed chair. "I know you're worried about what happened with Megan, but there's nothing to be concerned about."

"The neighborhood seems okay, and the price is decent," Jessica said. "I love that I could walk to campus. I just don't like taking chances."

"You wouldn't be taking chances. It's fine if you don't want to rent here, but I don't want you to have the wrong idea about our tenants. It wasn't Megan who kidnapped or killed anyone. It was her sister, her twin sister. Kristen."

Jessica let her jaw droop. "Her sister? Seriously?"

"Yes. See, Megan's aunt . . . I mean her great-aunt Evelyn Seaver had this old grudge against President Drake and Megan and Kristen's mom, Pamela. Twenty-something years ago, President Drake hit and killed Evelyn's daughter when she was riding a bike."

Jessica gasped. "Oh my heck, really?"

"It wasn't his fault at all, but Evelyn still blamed him. And Pamela—the mom—had been out drinking with Evelyn's daughter the night of the accident, and Evelyn blamed Pamela for not stopping her daughter from biking home drunk. They hadn't spoken to each other in decades."

"That's so sad," Jessica said, careful to sound horrified instead of bored. She knew about Evelyn's grudges. How could she angle to get new, twenty-four-carat gossip she could use against Megan?

"Yeah, it was awful. Still affects President Drake, from what I hear. He hates driving. He has a chauffeur do it for him."

*That* was something she hadn't known, that President Drake had a driving phobia. Kind of interesting, but off the top of her head, she didn't know how she could use it to soil Megan's reputation. "Handy to be rich if you're scared of driving."

"True."

"What does the accident have to do with the kidnapping?"

"It was the reason for it. Evelyn wanted revenge. She'd stewed about her daughter's death for years and finally hatched this plan to kidnap President Drake's daughter, Rachel, for ransom and to use Megan and Kristen as her stooges. She planned for Kristen to end up in prison and for Rachel and Megan to end up dead. To take one daughter from each of the culprits."

"Ohh. Taking their daughters because they took her daughter, right? Scary!" Jessica stroked her smooth brown wig, checking the curve of the hair over her cheek, under her jawline, and up to her chin. This A-line style would keep Adrianne from getting a complete look at the shape of her face. "But if the crazy old aunt hated Pamela, what made her think she could get Pamela's kids to work for her?"

"They didn't know anything about her daughter or the accident. It happened before they were born, and they'd never met Evelyn. But Evelyn had kept track of them all their lives, stalkerlike, I guess."

Jessica kept her expression riveted and said wow a bunch of times as Adrianne explained things Jessica already knew about the inheritance scam and how Kristen had fooled Megan into being her alibi. She needed new things about Megan, personal things, but the more ignorant she pretended to be, the more Adrianne would open up. "So Megan had no idea what was happening?"

"Nope. She was with Rachel when the kidnappers—Kristen and her boyfriend—grabbed Rachel, but Megan had no idea one of the kidnappers was her own sister."

"Uh . . . I hope this doesn't sound too rude, but how brainless is she?"

Adrianne averted her gaze and straightened a stack of mail on the table next to her. Was she stalling? *Hmm.* She hadn't quickly defended Megan's intelligence and now seemed reluctant to speak.

"Sorry," Jessica said. "It's just surprising she fell for that story."

"Yeah, it's . . . crazy. Evelyn wasn't dying, by the way. She wasn't sick at all."

"Megan didn't figure that out?"

"Not until things started going wrong and she started digging into Kristen's lies."

"Sounds like she had a mind-blowing case of gullible."

"She was gullible. A clueless doormat."

*Ooh. Nasty.* Jessica ditched her theory that Adrianne and Megan were close friends. Despite Adrianne's efforts to assure Jessica that Megan wasn't dangerous, she didn't seem to have much respect for her.

"Doormat?" Jessica prompted.

"Yeah, pushover. Her mother'd been manipulating her for years."

Jessica wanted to smile but held it back. Adrianne was getting blatantly gossipy. In the articles Jessica had studied, some of the quotes from Pamela O'Connor had given her the sense that Pamela was melodramatic and savored the limelight. Jessica might be able to use Megan's mother. "So her mother is . . . overbearing?"

"She's a self-centered drama queen. My sister, Larissa, had to deal with her when Megan first moved in, and Larissa said she was a piece of work, moaning about how her daughter had abandoned her and she was going to end up in poverty, dying of loneliness."

"Loneliness?"

"She's young, can't be older than midfifties, and healthy. But she spent years mooching money off Megan, pressuring her to live at home even though Megan wanted to go to college. That's why Megan's still an undergrad, even though she's older."

"Yikes." This was juicy information. While Jessica thought about what else she wanted to know about Megan's relationship with Pamela, she asked the question Adrianne would expect from Sabrina. "What happened to Rachel Drake? Did she escape?"

"Evelyn set it up so she would see Kristen without her mask on. Evelyn wanted Kristen to panic and kill Rachel for her while Evelyn killed Megan. But Megan had finally figured out what was happening. She escaped from Evelyn and stopped Kristen. Rachel got hurt, but she's fine now."

"You said someone got killed. Who was that?"

"A doctor named Gail Ludlum. A friend of the Drakes. Kristen had blackmailed her to get information about the Drakes and medical supplies she needed for the kidnapping."

"Who killed her?"

"Kristen. She got scared Dr. Ludlum would go to the police. But remember, Megan had nothing to do with it, and Kristen's in prison for life. There's no danger anymore for anyone. It's over."

Jessica set her glass on a multicolored ceramic coaster. "This is soooo wild. Scary!"

"Believe me, it's not normal for Britteridge. It's a quiet place. Very low crime."

"What happened to the old aunt?"

"She killed herself."

"Oh, wow. That's sad."

"Anyway . . . I know it's a crazy story, but Megan's not a danger to anyone. We wouldn't rent to someone who was dangerous."

"Yeah, sure, I get it. But, like, do people hate Megan? She doesn't get graffiti or rocks through her window?"

"No, people love her." Adrianne smiled, but it was lousy acting. "In fact, she just got engaged to Trevor, Rachel's brother."

"No way!"

"It doesn't make sense to me that he'd go for her." Adrianne kept the fake smile but sounded so scornful that Jessica excitedly added another fact to her list: Megan's engagement bothered Adrianne. Was she jealous?

"But she's great as a tenant," Adrianne added. "If you move in here, you'll hardly ever see her. You don't have to be friends. Do you think *I'd* live here if I thought there was any danger?"

"Good point." Yay for Adrianne for bringing up Trevor's name. Now Jessica could ask about him without sounding extra nosy. The more she could learn about Trevor, the better she'd know how to split Megan and him up. When she'd asked Noah for gossip about him, Noah had looked stumped and said, "What do you mean, gossip? You remember the guy from school. What's there to gossip about?"

Right.

"Megan totally scored, right?" Jessica said. "President Drake's son! Do you know him?"

"Yes."

One word answer. No eye contact. *Sore spot.* "What's he like? Is he hot?"

"He's handsome," Adrianne said curtly. "He looks a lot like his dad, if you've seen President Drake, but bigger and taller."

"So every girl on campus chases him?"

"He's not *that* great of a catch."

"Hot and rich, and he's not a great catch?"

"You'd never know he's rich. Well, he isn't, technically, but I know he has plenty of money of his own, and he'll inherit a ton someday. He just doesn't spend much. Frugal. Kind of a boring do-your-duty guy."

*Squeeze those sour grapes.* "You think he's boring?" Jessica skillfully portrayed herself as awestruck. Adrianne was cool enough to know *and* dismiss Trevor Drake! "Do you know him well?"

\* \* \*

Before he climbed into his truck, Trevor vowed he wouldn't get angry while talking to Bryce. With every block he drove toward Bryce's home, he had to remake the vow; his brain kept campaigning for him to kick down Bryce's door and punch him hard enough to hurl him into Massachusetts Bay.

He parked in front of Gail's house—Bryce's house. Trevor hadn't been here since Megan's hysterical call had summoned him with the news that she'd found Gail dead.

*Welcome back.*

He rammed his thumbs against his temples and rubbed circles into his aching muscles. Why had he been so egotistical as to think he had any valid idea whether or not Bryce would terrorize Rachel? He didn't know Bryce anymore. In assuming Bryce wouldn't set up that scare, he'd made Megan overconfident about meeting with him. Why hadn't Trevor done a better job at convincing her to wait until he returned from San Diego?

*Get in there and find out what you can. Keep calm.* He strode to the door and rang the bell. He hadn't warned Bryce he was coming. Why give him time to fortify his defenses? If Trevor heard Bryce approach but he didn't open the door, Trevor would camp out on the porch until midnight, ringing and knocking. He doubted Bryce would call the police and report him as a trespasser.

Bryce opened the door. His colorless face and the purplish bags under his eyes made Trevor wonder if his sleeves were covering new needle marks. "What do you want?"

"To talk. Civilly."

Bryce gestured at his clothes. "Not ready for visitors."

His sweatshirt was frayed around the neck, and drips and smears on the front looked like wood stain. That must be one of Charlie's old shirts he'd worn in his garage workshop. Gail must have kept it as a memento.

Bryce had chosen to wear it. His father's ratty shirt.

Anger scaled back its siege against Trevor's self-control. "I'm not the fashion police. Let's talk."

"You look like the something-police. FBI. Secret Service."

Trevor pinched the knot of his tie. "I haven't changed since church."

Bryce lowered his chin and twitched the toes on one sock-covered foot. Trevor suspected what was roiling in his thoughts: he didn't want to deal with Trevor, but he was leery of being too uncooperative. From what Trevor had heard, Bryce was performing stellar work on the Britt grounds crew. That meant he still wanted the job. He must already be worried that Trevor's father knew he'd insulted Megan, and he didn't want Trevor logging strike two by reporting that he'd refused to talk.

"May I come in?" Trevor asked.

Bryce edged backward. "I was, uh, doing the dishes."

Trevor stepped inside. Posture rigid, Bryce stood, waiting, not inviting Trevor to sit. Did he think he could dispatch this issue with a five-minute chat in the hall?

"Let's go in the kitchen, and I'll help you clean up." Trevor hung his overcoat and suit coat in the closet. Gail's white puffy coat and her white-and-red beret still hung there, evoking memories of Gail swooping into the Drakes' house at Christmastime, carrying a loaf of Finnish pulla or a platter of almond pastries.

"You don't want to do my dishes," Bryce said.

Trevor walked past him. In Gail's familiar kitchen, he stopped at the sink Bryce had filled with soapy water and rolled up his sleeves. Given the pile of dishes on the counter, cleaning the kitchen had to be a once-a-week activity. "You dry," Trevor said, washing a plate.

Scowling, Bryce picked up a dish towel. "Is dishwashing tonight's installment of the service project?" He took the plate from Trevor.

Trevor sank a couple of oatmeal-encrusted bowls into the water. "Service project?"

"Help Bryce adjust to post-prison life. Get him a job. Invite him for dinner. Wash his dishes."

"Our families have been friends since we were in elementary school. You call friendship a service project?"

"You know everything's changed." Bryce shoved the plate into a cupboard. "Go ahead and tear my head off for what I said to Megan.

If you can't see how obvious it is that's she's the one who scared Rachel, then you're love-stupid. I'll bet you told your dad what I said to her, but guess what? He hasn't fired me. He knows I'm right."

"Did he say that?"

"He hasn't talked to me. But if he *didn't* think I was right, he *would* have sacked me."

"He doesn't believe it was Megan. We know Megan. She would never do that to Rachel."

"I don't care if you believe her, but if you let her blame this on me and her lies get me arrested, I'll sue your family for every one of their gazillion dollars."

"No one is trying to blame it on you." Trevor scrubbed at a glued-on blueberry. "Unless you can shrink yourself and make your voice credibly female, you didn't spook Rachel."

"Megan wants me to take the rap as the mastermind. I get it. I recruited a female friend—one of the hundreds who follow me like groupies—to haunt Rachel."

"Can you drop the defensiveness?"

"Not when someone's plotting to send me back to prison."

Trevor rinsed the bowl and handed it to Bryce. "Did you send Megan that hate mail last month?"

"*No.*"

"Do you have any idea who did?"

Bryce clanked the bowl onto a stack in the cupboard. "No."

"Pretend you don't think Megan's lying. Now do you have any idea who'd harass her or Rachel?"

"I don't have friends here anymore. I don't hear gossip, except at work, and no one there is dumb enough to gossip about President Drake's future daughter-in-law. How would I know anything, except that I'm a scapegoat?"

"The only reason the police came to you is because you'd shown hostility toward Megan. Questioning you was mandatory if they wanted to do their work. No one wants to send you back to prison for something you didn't do."

"Sure."

Trevor passed him another clean bowl. "I understand why you suspect Megan of scaring Rachel. You don't know her well enough to see how out of character that would be for her. But accusing her of trying to frame you is paranoid." He shook bubbles off his hands and turned to face Bryce. "Insulting her like you did was completely out of line."

Bryce closed the cupboard and met Trevor's gaze. "You came to tell me if I don't apologize to her, you'll—"

"I'm not telling you to apologize. I'm not threatening you. Show some character and quit acting like a grade-A swine."

Bryce tossed his dish towel on the counter and walked away.

Trevor dipped a tomato-sauce-coated pan into the sink. Behind him, he heard chair legs drag across hardwood and Bryce thud into a kitchen chair.

"What did the police say to you?" Trevor asked, his back to Bryce. "Did they accuse you of anything?"

Bryce didn't answer.

Trevor had washed the pan and scrubbed peanut butter off half a dozen knives before Bryce spoke. "They didn't accuse me," he said wearily. "They asked me where I was on Tuesday night when 'Kristen' showed up at Rachel's. I was here, no witnesses. They asked me about the letter. I said I didn't send it. They interrogated me about how I felt about Megan. Did I blame her for Mom's death? I said no. They left."

"From that routine questioning, you decided Megan was framing you?"

Bryce stayed silent. Trevor looked over his shoulder.

"Maybe I overreacted," Bryce mumbled. "Thinking of going back to prison . . . Man, I hated it there. I've been careful, way careful. I don't even drink beer; it's all water and Coke and orange juice. I pass my drug tests. I'm on time to work every day and work my tail off. Hundred percent law-abiding citizen. But after one month of me being perfect, here come the cops. I guess I panicked. Stop washing those dishes. I can shove most of them in the dishwasher. I only wanted to do Mom's best pans by hand."

Trevor dried his hands on the dish towel.

"I swear I haven't bothered Rachel or sent any letters to Megan. All I do is work, come home, and watch TV. Sometimes run laps at the track at Britt. Why the—" He trapped the half-spoken profanity. It surprised Trevor that Bryce would care about keeping his language clean in front of him.

"Why would I risk going back to prison for *any* reason?" Bryce rested his fingertips against his eyebrows and pushed them up and down as though they were manually operated. "You think I like a grudge more than I like freedom?"

"You look exhausted. Got a headache?"

"Yeah, but not bad. I don't want to take anything for it."

"You sleeping okay?"

"Uh . . . not too good. Lotta nightmares. Last night I kept waking up thinking a SWAT team was bashing through the door."

Trevor walked to a cupboard near the phone. On the top shelf were still teas and cocoas, where Gail had always kept them. They all must be at least three years old, but he doubted out-of-date herbal tea would hurt them. He chose a box of lemon balm tea.

"You're making tea?" Bryce watched Trevor set Gail's copper teakettle on the stove. "Do you play shuffleboard too and yell at Megan to turn up the TV?"

"Don't fake it." Trevor took two mugs out of the cupboard. "I know you like this stuff. Your mom used to give it to you before school."

Bryce half grinned. "When I was a little kid!"

"Teenager."

"Hey, it helped me when I had tests that day. Made me smarter."

"Placebo effect."

"It worked!"

"Let's hope it makes you smarter now."

"I want honey in mine. It's in the cupboard over the sink."

Trevor set the jar of honey on the table, along with a couple of spoons and saucers. When the water was boiling, he poured it over the teabags and brought one of the mugs to Bryce.

Bryce fiddled with the string dangling from the teabag. "I haven't drunk this stuff in—" He choked, then swore under his breath.

Trevor sat at the table, his own lemon tea in front of him. He hadn't had this in years either, not since he'd drunk it here with Bryce. He focused on the cup while Bryce wiped tears off his face.

"I'm sorry," Trevor said. "It's got to be tough."

Bryce tapped the twisted handle of his pottery mug. "Did you know Mom didn't have any two mugs the same? Said she didn't want to take up cupboard space with duplicates when there were so many creative designs. All handmade stuff."

"I remember that."

Bryce rotated the mug. Trevor rejected the urge to ask a question or make a comment. He wanted to see where Bryce would go with the conversation without any lead from Trevor.

Bryce bowed his head over his mug. Either he wanted to inhale the steam, or he was safeguarding himself against any eye contact with Trevor. "Drives me crazy, thinking about what a sucker I was. Getting set up like that."

"Evelyn Seaver was an expert at fooling people," Trevor said.

"Yeah, but why didn't I see how nutty it was? This fussy old lady hiring me to do her yard, saying someone had recommended me. Who would recommend me? I was a mess. The only customers who hadn't dumped me were doing a favor for my mom."

"Maybe you thought Evelyn was doing a favor too."

"My mom said she didn't know her."

"Which still wasn't evidence that it was suspicious."

He lifted his head. "You want to knock off the saintly comfort thing?"

"Sure. You're an idiot. Like that better?"

Air puffed from Bryce's throat, a laugh that sounded like it had surprised him. "Yeah."

"You just said you were a mess. You weren't thinking clearly. It's not surprising you didn't realize Evelyn was setting you up."

"Yeah, but come on. After a month, this old lady tells me—tells this sketchy guy who's always breaking branches on her peony bushes or forgetting to mow the backyard or is too stoned to come to work at all—that she stores a bunch of cash under her mattress. Who'd do that?"

"Someone senile?"

"She didn't seem senile. Then she hands me a key so I can water her plants while she's out of town. I'd never robbed a house before, but, man, I was crazy with excitement at the number of fixes I could get if I stole her hoard. Didn't think about how it made *no* sense for her to trust me like that."

"Yeah, you should have caught on," Trevor said. "You should have realized she'd had a grudge against my family since before you were born, knew your mother was best friends with my mother, was planning to kidnap Rachel, and needed an inside source of information and a doctor's help, knew you were an addict, wanted you to think there were thousands of dollars in the house and no one was home so you'd try to rob it, planned to record you on security cameras, *and* set things up so when you went to swipe the cash from under the mattress you'd find her husband asleep on the bed."

Bryce resumed massaging his eyebrows. "Yeah, and when I saw him, I *still* didn't catch on. I should have run."

"Yeah, you should have. But she knew a feeble old man wouldn't be enough to scare you away when you thought there was a hoard under his mattress."

"*Feeble*. William Seaver was a stubborn loon. Almost broke my arm with his cane."

Trevor picked up one of the spoons and pushed his teabag deeper into the mug. Evelyn had known the husband she despised was stubborn and cranky enough to challenge a thief. They would fight; she'd hoped Bryce would kill him. Bryce hadn't, but William's tumble down the stairs during their skirmish had been enough. The paper had reported that an elderly man had died of head injuries due to a fall; video footage of the fight had convinced Gail her son had killed the man during an attempted robbery. Blackmail material. Even Bryce didn't know the fall hadn't killed William— Evelyn had, after Bryce had fled.

"Fine, no way could I have known what she was planning." Bryce grabbed the honey jar. "I just wish I'd . . . done different stuff. My mom must have been in agony over betraying your family. Like hurting so much it was killing her."

"I know that."

"No way would I mock her memory by scaring Rachel, and no way would I risk going back to prison. Maybe it wasn't Megan who did it. I don't know who it was. But I swear it wasn't me."

Trevor scrutinized Bryce's pallid face. On the wall, the enameled butterfly clock ticked.

He didn't want to believe Bryce. He wanted Bryce to be guilty. Crime solved, culprit punished, no further danger to the people Trevor loved.

Unfortunately, he believed Bryce.

# Chapter 10

HOLDING THE WALT WHITMAN ANTHOLOGY she'd found, Megan returned to her favorite study carrel in an out-of-the-way nook in the Britteridge College Library. Many times, she'd fantasized about how wonderful it would be to stay in the library for days, roll out a sleeping bag and spend the nights breathing the scent of books; wake when sunlight shone through the tall, arched windows; spend chilly evenings in front of the fireplace in one of the reading rooms; wander for hours, pulling from the shelves any book that caught her attention; study every painting on the walls and absorb the beauty of the artwork. She'd told Trevor she wanted a set of bookshelves for a wedding present. He'd responded that when they built a house, they'd include an entire room walled with bookshelves.

She opened the Whitman anthology but couldn't concentrate. She kept scanning the stacks around her, contemplating a home with Trevor and working to nourish the still-wilted confidence inside her.

A week had gone by since "Kristen's" visit. As far as Megan knew, Powell hadn't found any leads or enough evidence to charge Megan. Rachel and Peter had changed their locks. No one had bothered them. No one had bothered Megan. Rachel had called and texted her too many times with too many cheerful, trivial questions and remarks: *Cold day! When's spring? What are you having for lunch? I'm thinking minestrone. Is this blouse cute, or are the pleats weird? Ran out of milk! What do you think of hydrangeas in bouquets?* Was she still trying to drag her trust in Megan back up to 100 percent? Trevor showed no trace of doubting her, and when she said her prayers at night, exhausted from rigorous days, her fervent, long-winded efforts to express gratitude for Trevor resulted in twice waking up in the middle of the night, still kneeling by her bed with her legs and folded arms now numb.

What time was it? It must be dinnertime; she was hungry. She opened the pocket of her backpack to check the time on her phone. Five forty-seven.

The screen showed three missed calls from her mother. Three! That made four calls today, including the one that had come during class this afternoon.

She'd better call her back . . . after meditating, watching birds glide across a twilight sky, listening to ethereal Celtic music, and soaking in a hot bath scented with lavender.

*Very funny. Why waste relaxation techniques* before *you talk to her? Save them for afterward—if you need them. You'll do fine. She probably wants to tell you about some new shoes.*

Megan exited the library. As she trotted through the frigid wind, she tapped the screen to return her mother's call.

"There you are!" Pamela's voice rang in her ear. "I've been trying to call you all day."

"I've either been in class or in the library. Tuesdays are busy."

"Why didn't you call me back as soon as class ended? Or text me immediately?"

Megan restrained a sigh. "How are you doing, Mother?"

"Oh, I *was* fine until I found out my loving daughter has been lying to me."

So much for a lighthearted new-shoes conversation. "I assume that's hyperbole. What did I say that you think was misleading?"

"Your claims of being a poor college student! About how your stipend only covers books and necessities and you don't have money to spare."

Confused, Megan walked faster. This was obviously going to be a bewildering and irritating conversation, and she wanted to get away from campus to a less crowded sidewalk. "That's the truth. I don't know why you'd think otherwise."

"Is Trevor dressing you in emeralds and mink and filling your bank account with gold now that you're engaged? Did you think you could hide it since I'm marooned in Pennsylvania and hardly ever see you?"

Megan was almost jogging now, the cold air clawing her throat. "First of all, my finances are not your concern. Second, what you don't seem to understand, even though I've explained it many times, is that Trevor is not wealthy. His parents—"

"For heaven's sake, that's splitting hairs. His family is drowning in money. He'll always have anything he wants."

"That's not how the Drakes are. Trevor works hard for—"

"He gives you expensive gifts, doesn't he? What did he give you for Christmas?"

With no one in earshot, Megan slowed, trying not to pant into Pamela's ear. "I'd like to change the subject. You already asked me about my Christmas, and I already told you."

"I've forgotten. What was it? A Mercedes convertible? A trip to the French Riviera?"

"It was a new phone. Which I very much appreciated and needed."

"How big is that rock on your finger? Two carats? More?"

Megan glanced at the diamond solitaire on her hand, realizing she'd forgotten to put on her gloves. She didn't know how big the stone was. Trevor hadn't offered that information when he'd proposed, and she had no idea how to judge carats. "It's the size of a coconut," she said. "He also gave me a diamond tiara."

"Oh, hilarious. Here I am scraping by, and you make fun of how much money you have."

Bracing the phone between her cheek and shoulder, Megan tugged her gloves out of her pockets. "If you can't let go of the fiction that I have piles of money, I'm hanging up."

"Did he pay for your new leather coat?"

Jolted, Megan clutched the phone with a still-bare hand. How did Pamela know she'd purchased a leather coat? She'd never mentioned it. "No, he didn't," she said. "I bought that myself."

"You bought it *yourself.* You tell me you don't have money for anything but books and food and rent—certainty not enough money to help *me* out—and you buy yourself an expensive designer leather jacket."

The wind blew Megan's hair across her face. She slipped her gloves on and reached in her pocket for her fleece hat. "It wasn't that expensive."

"You don't think two thousand dollars is expensive? Two thousand dollars for a *coat*? You criticize me for spending fifty dollars on a scarf!"

"What are you talking about? It didn't cost two thousand dollars. It cost—" Megan stopped herself. "It did not cost anywhere near that much. What makes you think I spent thousands of dollars on a coat?"

"A friend of yours called me this morning. She was worried about you."

"A friend! Who?"

"She didn't give her name, dear. She didn't want you to be angry with her."

"What in the world did she say?"

"That you were blowing through money because you assumed you had lots coming, and you didn't understand that Trevor is a cheapskate and he'll never support extravagant spending. She hoped I could persuade you to be sensible."

Megan slid on a patch of ice and flapped her arms to hold her balance, nearly dropping her phone. She brought it back to her ear. "Some anonymous person called you and said I blew thousands on a leather jacket?"

"She said she was a friend from that church you joined."

Megan's mind made a blurry pass through the ward list, but she couldn't fathom anyone calling Pamela to spread rumors. "What's her phone number?"

"Oh, darling, she said she was calling from a pay phone at the mall."

"*Are* there pay phones at the mall these days?"

"Well, apparently so. She said she adores you and was so afraid you'd be mad at her that she didn't want to use her own phone in case you were visiting me and saw the caller ID. I told her there was almost no chance you'd be here; you hardly ever—"

"Mother, whoever it was, she's nuts. I have no idea why she thought the coat was so expensive or why it was any of her business." Megan decided not to waste time pointing out that Pamela was now claiming she'd called to warn Megan that Trevor was a tightwad after she'd started off by accusing Trevor of spending lavishly on Megan.

"Let's get to the point," Megan said. "If you're calling to ask me for money because you think the coat means I've been hiding how rich I am, the answer is no. We worked that out three years ago. We're both independent adults, responsible for our own expenses."

"Is that what I am to you? An 'independent adult'? I thought we were family."

"We are family. I love you. That has nothing to do with our finances."

"I can't believe you'd spend so much on a coat while telling me you can't spare—"

"The coat cost $125!" Irritated that she'd let Pamela goad her into sharing information that was none of her business, she said, "Hang on," and drew the phone away from her ear. Stalling for a few seconds, she fluffed her scarf up under her chin and pulled her fleece hat down so it completely covered her nonphone ear. *Don't let her rile you up.*

She raised the phone back to her ear. "The rumor is hogwash, and my 'friend' was wrong. How's work? Are things getting hectic with orders for Valentine flower—"

"Well, honestly, you always make yourself sound so broke I'm surprised you'd have *anything* to spend on a coat."

Megan waffled between refusing to say more about the coat and offering a brief explanation. Maybe a few details would clear away the rumor still stuck in Pamela's brain. "I needed a new dressy coat. My old one has holes in it, and the lining is falling out. I budgeted carefully. I set money aside from my TA job. I searched for weeks until I found what I wanted and could afford. I bought the coat *used* on eBay."

Pamela didn't speak. Thank goodness. She finally understood how outrageously she was acting.

Megan slowed her steps. Power walking in boots was hurting her shins. "So I imagine the floral shop is—"

"You can't claim a leather coat isn't a luxury. Apparently you're only frugal when it comes to helping your mother."

Submerged anger shot to the surface. "Don't you dare accuse me of being callous toward you because for the first time since Dad died I bought myself something a little indulgent instead of making your car payments so you could spend your money on manicures."

Pamela gasped. "What has happened to you? Did I accidentally dial the prison? Am I talking to Kristen?"

Megan slammed her thumb against the screen of her phone, disconnecting the call.

* * *

*Definite D minus on that conversation.* Stress had worn holes in Megan's self-control and good sense. She knew better than to let her mother's complaints grow and mutate so no matter what Megan said, Pamela could still relish being offended. She expected Pamela to call back promptly and berate her for hanging up. As she ate dinner, she kept glancing at her phone, the all-in-one, high-tech version of a rock and a hard place. If she answered the call, she'd have to deal with her mother. If she didn't answer, she'd have to deal with her angrier mother later.

After an hour of no contact, Megan started to relax. Pamela must have realized the rumor was absurd and she'd been rude to Megan. She'd likely call tomorrow—not to apologize but to chat about the florist's shop and her plans to get new accent pillows for the living room couch if she could find a light green that was more blue than yellow. If she wanted to act like nothing had happened, Megan was fine with that.

Who had called Pamela with that outlandish coat rumor? Megan had worn the coat for a couple of Sundays, and a lot of people had complimented it, but no one had mentioned cost. Should she text friends in the ward and ask if they'd heard gossip about it?

*Don't do it. What does it matter where the rumor came from? Whoever called Mother thought she was being helpful or, at worst, likes spreading gossip and feeling self-righteous. If you ask friends about it, it'll feed rumors and contention. Let it all go. It doesn't matter.*

She was on the couch, wrapped in a blanket and skimming through the Whitman anthology, when a text from Trevor asked if she could come to his parents' house as soon as possible; they needed to discuss some things. Would she mind driving herself? He was already there.

Puzzled, Megan started to call Trevor to ask about this short-notice invitation but stopped and reread the text several times, her anxiety escalating. Maybe Michael and Sandra wanted to discuss wedding plans, but on a weeknight, without making prior arrangements? They were busy, organized people, and this was a busy season at work for Trevor, especially with his needing to catch up after his San Diego trip. She'd thought he was at his office tonight. He hadn't mentioned plans to go to Andover to see his parents.

Megan couldn't think of a positive reason that Trevor, who was always courteous, would summon her without an explanation, without asking if she had time tonight, and without offering to pick her up. This wasn't a "let's talk about reception menus" meeting.

Michael and Sandra had reassured her that they didn't suspect her of terrorizing Rachel, but after pondering the incident further, had they changed their minds? Had they, like Bryce, decided she was the only reasonable suspect?

*Calm down. They'll be your family soon. Trust them.*

If this was going to be a nerve-wracking conversation, she didn't want to start it over the phone. She texted Trevor instead of calling. *I'll leave now. See you soon.*

During the twenty-minute drive, Megan tried to soothe herself with breathing techniques and learned she was a pro at counting her breaths *and* simultaneously getting more anxious over what Sandra and Michael wanted to say to her. If they thought she had maliciously tormented Rachel, they'd still treat her with compassion and respect, but their trust in her, their feelings about her becoming a member of the family, their view of her integrity and mental stability—

*Don't panic. They know you. They know you wouldn't hurt Rachel.*

Parking her junky car in the Drakes' driveway always seemed odd—talk about an anomaly for the neighborhood. It usually seemed odd *and* comical, but tonight it felt odd and uncomfortable. Had anyone ever asked Sandra who drove that hideous, rusty thing?

*What's wrong with you? You know the Drakes couldn't care less what car you drive.* She hurried to the front door and rang the bell.

Trevor answered. "Hey," he said. "Thanks for coming. I know you must be busy."

"You're busier than I am."

He smiled, but it was a polite smile, not an authentic one. No kiss hello. He even stood back a few feet.

Did he suspect her? Not just his parents?

"Come in to the living room," he said.

She walked next to him, the cramps intensifying in her stomach and making her feel like she'd caught a stomach bug in the last thirty seconds.

Sandra and Michael were sitting on the couch together. As Megan and Trevor entered, Michael rose to his feet.

"Good evening." His smile was kind, and his eyes had a solemn, contemplative expression. Sandra's smile was about as real as Trevor's.

Megan got queasier with apprehension, realizing Trevor—chivalrous Trevor—hadn't offered to take her coat for her as he always did. Awkwardly, she unbuttoned it. Michael moved forward to take it and draped it over the back of a chair.

"Please, sit down." He gestured toward the chairs facing the couch.

Megan sat. Trevor took the chair next to her, looking neither at her nor at his parents.

"Please understand this is not meant as an ambush." Michael returned to his seat. "We simply thought it would be beneficial if we were together when we discussed the e-mail you sent Sandra earlier today."

The e-mail? Megan tried to recall what e-mail she'd sent but couldn't remember contacting Sandra at all. As unobtrusively as she could, she inhaled and exhaled full breaths. She'd gotten so wound up thinking they were going to accuse her of playacting escaped-convict Kristen that she'd apparently muddled her brain. "I'm sorry. It's been a long day. I don't remember the e-mail you're talking about. What did it say?"

"The e-mail asking for money," Sandra said softly.

Baffled, Megan looked at Trevor. He met her eyes for a moment but didn't speak.

"I know you didn't want me to say anything to Trevor," Sandra said. "But it's only right—"

Michael held up a hand. "Megan, did you send Sandra an e-mail this afternoon?"

Megan reviewed her day. She'd gone to class, eaten leftover spaghetti that she'd heated in the microwave in the student center, gone to class again, graded tests, studied and hunted for books for that poetry research paper in the library, walked home at dinnertime, . . . fought with her mother over that nonsensical coat rumor . . .

A rumor about money. Had the Drakes heard it? Had the same person who'd called Pamela e-mailed Sandra?

But Michael had said the e-mail had come from Megan.

"I'm sorry," Megan said. "I might be losing my mind, but I don't remember sending an e-mail to Sandra today."

Sandra lifted her glasses from the top of her head and put them on. Michael picked up a phone from the lamp table and passed it to Sandra. She worked with the phone for a moment and brought it to Megan.

An e-mail showed on the screen:

*Sandra,*

*I'm so sorry about this, but I need to ask a favor. I feel so stupid. I went all crazy and spent a fortune on a new coat, and I forgot my car insurance and renter's insurance are due, and some other bills are coming up fast. Could I borrow some cash just for a few weeks? A thousand dollars would help me so much, and I promise I'll pay you back.*

*This is so embarrassing. I promise it will never happen again. Please don't tell Trevor. You know how boring and stuffy he is about money— never makes a mistake or an impulse buy and can't understand how the rest of us are human and blow it sometimes.*☺

*Thanks so much. This would save me! I could come by any time you say to pick up the money—hopefully at a time when none of the men are around, right?* ☺

*Love,*
*Megan*

Anger poured into what was already flood-level embarrassment. Who wrote this? Megan tapped her name in the from box. It showed her e-mail address. She handed the phone back to Sandra and reached into the pocket of her purse for her own phone. Fingers shaking, she accessed the sent box.

There it was, an e-mail to Sandra that she'd never written. The time stamp on the e-mail said she'd sent it at 3:24 p.m. She'd been in class at that time.

Megan lowered her phone. "Sandra—"

"We're not upset, sweetheart." Sandra touched her cheek. "It would be astounding if you hadn't picked up some poor financial habits from your mother, and I know you're usually a responsible spender. We're happy to help out when there's legitimate need, but this isn't that kind of situation. Trevor is excellent at budgeting and can teach you how to handle your money in a way that prevents issues like this."

Humiliation chewing her up, Megan wanted to say she knew how to budget as well as Trevor did, but Sandra didn't pause. "If you can still return the coat, that would be the best solution. If it's too late to do that, we'll help you work out a plan for fulfilling your obligations. Selling the coat online might be part of the answer."

"Thank you," Megan said hastily. "I appreciate what you're saying, but I didn't—"

"The money isn't the biggest issue." Sandra interrupted her again, a gaffe so unusual for gracious Sandra that it flummoxed Megan. "You know I regarded you as a daughter even before you and Trevor got engaged, so I hope we have a strong enough relationship that I can be blunt." She continued talking as she returned to the couch. "I don't think it's funny or appropriate when women mock their husbands. I assume you intended to sound joking, but even if it was a joke, it was unkind and inappropriate."

Megan nodded and opened her lips to speak, but another surge of words from Sandra stopped her.

"Sweetheart, you need to understand that unless the matter is something harmless and fun, like a birthday present, I don't conspire in keeping secrets from members of my family. Please don't ask me to hide things from Trevor. You need to communicate openly with him, not sneak behind his back. A strong marriage—"

"Sandra." Michael laid his hand on her knee.

"I'm sorry." Sandra removed her glasses and nestled them back in her curly brown hair. She gave Megan a thin but warm smile. "I'm not giving you the opportunity to say anything."

"I didn't send that e-mail." Why did she feel a hundred times more flustered defending herself to the Drakes than she had felt defending herself to her mother?

*Easy question.* Her mother was prone to silly accusations and exaggerations. The Drakes weren't, so this hurt more.

Hurt a *lot* more. Even Trevor had believed the e-mail. "Someone must have hacked into my account. Someone who knows details about my life." She eyed her caramel-brown leather coat draped over a chair and wanted to burn it. "I would never ask for money to cover irresponsible purchases. I don't *need* money. I'm fine. The coat— I'll show you."

She tapped at her phone until she'd accessed her bank account. "Here." She held the phone out to Trevor. "You can see I'm in the black. As far as renter's insurance, I paid that in August. Car insurance isn't due until April, and if you want, I can show you that information too. Click on the link for automatic bill payments, and you'll see what I've paid recently and that I'm up-to-date. Feel free to show this to your parents."

"You're not obligated to show us your private financial information," Michael said.

"I want you to see it. As far as the coat—apparently there's a rumor that I spent thousands of dollars on it. Someone even called my mother to ask her to talk sense into me, which is about as ironic as you can get."

Trevor took her phone but didn't look at the screen. Was he trying to indicate that he believed her? She couldn't see any emotion through the guarded expression on his face.

"Check the list of recent transactions, and you'll see a PayPal transaction for $125," she said. "That's what the coat cost me." She waved toward the coat. "It's in good shape, but if you look closely, you'll see it's not new. I bought it used on eBay. Trevor, I told you I bought it used. I told you it was a fantastic bargain."

Trevor passed the phone back. "I . . . missed that. I'm sorry."

Megan wanted to groan, but showing exasperation wouldn't help. She wasn't surprised Trevor had forgotten. His only interest in fashion was in remembering the handful of brands and styles he liked so he could replace a worn-out shirt via a click of the mouse instead of a shopping trip. He never commented on her clothes, and the details she'd told him about the coat had probably skated over his ears while his mouth said automatically, "It looks great, Meg."

She brought her phone to Michael and Sandra; she wanted *someone* in the family to study objective evidence. "I can also show you the receipt for the coat if you'd like. Maybe it's more than I should have spent, but I've been setting aside money for it, and it was within my budget. I'd be happy to show you the program I use for budgeting, and you can see exactly how I track my income and expenses." Megan blinked, frustrated that her eyes were stinging. She didn't want to cry.

Michael accepted the phone and put on his glasses.

"I will never stop being grateful for the opportunity you gave me to get an education," Megan said. "The last thing I would do is waste scholarship money, then come begging you for cash." *Actually, the last thing I would do is terrify Rachel by pretending to be her kidnapper. Do you suspect me of that too?*

"We know you work hard, sweetie," Sandra said.

Was she being hypersensitive to think Sandra's answer was vague? Michael was still studying her phone, periodically tapping the screen. Excellent. The more he searched, the more he'd see that the e-mail was a hoax.

"Would you like to see the budget program I use?" she asked.

"Thank you, but it's not necessary." After a few more seconds, he held the phone out to her. "I'm sorry." He patted her hand as she took the phone. "We've jumped to conclusions and embarrassed you."

Relieved, Megan headed back to her seat. "It's not much of a jump when the e-mail came from my account. How could you know it wasn't from me?" She forbade herself to add *Except that it was completely out of character for me.*

But was it out of character? When the Drakes had met her, she'd been seeking an alleged inheritance that she wasn't entitled to. Why shouldn't they think she was greedy? Did she assume three years was long enough to erase their first impression of her?

Even Trevor had believed she'd beg money off his parents because she'd gone into debt to buy an outrageously expensive coat. *And* that she'd labeled him boring and stuffy to his own mother. She pressed her thumb against the diamond on her ring.

"Obviously we have a problem." Michael rested his arm around Sandra's shoulders. "Someone—or more than one person—is putting intense effort into causing trouble for our family. First, that letter to Megan, then the scare Rachel experienced last week. Now this hoax e-mail."

Sandra closed her eyes. "Trouble again," she whispered.

"All the incidents seem very different." Megan kept her voice composed, but her eyes were still prepping for tears. She wished she could drag Trevor out of the room and talk with him alone, but since the e-mail had gone to Sandra, she'd better work this out with his parents first. "I'd guess multiple people are responsible."

"What did your mother say about the person who called her?" Michael asked.

Megan swiped her index finger under each eye, intercepting what she hoped would be her only tears. "She said it was a woman who claimed to be from church. The caller wouldn't give her name and was calling from a pay phone at the mall, supposedly because she was so nervous that I'd be mad at her. I can think of a few people who are gossipy or immature, who might spread a rumor about the cost of my coat, but I can't think of anyone who'd call my mother, let alone hack my account and send a hoax e-mail."

"Has anyone seemed hostile about your relationship with Trevor?" Michael asked. "Jealous?"

She'd warded that question off when Trevor had asked her earlier, not wanting to give the impression that she was accusing anyone, but at this point, she'd better not conceal anything. "I've received a few catty comments, but nothing really hostile, and just one-time cracks, mostly. The only person who said something unkind about our engagement and who is consistently cold to me is Adrianne Mullins."

Sandra opened her eyes. "Adrianne!"

Trevor frowned at Megan. "You didn't tell me Adrianne has been rude to you."

"She's not . . . Well, it's mostly low-key, mostly vibes. When she first moved in, she said something about being astounded that you chose me, but she hasn't been openly rude since then. But every time we interact, she seems cold. I guess she doesn't like me, but I'm *not* accusing her of harassing me."

"Why are you running into Adrianne so often?" Sandra asked.

"She took over for Larissa recently, managing her parents' properties," Megan said. "She lives upstairs from me."

"Oh!" Sandra said. "Did you know she used to date Trevor?"

Astounded, Megan looked at Trevor. He flushed, the red in his face brighter than Megan had ever seen it.

"Why didn't you tell me?" she asked.

"I didn't think it was relevant. It was years ago. I had no idea she was being hostile to you, because you didn't tell me when I asked you for names."

"I couldn't imagine she'd sent that letter. She's Larissa's sister!" The words made Megan feel ridiculous. Had she assumed Adrianne must be innocent because she had a nice sister? When Megan's own sister was a kidnapper and a murderer?

"They dated right after he got home from his mission," Sandra said.

"We weren't serious," Trevor said. "Not very serious."

*Serious enough to make you turn red,* Megan thought. Trevor had never been inclined to talk about past romances, but she was surprised Rachel hadn't gabbed about it. Maybe she had kept quiet because she hadn't wanted Megan to feel awkward with Adrianne.

"Adrianne is a nice girl, and she and Trevor broke up a long time ago," Sandra said. "I can't imagine she'd cause trouble for Megan now."

Why was Megan suddenly worrying the Drakes might think she'd brought up Adrianne's name out of jealousy? She hadn't even known about Adrianne and Trevor. "I'm not accusing her."

"We understand," Michael said. "We're not accusing her either; we're brainstorming. I assume that as property manager, Adrianne has access to your apartment."

"Yes." Megan wasn't sure if that was pertinent. She hadn't seen signs that anyone had entered her apartment while she was gone.

"Do you know if the police talked to her after the incident at Rachel's?" Michael asked.

"To see if she could testify I was home that night, you mean? I don't know. I do know she wouldn't be able to provide an alibi for me. There was a note on her door saying she was out of town until morning."

His expression thoughtful, Michael removed his reading glasses and tucked them into his shirt pocket. "I doubt Detective Powell knows there was a relationship between Trevor and Adrianne. This is old news and wasn't relevant to our previous experiences with the police."

"I can't believe one of the Mullins girls would . . ." Sandra's words dwindled. Was she remembering how she had liked Kristen initially? Or how she had trusted Gail?

"It would be premature to urge the police to investigate Adrianne." Michael grasped Sandra's hand. "She may well have an alibi for the night 'Kristen' showed up, and it seems unlikely she'd behave in a spiteful and immature way. But it may be wise to subtly seek information."

"Rachel is close friends with Larissa," Sandra said. "She might be able to ask Larissa casual questions about Adrianne's state of mind. Larissa might know if her sister is having a difficult time."

Michael nodded.

"We need to stop this nonsense before it . . . goes anywhere," Sandra said.

The fear in Sandra's voice wasn't apprehension about getting another hoax e-mail, and the stoicism in Michael's face wasn't masking irritation over pranks. They were thinking of Rachel's kidnapping. Gail's murder. "It might *not* be going anywhere," Megan said. "We don't know that these are markers on the same trail. They could be the work of different people with different motives—not one person with a grudge."

"I don't know." Trevor finally touched Megan, laying his hand on hers. "Is it more credible that our engagement or Bryce's return awoke a bunch of dormant kooks who all decided to harass us?"

"Maybe." Miserable at the misery in Sandra's expression, Megan added, "At least this kook or kooks doesn't seem to be dangerous. Even when the intruder broke into Rachel's townhouse, she didn't touch Rachel. This is a psychological game, not a deadly one."

"It's started out that way," Sandra said. "That means nothing."

* * *

Standing by the door of her car, Megan smiled at Trevor, a smile that reflected the desire she knew she should have to act charitably. They needed to talk, but this wasn't the place, freezing outside his parents' house. She hoped he'd suggest coming over to her apartment or invite her to his condo.

He didn't speak. She slid her key in the ancient lock on her car. "Are you . . . going back to work tonight?"

"No." He spoke quietly. "Meg, I'm sorry. I'm an idiot."

Megan filled her lungs with icy air, faltering in her effort to think of any compassionate words she could speak sincerely. "You thought I was irresponsible. Flaky. That after all your parents have done for me, I'd expect your mother to cover for my bad judgment and hide it from you."

"I'm sorry. It didn't seem like something you'd do."

That wasn't comforting. Maybe he'd doubted, but he hadn't doubted enough to lead off with a disclaimer about how her e-mail must have been hacked. "You believed I think you're such a stick in the mud that I didn't dare confide in you? And that I'd say so to your mother?"

Trevor's words thumped out so heavy and hard that they un-nerved Megan. "I *am* boring. I'm aware of that."

"Trevor! That's silly!"

"It's fact. Ask Rachel. She tells me every time we talk."

"She's teasing!" Rachel did have a habit of hounding her brother to try new activities or quirky adventures and razzing him if he declined. *Trev, for real—hula dancing! Meg will love it, and it would be sooo fun for you to take the class together. Don't be such a bore.*

Concern for him finally took precedence over Megan's stinging emotions. "You genuinely thought I felt that way about you?"

He hesitated. "I'm sorry. I messed up. I should have known you wouldn't send that e-mail. I should have told my parents it was a hoax. I should have talked to you privately instead of asking you to come here. I butchered the whole deal."

He'd bypassed her question. "I don't find you boring at all. I love spending time with you. I love talking with you. If you think you're boring, what does it take to be interesting? Spending money on things you don't want? Bungee jumping? Wearing Elvis suits to work?"

He smiled slightly and used his elbow to rub a streak of road salt off her side window.

"Are you sure you believe I didn't send that e-mail?" Megan gripped his hand and wished their hands were actually in contact, not separated by two chilled gloves. Two chilled gloves and two sets of insecurities. "You still look upset."

"I'm upset with myself. Not with you. You haven't done anything wrong, except be too nice to tell me Adrianne was giving you a hard time."

"She wasn't giving me a hard time. She wasn't friendly, but that wasn't enough to make me think she might send hate mail. If you had mentioned you had a history with her—" Megan's phone began to play "Every Breath You Take," the ringtone Rachel had programmed to alert her that her mother was on the line. Megan hit the button to reject the call.

"If you need to take that, it's okay," Trevor said. "I didn't mean to keep you here when you must have homework."

*Yes*, Megan thought. *I'd love to drive away while there's tension between us* and *take a call from my mother.* But they couldn't keep standing on the driveway; she was shivering. "Can you come over for a little while?"

"Are you sure you want my company?"

"Will you stop—" Her phone started playing an encore. "For goodness' sake."

"Might be easier to answer her," Trevor said.

"No, thanks." Megan switched off the ringer, wishing she hadn't switched it back on after leaving the Drakes' living room. "You'll follow me home?"

"Yes."

"See you there." Teeth chattering, Megan jumped into her car, tossed her purse and phone on the passenger seat, and started the engine.

Her phone screen lit up. She checked it to see if her mother had miraculously texted to apologize for hassling her about a ludicrous rumor.

*When will you be home?* the text read. *I'm in front of your apartment, freezing to death.*

# Chapter 11

Exhaust floated from the tailpipe of Pamela's car as Megan parked at the curb behind her. *Freezing to death.* Sitting in her car with the heat on. It was probably eighty degrees in there.

Trevor pulled his truck in behind Megan's car. She'd encouraged him to go home rather than deal with Pamela, but he'd insisted he come as backup. She was grateful; if her mother had driven six hours from Morris Glen to confront her, this would be a dreadful conversation.

Megan stepped out of her car and walked to where Pamela was opening her car door.

"*There* you are at last." Pamela embraced her. "I've been calling you for the last hour."

"My phone was off. I was occupied. You didn't tell me you were coming."

"You hung up on me. How could I tell you?"

"You could have opened the conversation that way." It hadn't been six hours since they'd talked. Pamela had been en route to Britteridge *before* checking the rumors with Megan.

Trevor walked to Megan's side. "Good evening, Mrs. O'Connor."

"I'm surprised you let Megan drive around in that eyesore in winter weather," Pamela said. "A well-to-do gentleman should buy her something more reliable."

"Mother, we're not married yet, and providing me with a car is not Trevor's responsibility. My car is reliable. Come inside and—"

"Oh, *this* is the new coat." Pamela caressed Megan's sleeve. "So lovely. I see why you gave in to the temptation to spend thousands—"

"If you drove to Massachusetts to repeat the same silly rumor, I'm sorry you wasted your time." Megan reached for Trevor's arm, and they led the way toward Megan's basement apartment.

"I can't believe you're still in this little dive," Pamela said as Megan unlocked the door. "How can you endure living in a basement?"

Megan switched on the lights. "I don't need a lot of space, and it's a great value."

Pamela tipped her head toward the narrow, high windows. "If you don't want to see daylight!"

Trevor helped Megan remove her coat. Pamela waited, and he turned to take her coat as well.

"Would you like something to drink?" Megan asked. "I have orange juice, or I could make some hot—"

"No, thank you. Excuse me; it was a *long* drive, and then I was stuck waiting for you." Pamela glided past Megan, heading for the bathroom.

As soon the door closed, Megan whispered, "I don't want to tell her everything that's been going on. I can't take the drama she'll give us. I'm done with stress for the night."

"I'm sorry. I shouldn't have let that happen." In his eyes, she saw the self-condemnation he showed whenever he thought he'd failed her. "I shouldn't have—"

"Trevor, I'll live." She kissed him, but it was a quick tap of her cold lips against his. "We'll talk it out later. Right now, what do we tell my mother?"

"We need to at least ask her about the call she got. It's connected to the hoax e-mail, so she might know something important, and I want to check the phone number to make sure it was a mall pay phone. Unfortunately, she does need to know what's going on in case she gets contacted again."

"Locking her in the bathroom is out of the question?"

"That might be a viable option."

At the click of the bathroom door opening, they stepped apart from each other.

"Dear, that's such lovely hand lotion you have." Pamela walked into the room, fluttering her fingers, spreading a light peach scent.

"Rachel gave it to me," Megan said, knowing Pamela was hinting that it was an expensive brand and another sign of Megan's hidden wealth. "Sit down. Are you hungry? I have some lentil soup I could warm up."

"No, thank you." Brows arched, Pamela inspected the couch, then the worn recliner as though deciding which piece of furniture was less likely to give her fleas. Megan automatically checked out Pamela's clothes. When their face-to-face interactions got too aggravating, Megan had learned to distract herself by making mental fashion notes. Admiring the bright teal of Pamela's sweater, the cut of her slacks, or the unique knot in her silk scarf helped inhibit Megan's stress. As a bonus, it also gave her wardrobe ideas; Pamela had stellar taste.

Pamela chose the chair. Megan and Trevor sat on the couch.

"I hope you don't think I drove here to ask you for money," Pamela said. "If you prefer to lie to your mother about—"

"Excuse me," Megan said. "I've already explained that the rumor you heard is not true. Someone is playing a prank." She explained about the hoax e-mail to the Drakes. "Considering the timing of the call you received, that wasn't a well-meaning friend who believed a rumor about the cost of the coat. Chances are it was the same person who e-mailed the Drakes. Can you tell me more details about the call?"

"My dear. Wouldn't it be easier to admit you've been fibbing to me about the amount of money the Drakes give you? I've always thought it was absurd how you pretend to live such a frugal life when a man like Michael Drake would do *much* better than a measly scholarship for the woman who saved his daughter's life!"

"Please stop calling your daughter a liar," Trevor said.

Pamela wasn't fazed. "Oh, gracious, we're almost family here. We can be frank with each other. It's absurd for you to go to bat for Megan's honesty since the first time you met her, she told you she was Kristen."

"That was a mistake she regrets and has fully put behind her."

"I'm glad she's not hurting *you* anymore, but I can't hide that it hurts me to learn my daughter views me so disdainfully that she chose to pretend she was a poor student rather than share—"

Trevor's voice stayed calm but moved higher on the scale of hardness. "Your daughter has told you the information you received about the coat was false. Stop accusing her of lying."

Pamela's cheeks flushed. "Do you speak for Megan now that you're engaged? You're in charge of her?"

"*Mother.* He's defending me because you are attacking me. If you can't stop, I'll ask you to leave."

"I apologize." Pamela's tone was brittle. "I didn't mean to offend you."

"Thank you," Megan said. "If you could please tell us anything you remember about the call, it might help. First, we'd like to look up the phone number. What is it?"

"She said it was a pay phone."

"I know. We'd still like to check it."

"I'm surprised you'd be this vindictive, dear. She meant well."

"I don't want revenge. I want to know what's going on."

Pamela took her phone from her purse. "Well, it was this morning . . . There it is." She recited the number.

"I'll look it up," Trevor said.

While he researched the number on his phone, Megan asked, "What did the woman sound like?"

"I don't remember anything special about her voice. She sounded young, not like a child, but maybe your age or mine. She *didn't* sound like she was playing a prank. She sounded very worried that your spending would ruin your chance to marry your knight in shining armor."

"If a friend was concerned, why wouldn't she come to me about it? Why would she call my mother?"

Pamela straightened the peacock pin that fastened her scarf. Megan remembered helping her father pick out the carved abalone pin for Mother's Day a few months before his sudden, lethal heart attack. *Dad, if you were here now, this would go a lot better.* His humor and down-to-earth attitude would mellow Pamela and help her see the situation from a point of view other than her own.

"Dear, she said she *had* tried to talk to you," Pamela said. "She told me you'd laughed and said it didn't matter if Trevor was a cheapskate; his parents would keep you rolling in cash."

Hearing Trevor get slighted again made Megan cringe, but this was helpful information. The caller was flagrantly lying, evidence she wasn't acting on a rumor spread by someone else but was instead an integral part of the scheme. "No one talked to me about this at all. That call to you was a hoax."

"Why would someone do that?"

"To cause trouble for me, I guess."

Pamela tugged at a loose thread on the arm of the chair, paused, and tugged again as though testing to see if the whole chair would unravel. "If someone wants to cause trouble for you, why would they contact me?"

Trevor glanced at Megan, and she quelled an impulse to roll her eyes. Pamela had called Megan to harangue her and had driven to Britteridge to attack her in person, yet she couldn't figure out how a call to her had played into the harassment of Megan?

The call to Pamela did reemphasize what Megan and the Drakes had been discussing: the culprit knew a lot of personal details. She knew Megan had recently purchased a leather coat; she knew how to sting Trevor, making him less likely to evaluate the e-mail objectively; she knew Pamela would have a fit if she thought Megan had been hiding money from her.

"Where are you staying tonight?" Megan asked. Knowing Pamela would decline, she offered anyway. "If you'd like to take my bed, I'm happy to sleep on the couch."

"A mattress that came used with the apartment? Ghastly. I've made reservations at the Marriott."

Megan squashed her lips together to prevent a smile. Pamela was repulsed at the thought of using a mattress others had slept on, so she was going to a hotel?

"Besides," Pamela said, "I wouldn't want to be underfoot, forcing you to hide the Belgian chocolate and caviar and live on dried beans because your fiancé won't let you tell your mother he's giving you mountains of money."

Megan sprang to her feet and stepped a little in front of Trevor before he could react. "I'll get your coat," she said to Pamela.

Pamela didn't stand. "Oh, for heaven's sake, I apologize. I was teasing."

No, she wasn't. Pamela had the capacity to tease, but it came with genuine affection, not miffed sarcasm. Megan fetched her mother's coat. "Go to the Marriott. We'll talk later."

"You're throwing me out into a February night after I drove six hours to see you? I don't see why we can't act like adults."

"Acting like adults means treating each other with respect, which you aren't doing. We'll talk tomorrow."

"I *apologized*. Are you this unforgiving?"

Trevor stood, took the coat from Megan, and extended it to Pamela. "Your daughter has asked you to leave. If you need assistance getting to your car, I'd be happy to escort you."

"Are you threatening to use those big muscles to haul me out of here? If you touch me, I'll call the police!"

"*Mother*."

"I can't *believe* how much you despise me." Pamela leaped from her chair and shoved her arms into her coat. "First, you cut me out of your wedding. My only chance to see a child of mine as a bride, and you choose to marry where I can't attend. Now you won't even *talk* to me. I thought you cared, but neither of my daughters seems capable of considering my feelings." She marched out the door. Trevor closed it.

Megan wanted to crack a joke, but she couldn't. Her mother hadn't been this obnoxious in years. At this moment, how could Trevor not want to snatch the diamond off Megan's finger and flee to Mongolia rather than deal with Pamela for the rest of his life?

# Chapter 1 2

FROM THE *YOU'RE GONNA STICK my artwork on the fridge, right?* expression on Jessica's face, she wanted Noah to applaud. He'd better say something nice. "Uh . . . that was great. That mother . . . Can't believe Megan didn't slap her."

"Wasn't she the worst? When I called her, I didn't know she'd drive all the way to Britteridge!" Jessica laughed and set the recorder on the coffee table. "I wish I could have recorded what happened when Sandra Drake got that e-mail. Too dangerous to break into *their* house though. Megan's is easy. Not that I have to jimmy the lock anymore since I copied her key."

Noah shifted on Jessica's cheap couch, picking at the zipper of the bulky black coat he hadn't removed. "Megan didn't change her locks?"

"Why would she? She doesn't know anyone was ever in her apartment, and everyone else thinks she pulled the Kristen stunt herself."

Why did Noah feel so deadened, laboring to speak or think? He should be pleased. Jessica was putting Megan through the wringer.

More breaking and entering? This was too risky. He needed to slow things down. Get Jessica under control.

"What's wrong?" Jessica jostled his shoulder. "Hello, this was another win for you!"

He should reprimand her for bumping him, but it was too much hassle. "Yeah, it's great. It's just . . . riskier than I thought. You're still sneaking into places. I didn't expect so much . . . law breaking."

"You *hired* me to harass someone! There's nothing legal about that. Make up your mind!"

What was his problem? When she'd scared Rachel, that had been serious stuff, but he'd been impressed.

"I didn't steal anything or vandalize anything," she said. "I only looked around Megan's apartment for ideas. The eBay receipt was on the counter. I used her iPad to send the e-mail to Sandra, and I didn't even move it off the table where she'd left it. Are you afraid I'm so stupid I'll get caught and finger you?"

Noah pictured the police pounding on his door. Pictured what his father would do if Noah got arrested. He'd hate Noah for life. No reconciliation—ever.

"I think you're reckless," Noah said.

"You think I'm stupid."

He hesitated. Jessica was smart in some ways, but if she were really intelligent, she wouldn't be living this loser life. "You're too cocky."

"I'm bold because I know what I'm doing. I'm good at this. Disguises—I use several different ones. Different voices too. When I go into Megan's apartment, I look like Megan. Wear the Megan wig, walk like her, wear a blue coat like her regular one—found a similar one at Goodwill."

"What if someone enters the apartment while you're there? Like a handyman or the landlady? If anyone sees your face—"

"Thought of that. When I'm actually inside an apartment where I shouldn't be, I always put my ski mask on. Extreme worst-case scenario: the plumber surprises me. I run. He tells police he saw an intruder in a mask. Nothing for the police to work with. Chill, Noah. If anyone saw a suspicious intruder, they would have told Megan, and she and Trevor would have talked about it." She gestured at the digital recorder. "You heard them. Nobody knows I was there."

Noah reached into his pocket and pulled out the envelope of cash he'd brought. "Five hundred, like we agreed for this round. I'm not covering expenses exceeding that."

Jessica snatched it. "I have some fantastic ideas for where to go next."

She was far ahead of him on the scheme *he'd* initiated. Using Megan's mother wasn't an idea he ever would have thought up. He loathed how intimidated he felt. He shouldn't feel intimidated. Hadn't he hired her because she was skilled at this garbage?

Did he want to end things now? He could tell her they were done and never deal with her again.

"You're a total chicken, aren't you?" she said.

Noah wanted to seize the envelope of cash, rip up the bills, and walk out. Let her scrounge for hundreds of scraps and curse her insolence while she tried to tape confetti into something a bank would accept. "I get that you don't care if you go to prison," he said. "What do you have to lose?"

Her eyes were fragments of glass. Pale green glass, shards of the wine goblet he'd broken when he'd been exploring the boxes that held his late mother's treasures. Shards he'd gathered too fast and shoved back into the box so his father wouldn't catch him. He massaged the scar on his right index finger.

"What do *you* have to lose?" Jessica said caustically. "A guy so pathetic he has to hire someone to hurt a girl's feelings."

Noah trapped his fury behind opaque dignity. "This is about retribution. About not letting a greedy bloodsucker win."

"Okay, whatever. Things are on the right path, but if we don't keep pushing them, they'll slide back to status quo."

"After what you've done, it should be enough to get Trevor to—"

"Not Trevor. He's a patient guy. Calm. If we quit now, he and Megan will work everything out and live happily ever after. After they throttle the mother-in-law."

Jessica's bushy, brown-striped cat peeked out from under the coffee table and crept toward Jessica. No noise at all. Living with a cat would give him the creeps. Uncanny stalkers and killers.

"No one's gotten hurt." Jessica lifted the cat to her lap. "Not even a scraped knee or a paper cut. I told you, I haven't stolen or damaged anything."

She must be telling the truth. Noah hadn't heard anything about vandalism or burglary. She was sticking to the job he'd given her, not becoming a loose cannon.

"Don't quit on your goal now," Jessica said. "Is that how you want to honor your aunt's memory? Give Megan a few bad days, then let her climb into her Cinderella coach with Prince Charming while Gail lies in the graveyard?"

Claws made a faint scratchy pop as Jessica lifted the cat's front paws clear of her jeans. Tenderly, she set the paws down again. Why didn't she push the cat to the floor if it was stabbing its claws into her legs? What made her think it would keep its claws retracted now?

"Don't quit," Jessica said. "You'll regret it."

His kept his gaze on the cat's furry paws and muttered, "What were you thinking of doing next?"

* * *

"Oh my heck, *nightmare!*" Rachel reached from the other end of the couch and squeezed Megan's arm. "You must have been dying. I am so, so, so sorry I haven't had a chance to visit with you in, like, a whole week. I am the worst friend on the planet."

"It's fine, Rach. We're both busy."

"Last week was super crazy—Friday *and* Saturday weddings. I kept thinking, *I need to go see Megan!* and getting distracted when the bride changed her mind about the table decorations two days before the wedding, then the mother of the other bride had a conniption over brown spots on the roses—a couple of brown spots the size of *pinheads* on about three out of hundreds of roses. I'm like, 'Good heavens, lady, if you wanted things to be *that* flawless, call Adam and Eve and see if the Garden of Eden sells roses wholesale.' I couldn't say that to her though. Anyway . . . your mom. How are you doing?"

"Fine. It was a nightmare though. I thought I was used to her, but this was a new depth of awful." Megan ate the last bite of the cherry and cream cheese mini cupcake Rachel had offered her when she'd arrived at Rachel's townhouse—a sample from a bakery owner who hoped Rachel would recommend the bakery to her clients. She was anxious to ask Rachel what she'd learned about Adrianne Mullins, but Rachel was still interrogating her about her mother's surprise visit.

"How long did she stay in town?" Rachel asked.

"Just overnight. I met her for breakfast the next morning, made it clear—again—that I had no money for her, and if she mentioned it one more time, I would cut off contact with her until she gets over this delusion."

"Did she manage that? Ooh!" Rachel gestured at her front window. "It's snowing!"

"We're supposed to get eight inches." It would be so relaxing to wrap a blanket around herself, turn on some tranquil music, and spend the rest of Monday afternoon watching snow fall from the gray sky. Forget stress. Ignore homework. Lose her TA job. Flunk out of school. Never mind; it wouldn't be relaxing at all.

"Anyway, sorry," Rachel said. "I get excited over snow. You were telling me what your mother did at breakfast."

"Once she gave up on the money rumor, she switched to hints about how I'd changed for the worse since meeting Trevor, and I was going to cut off contact with her anyway once we were married because he'd make me do it, and she's dated a few controlling men, so she knows what they're like."

"She called Trevor controlling? He's not that way! At all!"

"She knows it isn't true. Trevor's such a wonderful guy that she has trouble coming up with credible insults. She went home that afternoon; she had to work the next day. Since she didn't get any money out of me, she needs her job."

"What does she do?"

"She works at a florists' and is starting to do some consulting work in interior design. She's very gifted at it."

"That's great." Rachel plucked a mini cupcake out of the bakery box she'd placed on the coffee table and checked the sticker on the wrapper. "White-chocolate strawberry," she said. "Hey, I wanted to tell you, I'm so sorry about leading my mom astray on that crazy coat–e-mail thing. Did she tell you how she texted me the day she got that fake e-mail?"

"Yes. It's not your fault. You had no idea what was going on."

"For real. She asked, 'Does Megan have a new coat?' and I thought she was thinking ahead about birthday presents for you, so I texted back something like 'Yes! Leather dress coat! So nice! But she could use a new regular coat.' And she took that as evidence that the e-mail about going into debt for a coat was from you. Good grief! If she'd told me why she was asking, I'd have said, 'Are you kidding? Megan would never spend thousands of dollars on a coat! She's as cheap as Trevor' . . . no offense."

"As wise as Trevor, you mean."

"He's infected you." She touched her upper lip. "You have frosting on your lip."

Megan wiped the frosting off with her napkin. She didn't want to hurt Rachel's feelings, but this was an ideal opening. "May I say something sensitive?"

Rachel's eyes widened. "Oh boy. Sure."

"The way you tease Trevor . . . I . . . think sometimes it bothers him. I'm afraid he takes it more seriously than you mean it."

"What?" Rachel nibbled her cupcake. "We've always gone after each other that way. You know that. He lectures me about spending too much and doing impulsive things; I tease him about being a boring tightwad."

"Does it bother you when he says things like that?"

Rachel blushed the pink of the frosting on her strawberry cupcake. "Not really."

"Rach, I've seen you get prickly when you think he's questioning your judgment."

"Okay . . . sometimes it bugs me. Did he say something about me teasing him?"

"It came up when we were discussing that hoax e-mail. There was a line about how I didn't want him to know about my financial issues because he was 'boring and stuffy' and wouldn't understand my mistake. It hurt him, a lot. I didn't realize he was so sensitive about thinking he was dull, and I figured you didn't either."

Rachel took another bite of cupcake. Her face darkened to red velvet. "If he can't take it, he shouldn't dish it out."

Megan picked up a mini cupcake with a caramel-nut mixture on top. "I think he's tried to be better. Since you got married, I haven't noticed much of that type of teasing from him."

Rachel finished her cupcake. As she folded the wrapper and set it on the table, she said, "I hadn't thought about it, but you're right. He is holding back. Guess he figures my dingbat personality is Peter's problem now."

"He doesn't think you're a dingbat."

"You know, Megan, I am careful not to spend more than—"

"I'm not judging anyone's financial decisions—except my mother's since she tries to make her finances my problem. I'm just passing on to you that Trevor is worried that we genuinely see him as a Scrooge-like bore."

"Sorry." Rachel ran her fingers through her chocolate-brown curls, pushing them behind her ears. "I guess I'm getting prickly because I'm embarrassed. I'm mortified knowing I hurt his feelings. I think he's an amazing guy and will be an awesome husband, and I adore him, and honestly, most of the tightwad teasing is nonsense. I don't think he's Scrooge. In fact, he's super generous. He's like Dad—doesn't think material possessions are the most important thing in the world and likes to make sure it's something he'll value before he spends money. If it is something he'll value, he has no trouble buying it, and he's always generous with other people. I'm sure you know that."

"Yes."

"Though I do want to take credit for him buying you that iPad last month. He was worried that spending that much on you would make you uncomfortable since Christmas was past and it's not your birthday for a few months, and I'm like, 'Trev, she needs a tablet, and you're engaged, for Pete's sake. If you can buy her a diamond ring, you can buy her an iPad."

"In that case, thank you. It's really helped me with all my reading."

"Anything else you'd like? I'll talk him into buying it for you." She winked. "Just kidding. But I will totally talk to him and make sure he knows I worship him. He's one of the best three brothers in the world." She reached for another mini cupcake. "Whew, well, this conversation has been a double-headed cringer already, and we haven't even talked about my visit with Larissa this morning."

"Did you learn anything?" Megan asked, relieved to finally hit the subject she'd been waiting for.

"We met for brunch, then decided to go ice skating. Would you believe it? It was a hoot. I fell over about twenty times. While we were out for pie afterward, I asked Larissa how Adrianne was doing. Larissa's easy to talk to, right? It was easy to get her chattering."

"What did she say?"

"Things haven't been going great for Adrianne. She was an office manager in Boston, but her boss was a nitpicky micromanager, and she hated her job. When her parents asked if she'd be interested in taking over the property management job from Larissa, Adrianne said yes, even though she didn't want to come back to Britteridge."

"Did Larissa say why she didn't want to live here?"

"At first she said Adrianne thought Britteridge was too small and college-towny. So I prodded, and she gave me the scoop." Rachel sighed. "Adrianne didn't like the idea of managing properties that included your apartment building."

Megan tried not to sound as hopeful as she felt. It would be handy if a jealous ex-girlfriend was the culprit behind everything—a woman who would, as soon as she was confronted, confess, back off, and never bother the Drakes or Megan again. "So I'm not paranoid in thinking she doesn't like me."

"Nope, you're not paranoid. Larissa said it was tough for her when Trevor broke up with her, even though it was, what, like six years ago? Adrianne gets irritated when anyone mentions Trev: 'Didn't you used to date Michael Drake's son?' and Adrianne's eyes go all Medusa and turn the person to stone. Larissa says her family all thinks Adrianne thought Trevor was going to propose."

"He said they weren't that serious."

"Oh, I think Larissa was exaggerating, but Trevor's underplaying it because he feels guilty that he hurt her. So I said to Larissa, 'Wow, I can't believe she'd take the property job if it meant dealing with Trevor's fiancée,' and Larissa said Adrianne won't admit it bothers her, but she can tell. Larissa's take is that Adrianne doesn't care about Trevor anymore; she's just bitter because she's had a rough time lately, with the dud job, and then she was dating some snake who stole her credit card number and damaged her credit rating."

"Oh no. That's awful."

"Yeah, no fun."

Megan picked a nugget of pecan off her cupcake wrapper. "Were you able to get any hints as to whether or not she's likely to . . . lash out?"

"I did dig, carefully. 'That's so rotten for her. Is she hanging in there? Like, keeping her life together and everything? Sometimes people do weird stuff when they go through a betrayal like that.' But the best I got was, 'I think she's okay. She seems okay.'"

"Does she have any voice or theater training?"

"You mean could she have mimicked Kristen's voice? I don't know, and I couldn't think of a nonawkward way to ask. The Mullinses lived in Lexington while the girls were growing up. I didn't meet Adrianne until she was attending Britt, and she studied business there, not theater. I don't know her very well. I know Larissa much better."

Physically, Adrianne could pull off the masquerade in the dark. She was about Megan's size or maybe a couple inches shorter. "What's your opinion, then? Do we mention her to Detective Powell? This isn't much more than we had before, just confirmation that she dislikes me."

"Hmm." Pensively, Rachel monitored the falling snow. "You know, part of me wants to say talk to him, because if we have any ideas, we should pass them on, right? But here's the issue. Larissa and Adrianne's mother is wonderful, but she's even more chatty and gossipy than Larissa."

Megan nodded. She'd learned that when she'd met Eileen. "Oh, Megan, honey! How many scars do you have? Did your doctor tell you if they'll fade at all? It must be terrible, having those reminders right on your body that your sister tried to kill you. I have a brother-in-law who's a plastic surgeon; I'd be happy to give you his number."

"If Adrianne is innocent and we point the police toward her, she might vent her humiliation to her family, and the family will talk," Rachel said. "Oh gosh, Meg. Half of Massachusetts will know how we insulted her. And they might think we blamed her because, um . . ."

"Because you're trying to hide the fact that Trevor's fiancée is a manipulative, criminal lunatic," Megan said.

Rachel moaned. "Yeah. I feel stuck. Like if we do anything, we might make a mess into a giant mess."

"Maybe this needs to be a stealth operation. I could try to connect with Adrianne."

"How?"

"Just be friendly. Give her banana bread or something. If she hates me enough to lash out, that'll probably show. Even if she does hate me, maybe she'll soften once she realizes . . ." Megan didn't know how to finish. Realized Megan was a nice person? That it wasn't her fault Trevor had broken up with Adrianne several years before he'd met Megan? That it wasn't her fault Adrianne was having a tough time?

"Sounds like the best idea we have." Rachel plucked the last mini cupcake out of the box and offered it to Megan.

"I'm full," Megan said. "You eat it."

"Just take a bite and tell me what you think of it. I thought the one I tasted was too cinnamon-y. Meg, you should be careful. Even though the, uh, culprit has never done anything violent . . . that could change."

"I learned three years ago not to make assumptions about people." Megan accepted the cupcake. "I'll be careful."

# Chapter 1 3

"Hey, Jenna." Trevor tipped back in his office chair, glad for a breather from the applications he'd been reviewing. "Great to hear from you. How are things?"

"They're good." Over the phone, Jenna Elliot . . . Jenna *Anderson* sounded nervous.

Trevor waited a moment for her to tell him why she'd called, but when she said nothing, he said cautiously, "How's the family?"

"They're great. Stressed out sometimes. At least we're halfway through the week! But great. Aaron loves his program. I'm a little stir-crazy at home with Ella in the winter, but she's so fun, learning to talk; today she said *snow*. Or a word that had an *O* sound in it, so close enough." Jenna's voice quivered. "Don't shoot the messenger, okay? I debated what to . . . I don't like spreading gossip. I wouldn't tell anyone else."

Trevor massaged the back of his neck. "I'm assuming you didn't call to complain about why your child didn't get admitted. Not that she isn't a genius for a two-year-old."

"Nineteen months," Jenna corrected. "I . . . overheard something that bothered me."

*The coat rumor.* He'd wondered how far the troublemaker had spread it, but it surprised him his longtime friend Jenna would feel the need to bring it to him. "What did you hear?"

"You know that second-floor lounge in the Halverson Building where we used to hang out?"

"Yeah."

"I meet Aaron there almost every day, and we eat lunch on campus. It gets me out of the apartment, and Ella loves seeing Daddy. But when I got there a few minutes ago, I saw Megan."

Trevor's heart thudded. When Jenna didn't explain why a sighting of Megan on the campus of the college she attended was significant, he prompted, "You saw Megan?"

"She didn't see me. She was on the phone. She was . . ." Jenna drew a loud breath. "She was talking about you. I missed the first part of the conversation, so I don't know the context, but she said . . . she said . . . I'm sorry. This feels horrible telling you, but I think you should know."

Trevor fixed his gaze on the words of an admissions essay without seeing anything except random marks. "What did she say?"

"Like I said, I missed the first part, but when I walked past her, she was saying something about how at least it was some excitement in her life because she doesn't have much of that. Then she said something like, 'Trevor's so bland he'd make an accountants' convention look like Mardi Gras.' I, well, I sort of started loitering near her. She hadn't seen me; she was facing the other way, and I . . . was eavesdropping."

"I understand." Trevor controlled his voice. "What else did she say?"

"Something about how it will be worth it someday. And . . . she said . . . 'I'll find ways to keep occupied,' and she laughed. Then she said something like, 'Maybe I'll get lucky, and he'll get strangled by a crazy parent whose princess didn't make it into Britt, and I can retire to Rio with his money and a hot Latino guy.' I'm sorry, Trev. We've been friends for ages, and you know I wouldn't normally repeat something like this, but it makes me rabid thinking that she . . . I felt like you deserved to know before . . . Well, I mean, so you can . . . be informed. Ella, don't put that in your mouth!"

Trevor sat stiffly, listening to Jenna's daughter squealing in the background. *Was* it Jenna? If someone had mimicked Kristen's voice . . .

"I appreciate your telling me this," he said. "It helps make up for that Labor Day barbecue when you pushed me into the pool."

"I did not! That was Mindy McLeod! I told you that later! I took the rap for it because I knew you'd retaliate, and I was already wet, and Mindy didn't want to swim. I sacrificed myself to save her hairdo!"

It was Jenna. Those details weren't ones an imposter would know. His mouth went parched. His throat went parched. His lungs. All of him, mummified.

When Trevor didn't respond to her humor, Jenna sobered. "I'm sorry about this. It completely stunned me. Megan's always so nice. She's probably overwhelmed by school and wedding plans."

Trevor opened the water bottle on his desk. "You're *sure* it was her?"

"I wouldn't have called unless . . . Well, I didn't see her face. Her back was to me. She wouldn't have kept talking like that if she'd seen me. But her hair's so distinctive, that strawberry-blonde, and she was wearing that neon green scarf and hat. You know, the ones Rachel made her when Rachel went knitting crazy? And her coat, with that stitched-up tear on the back? I could hear her voice, obviously, and how many other women are involved with guys named Trevor who work in the Britt admissions office? I was so furious I wanted to tell her what I thought of her talking smack about you, but she hurried out of the lounge partway through her conversation, and following her seemed too aggressive. Besides, Ella had spilled my purse. I hope you're not mad at me. I don't want anybody to hurt you."

"I appreciate that, and thank you for calling me. That took guts. Listen, have you recently said anything public, maybe online, about how you always meet Aaron at the Halverson Building around lunchtime?"

"Um . . . yeah, did you see it? I posted a picture of Ella and Aaron in the lounge the other day with a 'Best part of every day: meeting Daddy for lunch' caption. Why?"

"You identified the place where you meet?"

"I can't remember exactly what I said, but I am *very* careful about my privacy settings, and—"

"I'm not criticizing you. This is a long story. I'll explain later."

"Are you okay?"

"Yes. I'll call you later, all right? And thank you. This is important."

"Okay. I swear I won't tell anyone what I overheard."

"I know that. Thanks, Jenna."

"Bye." Jenna hung up.

Trevor set his phone on his desk and closed his eyes.

Megan, tactlessly yammering on her phone on campus, insulting Trevor both by name and in a way that identified him by occupation. Megan, in the right spot to be overheard by a woman who had been Trevor's friend since preschool, in a building where Megan had no classes. Always keeping her face away from Jenna while wearing the most distinctive winter gear she owned: that scorchingly bright scarf and hat and a mended coat. A mended wool dress coat, when Megan owned both a much warmer parka and the new leather coat.

Trevor called Megan.

"Hey!" she said. "I hope your day is better than mine. I fell on the ice."

"Are you okay?"

"Fine. Just bruised and scraped. It was an impressive fall though—virtuoso landing."

"Meg . . . odd question. What coat are you wearing today?"

"My coat?" Megan's tone went wary. "I was wearing my regular one, the blue parka. I'm not wearing any coat right now since I'm inside."

"Scarf? Hat?"

"My blue fleece hat. The tartan scarf your brother sent me from Scotland. Why? There haven't been more coat rumors, have there?"

"When was the last time you saw your black dress coat and the green scarf and hat Rachel knitted for you?"

"Um . . . the coat's in my closet. It's too worn out for Goodwill, and I was debating if it was worth keeping for any reason. The hat and scarf are there too."

"When did you last see them?"

"I know the scarf and hat were there this morning. I didn't notice if the coat was there. I wasn't looking for it."

"But you're sure about the scarf and hat?"

"Yes. They glow like they're radioactive. What's going on?"

Trevor scooted back from his desk. "A woman was on campus a few minutes ago pretending to be you, wearing your green hat and scarf and your old dress coat."

"*What?*"

"I'll explain later." Trevor grabbed his coat and hurried out of his office. "I'm betting she won't want you to know she ever had your gear, so she'll try to return it before you get home. I'm going to your apartment now to see if I can catch her at it."

"I'm home now."

"*What?*" Trevor switched from jogging along the corridor to sprinting, his loafers hammering against the tile.

"My jeans got dirty and wet when I fell, so I came home to clean up. I decided I'd study here for once."

"Get out of there! You can't risk—"

"I'm fed up with this." Megan spoke grimly. "I'm not missing the chance to spot 'Kristen' or whoever this punk is."

"No! Meg—"

"This isn't a hardened criminal who'll shoot me. This is a prankster, and female."

"You're thinking it's Adrianne. You can't know—"

"You'll be here in a few minutes, right? You'll get here before—" Her voice lowered to a whisper. "She's here! Someone's unlocking the front door. I heard the knob—I'm in my bedroom, at the back of the house, so she wouldn't have seen a light on, wouldn't know I was home—I'm hanging up. Call 911 for me so she doesn't hear me talking." Megan disconnected.

\* \* \*

Megan crept out of the nest of blankets she'd curled around herself while studying and slid her phone into her pocket. It had to be Adrianne Mullins. Adrianne's coldness, including yesterday's terse rejection of the banana bread Megan had tried to give her, weren't proof, but what other woman had a grudge against Megan? What hoax had Adrianne pulled today while wearing Megan's coat?

Megan rapidly scanned the room for anything she could use as a weapon. She grabbed her backpack, lead-heavy with books. Once Adrianne knew she'd been busted, she couldn't be foolish enough to do anything that would get her in more trouble with the law, but it would still be better not to confront her empty-handed. With a swing of her weighted backpack, Megan could keep distance between them.

She had to hurry; it would take Adrianne only a few seconds to hang the hat, scarf, and coat in the closet. She'd know Megan was here as soon as Megan opened the creaky bedroom door that she'd closed to trap the heat.

Megan yanked the door open, hurtled into the dim basement hallway, and smacked the light switch.

Standing at the hall closet was a figure in a white ski mask and blue coat, holding Megan's old dress coat.

*No!* She had to see the intruder's face. Megan sprinted past the intruder, heading toward the front door. At the door, she whirled around, shielding herself with her backpack. The intruder was maybe three strides behind her. "Don't come closer!" Megan shrieked.

The intruder lurched a couple of steps backward. She must have expected Megan to flee out the door.

"This is over." Megan held the straps, ready to swing her makeshift weapon if she had to. The intruder had a backpack over one shoulder, but it was smaller than Megan's. From the deflated look of it, it didn't have much inside. It wouldn't beat her wrecking-ball pack. "If you have a problem with me, let's deal with it face-to-face."

The intruder slipped the free backpack strap over her other shoulder and stayed where she was, not retreating farther. Megan stood her ground. She couldn't miss this chance. If she let a still-anonymous culprit escape, she'd be foundering again with no evidence, and the harassment would continue.

"Take the mask off, and let's talk." Megan doubted she'd do it, but if Megan could stall for a few minutes, the police and Trevor would be here. "Quit what you're doing, and I won't press charges.

I know Rachel won't either. Let's work it out." She thought about addressing Adrianne by name, but if the intruder wasn't Adrianne, calling her by the wrong name would make her more confident.

Was it Adrianne? She might be too tall. Megan didn't dare look down to see if she was wearing thick-soled boots, and with that padded parka, it was hard to tell whether she was slim or heavy or even a man or a woman.

Megan's resolve started splintering. Her statements to Trevor repeated themselves in her brain: *Not a hardened criminal . . . Female . . .* Neither Kristen nor Aunt Evelyn had been a hardened criminal. Each had tried to murder her and had nearly succeeded.

*I am unbelievably stupid.* She'd been too determined to identify the prankster. She shouldn't have challenged her before the police—

The intruder backed up next to the kitchen table. Megan's terror lessened. "Sit down, and we can—"

The intruder snatched a wooden chair, swooped it into the air, and charged. With a scream, Megan dodged to the left.

Holding the back of the chair, the intruder swung it toward Megan. Megan slammed her backpack into the chair, bashing it aside, but she'd put so much force into the swing that the collision knocked the pack out of her hands. It thudded to the floor.

The intruder regained her balance and swung the chair again. Megan seized the legs of the chair, a gesture that shocked the nerves from her fingers to her shoulders. She fought to wrench the chair out of the intruder's hands. "You are *crazy!*"

The intruder ripped the chair free, dropped it, and swung her gloved fist at Megan's face. Evading the blow, Megan inadvertently jumped back in front of the door. She needed to move *away* from the door, let the intruder leave.

The intruder's fist crashed into Megan's stomach. Gasping, her entire body cramping around the agony in her gut, Megan tried to punch back, but she couldn't aim, and her knuckles barely grazed the intruder's coat. A fist rammed into her face near her eye, knocking her on top of the fallen chair. Lights twinkled in her skull; the doorknob clacked and boots banged against the outside stairs.

\* \* \*

In front of Megan's apartment, Trevor leaped out of his truck. A patrol car pulled in behind him, but he didn't wait for the officer to get out of his car or give instructions; he ran toward the open basement door.

On the living room rug, Megan lay coiled in a ball near an overturned kitchen chair, her face against her knees. Fear pulverized Trevor's heart as he knelt next to her and lightly touched her shoulder, afraid to jar her until he knew what her injuries were. "Megan."

She wriggled, lifting her head and attempting to straighten her knotted body. "I'm . . . okay," she squeaked, a noise so soft Trevor instantly stared at her throat, fearing her windpipe was damaged or her lungs. Her throat didn't look injured, but that bump near her left eye—fractured eye socket? Concussion?

A police officer, gun drawn, stepped through the doorway.

"She . . . left just a moment ago," Megan rasped to the officer. "I don't . . . know which way she went." She inhaled hoarsely. "Blue parka. White ski mask. I didn't . . . see her face."

The officer lifted his radio. Trevor felt a wrathful craving to personally hunt down the assailant, but he didn't want to abandon Megan or get in the way of the police.

"An ambulance is coming." A different officer leaned over Megan. "Ma'am, can you tell me where you're injured?"

"I'm fine." To Trevor's relief, she spoke with increased volume; she was getting more air. "She punched me a couple of times." She pressed her hand against the rug, lifting herself. Still not sure what contact would hurt, Trevor kept his touch gentle as he helped her sit up.

"What happened?" Trevor asked.

"I . . . was blocking the door, trying to convince her to talk to me," Megan said. "I was desperate to see who she was . . . to keep her here until you and the police arrived. I guess she panicked. Or . . . I guess it could be a man. With that coat and the face covered . . . I don't know."

"You blocked the door? Meg!"

Megan moaned. "I know it was stupid."

"She, or he, never spoke?" the officer asked.

"No. I didn't hear a voice at all."

Two paramedics entered the apartment. Trevor stepped back and watched Megan's white face as she talked to them. *She blocked the doorway? Cornered an unknown intruder?*

Why had he sat uselessly in his office and listened to Jenna's entire story before alerting Megan? The instant he suspected the prankster was at work, he should have warned her. He would have learned she was home; he would have arrived here in time; he would have caught the prankster; he could have protected Megan and permanently ended this harassment. Instead, he'd left Megan without help, so frantic to identify the intruder that she'd gotten reckless.

A hand tapped Trevor's shoulder. He pivoted.

"Mr. Drake." Detective Powell held out his hand. Trevor shook it, wishing he'd traveled a better route to getting acquainted with the police detective. Powell was a good man. Too bad they hadn't met as next-door neighbors or when shoveling mulch together at a community service project. Not through kidnapping, murder, and assault.

"Would you mind stepping outside with me for a moment?" Powell asked.

Trevor didn't want to leave the apartment until he was sure Megan wasn't seriously injured, but it was pointless to delay answering Powell's questions so he could stand here and do nothing.

On the sidewalk in front of the apartment, Trevor explained Jenna's call, gave Powell her number, and shared what Megan had told him. He added a report of the hoax e-mail and call to Pamela. Megan hadn't wanted to call the police about it—what could they do about a hacked e-mail and a practical joke about a designer coat?—but now it seemed starkly relevant.

Uncomfortably, he finished his report with words that felt concurrently necessary and unfair. "This is not an accusation, but the property manager who lives upstairs, Adrianne Mullins, and I were involved several years ago, before Megan moved to Britteridge. I haven't talked to her in years, but Megan mentioned she's been . . . unfriendly." Trevor tugged the knot of his tie. "No open conflict. Just sending signals that she doesn't like Megan."

Powell nodded and wrote on his pad. "Was it a difficult breakup?"

Here came the burning in his neck. Why couldn't he talk about Adrianne without his nervous system displaying his embarrassment? "The breakup was civil, and we didn't contact each other afterward. But it was my decision. It . . . surprised her."

"I appreciate your telling me. Ms. Mullins isn't home at the moment, or at least didn't answer her door when we knocked to ask if she'd seen anything. We'll follow up."

"Thank you." Trevor flipped his hood up to cover his chilled ears. "As I said, this isn't an accusation or even a significant suspicion."

"I know that. We'll be tactful."

He and Powell returned to Megan's apartment. The paramedics were already packing up, and Megan sat on the couch, holding an ice pack above her eye. Powell approached the officer in the kitchen; Trevor hurried toward Megan.

"Are you all right?" he asked.

"Fine. Sore. I'm supposed to call if I experience dizziness or other problems, but everything looks okay right now." Megan pointed at a pile of vivid green yarn on the carpet. "Polite of her to return my stuff."

Trevor sat next to her. Megan rested her head on his shoulder and shut her eyes. "What did 'I' do on campus?"

Trevor slid the ice pack out of her hand and held it against her forehead so she could relax her arm. "Another prank phone call. Take it easy for a while."

"*I* made the call?"

Powell and the officer ended their discussion, and Powell started toward Megan and Trevor. Grateful for a reason to delay rather than answer Megan's question, Trevor waited without speaking.

Powell sat on the other side of Megan. She straightened and reclaimed the ice pack from Trevor.

"Any luck on catching her?" Megan asked.

"Not yet. We've searched the neighborhood and are checking with neighbors to see if anyone has information."

"I didn't give you much to work with. I'm sorry. I didn't even notice what color pants or shoes she was wearing."

"Are you up to answering some questions?"

"Yes."

Guessing Powell would want to talk to Megan alone, Trevor stood. "I'll wait in my truck."

Outside, Trevor changed his mind about the truck. Too restless to sit, he paced the sidewalk. How could he have let Megan get hurt? How could he be this inept? He scanned houses, apartments, and yards, even knowing the police had already searched the area and would have noticed fresh footprints in the snow or a dropped white ski mask or any other evidence.

What other evidence could exist out here? None of them had any inkling how the intruder looked or what vehicle he or she drove.

Gloved hands in his pockets, he accelerated his pacing to warm himself up, retracing the same few hundred feet so he wouldn't get too far from Megan's apartment. His toes were numb in his loafers by the time Powell walked up the stairs leading from Megan's door.

Trevor hurried toward Powell. "Is she okay?"

"She's fine. Feel free to go in. For your information, we contacted Adrianne Mullins. She's in Plymouth taking pictures of a property her family is interested in buying."

"Has anyone confirmed—?"

"The Plymouth police already met her at the site and verified that she's there."

"Thank you." Plymouth was over an hour away. Adrianne couldn't have attacked Megan.

"I'm sorry to say we haven't yet located the assailant," Powell said.

"Witnesses?"

"Not yet."

The culprit had disappeared. Trevor's only guess about her identity had disintegrated. Megan was injured and still in danger.

He'd be a champion of a husband, defending his family, reaching for a sword and grabbing a handful of rust.

# Chapter 14

THE DAM-BREAKING WALL OF adrenaline had drained, but Jessica's nerves remained bent and waterlogged. *She's never home in the afternoon! Why today?* In the crowded Britt student center, Jessica hunched on a bench, pretending she was reading the student paper and frantically wringing ideas from her brain. She wanted to peel her gloves off her sweaty hands, but that ache in her knuckles might mean bruises passing students could see.

*You're all right. Megan won't be able to tell the police anything that identifies you.* Her escape had been flawless: out of Megan's apartment, around the house, along the sidewalk that led to the back fence—no footprints. She'd slid between the pine tree and the other side of the fence; shed her coat to show a gray fleece pullover; hid the coat, ski mask, gloves, and boot covers in her backpack; put on her brown wig, striped beanie, glasses with dark rims, different gloves; crammed the backpack itself into the large, crocheted tote formerly folded inside the backpack. No longer resembling the intruder at all, she'd headed for campus.

Pro job on the escape, but the rest of Jessica's work had collapsed. The rumors, suspicions, and tensions she'd bolted together were now mangled chunks of debris, thanks to Megan's attempt to trap Jessica like a house cat cornering a tiger. She'd coerced Jessica into a fight, and now Megan had at least a black eye and probably other big bruises. Visible evidence that someone *was* harassing her, that there *was* another possible Kristen, that it might *not* have been Megan with the money-grubbing e-mail or Megan trashing Trevor on the phone.

When Jessica reported to Noah tonight, he'd rant about how she'd failed, what a cocky loser she was, and how she should return his money because they'd been kicked back to the starting line. Kicked off the track completely. If Jessica targeted Megan now, everyone would peer sympathetically at her black eye and believe her when she claimed she hadn't done whatever Jessica was framing her for. If Jessica hadn't had to fight Megan, maybe Trevor would have thought Megan had made up the story about an intruder because she'd gotten scared someone would rat on her for that phone call.

Made up the story.

*Damage control, damage control, damage control.* Jessica started to fold her newspaper but blundered with it like it was complicated origami, dropping the inserts. She crunched the paper in her trembling hands and tossed it under the bench. *Damage control. Make this into a win.*

* * *

Noah's jaw opened with an abrupt, mechanical motion and wouldn't close again. He wanted to speak, but his tongue wouldn't move.

"It's not my fault." Jessica tapped her fingers on the steering wheel of her parked Saturn. "She's never home at that time of day. She's always in the library."

Noah swallowed. Meeting in this always-busy shopping-center parking lot after dark had seemed safe to him, better than driving to Lowell again, but now he regretted meeting Jessica anywhere public. Or ever meeting her at all. "You should have made sure—"

"How? Do you have any idea how complicated these ops are? How much I have to keep track of?"

"Her location is the *first* thing you should have kept track of."

"I was busy setting up that scene for Trevor's friend. I didn't have time to hunt down Megan. She's always on campus at that time of day. This isn't math or a computer program. Sometimes plans go weird." She kept tapping her fingers in a fast, upbeat rhythm, and twitching her shoulders. If she was dancing to a song in her head, it wasn't a song of regret.

"You bungled this," Noah said.

"I fixed it and—"

"By hitting her?"

"What was I supposed to do? She barricaded the door."

Revulsion sliced Noah's stomach. "You weren't supposed to hurt her. That was one of my rules. No injuries."

"Ooh, you're such an idealistic cutie pie. Was I supposed to let her yank off my mask? I know you don't care if I end up in the slammer, but you'd care when I ratted you out, which I would. I only hit her a couple of times, enough to push her down so I could run. I was careful not to hit too hard. She's fine. Stop whining, and let me tell you how I fixed this because you'll love it."

No twist on this disaster could make him love it. He jiggled a broken vent on the dashboard, straightening the slats. "Wasn't her car there?"

"*Hello.* Do you think I'm brain dead? She walks to campus; she always leaves her car there when she's at school. That wasn't a tip-off. I didn't want to hurt her, but I had no choice."

*I didn't want to hurt her.* Kristen O'Connor's attorney had told that to the judge at Kristen's plea bargain. Kristen hadn't wanted to hurt Gail. Gail's murder had been an unplanned crime, spawned by desperation.

That was true. Kristen hadn't planned to kill Gail or fire a bullet into Rachel's leg or knife her own sister.

Jessica hadn't planned to hurt Megan.

*Careful not to hit too hard?* Jessica thought he was a numbskull, expecting him to buy that. She hadn't been careful. She'd panicked and swung as hard as she could. If, in order to escape, she'd had to leave Megan on the floor in a pool of blood, she would have done it.

But if she hadn't fought and escaped and the police had caught her, his father would have learned he'd hired her, given wads of cash to a skanky musician. He'd get arrested. The Sahlberg name would be dirtied for generations.

"Listen," Jessica said. "It gets awesome. After I got back to campus, I sneaked a cell phone out of a random gym locker and called the property manager, Adrianne Mullins, using my Sabrina voice."

"You stole a phone?"

"I used it and put it back in the locker. The girl will never know. I told Adrianne I'd been in her neighborhood this afternoon and decided to see if she was home so I could take another look at that apartment. She said, oh sorry, she'd been gone all day, which was *great*. I was hoping she hadn't been home so there was no way she could have witnessed anything herself. Then I told her I hadn't ended up knocking on her door at all because I'd decided to knock on Megan's door first to get my own impression of her."

Jessica's eager tone disgusted Noah. She thought this catastrophe was exciting, fun because it was dangerous.

"Then I told her that when I got to Megan's door, I heard this crash, like something breaking, then a woman giggling and saying, 'It's not enough to throw things; you have to hit me. I need bruises for sympathy.'"

"What? I don't get—"

"If you can't keep up, we'll do a remedial session when I'm done. Then I told Adrianne I heard this thump, a yelp, and the woman saying, 'Now, go quickly.' I realized someone was coming out the door and ran, but I saw a man—not his face very well but enough to see he was young with brown hair and wearing a tan jacket. So I wanted Adrianne to know that Megan is a freak and she's wrecking her apartment. And I begged Adrianne, 'Please, please, don't tell anyone I told you this because I don't want trouble with the Drakes.'"

Noah gaped at Jessica's silver-screen grin. "Did Adrianne believe you?

"*So* totally believed me. See how I fixed everything? Victory! It's even better than the original plan. Right?"

"Victory," Noah said faintly. She'd escaped *and* might have damaged Megan's reputation even worse. But Gail would never have condoned physical violence. She hated violence; she wanted to love everybody, heal everybody. "I didn't want Megan getting physically injured. I just wanted everyone to know she's garbage."

"We're almost there! How can you be this big of a wimp? Megan is part of the reason your aunt is dead. What do you care if she gets a few bruises?"

*I don't.* Noah wanted to say the words but could imagine the sorrow in Gail's eyes if he did. No matter what, she *still* wouldn't like Megan getting hurt.

"I don't know how the conversation went at Megan's since I already took the recorder back," Jessica said. "So I'm not sure if Jenna Anderson has squealed to Trevor yet. But she will. It was so obvious she was skulking behind me. Hard to be sneaky about eavesdropping when you're holding a giggly kid."

Clever. Jessica was clever. Searching Megan's social media accounts on her iPad. Finding that post from a friend of Trevor's. Staging a conversation that showed Megan as a conniving cheat. *And* salvaging a situation that could have sent them both to prison.

But she wasn't supposed to hurt Megan.

"Once Jenna talks to Trevor, he'll dump Megan," Jessica said. "Once Adrianne spreads the news that Megan staged the attack, the whole town will chatter about how loony she is. Even her friends will share the rumors, pretending they feel bad for her: 'Did you hear the kooky things people are saying about Megan? Poor girl!'"

Jessica was right about the gossip. People would relish this bizarre tale.

"As soon as I ferret out info about how everything shook out, I'll decide what to do next," Jessica said. "I think I can finish it in one more operation. I'll make sure that no matter how much Megan bawls and denies things, Trevor will never take her back. In fact, I'm positive I can get Saint Michael to kick her out of Britt. Great, right?"

Was he shaking? Humiliated, Noah folded his arms and pushed his spine against the seat. Megan could have been killed. Or if Megan had gained the upper hand, Jessica could have been killed. Gail despised Jessica, but she'd still be devastated if a young woman died while working for Noah.

What if plans went wrong—worse—next time?

He couldn't control Jessica. Or Megan. He couldn't control the circumstances that might once again stir violence.

He tried to see himself at Gail's kitchen table, explaining tonight's glitch, and Gail smiling. *I appreciate the effort, kiddo. It's not your fault that girl hit Megan, and don't tell anyone I said this, but Megan deserved it. Thanks for doing some payback for me.*

He couldn't see it. Gail wouldn't praise him or wink at what had happened. She'd be horrified. Livid at him for hiring Jessica. Heartbroken.

Would she have wanted him to do any of this?

Even send the letter?

*The things I wrote were true. Megan deserved those.*

His certainty that he was honoring Gail contorted and snapped. "We're done."

Jessica shook her head. "We're an *inch* from the finish line. I can nail this. She'll get dumped, expelled, her reputation—"

"We're done for real." Sharp edges gouged his stomach. "I'm not paying you for anything else. Stay away from her."

Jessica swore. "I'm fired because I couldn't do this in a business suit and heels? I'm doing an *awesome* job, much better than you—"

"You're working for me. If I say we're done, we're done."

"You *coward*." Jessica's voice emitted such intense rage that Noah thought of radiation, gamma rays, something unseen that could kill him. "At least I have guts. If it had been you in Megan's apartment, you would have curled in a ball and cried for Auntie Gail while Megan called the cops."

He turned away and reached for the door handle.

Jessica grabbed the collar of his coat, her fingernails spearing him in the neck. "You haven't paid me. Pay up, or I'll smash your dainty nose."

He reached into his pocket, took the envelope of cash, and slapped it on the console between them. "I should have known if

I bailed you out of the gutter, I'd end up with a bucket of scum."
As fast as he could without making his actions conspicuous, he
stepped out of her car and walked away.

* * *

By the time Jessica staggered out of bed for her four a.m. donut
shift, her rage at Noah's arrogance had transformed to snickering.
She'd known since high school that he was as adventurous as a clam
buried in the sand, and she should have known anything more
intense than a prank phone call or an escaped-convict masquerade
would scare his shell shut. She'd become way too invested in
finishing that job, way too driven to show off how brilliant she was.
He had been impressed, but he'd never admit that to his gutter-
scum employee. Getting fired was good.

It was time for her to take control and get rich.

# Chapter 1 5

Eyes as blue and icy as the glaciers he'd seen in Alaska last summer evaluated Trevor. "I don't appreciate your fiancée telling the police I attacked her," Adrianne said.

"Megan didn't say anything about you to the police." Trevor wished he could telepathically trigger a call from an overprotective parent or a knock on his office door from an applications processor who urgently needed his input. He'd like a reason to excuse himself and wrack his brain for how to make this less awkward. At least now that Adrianne had come to see him, he could stop feeling guilty that he hadn't called to explain what had happened yesterday.

"You don't know what she told the police about me," Adrianne said. "They wouldn't have tracked me down in Plymouth if she hadn't accused me."

"I'm the one who told Detective Powell we used to date and that you'd indicated to Megan that you didn't like her or approve of our engagement. I didn't accuse you of anything, and I'm sorry for the embarrassment and the hassle you've been through. The police already wanted to talk to you in your role as property manager, and for me to hide the history between us or avoid mentioning your attitude toward Megan would have been deceitful and obstructive."

"They already knew the history between us. This is the second time they've talked to me. They came a couple weeks ago to ask who might have keys to Megan's apartment and if I knew of anyone who might have a problem with her or your sister. They didn't tell me anything specific, just that there had been harassment."

"You told Detective Powell we'd dated?"

"Did you expect me to act like it was a guilty secret? He asked how well I knew Megan, and I said not very well. He said he'd heard my family was friends with the Drake family and asked how well I knew Rachel. I said I knew her, but Larissa knew Rachel and Megan a lot better than I did. And I told him I'd dated you a while back. I didn't want him to learn that from Larissa or someone else and think I'd hidden it."

"That makes sense," Trevor said, irritated that pleasantly poker-faced Powell hadn't indicated he already knew about Adrianne and Trevor when Trevor had brought her up.

"I don't appreciate your telling him I don't like Megan," Adrianne said. "If Megan thinks that, she's hypersensitive. I've been completely polite."

*Oh brother.* Megan was not hypersensitive, and Trevor had seen Adrianne be standoffish or rude to people who bothered her. The asymmetrical silver bracelet on her wrist reminded him of listening to her complain about a clerk who'd neglected to give her the sale price on a necklace, then watching her criticize a customer service worker who couldn't figure out how to refund the percentage the clerk should have deducted. Trevor empathized with her annoyance— neither worker had been competent—but her curt impatience had elevated his uncertainty and misgivings into a solid decision: he didn't want to continue a relationship with her.

"I'm not here to berate you because your fiancée is intimidated that she's not the first woman you dated," Adrianne said. "I came to tell you something I didn't want to share over the phone."

"What's that?"

"Not too long ago, I showed a girl the vacant apartment upstairs from me. She was edgy because she'd heard rumors about a criminal living in the house. I reassured her Megan was not a criminal or at all dangerous."

Trevor nodded. Adrianne would have tried to give a positive impression about Megan; she wanted to rent out the unit.

"She called back yesterday afternoon and said she'd stopped by the house again, trying to make up her mind about renting, and decided to talk to Megan in person to check out the vibes, get her own opinion on her."

Trevor braced himself. This story wasn't going to have a happy twist like "And they turned out to be best friends from kindergarten!" "Did she talk to Megan?"

"She was about to ring the doorbell but heard thuds, like someone throwing heavy things or knocking them over. Then she heard a woman laughing and telling someone to hit her." Adrianne hesitated, maintaining eye contact. "The woman said she needed the injury for sympathy."

"What did your friend do then?" Trevor asked, speaking with punctilious composure.

"Got scared and ran, but she saw a man leaving Megan's place. He was young with brown hair."

"Could she identify him?"

"She says no; she only got a glimpse. She called to let me know she definitely didn't want the apartment and that Megan is a loon."

More than one spring fed the rising stress inside Trevor, but he didn't want to trace and explore the sources now. It didn't matter yet; all he planned to show Adrianne was equanimity. Was this story her invention? She didn't sound vindictive. She sounded businesslike. "Your friend must have misheard," he said.

"I know this is awful for you. I have no idea what's happening. I hardly know Megan. I felt obligated to tell you because I respect you and your family, but it's your business what you do about it."

"Your friend is sure it was Megan's voice she heard?"

"She's never met Megan, but what other woman would be speaking from Megan's apartment, joking about getting hit on the day Megan ends up with a black eye?"

"Forgive me, but if your friend is not mistaken, she's lying."

Adrianne sighed and slid a finger along a wisp of straight blonde hair. "Why would this woman lie? I just said she doesn't know Megan, and she's not my friend. I've met her once, when she came to tour the apartment. She's not connected to any of us."

"Why would Megan and a . . . co-conspirator . . . stage something like that?"

"How would I know? She's *your* wife-to-be. Maybe she wants more attention from you and thinks pretending to be in danger will help. Ask a psychologist. I'm only telling you what an eyewitness told me."

"What is your source's name?"

"I promised to keep her anonymous."

"This is a police matter."

"Are you sure you want the police more involved? If you don't want to hit the tabloids, there are more discreet ways to deal with it."

"If your source isn't willing to—"

"She made me swear I wouldn't tell anyone her name. She's a Britt student and scared to death about getting on the wrong side of your family." Empathy warmed Adrianne's eyes. "I'm sorry. You're a nice guy. But are there any witnesses to testify it wasn't Megan staging this?"

"The police are investigating."

"You mean there are no witnesses, and you don't want to admit it. I don't know what other harassment Detective Powell was talking about, but have there been any witnesses to testify that Megan's been harassed at all? That she didn't make everything up?"

"Megan would not—"

"Oh, good grief. You met her when she was pretending to be her sister so her sister could have an alibi when she *kidnapped Rachel.* Yes, I know Megan wasn't aware of what was going on, but being oblivious doesn't equal being trustworthy. Her sister is in prison for kidnapping and murder, her mother is a toxic drama queen, and you're surprised Megan isn't stable?" Fluidly, Adrianne rose to her feet. "Maybe she doesn't know she's doing it. No matter what, it's your problem. I've done my duty. I warned you." She walked to the coat tree in the corner of his office.

"Wait." Trevor stood.

"I'm not throwing an innocent student under the bus because you can't cope with the fact that Megan is having a breakdown and is probably cheating on you. Thanks for your time." With smooth dignity, she walked out the door and closed it behind her.

\* \* \*

"This is absurd." Anguish in her eyes, Sandra looked at Trevor sitting on other side of her sewing table. "We've embarrassed poor Adrianne enough times."

"That's why Megan and I decided to run this by you and Dad first. Would you prefer to personally contact Eileen and Calvin and see if they'd like to talk to Adrianne before we tell Detective Powell what she said?"

Sandra adjusted the white fabric she was stitching into an astronaut costume for one of Evan's kids; Trevor couldn't remember which of his little nieces was obsessed with rockets and outer space. "Is having us talk to the Mullinses first what you wanted or what Megan wanted?"

"We both agreed on it." It had been Megan's suggestion, but he didn't specify that. He'd called Megan this afternoon, telling her he wanted to go directly to Powell. Horrified at Adrianne's tale, Megan had urged Trevor to contact his parents first. He suspected her main reason for delay was fear that Powell doubted her, and she wanted more information before they called the police. He wished Megan and his father could have been here for this conversation, but his father was in a meeting, and Megan had an exam in her evening class. Trevor hadn't wanted to wait.

"We know Adrianne couldn't have attacked Megan," Sandra said. "The police verified she was in Plymouth."

"I'm not accusing her of attacking Megan, clearly. But either she's holding back the name of the person who lied about Megan, or she is the one lying. I think it's the former."

Sandra snipped a couple of threads and set the unfinished costume aside. "You're suggesting I call Eileen and ask her to interrogate her daughter about what she's hiding."

"You're friends with Eileen. If Adrianne's parents can persuade her to cooperate, that would be more tactful than sending Detective Powell straight to her door."

Without answering, Sandra picked up the instructions for the costume, folded them, and slid them into a Ziploc bag. She opened a drawer on her sewing table and put the bag away.

"Mom," Trevor said as she picked up her scissors and pincushion.

She stored the tools in the drawer and closed it. "Sweetheart, there's something else we need to think about. Adrianne and her friend could be telling the truth."

Trevor linked his fingers. He dug his fingertips into one set of knuckles and then the other, back and forth as though the rocking movement could help him resist the temptation to get defensive. "Okay," he said. "Objectively speaking, Megan could be lying. However, she isn't."

Sandra switched off the power on her sewing machine and came to sit in the overstuffed chair next to Trevor. She rested her hand on his arm for a few seconds, then leaned back in her chair, a preoccupied glaze over her face.

Trevor spoke in the same convincing-but-fake-calm voice he'd used with Adrianne. "Staging an attack to gain sympathy is so far out of character for Megan that it's ludicrous."

"I . . . almost agree with you." Sandra lifted her glasses and rested them on top of her head. "But . . . a vindictive, violent person targeting Rachel and Megan again? Is it . . . truly likely that we have a new Evelyn Seaver?"

"This isn't that extreme." Was Sandra partly relieved that Adrianne had presented an explanation for yesterday's attack that didn't involve a dangerous new adversary? If Megan had staged yesterday, it was a given that she'd also played Kristen in the prison-break hoax.

Sandra loved Megan. It must be acutely painful for her to suggest that Megan was responsible. Painful but not as terrifying as worrying her family was under siege again.

"I'm worried we're fighting to avoid confronting a real possibility," Sandra said gently.

"Megan wouldn't do any of these things. Scaring Rachel—"

Sandra touched his hand. "She's done a marvelous job coping with the stress in her life, but think about what she's been through. Think about the timing."

"Bryce?"

"Bryce returned to Britteridge, which stirred up everyone's memories of the kidnapping. You two got engaged, which put her in a different spotlight."

"How would notoriety lead her to act outrageously?'

"I don't know. It may have exacerbated self-esteem issues. Maybe she doesn't dare admit she's struggling for fear you'll reject her, but the turmoil is . . . more than she can rationally cope with."

"Terrorizing Rachel," Trevor said flatly. "She wouldn't do that no matter how stressed she is."

"We don't always know what's going on inside someone's head. We don't ever know everything, and sometimes we know nothing, even when it's someone we love. I thought I knew Gail. I believed with every cell in my body that Gail would never harm our family."

"We all trusted her." The kidnappers had found Gail's weakness and used it. His mother thought stress was pounding Megan in a weak spot, and unable to cope, she was doing things they'd never fathomed she could do.

Did he think that?

Absolutely not.

*Absolutely not? Be unbiased. Assess her as though you don't have personal feelings for her.*

Not possible. Not anymore.

"Megan is an extraordinary woman," Sandra said. She didn't add what Trevor figured she was contemplating: Did Megan's out-of-the-ordinary qualities include out-of-the-ordinary insanity?

*Extraordinary.* She was extraordinary, but that imposing word described only a fraction of why he loved her. He loved the ordinary things, little things, everyday things. He thought of when he and

Megan had been dating for a few weeks and she'd dozed off doing homework and slept with her face on her notes and her arm flopped across the keyboard of her computer. He'd stopped by to bring her apples from the farmer's market and found her with pen smudges on her cheek, glassy eyes, and cute messy eyebrows—he'd never known fine, light eyebrows could get scrambled. He'd tinkered with the frozen keyboard, enjoying her comical story of how she'd face-planted on top of her homework. And he'd realized during that simple afternoon how deeply interested he was in Megan O'Connor.

"I'm sorry." Sandra pulled a tissue from her pocket. "But if it's possible Megan is suffering, we need to help her. Her own mother won't. I doubt she's capable of noticing when others are in pain."

"That call to her mother about the two-thousand-dollar coat," Trevor said. "The e-mail asking you for money. We know those hoaxes weren't Megan's doing. Her finances are fine. Dad checked her account."

"I'm not sure her finances are proof, honey. The fact that she's not financially under water doesn't mean she didn't claim to be."

"Why would she willingly embarrass herself and get her mother riled up?"

"I have no idea. I'm not saying she's done any of this." She rubbed around her eyes. "I'm trying to balance so many critical factors that I'm afraid I'll drop them all. Or drop the wrong ones, at least. I don't want to risk wounding Megan and damaging my relationship with her, but if she is struggling, I don't want to risk not getting help for her. That would be a disaster for her *and* for you." She sighed. "The best balance I can come up with is to open our minds and consider the possibility that Megan is staging things. We'll talk to her. Then we'll work from that point."

Trevor stared at his feet, immobile against the Berber carpet. Big, incompetent feet in brown loafers. Why couldn't he fix this? He didn't want to agree that his mother had a valid point, but rejecting what she'd suggested wouldn't erase reality. Was he missing something in Megan's behavior? Was she falling apart, but he, thickheaded, kept blaming Bryce or Adrianne?

"I'll take the heat," Sandra said. "I'll talk to her privately and make it clear I'm expressing my concerns and leave you out of it. Let her be angry with me, not you. But I should talk to her before we talk to the Mullinses or the police about what Adrianne said. If these problems are coming from Megan, we don't want to make the situation worse for her. *If*," she repeated. "I hope I'm 100 percent wrong."

"I know that."

Sandra's worry-crimped face relaxed a little at his nondefensive answer. "I'm afraid of . . . I don't want to make the mistakes I made with Gail, oblivious until it was too late for her."

Megan . . . knotted in agony on the floor of her apartment. What if she hadn't been okay? "Thank you for offering, but I'll talk to Megan myself." Trevor tried to collect his thoughts and remember what he'd wanted to accomplish here. He'd wanted to ask his parents to talk to the Mullinses. *Check that off the list. Or rip it off the list and burn it.* He'd also wanted to brainstorm new ideas for who might be responsible for this chaos.

"Setting aside Megan, Adrianne, or Bryce," he said, "who else might have been stressed by recent changes?"

"Meaning Bryce's return or your engagement?"

"Both. Let's start with Bryce's return. Tell me about Gail's family, besides Charlie and Bryce. Was she close to any of her siblings?"

"She has a brother, Louis, who lives in British Columbia. They had a friendly relationship, but she didn't see him very often. Her only sister was Rosemarie, Noah Sahlberg's mother, who died before we even met Gail and Charlie. Noah's father, Kurt, still lives in the area."

"Bryce said he hasn't seen his uncle since his release."

"Or for years before he went to prison, I'd guess. Kurt wasn't close to Gail or Bryce. He has a . . . thorny personality. Gail said losing Rosemarie overwhelmed him, and he never got himself together emotionally. He's successful financially. He owns a home improvement business or something related to that, but he . . . never figured out how to relate to his son. Lots of criticism, no patience. Gail did everything she could to love Noah in Rosemarie's place."

Noah. Tall, smart, always wore polo shirts in high school. Decent guy, reserved, sometimes abrasive.

Sandra picked up a scrap of fabric from the carpet. "I'm trying to remember if I saw Noah at Gail's funeral, but . . . you know, I was so in shock that I wasn't thinking about her family as much as I should have. I should have reached out to him."

Quintessential Sandra Drake, reproaching herself because she hadn't been focused on serving the family of the friend who had aided her daughter's kidnappers. "It was a rotten time for you," Trevor said.

"He's a hardworking, reliable boy." Sandra rolled and unrolled the scrap of fabric. "Never a troublemaker. To be honest, he was a relief to Gail when Bryce was out of control. Noah is not someone I'd suspect of doing these bizarre things to Megan."

"Yeah, from what I remember of him, I agree." Trevor checked his watch. "I told Megan I'd pick her up after her exam. I'd better go."

"She's not staying at her apartment, is she? She's welcome to stay here."

"I told her you'd be happy to have her, but she said she'd rather stay in her own place. She just wanted the locks changed."

"That's not much of a security upgrade."

"She said she isn't worried, that whoever is doing this doesn't want to come face-to-face with her, and the reason there was a fight last time was because the intruder panicked when cornered. I tried to persuade her to go somewhere else, but she was stubborn."

Sandra hesitated. Trevor knew she was thinking. *Maybe she isn't worried because she knows there wasn't an intruder, so why inconvenience herself by moving?* "I can see why it would be important to her to feel she's handling things," Sandra said graciously. "Kristen tried to make her feel weak and incompetent, and Megan still wrestles against feeling that way about herself."

"She does. I sent a locksmith to replace the locks on the front door and bulkhead doors and to install new window locks."

"Without permission from the Mullinses or giving them keys, I assume."

"If they don't like what I did to their property, I'll pay to change it to whatever they want once this is over." He rose to his feet.

Sandra stood and hugged him. "We'll do anything we can to help Megan, in whatever way she needs."

Trevor kissed her cheek. "I'll be in touch." He headed for his truck, getting clumsier with each step as he thought about what he was going to say to Megan.

* * *

Megan hurried out of the classroom, eager to escape artificial lighting and relieved it was dark outside. After one day, the swelling on her forehead and eyelid had shrunk, but the area was still misshapen, and the bruising was so dark that even repeated retouching of her concealing makeup didn't avert stares and questions. How to respond was a dilemma: if she explained about the break-in, she'd stir a hurricane of curiosity. If she refused to explain, gossip would spread that Trevor Drake's fiancée had an unexplained black eye. She'd decided to smile at questions, say it was a ridiculous story that she'd share as soon as she could figure out a way to make it less embarrassing, and change the subject. It earned a C in effectiveness and a failing grade in peace of mind. Weaseling around the truth reminded her of claiming that a fall down the stairs had scraped and bruised her, rather than risking Rachel's safety by admitting kidnappers had inflicted her injuries.

She spotted Trevor approaching her. "You didn't have to walk across campus," she said as they met. "I was going to meet you at your truck."

"These days, I don't like you walking alone in the dark." Trevor took her backpack, and they headed toward the staff parking lot behind the administration building.

"Everyone walks alone in the dark in winter," Megan said. "It's dark at five o'clock." Desperate to ask what Trevor's parents had said, she accelerated her pace, figuring she shouldn't discuss it until they were alone. She couldn't think of an alternate subject, and apparently neither could Trevor; they walked in silence until they were nearly to his truck.

"How was your test?" he asked as he took his keys from his pocket.

"I think I did well, but my focus wasn't the best. Surprise."

"I'm sure you aced it." Trevor opened the door of his truck, and Megan climbed inside. Once he was in his seat with the door closed, she expected him to immediately tell her what had happened, but he didn't speak as he backed out and headed for the road.

"Did you talk to your parents about Adrianne?" Megan asked.

"My father wasn't home, but I talked to my mother."

Megan waited. Trevor didn't elaborate.

"Did . . . your mother think it was a good idea to contact Adrianne's family?" Megan asked.

"At some point. Do you want to come to my place?"

"If you don't mind feeding me. After that exam, I need a snack." *He's nervous*, Megan thought. He kept waiting for her to tug information out of him even though he knew she was anxious for a report.

Mouth dry, she pulled at a snag in the yarn of her glove. *You know what the problem is. Deal with it.*

She didn't want to deal with it.

She shut her eyes, needing another round of painkillers but too weary to unzip her backpack and dig up her bottle of ibuprofen.

"You okay?" Trevor asked.

"Your mother thinks I'm the culprit in all these problems. She thinks Adrianne is telling the truth."

"No. She . . . just suggested we should examine all possible explanations."

"You don't have to tiptoe." Megan looked at him. "This is far from being the most awkward conversation we've ever had. At least she doesn't suspect me of murder."

Trevor gave an edgy smile and didn't comment. Wanting to give her nerves a break before she asked another question, Megan stayed silent as well and thought about sitting in this truck, rain slamming against the roof, as she admitted to Trevor she wasn't Kristen and learned Trevor had already figured out her identity and suspected her of killing Gail. *Perfect thing to dwell on if you're trying to give your nerves a break.* If a guest at her bridal shower said, "Tell us how you met!" Megan planned to hide her face in a bowl of pastel M&Ms.

"Do you think I'm doing these things?" she asked as Trevor pulled into the parking space in front of his condo.

"No."

It was a credible no—not hesitant or too quick or exaggerated. Megan still didn't believe it. Her headache hammered her skull. Trevor thought she might be . . . crazy? Manipulative? Evil? A little of each?

*Handle this calmly,* she told herself. *Look at it from his point of view. From Sandra's point of view. They've known Adrianne Mullins longer than they've known you, and you showed up here lying and fooling them. No matter how much they love you, that doesn't mean they've completely forgotten what you did.*

"Megan." Trevor grasped her hand. "I'm sorry. You're angry."

*Yes. I am.* She wanted to snap, *I can't believe you suspect me of being that cruel to Rachel,* but she restrained the words. "Don't apologize. I earned this three years ago. I've worked to do the right thing since then, but that doesn't mean it's fair for me to expect you to pretend I've always been trustworthy."

"My mother isn't blaming . . . I already told you I don't think that—"

"Let's go inside." Megan opened the door. Trevor all but lunged around the front of the truck to help her to the ground and escort her to his condo.

Inside, he took her coat and switched on the gas fireplace. "What would you like to eat?"

"That." Megan pointed at the sunflower-seed-covered loaf of whole-wheat bread on the counter.

"Toasted?"

"Thanks." She sat on the couch, unzipped her backpack, and found the bottle of pain reliever. Neither of them spoke while Trevor toasted and buttered the bread and brought it to her with a glass of milk. She swallowed the medication with the milk.

He sat next to her but left a few more inches between them than he usually did. Was he squeamish about being too close to her, or did he think she didn't want to be too close to him?

She took a few bites of the toast, evaluating her thoughts, defying the impulse to cry. "Here's where I'm at. I have been absolutely truthful with you from that horrible night Gail died, when I realized how wrong I'd been to masquerade as Kristen."

She set the plate of toast on the square table in front of her. "I received hate mail a month or so ago, and I did not write it to myself. I did not sneak into Rachel's house and pretend to be Kristen to scare her. I did not send your mother an e-mail asking for money or start a rumor about the cost of my coat. I did not hold a tacky, insulting phone conversation about you in the lounge at the Halverson Building, then come home and egg a secret boyfriend into smacking me so I could role play a victim. No, I am not having blank spells or anything like that. Yes, I'm stressed. Yes, it's been hard lately with Bryce's return. No, I have not had a breakdown."

Trevor's hands curved around both of hers. "I wish you believed that I'm not accusing you."

She blinked. If she cried, Trevor would feel like a jerk. The worse he felt, the less forthright he'd be. "You're stating that my guilt is a possibility. I'm sure that's how Detective Powell sees it. He'd be a lousy investigator if he didn't view me as a suspect. Your mother must be scared silly, and I don't blame her. If you were my son, I'd be petrified that you were engaged to a manipulative nut."

"She knows you're not a manipulative nut."

"She hopes I'm not. What do I need to do to reassure her—and you—that I'm not staging things? I'm happy to do whatever you want. Would you like me to meet with my bishop? The counselor who helped me cope with that tense family-history moment when my twin sister tried to kill me? A psychiatrist? Detective Powell? All of the above? Would you like to hire a private eye to follow me around?"

"Meg . . ."

"None of that was sarcastic. I'm serious with every one of those suggestions. I'll do whatever would reassure you."

Trevor released her hands and wrapped his arms around her. Megan leaned her head against his shoulder, her hold on her tears slipping at last.

"I love you," he said.

If she could keep her voice relatively steady, maybe he wouldn't know she was crying. "I didn't give your family the best first impression."

"You got pulled in by the promise of things you'd wanted for a long time, and you made a poor judgment call."

"That's a colossal understatement."

"You did everything you could to set it right, even when that included nearly getting killed, and you've done everything you can since then to get your life on the best possible path. I've watched you do that for three years, Megan. Long before we started dating."

If he'd been watching her, if he knew her, why did he doubt her now—even a tiny bit?

Abruptly, he drew back. Lacking a hasty, subtle way to wipe her face, Megan couldn't keep her tears secret.

With a fingertip, he collected the tears from her cheeks. "You can do better than me."

"Trevor! That's absurd! You are the most incredible man I've ever met." Were his insecurities part of his doubts about her? The prankster's references to his being dull and miserly, the hints that Megan was marrying him for access to the Drake money, the lurid rumor of a mysterious man conspiring with her. Did he know in his head that she'd never do these things, but in his self-doubt, he couldn't help fearing maybe she *didn't* love him as much as she claimed?

Why was he like this? Was it the pressure of growing up a Drake, knowing everyone expected him to be exceptional like his father? Who was likely to be aware that Trevor—confident, successful, compassionate, funny, handsome—doubted himself?

Adrianne. She couldn't have been the attacker, but that didn't mean she wasn't involved. The ingenious emotional manipulation, the sensitivity to personal ways to stir up a ruckus, like goading an oblivious Pamela . . . Was it sexist that Megan thought this was more female strategy than male?

She picked up the remainder of her toast. "I'm happy to do whatever your mother would find reassuring." She would never have made that offer to her own mother; she could imagine what Pamela would suggest as proof that Megan was innocent. "Well dear, if you moved back home so I can keep an eye on you, and signed over control of your bank account . . ."

"I'm reasonably sure my mother won't go for the Sam Spade option." From the trace of humor that animated Trevor's tone, Megan knew he was relieved. He'd been afraid she'd be hurt and offended. She was hurt, but getting offended over this was senseless.

"If your mother sent a private investigator to tail me, she'd send him with jars of homemade applesauce and loaves of cinnamon bread to leave at my door and add a card at the end saying, 'Thanks for a great case!'"

Trevor laughed. "True."

Megan ate the last piece of crust. "I'll talk to your parents."

"Do you . . . want me to be there when you do?"

"Of course I want you to be there. There's nothing I'd say to them that I wouldn't say in front of my—"

*My future husband.* Megan reached to grasp the words, but they fell, grazing her fingertips, plummeting toward the ground.

Trevor's arm circled her shoulders. He tilted toward her and rested his cheek against her temple.

Megan waited for him to say something. Did he want to tell her the wedding was off, at least temporarily? Should she joke about cold feet, make it less awkward for him, tell him it was okay, even though there wouldn't be a miniscule fragment of okay anywhere in their broken engagement?

He didn't speak or move. He held her, silent, gentle, until Megan relaxed, dwelling only on his quiet breathing, the warmth of his body, the warmth of his soul.

Light strengthening her.

"I'm moving forward with Adrianne," she murmured.

Slowly, Trevor lifted his head. "What do you mean?"

Megan straightened her spine. Trevor drew his arm away and sat straight as well.

"I understand your mother is reluctant to approach the Mullinses," she said. "That's fine. I thought it might be a more sensitive way to handle things, but if it's not happening immediately, I'm not waiting. Either the culprit is using Adrianne, or she *is* one of the culprits. No matter what, she has critical information. I respect that you don't know that for sure and neither do your parents, but I do. I know what happened yesterday afternoon."

"I don't know her parents that well," Trevor said. "But I'll talk to them if you want."

"Adrianne will have to give evidence to the police, even if we coax the name of her witness out of her first. I'm calling Detective Powell. We should have done that right away, like you suggested."

She waited, striving to lock her thoughts on hope, on sunlight, not on rising wind. If Trevor acted reluctant or said sending Powell to Adrianne now would embarrass the Mullins family, churn up rumors, or embarrass the Drakes, this change of heart meant he had significant questions about her innocence. He worried an investigation would confirm Adrianne's report.

"Yes," he said. "Absolutely; let's call now." He took his phone off the table. "I'll do it since I'm the one Adrianne talked to."

"Thank you." Megan went slack against the couch and pillowed her head on the top of the cushions. "I can't believe we're dealing with the police again. I like Detective Powell, but I would be grateful if we never needed to speak with him again. I thought life was normal, that it would stay normal!"

"I thought that too." Trevor searched for Powell's number. "We need to give up our hobby of collecting lightning strikes."

# Chapter 16

ADRIANNE DIPPED HER FORK INTO her bowl of fruit and glanced at her phone. A missed call and a voice mail from a number that jiggled her memory. She'd seen it before but couldn't identify it. The call must have come while she was in the shower. She swallowed a mouthful of breakfast, poked the fork into the bowl again, and stared at her phone. Sabrina Erickson . . . ? No, when Sabrina had called a couple of days ago, Adrianne had noticed she had an out-of-state area code. This number was local. She should just listen to the voice mail, but things had been so weird lately that she was jumpy about—

A cold, wet object hit her foot. Startled, she gave her foot a savage shake; a slice of peach dropped to the floor. A few grapes rolled along the table. A half-frozen strawberry, a pineapple chunk, and three blueberries sat next to her bowl.

*Get your act together, sister.* Adrianne set her fork down and gathered the spilled fruit in a napkin. She should focus on breakfast instead of goggling at her phone while she knocked fruit from her overfull bowl.

She tossed the napkin into the trash and picked up her phone to listen to her voice mail.

"Hello, Ms. Mullins. This is Detective Aaron Powell of the Britteridge Police Department. I need to speak with you as soon as possible. Please call me." He gave his phone number.

She groaned, smacking her phone onto the table. Trevor had obviously called the police after their meeting yesterday—Adrianne's grand prize for giving him the opportunity to help Megan discreetly. He'd probably told Powell that Adrianne was lying out of jealousy and his adorable Megan never told lies, that the whole pretend-to-be-her-sister-during-Rachel's-kidnapping scam was a fluke. Since when did Trevor go mush-brained because a woman was attractive?

Adrianne wasn't jealous. She was irritated. It bothered her that Trevor had rejected her because they "weren't right for each other"— *dumped via cliché*; he'd never explained what wasn't right—and he'd chosen a deceitful, semicriminal, crazy woman instead. She wouldn't take Trevor now, but, good grief, how insulting. *I hope you're still enthralled by that pretty face after Megan's demolished your life.*

If Adrianne called Detective Powell and repeated Sabrina's story but refused to identify her, could she get in trouble for withholding information? She didn't want to betray Sabrina. If Megan learned Sabrina's name, she might bamboozle Trevor into chucking her out of Britt. Before Megan, Adrianne wouldn't have worried that Trevor might get vengeful, but now she had no idea what he'd do for his femme fatale. If Megan could bewitch him into proposing to her, she could effortlessly enchant him into punishing Sabrina for "lying" about her.

But if Adrianne didn't give Sabrina's name to Powell, he might assume—he would assume—Sabrina didn't exist and Adrianne was maliciously slandering Megan.

She'd agreed to keep Sabrina's identity confidential, but she hadn't agreed to stand near the crater of an active volcano and hope it wouldn't erupt. Since Trevor had taken Sabrina's report to Powell, Sabrina would have to deal with it. Even if Trevor did get vengeful, surely his father would intervene. President Drake was an intelligent, honest, compassionate man. Which Trevor *had* been, before Megan.

Adrianne scrolled through her recent calls until she found Sabrina's number. She'd apologize to Sabrina and tell her this situation was too serious for Adrianne to hide any information, and if Sabrina didn't go to the police, Adrianne would have to give her name to Powell. She'd reassure Sabrina by sharing that her parents were friends with President and Mrs. Drake, and if Trevor or Megan tried to cause trouble, the Mullinses would advocate for Sabrina.

Adrianne called her.

"Hello?"

"Hi, Sabrina, it's Adrianne Mullins, the property manager."

"Who did you want to talk to?"

"Sabrina?"

"Wrong number," the girl said cheerfully. "Sorry."

"This isn't Sabrina Erickson's number?"

"Nope."

"I'm sorry to bother you." Adrianne disconnected. Puzzled, she checked the number she'd called. She was certain it was Sabrina's. It was the only number from that date with a non-Massachusetts area code. 602. Quickly, she looked it up. Arizona. Had Sabrina said she was from Arizona? Adrianne couldn't remember. The time of the call was correct. Maybe the data had gotten messed up, a mistake in the cell service? Did that ever happen?

She tried again.

"Still not Sabrina!" The same voice answered.

"I'm sorry. I wanted to double-check." Adrianne recited the number she'd called. "Is that your number?"

"Yep, but I'm not Sabrina."

Impressed that the girl still sounded friendly instead of impatient, Adrianne asked, "Did you get this number in the past few days?"

"No, I've had it since, gosh, I was a freshman in high school. That was . . . six years ago."

"Do you by chance have any friends named Sabrina who might have borrowed your phone?"

"Nope. I don't know anyone named Sabrina. Could you look her up online?"

"I'll try that. Thanks. I'm sorry to bother you again." Adrianne hung up and went to her computer. After a few minutes of fruitless Googling, she gave up and checked her calendar to find the date she'd shown Sabrina the apartment, the same day Sabrina had first called her. February sixth.

She scrolled back further through her list of calls. No 602 calls on the sixth. She remembered talking to Sabrina in the late morning, a few hours before she came over. The only call at that time of day was from a local area code.

She called the number and paced the kitchen while the phone rang. Six rings; no answer. She'd have to leave a message. Three more rings. Didn't she have voice mail set up? Why was she so hard to—

"Heyyyy!" A male voice answered. "Can I help you?"

"Sabrina Erickson, please."

"Sorry. The only person I see is a guy sitting by the drinking fountain, pigging out on an apple fritter. Dude, do you know Sabrina Erickson?"

Faintly, Adrianne heard a "Never heard of her."

"Sorry, she's not here. Did she tell you to call this number?"

"She called me from it before. I thought it was her phone."

"Nope. You've called the only remaining pay phone on campus. The last relic of the technology of the caveman."

"This is a public phone?"

"Yes, ma'am. Third floor of the student center. How much are you willing to pledge to help get this artifact bronzed?"

Too tense to joke back, Adrianne hung up. Two numbers that didn't lead to Sabrina? Sabrina might have used the pay phone if her own phone needed charging or she'd misplaced it, but what about the 602 number?

*Don't panic and assume Trevor's right and Sabrina's part of a conspiracy. The woman didn't even know anything about Megan except vague rumors.*

Unless she was pretending she didn't know anything. But why waste her time asking for information she already had? If she had a grudge against Megan, she knew enough to hate her. If she wanted to smear Megan, she could have given the police an anonymous tip about the faked attack. No need to go through a charade with Adrianne.

Sabrina had said she was a grad student in math and knew Dr. Mark Jenkins. Adrianne didn't have his cell phone number, but she could call the math department. She gobbled a few more bites of fruit, shoved the bowl into the fridge, and found his contact information online. Seeing the faculty picture of her friend made her feel less anxious and less alone: Mark had a genial smile and a genius brain. He'd help her.

She tapped his number into her phone. He probably wouldn't be in his office right now. She'd have to leave a message and wait for him to call back.

No. She couldn't wait for answers when the police might bang on her door at any time. If he didn't answer, she'd go to campus and track him down.

After one ring, he answered. "Good morning, this is Dr. Jenkins."

"Mark!" Relieved, she spoke in a hyperhappy voice. Cringing, she spoke more composedly. "It's Adrianne Mullins."

"Adrianne! Lady, it's good to hear from you. It's been a while. How are things?"

"Okay. I'm living in Britteridge again, doing property management for my parents."

"Excellent! Welcome back. What can I do for you? Math question? My neurons are warmed up. I'll prove the Riemann hypothesis right here on the phone and win myself a million bucks."

"I have *no* idea what that means."

"It means I have delusions of grandeur. What can I really do for you?"

"It's tangentially math related," Adrianne said.

"Extra points for use of *tangentially* in a sentence."

Adrianne laughed. "I'm trying to contact a girl who came to view an apartment a little while back. Her number isn't working, and I need to talk to her. She's a math grad student. Sabrina Erickson."

"Sabrina Erickson?"

"Yes."

"Uhhhh, do you know what program she's in?"

"She just said math. But she knows you. Said you were a great teacher."

"Bless her. Sabrina Erickson? Looks like I lied about those warmed-up neurons. She's a grad student here now?"

Relief began to wither. "Yes. She's very tall, Caucasian, brown hair, dark eyes, round glasses."

"I am one embarrassed nerd. Her name's not ringing a bell. Don't tell her this happened. Tell her she's my favorite student. Hang on."

Pacing into the living room, Adrianne waited. Mark must be checking rosters.

"Are you sure you have her name right?" he asked after a moment.

"I . . . might not. Maybe I made a mistake."

"She said she knew me?"

"Maybe she was exaggerating and meant she'd heard of you."

"Usually the only person who's heard of me is my mother. Sorry to be no help, but I can't find her."

"Thanks for checking."

"Gotta go teach. Stay in touch, Adri."

"I will." Adrianne hung up, trudged into the bathroom, and switched on her hair dryer.

Half an hour later, she walked into the Britteridge College admissions office and approached the reception desk. A young woman wearing a purple silk hijab smiled at her. "Can I help you?"

"My name is Adrianne Mullins. Is Mr. Drake available? I don't have an appointment, but I need to talk to him."

The girl touched a few keys on her keyboard. "Is this about a current application?"

"No, it's not related to admissions. We're old friends. He was asking me for some information. I have it now, and he'll want it immediately." *I sound like a kook. Barging into the admissions office, claiming to be an "old friend" of the associate director, with information he'll want "immediately."* She tried to think of a more plausible way to explain why she needed to see Trevor, but the receptionist didn't look troubled.

"I'll see if he's available," she said politely. "Just a moment."

"Thank you." Receptionists probably had to certify in kook handling to work in a college admissions office.

The girl picked up the phone. "Hi, Mr. Drake, it's Rimsha. Adrianne Mullins is here and would like to see you regarding some information you requested."

Adrianne tried not to appear apprehensive. Would Trevor assume she was here to repeat her accusations against Megan and tell Rimsha to eject her?

"Thank you." Rimsha hung up and smiled at Adrianne. "Go right back. If you'd like to hang your coat up, there's a rack there." She gestured behind Adrianne.

"Thank you." Adrianne hung up her coat. Facing Trevor was going to be mortifying, but less miserable than putting it off.

"His office is the second door on the left."

"Thank you." Adrianne headed down the hallway.

Trevor stood in the doorway of his office, a neutral expression on his face. "Come in," he said. "Please, sit down."

She sat in one of the leather seats facing his desk. He closed the door.

Adrianne got to the point before Trevor could even reach his chair. "I need to know if someone is a graduate student here. If you can't give out information because it's confidential, fine, but at least look it up so you'll know."

"What's the name?"

"Sabrina Erickson. Erickson with a *C* and a *K.*"

Trevor typed for a few seconds. "There is no Sabrina Erickson enrolled here."

"Thanks," Adrianne said dully. Her last hope had been wishful thinking.

Trevor took the chair next to her. "Is that the name of the woman who told you Megan staged the attack?"

"Yes." She'd been wrong. Sabrina had fooled her. Fooled her ego, the ego yearning to believe Trevor's bride-to-be was a manipulative liar.

"Thank you for telling me." He sounded genuinely grateful, with no smidgeon of contempt for her gullibility. "Do you know how to contact her?"

"No. I have no idea who she really is." Adrianne explained her interaction with Sabrina and her attempts to contact her. "I'm sorry. You were right. She's a phony. I was extremely rude yesterday."

"Forgiven. The number she called from the second time—can you give it to me?"

Adrianne pulled out her phone, found the number, and handed the phone to Trevor.

He wrote it down. "I'll pass this along to Detective Powell. If the owner of the phone isn't involved, 'Sabrina' may have stolen her phone, used it, then returned it."

"I need to call him back. He left me a message this morning."

"Tell me everything you know about Sabrina. How did she look?"

"Very tall. Five ten at least, maybe six feet. Slim. Dark brown hair, cut in an A-line."

"An A-line?"

Adrianne held her hands flat and angled them on either side of her jaw. "Longer in front than in back. Glasses—round glasses. I'm not sure of the shape of her face, and I don't have a clue what her nose was like or her mouth or whatever else sketch artists ask about. I don't remember any specific accent either. Sorry. I'm not good at describing things."

"You're doing great. If you can name her hair color, you're better at it than I am."

"Dark eyes? At least not light. Brown, I think, or hazel? Do you have any idea who she is?"

He shook his head. "Maybe Megan will recognize your description. I doubt it though. If she's the same person who's been causing trouble, she was likely in disguise. We already know she's a good mimic, so the voice might not have been her natural one either."

"This isn't much help to you, then."

"Are you kidding? This is a treasure trove compared to what we had before." His smile made Adrianne feel guiltier for believing

Trevor would let himself get duped by a cunning woman and even punish a student on her behalf. She knew he wasn't like that, but she'd wanted to despise Megan and throw it in Trevor's face that he'd chosen a lunatic.

"I *am* sure she wasn't Megan in disguise," Adrianne said. "Just in case Detective Powell wonders if Megan's that, um, creatively crazy. After Sabrina toured the apartment and we chatted, I walked her out to the porch. While I was getting my mail, I saw Megan coming up the stairs from her apartment."

"Did Megan see Sabrina?"

"I doubt she noticed her. Sabrina was walking away—she was already past the house, and she was walking fast. I figured she was in a hurry to get to her car because it was about twenty degrees outside, and she'd said she'd parked far down the street because she got confused on the address. Megan didn't look in her direction. I . . . noticed that because I was a little self-conscious at how much I'd told Sabrina, and I didn't want them to notice each other right then. Megan got in her car and drove away in the opposite direction from Sabrina, so she probably didn't see her at all, and she definitely didn't see her with me." Too bad she hadn't shouted to Sabrina to come meet Megan and introduced them. Then Megan would be a witness now. "Do you believe me? Or do you think I'm making this up and there is no Sabrina?"

"We know you weren't in Britteridge when Megan got attacked."

That didn't mean he didn't suspect her of working with someone to harass Megan. She had a key to Megan's apartment.

Could she hide this fiasco from her family? She didn't want them to know what a flake she was. Of course, if she got arrested for stalking Megan, that would be exciting news to the whole town. *Jealous ex-girlfriend of Trevor Drake harasses his new love!*

"This is excellent progress," Trevor said. "We're on our way to solving this."

Adrianne nodded, trying not to look dejected. Excellent progress toward finding the real culprit? Or excellent progress toward convicting her?

\* \* \*

"You guys again?" Bryce glared at the lanky detective standing on his porch and the younger officer with him, wishing he could drive them away by yelling and flapping a pizza box at them like he had the raccoon skulking around his garbage can last night. "What do you want?"

"Good evening, Mr. Ludlum," Powell said. "May we come in?"

"This better not be about Megan O'Connor again. I haven't bothered her."

"It does relate to her, but we're not here to make accusations. We'd like your help."

*I'll bet.* Bryce could refuse to let them in; Powell didn't have a warrant. But defiance would make him appear guilty of whatever Powell wanted to accuse him of. He escorted the detective and Officer Mendoza into the living room.

"Have a seat. Want something to drink?" Even though these guys were cops making pests of themselves, his mother would have offered coffee or water or lemonade. Or ice cream sundaes. Powell could use some body fat.

"No, thank you," Powell said. He and Mendoza sat on the couch and removed their overcoats. Bryce should have asked if he could take their coats, but maybe he shouldn't do that with cops. They might keep cop stuff in the pockets.

Bryce took a chair. "What's up?"

"Do you know a woman who goes by the name of Sabrina Erickson?" Powell asked.

Powell had a question about someone besides Megan and maybe had a suspect besides Bryce? Bryce ought to pull out his phone and snap a picture of this great moment. He considered the name. "Sabrina Erickson. Doesn't sound familiar, but it's been a while since I lived here, and longer than that since I was here *and* had a functioning brain. Off the top of my head, I don't know her, but if you tell me about her, that might jog my memory."

Powell reached into the pocket of his coat, drew out a piece of paper, and unfolded it. He brought the paper to Bryce. "Sabrina Erickson is probably a fake name, so don't let that throw you."

Bryce examined the sketch of a woman with straight dark hair that came to points on either side of her jaw, half covering her chin. Glasses. Dark eyes. He wanted to recognize her and tell the police where to find her, but . . . Did she look familiar? Sort of? Maybe not? "Sorry. I don't know her. What did she do?"

"She may have information regarding a breaking and entering and an attack."

"On . . . Megan?"

"Yes."

"Is she all right?"

"Minor injuries." Powell handed him a second picture. This woman had lighter, longer hair; lighter skin; lighter eyes. No glasses.

"I don't know her either," Bryce said.

"It's the same woman. We think we're dealing with someone gifted with disguises and mimicking voices."

*Seriously? Then why waste time showing sketches?* "That makes it tough."

Powell took the pictures and returned to the couch. "I've asked you this before, but I need to repeat it. Do you know anything about the harassment of Megan O'Connor?"

"I still don't. If she's blaming me, she's a liar." *Watch it. Don't get vicious.* "*Liar*'s the wrong word. She's making a mistake."

Powell's affable smile irked Bryce. "I know you suspect Megan of staging the harassment, but let's set that aside. There's at least one other person involved—this so-called Sabrina Erickson—and we've confirmed Sabrina isn't Megan. I'll repeat another question I asked you previously: do you have any idea who has a grudge against Megan?"

Bryce wanted to ask if Powell thought Megan might have conspired with Sabrina, but the harder he pushed his suspicions, the guiltier he'd look. "I still don't know. I haven't learned anything new since the last time you bugged me." His thoughts shot to Noah. He'd avoided mentioning Noah to Powell last time. Yeah, he'd sent that hate mail. But spooking Rachel with a fake Kristen? Not Noah. Besides, this Sabrina woman was involved. No way would Noah have a girlfriend who'd do risky stuff. Noah's type would measure her pancakes with a ruler to certify that they were identical and scold other people for breaking the speed limit.

But if he told Powell that Noah hated Megan, that would give the police new prey instead of him—

*I can't believe you!* His mind created an image of his mother, her jovial smile gone. *You threw Noah to the cops just to get them off your back? Your own cousin? We're family! We help each other!*

"Sorry," he said. "I don't have a clue."

"Your cousin," Powell said. "Noah Sahlberg. I understand he was close to your mother?"

Thrown and hoping Powell didn't have ESP, Bryce said, "Yeah, they were close. His mom died when he was eight, and he was pretty lonely. He was over here a lot."

"Your mother's death must have been difficult for him."

"Yeah, of course."

"Has he ever said anything to you to indicate that he blames Megan, even partially, for what happened?"

"Nope." *You owe me, Noah.* "I've only seen him once since I got out. We were friends as kids, but not much anymore."

"Where were you this Wednesday between noon and two o'clock?"

"At work, and I have witnesses." Bryce wanted to feel this was a triumph, but even if he could prove he hadn't done anything to Megan at that time, Powell wouldn't be convinced he hadn't conspired with Sabrina.

"Names, please?" Powell lifted his pen.

"Hang on. I'm trying to remember who I was working with. And eating lunch with." Wednesday afternoon . . . fixing that fountain that should have been shut off but kept leaking and freezing. "Okay. There were four of us." He gave Powell the names.

"Thank you." Powell slid his pen and notebook into his pocket and set a card on the lamp table. "If you think of anything else that might be relevant, please contact me."

"I will." Bryce took that as the end to the interview and stood.

When he'd locked the door behind Powell and Mendoza, he wandered to the player piano and banged random keys, thinking of how many times his mother had chewed him out for manhandling her antiques. They were his antiques now. His house, his antiques, his money. He didn't need income, but he was there five days a week at Britteridge College, clearing snow off sidewalks, fixing leaks, emptying trash cans. If he didn't keep busy, he'd cartwheel back into the habits that had sent him to prison.

Was that hard work a waste? He was staying clean, doing everything right, but that was twice the police had shown up at his house, hunting for an excuse to lock him up again.

Never mind that they had no evidence against him. Since Megan had the support of the Drakes, the cops probably weren't even investigating Bryce's accusation that she was faking everything.

No wonder Noah hated her.

Bryce ambled out of the living room and into his mother's study. He flicked the switch to illuminate the glass case holding her silent-movie memorabilia and inspected a collection of Charlie Chaplin figurines. He remembered teenage Noah laughing his head off at Chaplin's slapstick but declining when Gail offered to lend him a DVD. "Can't watch it at home. It would annoy my dad."

Would the cops talk to Noah? Why would they? Noah was a respectable, brainy, quiet guy.

Who held grudges.

Could he be bothering Megan with more than an anonymous letter? If he was committing crimes and letting Bryce get in trouble for it . . . maybe he should hint to Powell that—

*Nah. You know it's not his style.* He couldn't sic the police on Noah. He'd tortured his mother enough without causing trouble for the nephew she'd loved like he was her kid.

# Chapter 17

MEGAN'S PHONE THAT SHE'D SET on a folded bath towel began to ring. She dropped her lipstick into her makeup basket and picked it up.

Adrianne Mullins. Gingerly, she accepted the call. She hadn't spoken to Adrianne in the two weeks since Adrianne had given the police information about Sabrina Erickson. With no idea if Adrianne still despised her, Megan hadn't been inclined to seek her out, and clearly Adrianne hadn't been inclined to seek Megan out. "Hello?"

"Megan, this is Adrianne. I'd like to talk to you, if this is a convenient time."

Her tone was courteous but not congenial. Megan promised herself that no matter what Adrianne said, she would respond with a Sandra-Drake level of classiness.

"Yes, I have a few minutes." Trevor would be here to pick her up soon, but she doubted Adrianne wanted a long chat.

"First, I'm overdue to apologize to you," Adrianne said. "I was unfair, unkind, and rude. I'm sorry."

"Thank you." Megan wiped speckles of eye shadow off the rim of the sink. Adrianne still sounded more no-nonsense than contrite, but that didn't mean it wasn't a sincere apology. "I'm sorry you got pulled into this nonsense with me and Sabrina."

"I'm guessing you doubt there's a Sabrina or that I got 'pulled' into anything. You think I created the entire fiction."

Megan assessed herself in the bathroom mirror, noticing how pink her face was becoming as she debated how honest to be with Adrianne. Detective Powell hadn't found any information on Sabrina, and the tips to the police hotline regarding the sketch of her had all been useless.

Adrianne was the only witness.

"I have no idea what's going on." Megan added a dab of concealer to cover the last faded trace of bruising around her eye. "But I'm not blaming you for anything." Suspecting wasn't blaming, and even *suspecting* was too emphatic of a word. She knew Adrianne was a possibility. That was it.

"I want you to know I had nothing to do with any harassment," Adrianne said. "I would never do anything like that."

"Neither would I," Megan said. "To myself or anyone else."

"Are you planning to stay here, or do you feel the apartment no longer works for you?"

"Would you *like* me to move out?"

Adrianne gave a sharp laugh. "No. I assumed you would want to go, that you might not feel safe living next to me."

Disconcerted, Megan again fished for something diplomatic to say. She'd talked several times with Trevor about whether or not she should move out. At first Trevor had, without accusing Adrianne, been adamant that Megan move somewhere with more security: move in with his family in Andover, move to a condo with a security service, move somewhere with multiple roommates, adopt a Doberman—anything to keep her safe. But they'd both calmed down. It was plain to Megan and becoming plainer to Trevor that the culprit hadn't planned to attack Megan. She doubted "Sabrina" would bother her again, even in minor ways. Megan's efforts to trap her and their ensuing fight would have shaken her, and she must know her attempts to smear Megan hadn't worked. You could only try a frame-up so many times before it became comically worthless.

"Megan." Adrianne spoke tersely, and Megan realized her long pause had embarrassed Adrianne.

"I'm sorry. Being spacey. No, I don't think I'm unsafe here. If I thought I was in danger, I'd be gone."

"A reporter called me today, offering me cash to do an interview on you, Trevor, and the Drakes. She obviously thought I'd want to give her dirt."

Megan winced. "I've never spread any rumors about you or talked to the press."

"I believe you. Larissa keeps insisting you're the sweetest person she's ever met. Sounds like you're a good match for Dudley Do-Right Drake."

"Should I tell him his new title, or are you mocking him?"

"Teasing him, but it's a compliment. He's a good guy. Not right for me but a good guy."

"The Drakes have all told me nice things about you," Megan said.

"They're compassionate people. When they testify against me in court, they'll emphasize that I'm the nicest jealous psycho they've ever met."

"They're not accusing you." Megan decided to go for full honesty. "This whole thing has boggled all of us, and we don't have answers. There's never been malice toward you or finger pointing. It's just that your recent move back to town, your access to my apartment, and your former relationship with Trevor would have made it stubborn denial on our part if we hadn't considered you."

"I agree. And given the dishonest way you slinked into town three years ago, and given your screwed-up background, it would have been stubborn denial on my part if I hadn't considered you."

"I agree." Candor without accusation felt liberating.

"There truly was a woman claiming to be Sabrina Erickson, who pretended to be interested in renting an apartment," Adrianne said. "I'm sorry I'm bad at remembering details of faces. I don't know if that police sketch looks anything like her. I'm sorry I didn't get suspicious of her earlier. When she kept digging for information about you and Trevor, I just figured she liked sensational gossip. The kidnapping saga is a crazy story."

"No kidding," Megan said.

"I got gossipy and told her too much. I'm sorry."

"You had no idea what she'd do with that information."

"That doesn't justify gossiping. Listen, I know it's not possible for you to completely trust me right now. If you're not comfortable living here, I understand. I'm not asking you to leave. I'd rather you didn't, because people will assume you ran because I'm a monster."

That was true, and a factor Megan and Trevor had discussed. If she moved out midsemester, the grapevine would label that as a Drake family declaration that Adrianne was guilty.

"But if you want to go, I understand," Adrianne said again. "I'll let you out of your contract. No penalties. You decide."

"Thank you," Megan said. "If I did leave, we'd cover the remaining months of the contract. We wouldn't expect your family to take a loss on this. But at this point, I'm staying. Assuming everything stays quiet, I'll finish out my contract. I think it *will* stay quiet. It better. We've already used up far more than our share of panic. Use any more and we'll cause a worldwide shortage."

"Let me know if you change your mind."

"Thank you. I will."

"As I said, I've been rude to you. You tried to make friends with me when I arrived here, and I didn't respond well. And I actually do like banana bread; thank you for being thoughtful, and I apologize for being a jerk. I doubt you want to give me another chance, especially after the way I accused you to Trevor, but . . . I would like the chance to get to know you."

"Are you sure you want that?" Megan was careful to sound frank, not sarcastic. "I promise I'm not offended if you'd rather limit our interaction to tenant-landlord business."

"Like I said, from what I hear, you're a nice person, and I'm sorry I misjudged you. But I understand if you want nothing to do with me."

"I've been given huge second chances in my life. I don't like being stingy giving them to others."

"Would you like to meet for lunch tomorrow? In a public place, of course, in case one of us is dangerous."

The dry humor in Adrianne's voice made Megan laugh. "Yes, I'd enjoy that."

"I'll text you a few suggestions, and I can work around your schedule. You pick the place. My treat."

"Thank you. I'll look forward to that."

"Good night." Adrianne disconnected.

Partly pleased, partly wary, Megan picked up her lipstick tube. The last time a formerly cold person had been unexpectedly nice to her was when Kristen had come to trick her into supporting a kidnapping scheme.

*If Adrianne starts telling you she's found an easy way to make money and all you have to do is pretend to be her, say no*, Megan thought sourly.

# Chapter 1 8

WITH MEGAN STILL LIVING IN Britteridge, it was a no-brainer which of Jessica's preliminary plans would work best. She added dozens of pages to her notes and kept them stashed inside a spike-heeled boot. She repeatedly got so excited working out details and checking out apartment listings in New York that she couldn't fall asleep until a couple of hours before work. In the early mornings, while plopping glazed donuts and cinnamon rolls into bags and filling coffee cups, she kept herself feverishly alert by fantasizing how Noah would react when he realized Jessica owned him.

In her time off, she jumped into preparations: doing recon, contacting her old friend Shane and negotiating with him for the items she needed and carping about what a greedy pig he was so he'd think he'd talked her into paying too much, more prep, more adrenaline rushes. When she got stressed, she'd decompress with her guitar, composing a song in honor of Noah and Bryce. Soon she'd be in a New York recording studio singing "I Win, Sucker," then fibbing when fans asked if her number-one hit was inspired by anyone. "Nope. It's a song for all girls who are sick of getting used."

She finished the prep with such skill that she wished she had someone to boast to. At least Gibson would listen. A cat that couldn't understand human speech was better than a snob who thought she was too subhuman to say anything valuable. If purring was the only applause she could get, she'd take it.

The first step in executing her plan was to charm Bryce. Two and a half weeks after Noah had stalked away from her car, leaving her his contempt, an envelope of cash, and his soul, Jessica parked out of sight of Bryce's house. Keeping the hood of her coat up to hide her hair and face, she strolled to his front door.

When Bryce answered, she edged her hood back a couple of inches so he could see who she was. His grimace sparked an idea for a new line for her song: the contempt on the face of a loser who thought he was better than she was—until she owned him. She smiled.

"Hey, Jess." He was wearing a Yale sweatshirt and baggy sweatpants. He hadn't gone to Yale; that was an old sweatshirt of his father's. Slumping around his mother's house in his dad's oversized clothes. He was clean-shaven, though, and his hair was trimmed. Still working to impress Saint Michael Drake while shoveling snow around campus.

"I was in Britteridge and wanted to see how you're doing," Jessica said. "I would have texted, but I don't have your number." *Because you wouldn't give it to me.* Which was fine; she didn't want to text him now. No electronic links between them for the police to trace.

"I'm okay," he said. "Thanks for checking in."

Jessica kept smiling. He knew she wasn't looking for a doorstep visit, but he didn't want to invite her in. Ooh, high standards. Jessica was too contaminated to cross his threshold.

"Mind if I come in for a little while?" she asked. "I'm freezing. I swear March weather is always worse than February's."

"Hey . . . Jessica . . . uh . . . I don't want you to think . . . "

"Thanks!" Jessica zipped past him into the house.

Bryce closed the door in slow motion.

She removed her coat. She'd chosen jeans, a sweater that fit closely but didn't dip low in the front, and a blue-and-gray swirled scarf she'd picked up at Walmart for four bucks. Surreptitiously, she watched Bryce check her out. She looked hot *and* dignified. This was an outfit prissy Megan could have worn.

Not asking if she could sit down—it would be dumb to give him a chance to refuse—she walked into the living room. Avoiding the couch so he wouldn't think she was scheming to sit close to him, she chose a wingback chair near Gail's player piano. She had never been able to comprehend having enough money that you could pay extra because something was ancient and used, but people paid unbelievable prices for some antiques. Yep. Unbelievable prices.

She hoped Ghost Gail would see her victory and regret the summer afternoon when she'd thundered into that coffeehouse in Gloucester and interrupted Jessica's gig, seizing Bryce from his table at the front and forcing him outside. Jessica kept singing, but no one listened; they were rubbernecking at Gail and Bryce standing on the sidewalk, yelling. "You promised me you were finished with that hussy! That was our deal! What are you doing to yourself? She's flesh-eating bacteria; she's killing you." When the manager had asked Gail to move on, she'd yelled back that she was appalled a fair-trade-coffee-beans and recyclable-cups place would invite a drug pusher and a thief to perform.

Drug pusher? She'd never sold drugs. Thief? As if Bryce had never shoplifted anything?

No friends or new fans had come to talk to her afterward. The manager had thanked her but hadn't mentioned the future gigs he'd been chatting about when he'd hired her. Gutted by humiliation, Jessica had spent most of her earnings on a taxi; Bryce had been her ride home.

Bryce had never called her again or answered her calls.

*I'm sitting in your elegant chair, Mommy Gail, and talking to your son. Too bad you can't get rid of me now.*

Bryce sat on the couch. Silently he adjusted the toe of one of his socks as though a seam was chafing him.

"So you're doing okay?" Jessica asked.

He glanced at her and muttered, "Thanks for the cookies."

Jessica crossed her legs. "Can we be honest with each other?"

Bryce eyed her, then eyed his socks again.

"I'm not trying to start something with you," Jessica said. "I just want you to know I'm still a friend. I don't think you have a lot of friends right now. Neither do I."

"Parties every night," he said. "I'm not lonely."

"You don't party at all, do you?"

"You have no clue how hard I work to stay clean. Every day. Or how hellish it was getting this far. I'm not going back into that world. You were the lucky one. Do a little here, a little there, but you never got hooked on anything. You never had trouble."

"Never had trouble?" She'd never experienced anything but bad luck and people using her, and spoiled-baby Bryce was claiming she was lucky? "Are you kidding?"

He shrugged.

Keeping her fury inside and a relaxed expression on her face, she said casually, "How's your job?"

"It's okay. It's not bad."

"I hope you're not planning to shovel Saint Michael's snow and mow his lawns forever. You should start your own business."

"I'm an ex-con. I don't have many options right now, and it's hard to think about the future anyway. I'm surviving, readjusting."

"I'm glad you're getting your life together." She touched the stained-glass floor lamp next to her chair. If she had Bryce's money, she wouldn't be chipping ice off sidewalks.

"How are you doing?" Bryce asked.

"Bored."

"Got a boyfriend? Can't imagine you wouldn't."

"Haven't found a man worth anything."

"Since when have you cared about more than the eye-candy factor and how much beer he's bringing to the party?"

Jessica clenched her jaw but quickly released it. "I'm not a kid."

"Sure."

"You can grow up, but I can't?"

"You can grow up. I never thought you wanted to."

"At least I've never been to prison. Stop being a skunk. I know you're trying to change, but so am I."

"By trying to wring cash out of me?"

She rolled her eyes. "You have tons of dough, and you're insulting me because I hinted you might want to help an old friend? How many times did I pass you twenty bucks when you were broke and your mom wouldn't give you a penny?"

"Money you swiped from your mother's rich boyfriends."

"Whatever. I'm not asking you for money now. It was worth a try. It didn't work. We've been friends long enough to get past it."

Bryce lowered his gaze back to his socks. "We're not friends."

The ghost of Gail must be floating around the room, whispering warnings in his ear. *She's flesh-eating bacteria!* Too bad Jessica couldn't slap a ghost. "Want to hang out anyway?"

He didn't answer.

"Or are you too busy chasing college girls?"

"I'm too old for that. Most of them are kids."

"Chase a grad student."

"What the heck kind of grad student would want me?"

"What the *heck*? You've been hanging around Saint Michael and Pope Trevor."

"Nah, I'm just rusty on swearing. Prison is a high-class place. Inmates all spoke in poetry."

"That's what I've heard. If you're going to open your mouth in the cellblock, it better be to quote Elizabeth Barrett Browning."

He laughed. Excellent. He was relaxing.

"I'm not into you," Jessica said. "Not like we were. But maybe you'd like a friend who doesn't judge you. Who isn't embarrassed to talk to you."

Bryce didn't say anything. Jessica figured that was positive.

"You're lonely," she said. "Admit it."

"I'm lonely."

*Yes.* "How about this? Next Wednesday, the Crew Socks are playing in Lawrence."

"No way! They're still together?"

"Yep. Blast from our past, right? Go with me. I don't have anyone to go with, and we're both bored. I'll pay. Deal?"

"*You'll* pay?"

"I do have some money," she said caustically. "I'll pay, and I'll bring dinner beforehand. Italian."

"I'm busy."

"No, you're not. Go with me. If you end up hating my company, fine. I'll stay away after this, and you can be buds with your mom's silent-movie collection."

Bryce rubbed the wood floor with his heel. "Jess, I'm not financing whatever trouble you're up to now."

"I don't want money. I want a *friend.* I won't push anything at you. All I ever have now is a little beer or wine anyway, and I'll even stay away from that at the concert. We'll drink vegan, organic, non-GMO ginger ale."

"Uh . . ."

"Stop being so pitiful."

"Jess . . ."

"Get a life."

"I have one."

"Ha. I still have connections in Britteridge. I hear gossip." She stood and picked up her coat. "I'll see you on Wednesday at seven."

Bryce's mixed feelings were so bare in his face that Jessica imagined him in front of a drama class. *Let's role play anxiety, kids. Look how my eyes got narrow and my eyebrows squeezed together. Nice job. Model confusion for me. Nice job. Now look hopeful, like you're thinking something exciting might happen.*

"One time," Bryce said. "You pay. You'd better bring cannoli for dessert."

"Deal. See you then." Jessica headed toward the door.

As soon as she was on the sidewalk, she smiled and whispered, "My turn, sucker."

Time to visit Noah.

* * *

The doorbell rang while Noah was cutting a second piece of carrot cake for his father. Kurt, seated at Noah's kitchen table, raised his eyebrows. "Your friends visit you uninvited?"

"Must be a salesman," Noah said. "I'll ignore it."

His father scooted back from the table and marched toward the door. Noah grinned. If he'd thought it was a friend, he'd have been worried, but it would be entertaining hearing his father lecture some kid hawking coupon books.

"Oh!" A female voice. "Gosh, you must be Noah's dad!"

"Who are you, young lady?"

"Noah's friend, Melanie."

The voice had a Southern twang. Noah didn't recognize it, nor could he think of any friend named Melanie. He didn't have so many friends he could lose track of their names. Bewildered, he set the cake knife down and went to the door.

"Hi, Noah!" She pointed at his apron. "Oh, sorry, sugar, did I interrupt your dinner?" Young, tan, long blonde hair and rectangular glasses. He had no idea who she was.

"We're just having dessert," Noah said, hoping he could wing this conversation. He'd feel like an imbecile in front of his father if he said, "Who are you?"

"Oh, well interrupting dessert is an even bigger etiquette fail, right?" She winked.

"Plan ahead next time, and you can avoid being a nuisance," Kurt said.

"I'm *so* sorry!"

*Melanie.* What had happened to his brain that he couldn't recognize a girl who obviously knew him—

Jessica Barnett.

"I'll come back another time," she said. "I just wanted to tell Noah that I destroyed that test today." She smiled at Kurt. "I'm a nurse. RN working on my master's degree. Call me, 'kay, Noah?" She sauntered away.

So blindsided that he could think of only foul words he couldn't say in front of Kurt, Noah hastily shut the door. "Sorry, Dad."

"She's a girlfriend?" Kurt asked. "Why didn't you tell me you were dating someone? You hiding her?"

Noah hurried to the counter and retrieved his father's cake. "We're not dating. She's a friend." He set the cake on the table. "She . . . lives in a condo at the other end of the street. We run into each other sometimes."

"Good looking." Kurt returned to the table. "But too tan for winter. That's not from sun. Does she use those tanning places?"

"I don't know." Noah felt so weighted that his knees shook trying to keep him standing. If Kurt had any inkling who Jessica was, the mud Noah had wallowed in . . .

"A nurse ought to know better. But you should date her anyway. Tell her to knock off the tanning."

"I'm not sure she's my type."

"You need to find a wife. Single at your age. You look like a reject."

"I'll find someone. There are some interesting women at work." *Keep cool. He'll leave soon.* Kurt came over every few weeks to eat a homemade meal, interrogate Noah, criticize his apartment, and leave immediately after dessert.

At least the apartment-criticism part had ended. In his peripheral vision, Noah caught sight of the dozen dog figurines on the lamp table. *You kept those useless toys? When are you going to grow up?* He'd meant to put the figurines away before his father arrived, but when he'd realized he didn't have any cream cheese for the frosting, he'd had to rush to the store and rush to finish the cake so Kurt wouldn't harangue him about how people who couldn't prepare things on time were lazy buffoons. He'd forgotten to inspect the living room and hide anything Kurt wouldn't like.

While Kurt finished eating his cake, Noah fabricated information about how the woman in the cubicle next to him at work had flirted with him and he was thinking of asking her out. The only woman who sat near him was married and had grandkids, but his dad wouldn't follow up on the story, and lies would placate him. For tonight.

Kurt finally rose, leaving his empty plate on the table. "You need a better table." He leaned over and rattled a table leg. "This thing is flimsy. Makes you look like you can't afford anything decent."

"I'll find something sturdier." Noah hurried to get Kurt's coat. "Thanks for coming over."

"The pot roast was too greasy. Get a better cut next time."

"I will."

As soon as Kurt exited, Noah lumbered to the sink and started scraping dishes. He wanted to flop onto the couch, but once, his father had come back for forgotten gloves and caught Noah playing a video game while the kitchen was a mess. *Yeah. Fun memory.*

What did Jessica want? To coax him into hiring her again? Hadn't he made it clear their deal was finished?

The doorbell rang. Noah accidentally whacked a plate against the edge of the counter, shattering it. He swore, grabbed the three biggest pieces of glass and shoved them in the trash, then went to look out the peephole. Had his dad—

He yanked the door open. "Get in here," he whispered. "What do you want?"

Jessica breezed inside. "You look precious in that apron," she drawled.

He closed and locked the door. "I told you I was finished with . . . things. I don't have any jobs for you. I don't want you around here."

Jessica handed her coat to Noah. He threw it on a chair.

"It was fun to meet your daddy. What a sweet man." She picked up a porcelain bulldog. "Ooh, this is darling. One of Gail's pieces?"

"Put it down *now*."

"Bless your jittery heart. I'm not going to break it." She set the bulldog down, clacking it against the table. Noah cringed.

"What do you want?" he asked.

She petted the bulldog's painted head with her index finger. "To hire you."

"Get your hands off that." Noah stood close to her so he could keep his voice quiet. "Are you insane? You don't have any money, and I wouldn't do anything for you even if you could pay. Get out of here, and never come near me again."

"You sure are a cold man." She stroked the ear of a stone resin bloodhound. "Hurting my feelings."

"Get out."

"I'm here to discuss our job."

"We aren't working together anymore."

"Maybe you should call the cops on me, sweet pea." Jessica drew her hand away from the dog collection and sat on the couch.

"You thought I'd disappear." She spoke without the Southern drawl. "You thought you could use me, then fire me, and I'd return to frying donuts and mopping floors or playing dumb gigs for tips that my stepfather steals or bit parts in community theater for free. If anything went wrong, you'd have denied everything and fed me to the cops. Right?"

"I paid you what we agreed on and bonuses too. I don't owe you anything. If you came here for money, forget it."

The Southern accent returned. "I should visit your papa and tell him what a rascal you are."

"Stay away from him!"

"I could tell him I supply you with cocaine and you owe me money and won't pay. Or I'm your girlfriend and we have a baby you won't support. You already know I'm a good actress. You already know I'm smart and could make him believe me."

Taking a step backward, Noah strove to control himself. "Get out before I snap your neck."

"My word, darlin'. I'd be a lot more scared if I didn't know what a wimp you are about violence. A couple of bruises on Megan and you panic and cancel the whole deal while she's still *here* and still *engaged.*"

"Get out."

"Toss me out and I'll wreck things with your dad so he'll cut you out of his will and never talk to you again. It would be so easy to set that goon against you. Much easier than making trouble for Megan, and I did that like a boss. I'm here to hire you."

He'd had nightmares like this, walking up a road that got steeper and steeper until it was almost vertical and he was stuck, body pressed to the asphalt, terrified he'd fall. "I can't work with you. After that fiasco at Megan's last time, the police came to me."

Jessica's mouth formed a lopsided hole.

"See?" Noah said. "It's too dangerous for me to do anything else. The cops are already interested."

"What did they want?"

"To ask me if I had any idea who might have a grudge against Megan."

"Did you do something to make them suspicious? Or is it only because you're Gail Ludlum's nephew?"

"They didn't say. The cop was faking sympathy about how it must have been hard when Gail died and asking if I knew of anyone who had a grudge against her killer's identical twin."

"You didn't go brainless and admit you hate Megan, did you?"

"*No.* But they asked about Sabrina Erickson. They have a police sketch of you."

She smiled. "I saw it on the news. It doesn't look anything like me."

"On the news?"

"Yep. 'Wanted for questioning in relation to an attack on a Britt student.' Time to compliment me on my gift for disguising myself. I knew Adrianne Mullins might get suspicious at some point and tell the cops about me, so I went all out on the disguise the one time I met with her. That sketch is a joke. Admit it, champ. It doesn't look like me at all."

It didn't look like her. That was fortunate, but he'd hoped to frighten her.

"Did Bryce tell the cops you hate Megan?" she asked.

"I asked him. He says he didn't, even when they brought up my name, but I'd better not be the one bothering her. I know he suspects me of sending that letter."

"That's what you get for having no imagination. Calm down. He won't rat on you, and even if he did, he doesn't have proof. The cops' visit to you was routine. They don't suspect you of anything, but Saint Michael is breathing down their necks, so they strut around intimidating people and pretending they're solving the case. You're related to Gail, so they harassed you. Unless they get evidence against you, they won't be back, and they won't get evidence against you. We're fine."

"We're *not* fine."

"Sit down. It's time for us to hook whales instead of goldfish. Don't worry, you'll get your cut of the catch. Not a big cut, but you'll make money."

Noah didn't want to sit with her, but his vertigo wasn't easing, and it would be mortifying to lose his balance in front of her. He sank onto the couch. "I'm not doing anything with you or for you."

"I kept that original note you sent me, the one I said I threw away. Your handwriting, sugar. And I recorded our conversations."

"You recorded us?"

"I'm sorry. Did I forget to ask your permission? Golly, let's ask a lawyer if it's admissible in court."

This trashy girl would not intimidate him. "That evidence is useless to you."

She examined the back of her hand. "Do you think this bronzer is too orange? It looked better when I put it on in the car."

"If I go to prison, so do you."

"I have plans for how to disappear. I'd rather do it *after* we make our fortune. But if you won't cooperate, here's what happens. First, I'll make sure your dad disowns you. If that doesn't get you to help me, I'll turn my evidence over to the cops. You'll get locked up, and I'll slip away and start a new life in a new place. I know how to do that, I'm prepared to do it, and as you pointed out, my life here is so lousy what do I care if I leave it behind? But you don't have any idea how to escape. Do you know how to get a forged ID? Nope. You'd go on the run in your own car, use your American Express to buy gas, and rent a room at the Marriott. You're stuck, snickerdoodle."

Shards of glass glittered on the kitchen floor. He should sweep them up. What if his father returned and saw the mess?

"You thought you could use me," she said. "Here's what you did, Noah. You sold yourself to me. You're mine now. Do what I say, and soon I'll be gone, and you'll never see me again. Fight me, and I'll make your life worthless. Ready to listen?"

# Chapter 1 9

"YOU SUUUURE EVERYTHING'S FINE?" A few spots of apprehension still stained Rachel's teasing tone. "Or do you think you can get away with fibbing over the phone because I can't see your new black eye and five-foot-high pile of nasty letters?"

"No new black eyes. No poison pens." Megan set her iPad on her nightstand and snuggled her blanket around her shoulders. "Everything's been peaceful."

"Nothing else freaky has happened? Like someone disguised as you yodeling insults at neighbors?"

"Yodeling?"

"Rapping, maybe?"

"I'll try both and see which I'm better at."

"I'll be first in line to buy your album. How did your lunch with Adrianne go?"

"It was great. Uncomfortable at the beginning, but we got over that. She's fun. Interesting to talk to."

"Larissa told me Adrianne enjoyed it."

"I'm glad to hear that. We want to do it again."

"You're both trusting each other okay?"

"Neither of us tried to ruin the other's reputation while we were eating our grilled salmon, so that's a positive sign."

Rachel laughed. "You've been so calm about all this loopiness."

"I'm hoping there's nothing to be not calm about now. I think that smackdown in my apartment scared Sabrina off. It's been almost three weeks since there's been trouble."

"But we still don't know who she is or why she did this, so I'm still nervous, and I'm nervous for you. Your creepy apartment . . . Oh my gosh, I sound like your mom, criticizing your place. I didn't mean it's creepy. It's adorable. I meant it's a basement, you know, not much light from outside—"

"Shush, Rach. I'm not offended."

"Trev should hire you a bodyguard."

"You haven't hired *you* a bodyguard."

Rachel sighed. "Peter and I were over at my parents' house last night. My mom was saying she appreciates how levelheaded you've been about everything."

"I appreciate how levelheaded she's been." Acting rational about the Drakes' doubts about her wasn't hard. *Feeling* rational was the part she hadn't mastered. At least with Adrianne's testimony about Sabrina, there was eyewitness evidence that Megan wasn't inventing everything. "I know your parents want the best for both Trevor and me."

"You're a total angel. Oops, I'd better go. Mother-of-the-bride calling me *again*. Which reminds me, I wanted to ask where things are with your mother and the dress shopping, but I'll call you tomorrow. See ya!" Rachel hung up.

Megan set her phone on top of her old clock radio. Dress shopping. Pamela's response when she'd brought it up: "I'm not sure I want to help you find a gown for a wedding I'm excluded from. I'll have to think about it."

That had been over a month ago, before the coat dustup. After Pamela had stormed into town and accused her of lying, Megan hadn't felt like discussing wedding dresses with her.

She could go ahead and dress shop with Rachel and Sandra. Sidestepping Pamela's involvement would be a relief—the momentary, shallow relief of putting something off while knowing procrastination wasn't fixing the problem.

Shopping with her mother used to be enjoyable. Trying on new styles or colors at Pamela's recommendation, clothes Megan never would have tried otherwise, and being thrilled at how they flattered her. Stopping for an éclair or a strawberry shake. Going home and watching a Cary Grant movie.

Megan unfurled her blanket and went to her closet. From behind her clothes, she lifted a large framed portrait.

She chose an unmatched sock from her drawer, returned to her place on the bed, and used the sock to wipe dust from the hand-carved ripples of the frame—her mother's choice of frames to hold the family portrait taken the spring before Megan's father died.

Pamela had tried to throw the portrait away after Kristen's sentencing; she didn't want a picture of a murderer and kidnapper hanging on her wall. Megan had intervened. Kristen's crimes didn't erase their relationship, and throwing away the last portrait of their family together seemed like a sorrowful choice.

Megan hadn't hung the portrait up; she wasn't ready to gaze daily at herself smiling next to Kristen. She wanted the portrait, but she didn't want to look at it too often—yet.

Megan polished the top edge of the frame and studied her family's faces as they posed in front of a flowering cherry tree.

Her father was dead. Her sister was in prison.

Her relationship with her mother was disintegrating.

She picked up her phone and called her mother.

"Darling!" Pamela exclaimed. "Has something happened?"

Megan had never told her about the fight with Sabrina and didn't plan to tell her ever. Why frighten her and provoke a lecture about why Megan should leave Britteridge and come home? "I'm fine. I want to talk."

"Oh! That's a surprise. After the way you treated me when I came to visit you, I thought the only reason you'd call me would be if you were bleeding to death."

Megan couldn't help looking at Kristen's picture. She wore a mint-green sweater and cream-colored scarf that complemented the baby-blue sweater and mint-green necklace Megan wore. Kristen had griped about the coordinated outfits their mother had selected, ridiculing them as childish. Given a choice, she would have worn purple or black or neon yellow—anything to issue the statement *We're not a pair.*

Kristen's graceful hand, resting with photographer-directed affection on their father's shoulder, was the hand that had spilled Megan's blood on the floor of Rachel's cell and splashed it across that rainy dock.

Megan set the portrait on the floor, balancing it against the nightstand with the back of the canvas facing out.

"Are you there?" Pamela asked.

"I'm here. I'm not bleeding to death. I want to talk about our relationship. We were doing better with each other a couple of years ago, treating each other like adults, and now we're slipping. That needs to change."

"Was it treating me like an adult when you threw me out of your apartment after I'd driven six hours to see you?"

"Yes. I'd require any adult to act respectfully in my home."

Pamela didn't speak. Megan waited, hoping, but doubting, she'd apologize.

"It's hard to treat that man respectfully when he's so determined to cut me off that he won't even let me attend my daughter's wedding," Pamela said.

"You know our choosing to marry in the temple has nothing to do with not wanting you there."

"Oh, honey, we both know this all comes back to what he wants. You only joined that church because he's such a fanatic he wouldn't get involved with you otherwise."

"Is that what you think my motives were?" Megan kept her tone tranquil. Pamela wanted to upset her; this time, Megan wouldn't cooperate. "Do you think I'd claim a belief I don't have and make covenants I don't mean—lie to God—and shape my entire life in following what I think is hogwash, all so I could snare Trevor Drake? If that's what you honestly think of me, say so, and we'll start from there in understanding each other."

"You don't have to phrase it like *that*, honey. I just meant your feelings for Trevor influenced you."

"It was over a year after I joined the Church that I even went on a date with him. I didn't join for him. Mother, I love you, but I will not allow you to be a source of stress in my marriage. We need to agree on—"

"Is that what Trevor told you to say?"

Megan flopped back on her pillow and stared at the light fixture. How did so many flies sneak in there and die? She should wash it out.

"Hello? Did you hang up on me?"

"Do you think I would marry a man who orders me around?"

"Well, honey, you know you sometimes have trouble standing up for yourself. I worry that—"

Disbelief and amusement washed Megan off her rickety tower of tranquility and spun her around, under the water, above the water, salt in her eyes.

"What's so funny?" Pamela asked.

"Mother . . . you . . . are the last person . . . who wants me to stand up for . . ." Laughter compacted the rest of the sentence into a squeak.

"Megan!" Pamela snapped. "Do you need a doctor?"

Megan breathed deeply and let her body go limp. "No," she said. "A counselor, actually. We both do." She inhaled again, repressing the giggles. "This spring, after the semester ends and my schedule is freer, I will drive to Morris Glen once a week, and you and I will see a family counselor together."

"Oh, for goodness sake!"

Megan wiped tears off her face. "I want a healthy relationship with you. I want you to have a healthy relationship with Trevor and, eventually, with your grandchildren. We need help with that."

"I thought you already saw a counselor after Kristen almost killed you. Are you saying that was so useless that—"

"We need to see a counselor *together*. I'll set it up, and I'll pay for it."

Pamela didn't respond.

"I know it's been hard for you since Dad died," Megan said. "I don't think you've ever adjusted to living without him. Our relationship didn't used to have this much conflict. We can be better."

"Since you're already analyzing me, I don't see why we need a counselor. We need to spend more time together."

*More time together.* Quickly Megan began a breathing exercise, but it turned out to be useless at averting hysterical laughter. Water streamed down her face; she licked salt off her lips. Was she laughing or sobbing?

"*Megan*! What is wrong with you?"

Letting the hand holding the phone fall to the bed, Megan pressed her other hand against her aching stomach muscles. Laughing hushed to panting, then gradually to breathing steady enough that she could speak. She raised the phone to her ear.

"Sorry about that. Are you still there?"

"*I* don't hang up on people. Are you sick?"

Full breath, as much air as her lungs could hold. Eyes closed. Chest relaxing. Air easing back out. "Lack of time together is not the problem. Last time we were together, you couldn't stop accusing me of hiding money from you. How will more of that benefit us?"

"How can you blame *me* for that? From what you say, I was tricked!"

Using the edge of her blanket, Megan blotted her tears. "And when I explained you'd been tricked, you still thought I was lying. We need to be able to trust and respect each other. If you want to be part of my life after I'm married, we're going to counseling."

"I can't believe you'd give your own mother an ultimatum. You really do want to cut me off. You think you're a Drake now, and I don't measure up."

Megan ignored her mother's attempt to compel her to defend herself. "Let me know your choice. Go ahead and think about it for a few weeks."

"I . . . lost your father." The words were ragged; she'd started crying. "I lost Kristen. Do you know how it hurts to hear you threaten to shut me out of your life? You're all I have."

Megan leaned over the side of the bed and tipped the portrait back so she could study it again. "I don't want to shut you out." Her gaze stayed on Pamela's photograph. "But you're trying to hold on to me in ways that are destroying our relationship." Megan released the portrait and relaxed on her pillow. She felt floppy and serene. "Let me say it like this. I love you. But if having you as part of my life means letting you insult me, insult my husband, and create drama and conflict, that's not healthy for any of us. I won't put up with it."

Pamela sniffled. "For heaven's sake, I didn't mean to insult either of you."

"Let me know your decision," Megan said. "I'll start researching counselors in Morris Glen, and I'll be in touch."

\* \* \*

"We start here." Jessica switched on an electric camping lantern and held it high so Noah could see the room. He'd rather have kept the room dark; from the reek of old cigarettes and mildew, he'd already known it would be repulsive. Dirty wallpaper had bubbled and peeled off the drywall. Yellow grime stained the ceiling, and footprints in the dust marked where Jessica must have walked across the wooden floor earlier. He hadn't known there were derelict places like this in Britteridge.

"This is the site the cops will never see," Jessica said. "But we'll mop the floors in the places where we'll walk so we won't leave footprints."

Noah attempted to lock the rotting front door Jessica had closed. The past twenty-four hours had been agonizing: no sleep; shoving himself through his Saturday routine of cleaning, grocery shopping, and laundry; waiting for nighttime so he could meet Jessica at the house she'd wanted to show him and convince her to abandon this catastrophic plan.

The latch bumped into the doorframe instead of fitting into the strike plate. The door wouldn't lock and only stayed closed because it was so crooked that it pressed against the doorframe. "We can't do this," Noah said. "It's too dangerous."

Jessica removed one glove and ran her fingers around the border of her knit cap, making sure no hair was slipping out. He wanted to check his own hat but didn't want to imitate her like a copycat child.

"I made my terms clear." She put her glove back on. "You fight me, and I'll ruin you. If you want, I'll start torpedoing your life tonight. I already decided on the story I'll tell your dad. It's a nail-biter; he'll be on the edge of his seat."

Even though there weren't other houses among the trees near this decrepit cottage, Noah didn't want to take any risk of being overheard. He moved close to Jessica and whispered, "This is a farce. You got greedy reading about Kristen O'Connor's schemes, and you're so arrogant you think you can pull off what she failed to—"

"Stop whining." Jessica swung the lantern so close to his face that he jumped back. "Did you listen to me last night? We're not making the mistakes they made. We're not going for a tough target. We're going for an easy one who'll willingly cough up money."

Noah took another step away from Jessica, the warped floorboards creaking. *An easy target.* She was delirious with gold fever. "We'll go to prison," he said. "For life."

"For life! What, are you planning to kill someone?"

*You.* He could murder her. Hide her body in this dilapidated house. No one would find her for years.

Jessica was a threat. Wasn't he justified in protecting himself?

Kristen had considered Gail a threat, and she'd felt justified in smashing Gail's skull.

His head hurt as though his own bones were fracturing. "Kristen didn't plan to kill anyone either, and Gail's dead."

"No one forced Kristen to do that. She made that choice. You don't want anyone to get killed, don't make that choice." She pivoted. Noah followed her up an uneven staircase.

"Kristen failed for two reasons," Jessica continued. "She was too greedy to realize ancient Auntie Evelyn had an ulterior motive, and she underestimated her sister. If you underestimate me, you *will* go to prison. Don't do that, and you'll be safe." With her hip, she knocked a door open. The lantern lit an empty bedroom. "This'll work for her temporary quarters."

This would work for a bonfire; setting the place aflame was a safer idea. "Look . . . you want money." He detested himself for making this offer, but he was out of options. " I'll pay you to let this go."

"Oh, nice!" She beamed. "How much?"

Knowing she'd bargain up, he started small. "Five grand."

She snorted.

"Come on. Five grand with no risk."

"You were fine taking risks when you hired me to bother Megan."

"This is much bigger—"

"At least this time if we go to prison, it'll be for something impressive. Not because you were a sulky coward who outsourced your revenge."

"Ten thousand," he said.

"This scheme will earn me a lot more than that."

"It's ten thousand without risking prison."

"So what?"

"Twenty-five," he said bitterly. Emptying his savings account for Jessica. She'd take the money he'd worked hard for and blow it on partying. "That's all I have."

"Nope."

"I can go higher if we do installments. Ten thousand a year for five years. You can't turn that down. Fifty grand with no risk."

"Oh, please. That is risky, you moron. You think I'd trust you for five years?"

"I couldn't betray you without—"

"You know how it feels to get used, Noah? To be so desperate that you *let* people treat you like garbage? That's what you did to me. That's what *everyone* has done to me."

"I never said you were garbage."

"The word you used was *scum*. But now I'm Queen Scum. This isn't only about money. It's about payback. I want money, but I also want to make you do this." She smiled. "I'll make you do whatever I want."

# Chapter 20

BLACK T-SHIRT. BRYCE STARTED TO slide it off the hanger. *Nah, boring.* He hung it back up. A Boston Celtics sweatshirt? No. He wanted something more, uh, more . . . more not a Boston Celtics sweatshirt.

*You've lost it, bro.* He'd never cared about what he wore; why did he care tonight? He didn't want to impress Jessica. Why hadn't he turned her down? Because she was hot? Because he was lonely?

*It's go to the concert or veg here and watch TV again.* Yeah, Jessica was a screw-up, but at least she didn't treat him like an outcast. She was the only old friend who'd contacted him. The only old friend besides Trevor. Trevor was good at pretending, but no way did he genuinely want to hang out with Bryce.

Bryce tossed his work clothes into the hamper and grabbed jeans and a blue hoodie. Tonight would be fun. Jessica's smart-alecky wit always cracked him up, and, whew, she'd gotten even prettier. But this was the *only* time he'd hang out with her. He wasn't getting involved again. Yeah, he needed friends, but he didn't need Jessica pushing the button for nuclear life meltdown.

The doorbell rang. Bryce tied his sneakers and trotted downstairs.

"Hey," Jessica greeted him. She was holding a plastic bag of takeout containers.

"Hey, Jess. Come in."

"Thanks."

He closed the door, and she lowered the giant hood of her parka. "How was work?" she asked.

"Not bad."

"Groundskeeping in winter. I hope they pay extra for the frostbite."

"It's not bad. Feels good to be outside."

"Yeah, with no concrete walls." Jessica walked toward the kitchen. Bryce followed her.

"Saint Michael treating you well?" she asked.

"It's not like I check in with the president of the university every day."

"How many people does he have spying on you?"

"A lot, I hope, so they can tell him I'm the best employee in groundskeeping."

"Getting spied on doesn't bother you?"

"I don't know if I am getting spied on, but if I am, who cares? I just got out of prison. I'm used to it. And I'm not doing anything wrong."

"Yeah, I guess having coworkers watching you isn't so bad compared to armed guards on watchtowers." She took five Styrofoam containers out of the bag and set them on the table.

"Two dinner choices," she said. "Fettuccine alfredo or chicken parmesan."

"I'll take the chicken."

She passed him one of the boxes, and they sat at the table.

"Got you Italian soda," she said. "No choice there. Sorry." She handed him a plastic bottle of blood-orange soda and took one for herself.

"This is great." Bryce twisted off the cap. "Thanks."

Jessica opened the third Styrofoam container. "Calamari. Not as nice as the calamari they fed you in prison, but it should be okay."

He laughed and reached for a ring of deep-fried squid. Had he laughed at all since his mother had died? Had he had any fun?

He sipped the soda. "I forgot how good this stuff is."

"I wanted to get you that vanilla kind you like, but they were out."

"This is great too. How's the music world? Any progress on putting a band together?"

Jessica opened the fourth box—garlic bread—and passed it to him. "Not really. The guys I used to play with sometimes have moved away or are too busy. Do you want to sing with me?"

He snorted. "You'll never be desperate enough to take me on board."

"You have a decent voice. Rocked the auditorium in *Hello, Dolly.*"

"Like fifteen years ago. I haven't sung in public since then. My mom's not here to bribe me to audition."

"I can't afford to bribe you. I'll stick with solo gigs. I'll keep *searching* for solo gigs, actually."

"You should go back to school."

"Yeah. Who's paying?"

"Loans. Grants. Work during the day, and go to night school."

"I have to be to work at 4:00 a.m. I'm not going to school at night. Is that what you're planning to do? Go back to school? You have the dough."

"Someday I'll go back, yeah." He wound linguini around his fork. "Sounds like too much right now."

"You could stick to groundskeeping and become head sprinkler-repair guy for Saint Michael. Maybe he'll knight you Sir Trimmer of Bushes."

"Not sure I could handle that much glory."

Jessica drank from her bottle of soda. Bryce tried to look like he was staring into space while he watched her. That shorter, messy-on-purpose blonde hair looked amazing. That silky black shirt. She had better curves than she had in high school.

*Nuclear meltdown. Don't do it.* He guzzled soda and took a few more forkfuls of the pasta he was eating at a fast pace—best food he'd had since that lasagna at Trevor's.

"Man, this is good." He dunked more calamari into the sauce. "Thanks for bringing dinner."

"No problem. It's nice not to eat alone."

"Yeah." Incredibly nice not to eat alone. Bryce lifted his soda bottle to his lips, wishing he could wipe out an undercurrent of squirminess. *Relax.* Spending one evening with Jessica wouldn't cause backsliding. They would eat dinner, go to the concert, and part ways. No illegal substances or anything else his mother wouldn't approve of.

He'd keep himself on a successful track. His life had calmed down; he hadn't heard from the police in three weeks. Maybe they'd found Sabrina Erickson, but even if they hadn't, they couldn't keep hassling him just because he was a felon and recovering junkie.

"I'm thinking I'll study landscape architecture," he said. "You really should consider school too, Jess. You have brains."

"My brains have other plans. Give me four years. Recording contract. Hit songs. Broadway shows. Movie roles. Starring roles, not just walk-ons. Awards. I'll succeed. I'll do it."

"Four years. Good luck. Send me a picture of you holding your Grammy."

"I will."

He jiggled his empty soda bottle. "You got more of this?"

"Sorry. I only brought two." Jessica went to the fridge and took out a Coke. She popped the top and handed it to him.

"Thanks," he said. "I'll leave a big tip."

"A stack of fifties would be best." Jessica sat and chose a piece of garlic bread. Bryce took a fourth piece but set it on his napkin. Scarfing all that rich food when he usually had a sandwich or a frozen dinner . . . he should have slowed down. And saved stomach space to eat that cannoli waiting in the last box.

Jessica tore the crust off her bread. "I'm working on a new song."

"Nice." He sipped Coke, hoping that would dilute the grease. "What's it about?"

"It's a woman-power thing. I'm fed up with getting used; it's my turn. Grab your dreams."

"It'll go viral." Drinking was making him queasier. He set his Coke down. "I remember the song you wrote for that talent show, the glass song . . . haunting song, all minor. Record it, and there's another hit for you."

He expected Jessica to grin, but instead, the energy in her face dropped to low and shadowy. Confused how a compliment had unplugged her cheerful mood, Bryce said, "It was a nice song. 'I chip away at dirt and stone; my arms fall tired and weak. All I find is broken glass where diamonds ought to be. Is there nothing else inside—'"

"I can't believe you remember the lyrics." She set her garlic bread and knife and fork inside her half-full container of fettuccine.

"You practiced it over here, remember? I heard it a hundred times . . ." Ripples of dizziness spread through his skull. "Man, I don't feel good."

"You okay? You look pale."

"Just . . . dizzy."

"You'd better not have food poisoning! I ate this stuff too!"

"Food poisoning wouldn't . . . hit this fast . . . I . . . lightheaded . . . lie down . . ."

Jessica stood. Bryce thought she'd help him to the couch, but she gathered the bottles and food containers, including the uneaten box of cannoli, and stuffed them into the plastic bag she'd brought. Straining to keep his eyes focused and his head steady, Bryce tried to stand. Climbing out of a swimming pool, gravity newly dragging at him. He thumped back into his chair.

"Something . . . wrong with me," he mumbled.

"You need a doctor." Jessica approached him. "I'll take you to the hospital, but we'll have to use your car. Mine's almost out of gas."

What was wrong with him? He'd never been sick like this before. What kind of flu would—

He felt doped.

With a lead-heavy hand, he grabbed Jessica. His fingers slipped along her wrist, quivering instead of gripping. "What did . . . what did you . . . give me . . . Drugged me . . . What was in that?"

"What?" Her face blurred. "How could I drug you? I let you choose which meal you wanted, and mine wasn't drugged. We both ate the appetizers, and the drinks were in unopened bottles!"

Bryce tried to herd thoughts that kept scattering. "What's . . . something . . . don't feel—" Where was she? He swiveled his head, blinking. The counters whooshed in curves.

She was next to him again, bending down, lifting his arm and resting it around her neck. That was his coat . . . She was wearing his coat.

"Come on." She hoisted him out of the chair. "I'll get you to the hospital."

Bryce leaned on her. She steered him toward the garage.

# Chapter 21

NIGHTMARE. WORSE THAN NIGHTMARE. NOAH would choose any bad dream he'd ever had over lying under Megan O'Connor's bed in the dark, waiting to commit a felony, his shoulder touching Jessica Barnett's. Pain clanged back and forth between his mind and his chest, regret slamming against rage; guilt battling blame. Gail would be furious with him; he was furious with Gail. If she'd refused to surrender to blackmail—

If he'd refused to surrender to blackmail—

*Do you want to wreck your life and go to prison? Do what you have to. Do it efficiently, with no mistakes. Jessica will get her money. She'll leave the state. Finish this, and be rid of her.*

Jessica had given him instructions for how to sneak away from his condo: "Park in your reserved space, go inside, turn on the TV and lights plugged into timers. Put food in the oven on timed bake, a frozen casserole with strong odors like bacon and garlic. If the police question you—which won't happen—claim you were home watching movies, and make sure you know in advance which films you'll say you watched. Go quietly out your back door, keeping your hood up, and meet me at the rendezvous spot."

His pride shriveling, he'd obeyed her meticulously, and so far things had worked. All the window blinds on the back of the building had been closed. He doubted anyone had seen him leave or noticed him walking to where Jessica had picked him up. Claiming he'd been home alone was a fragile alibi, but it matched his habits, and Jessica said it was the least complicated. She was paying a friend to say she'd been watching movies at his place, but Noah didn't have shady friends who'd lie to the cops for him.

"This isn't going to work," he whispered. "Our alibis—"

"Those are worst-case-scenario plans," she hissed. "The cops aren't even going to question us. You know that. You aren't the type to kidnap someone, and I have no connection to Megan."

"What if Megan doesn't get home for—"

"She'll be home any minute. They had reservations at that fondue place at eight, and they're only doing dessert, as a break; they're both busy. I read their whole pukey text conversation."

"What if Trevor stays when he drops her off?"

"Will you chill out? He's swamped figuring out which kids are perfect enough to let into Britt. Shut *up* about stuff we've already settled."

Loose fabric dangling from the box springs brushed across one eyehole of Noah's ski mask. He groped for the piece of fabric and ripped it off. Stuff they'd already settled. How settled could anything be? *Jessica's clever. Trust her.* She'd copied Megan's new key the way she'd copied the old one, snatching it from her gym locker while Megan was jogging and returning it before she noticed. And though Megan had finally put a password on her phone and her iPad, she hadn't put one on the laptop in her locker. Jessica could still access her calendar and texts.

Megan was underestimating her enemy, and Jessica was fearless and devious. Jessica could pull this off.

"You're sure Bryce won't wake up and get away?" Noah whispered.

Jessica swore under her breath. "Shut *up*."

Distantly, Noah heard voices. A lock clicked.

"Stop panting," Jessica said in his ear. "You're worse than a dog."

Making his breaths deeper and quieter, Noah listened to the conversation coming from the living room: chatter about Megan's essay, due tomorrow. Trevor offering to check the apartment. Megan laughing and saying it wasn't necessary. Trevor's insistence and his weighty footsteps in the hallway.

Noah tensed. He'd never broken a bone, so he had no idea how much it would hurt when Trevor—

"Easy." Jessica's nearly noiseless breath touched his ear. "He won't find us."

*She's right*, Noah told himself. *We're fine.* Jessica had arranged Megan's storage boxes around them, so even if Trevor did look under the bed, all he'd see was cardboard. But if he moved the boxes . . .

The light went on in the bedroom. Footsteps crossed the room. Trevor must be checking the window lock. More movement. The closet door creaked; a moment later, it clicked shut. Footsteps. The edge of the quilt lifted, letting more illumination under the bed. Soaked inside his ski mask and sweatshirt, Noah held his breath.

The fabric flapped back into place. Trevor exited the room, and Noah heard the scratch of shower curtain rings sliding along a rod. Checking the bathroom.

"All clear?" Megan's voice.

"All clear."

Silence. They must be kissing. Farewells, Trevor's reminder to lock the door, Megan's joke about how she wasn't likely to forget. The front door closing.

Noah closed his eyes. He was cast iron. Dented but solid. He'd be the muscle Jessica needed, and in a few hours, he'd be done with her.

Jessica breathed words into Noah's ear. "Don't move until I say so."

Noah inhaled, careful to keep it silent, tasting dust.

\* \* \*

Megan unzipped her boots and replaced them with ratty canvas tennis shoes, warm from where she'd left them near the kitchen radiator. Forty-five minutes of dipping strawberries and cheesecake squares into chocolate fondue was indulgent when she and Trevor both had work to do, but she felt rejuvenated. Time to finish that essay that was due tomorrow. Usually she didn't let deadlines catch up with her, but she was recovering from a few distracted weeks. From her first day at Britt, she'd vowed she wouldn't take a single moment of this opportunity for granted and she wouldn't waste a single cent of her scholarship money. Three years in, she didn't plan to let her grades drop due to Sabrina's spiteful harassment.

*In that case, you'd better make this an A-plus essay.* She settled at the kitchen table, opened her laptop, and reread the notes she'd added to her first draft.

Beeping from the back of the apartment made her jump. Clock radio. Had she goofed up the settings again? She sped down the hall and whacked the button on top of the clock, canceling the noise. *User-unfriendly piece of junk.* She should toss it and use her phone for—

A hand clamped over her mouth. An arm lashed around her, trapping her arms against her body.

Shock jolted her survival instincts; Megan twisted as hard as she could. The hold stayed tight, but her momentum propelled both her and her assailant into the closet door. Sabrina—no, not with the size and strength of the arms pinning her; not with the height and the hardness of the body. Bryce?

"Keep it *quiet*!" A woman's voice spoke behind them. Sabrina? Megan hurled herself away from the closet; she and her assailant collided with the nightstand. The lamp crashed to the ground.

Her assailant dragged her backward and swung her around so she faced the female intruder. Black ski mask. *Who is she?* Megan arced her heel into the shin of the man holding her, then stomped down as viciously as she could, hoping to crack foot bones. His yell quieted immediately to a gruff, dry groan; he didn't want noise. Megan did. If she could knock his hand off her mouth and scream
. . .

The masked woman lunged at Megan, a syringe in her hand. Letting the arms of the first intruder hold her up, Megan raised both feet off the floor and kicked. She aimed for the knees, but slipped too low—the man hadn't been braced for her shift in weight. Her feet collided with the woman's shins; the woman fell backward.

The man dropped to his knees, dragging Megan with him, his gloved hand still stifling her attempts to scream. The woman crawled toward her, clutching the syringe. Megan ripped one arm free and punched. Her fist struck the woman's shoulder. She swung again and hit the mask, feeling hard cheekbone under her knuckles. The woman recoiled, wobbled momentarily, and hit back, ramming her free hand into Megan's gut.

Shaking, gasping, Megan tried to strike again, but pain devastated her coordination; her arm flailed and missed. Tensing her muscles, she reached out and clawed the woman's masked face and neck, sinking her nails in. She caught the edge of the mask and wrenched it upward. The mask shifted, exposing a flushed cheek and a lock of short blonde hair.

The man clamped his hand around Megan's wrist and yanked her arm back. With one hand on her mouth and one on her wrist, he couldn't effectively restrain her other arm; Megan swooped that arm from under his and tried to grab—

The needle punctured her shoulder.

She thrashed, but the man leaned forward, forcing her to the floor and using his body to pin her there. She tried to elbow him in the chest or slam the back of her head into his jaw but couldn't get enough range of motion to strike at him.

Dizziness swished into her brain, bright, popping sparklers. She pressed her forehead against the floor and struggled to focus, praying she could fight whatever drug . . . could stay conscious . . . call for . . .

* * *

Fidgeting with the contract she'd been about to file, Adrianne frowned at the floor. She'd heard a crash from the basement, but now it was quiet. Megan was home alone—Adrianne had seen Trevor's truck drive up, both of them go inside, then Trevor drive away. She *wasn't* spying, but for the last few weeks, when she heard vehicles stopping nearby, she'd glance out the window. She'd be an idiot not to keep an eye on things. If Sabrina returned, Adrianne might get blamed for any trouble she caused, and there were enough rumors about Trevor's bitter ex already.

Was Megan okay? Sabrina couldn't be so reckless that she'd return to Megan's apartment while Megan was home, and it would be ridiculous for Adrianne to call the police because her tenant had tripped and broken a dish or knocked over a lamp.

What if Megan was in trouble?

*You're overreacting. Getting paranoid.*

Adrianne slapped the contract onto her desk, snatched her phone, and texted Megan. *You okay? I heard a crash.*

She tried to wait for Megan to respond, but the chance—tiny chance—that the woman who'd made a fool of Adrianne and injured Megan might be downstairs trounced her patience.

She grabbed her coat and hustled out the door, down the porch stairs, and down the second set of stairs to the basement apartment.

She rang the bell and waited, absently counting the seconds, though she had no idea how many seconds a normal wait would be.

Not *this* long, and Megan hadn't answered her text yet. Adrianne rapped hard on the door. "Megan?"

A soft clang came from the back of the house. What was that? Metal striking something but so quietly Adrianne wouldn't have heard it if the night weren't hushed and bitter cold with everyone inside, all windows closed, and not even any cars passing at the moment. A faint screech and another clang, still quiet—noises similar to the opening or closing of the bulkhead doors that shielded the stairs leading up from the basement to the backyard. But why would Megan be using the bulkhead? And those doors made a much louder bang. Unless someone swung them open with slow, gentle stealth.

First a crash, now a furtive exit out the back?

*Sabrina.*

Adrianne whisked her phone out of her pocket and raced around the side of the house, running through the snow so her flat-soled shoes wouldn't slip on the sidewalk. One hand fumbled to dial 911. "Megan!" she yelled.

Megan responded in a strained, out-of-breath voice. "I'm all right. Airing out the laundry room. I spilled bleach."

Relieved Megan was fine but guiltily disappointed that she couldn't confront Sabrina, Adrianne slowed her pace, cancelled the unfinished call, and wished there were an instant way to cancel unneeded adrenaline.

She would have liked to tackle Sabrina into the snow and trap her there until the cops arrived. Then again, she could be imagining herself as tougher than she was. Fighting Sabrina might not have worked out well. It hadn't for Megan.

Adrianne reached the corner of the house and turned toward the backyard. "You sound like you've breathed too many bleach fumes. I'll help you clean up the—"

A dark flicker to her left. She whirled to—

What? Snow chilling the back of her head . . . darkness. Stars. Her muscles weren't working. Air cold on her face but not in her chest. Suffocating.

Had she slipped? There had been an impact, she'd collided with something, or tripped . . .

An apparition next to her . . . shadowy, moving, reaching over her.

Lightning. Bright, silent bolt.

Black sky.

# Chapter 22

"You've got to help me spread Bryce's prints around," Jessica whispered. "I can't do that on my own. You're the muscle. That's our deal, remember?"

Noah couldn't answer. He slumped against the shredded wallpaper, thinking blearily that he should go outside instead of vomiting in here. He might not reach the door though. "Stupid kid. Eleven years old and you can't make it to the bathroom? Now the whole house stinks. Wipe it up. You'll earn the money to get that rug steam cleaned."

"You have to stop freaking out." Holding the camping lantern, Jessica squatted in front of him. The puffy bruise on her cheekbone made her face asymmetrical, and the crimson gouges in her skin made him think of rabid animals. Megan had clawed so hard she'd scraped Jessica through the mask. Almost pulled the mask off.

"We didn't have a choice, okay?" Jessica said.

He'd never felt this sick, his whole body, his brain, his soul so fevered that drips of molten iron burned his chest. "We could have . . . left Megan . . . run . . . We were wearing masks . . . She wouldn't be able to identify us . . ."

"You nitwit. Don't you know what Bryce would tell the cops if we canned this thing now?"

He didn't know. His brain was too scorched to remember.

"He knows I tricked him and drugged him," Jessica spelled it out. "Megan knows two people jumped her and drugged her. If I hadn't tackled Adrianne Mullins and knocked her out, she would have seen us with Megan, and when we ran, she'd have called the police. The masks wouldn't have helped. Once the cops got Bryce's story *and* Adrianne's story, they'd put the pieces together and find us."

"You . . . Her head . . . The rock you . . . She might be . . ."

"This is *your* mess, honey." Jessica's whispery voice got venomous. "You let Megan make too much noise."

Noise. She'd fought. His foot ached. His shin.

"Adrianne heard you," Jessica said. "I *saved* us. I didn't *want* to touch her. I had no choice."

"You killed—"

"I didn't. She was still breathing."

"You sounded . . . sort of like Megan . . . when you called to her . . ."

"Uh, hello. You knew I could imitate her. I know it wasn't my best, but talk about performing under pressure, and Adrianne believed it anyway."

"We should call . . . ambulance . . . tell them to go get her . . . maybe they can save her . . ."

"Are you *crazy*?" Jessica's voice rose. "Call them from where? Your phone? Want to go to prison for life?" She reverted to whispering. "Besides, we can't let the police know Megan is missing until we're done setting things up. If we call about Adrianne, they'll start scouring Britteridge. Then everything falls apart, and we get arrested. We can't quit. I already owe a bunch of money to the guy who got me the drugs."

Arrested . . . prison . . . his father disowning him . . .

"She'll be okay," Jessica said. "Scalp wounds look serious because they bleed so much, but I just knocked her out."

She wouldn't be okay. Hadn't Jessica noticed how Adrianne's head had looked when they'd carried her inside Megan's apartment? Caved in in that one spot?

Had Jessica dropped the rock she'd used and left it? He couldn't remember what she'd done with it.

A new burst of heated air hit the blast furnace in his gut. "I'm going to throw up," he whispered. "Gotta go outside."

"No! You can't leave puke around here. That's evidence. Take deep breaths. You'll be fine. We'll be fine if we stick to the plan."

Noah drew a musty, chilled breath. Sweat streamed down his back.

"Adrianne will be fine, Megan will be fine, we'll get our money, you'll never see me again," Jessica said. "Sound good?"

He shut his eyes.

"It's not our fault Adrianne got hurt," Jessica said. "She shouldn't have butted in."

"We left prints in the snow. Our boots . . ."

"I took care of it. Remember?"

Oh . . . yeah . . . while he'd been hauling Megan to the car, Jessica had grabbed the snow shovel leaning against the house, churned up the spot where Adrianne had fallen, and wiped out their tracks where they'd carried her across the lawn. They hadn't left footsteps between the house and the back gate; there was a shoveled sidewalk to the fence. The police wouldn't—

Blood drenching blonde hair. Face white. Body inert. If Adrianne wasn't dead yet, she would be soon, dying in a puddle of red on Megan's laundry room floor. That must have been how Gail had looked when she'd died.

"You're evil," he said. "*Evil.*"

"I'm *evil?*" Jessica straightened. "You hypocrite! Who hired me in the first place? Who started this?"

"I never wanted anyone to get hurt."

"All you wanted was to hurt someone, but you wanted to do it like a coward, using me as cheap labor. It was your fault Adrianne heard us. Your fault I had to hit her."

"It was *not* my fault." Noah pulled himself to his feet. Pain burned in his leg and foot. "You swung that rock! No wonder Gail despised you. She looked past that Barbie-doll face and knew you were rotten—"

Jessica grabbed his shoulder. "Shut up," she whispered. "We're in the middle of a kidnapping, and you're shouting?"

"You raised your voice first."

"Let's finish with Bryce before Megan wakes up." Jessica released him. "Then we can move her, and we'll be almost done."

Almost done. Noah tipped his weight onto his left foot to reduce the pain in his right.

He didn't want to finish this.

He didn't have to finish this.

If he walked out the door, Jessica couldn't stop him. He could send an ambulance for Adrianne. Even call the police for Megan and Bryce.

With the camping lantern on its lowest setting, the room was dim, and Jessica's blue eyes were murky. "If this falls apart," she said softly, "and if Adrianne does die, we'll get charged with murder."

"You will."

"Both of us. We were both involved. But I won't be here. I'll disappear tonight. Do you have an escape plan? You don't. Life sentence. Kidnapping and murder."

It wasn't his heart thudding. It was his entire body jolting as it fought to break away from an inferno that moved with it. Prison. For the rest of his life.

A miserable, useless, humiliating life trapped with a mob of violent scum like Jessica.

"Come on," Jessica said. "Let's get it over with."

Noah took a step toward her and winced. Was the pain increasing, or had he been too dazed to notice it before? "My foot," he said. "My leg. I'm injured."

"Oh no! Do you want a Mickey Mouse Band-Aid?"

He lifted his pant leg and folded down his sock. A bruise swelled horizontally across his shin, and Megan's heel had scraped off a thin layer of skin.

The thrift store boot was squashing his right foot, but the boots should be loose—he'd purchased them too big so if he left footprints, they wouldn't match either his shoe size or the tread of anything he owned. He started to unlace his boot.

"Not now." Jessica swatted him on the shoulder. "Come on."

"My foot is swelling. What if bones are broken?"

"You've been walking fine. Your foot isn't broken. Stop complaining and help me."

Even if he did have fractures, what could he do about it? Nothing now. His boot crushing seared muscles and white-hot bones, he trudged beside Jessica to where Bryce slept near the front door, tape over his mouth and a blindfold over his eyes. They each grabbed an arm and pulled him to his feet. He wriggled feebly and tried to balance, then sagged.

"Perfect," Jessica whispered. "He's conscious, but he won't give us any trouble, and he won't remember any of this. Wrap his arm around your shoulders."

Noah did so. Bryce leaned against him, head lolling. Jessica took Bryce's bare hand in her gloved one and curved his fingers around the front doorknob.

# Chapter 23

WHERE . . . ? WHAT WAS . . . ? FREEZING . . . COULDN'T roll over. Megan strained to nudge herself out of a paralyzed, half-asleep state. Couldn't see . . . Couldn't make her body obey . . .

A twitch of movement. A smidgen of control, but not enough to work her arms; she couldn't push herself up. She writhed. Metal clinked, digging into her ankles.

She tried to scream herself awake. Her lips stuck together.

She blinked. Her eyelids rubbed against fabric.

A blindfold. Gagged, blindfolded, tied up. Facedown on a cold, hard surface that smelled like ammonia. Where was she? She'd been in her apartment . . . the beeping of the alarm clock . . . someone grabbing her . . . the needle . . .

Kidnapped.

*Not again. This can't happen again, not after Rachel. Evelyn is dead . . . Kristen is locked up . . . but Sabrina . . .*

*Who is Sabrina?*

*Not someone scared off by your swinging a backpack at her.*

*Where am I now? How much time has passed?* She felt she'd walked into her bedroom seconds ago, but that plainly wasn't true. Had it been hours? Days?

*This isn't real. It's another stress dream.* She stopped squirming, hoping she'd awaken at her kitchen table, her head on her arms and an unfinished essay on the screen of her computer.

Her alertness sharpened, but the floor beneath her cheek didn't transform into her kitchen table, nor did her eyes sense any light. She jerked her wrists against whatever was binding them—duct tape? Her fingers were numb.

Who was Sabrina's crony? What did they want from Megan? A ransom . . .

*No. Not the Drakes. Don't do this to them. They can't go through this twice.*

Wisps of the past, a hazy swirl of Rachel being yanked out of her car, Trevor's bloodless face and bloodied sweatshirt, Sandra's tortured eyes, Evelyn's prim voice telling her she wouldn't feel a thing, rain whipping her in the face, Kristen with a knife— *"You really asked for this one, Meggie."*

Dizzy, Megan quit fighting to free her hands and lay motionless, collecting her thoughts. If the kidnappers demanded a ransom from the Drakes, they wouldn't get it. The Drakes would call the police and use every resource to find her, but they wouldn't cooperate with kidnappers again.

A rattle, a bump, more rattling, a scrape—someone pushing a stuck door open. Footsteps approached her, vibrating the floor under her ear. She braced herself, wishing she could see what was happening. No—she didn't want to see anything. The less she saw, the higher the odds they'd release her.

A hand clamped onto her shoulder and flipped her onto her back. She wriggled, adjusting her hands so she wasn't compressing them so painfully between her body and the floor.

The footsteps moved away from her, and a voice whispered, "She's awake."

More whispers, but she couldn't distinguish the words. Floorboards squeaked, and the next whisper was so close to her ear that she flinched. "If you give me any trouble, you'll regret it. Understand?"

She nodded. Under the circumstances, she couldn't win any fight, couldn't even yell for help, and she didn't want to anger the kidnapper for no gain at all. The kidnapper hauled her to her feet and tugged her forward. She tried to take too big of a step, and shackles seized her ankles, jerking her off balance. The kidnapper's hand kept her on her feet, but lightheadedness made her sway; her head knocked into his shoulder—or her . . . no, *his* shoulder; from the size, it was the man.

"You think I can't handle you?" he whispered.

Megan twisted her lips behind the gag, desperate to tell him she was dizzy from the drug; she wasn't fighting him. His hand shifted on her arm, and she heard him step in front of her. His shoulder dug into her abdomen, and he lifted her over his shoulder.

Being carried head down generated a thumping pulse in her skull. His descending footsteps told her they were going down a staircase. Another door opened; frosty air smelled of bark and snow. Where was he taking her?

\* \* \*

Trevor reread Megan's text: *This homework is crushing me! Gotta go radio silent. I'll talk to you tomorrow.*

When he'd received it, he'd been preoccupied with making a decision on a borderline application and had accepted her text with a quick *Good luck. Love you.* He'd ruled on half the applications the processors had sent him to review before it started to trouble him that Megan hadn't responded. She didn't have time for chatting, but normally she'd have written back *Love you too* or at least *Thanks!*

He almost texted her but put his phone down. She didn't want to be interrupted. Contacting her would appear demanding and overprotective. He opened the next application and resumed working.

His mind kept wandering. Yes, she was busy, but she'd been swamped many times, and this was the first time she'd ever sent him a "don't contact me" message. On evenings like this, she'd usually send him occasional texts: *"Another page done!" "Going crazy here, and I'm out of chocolate." "I'm writing the rest of this paper in Esperanto."* He'd respond in kind. Scraps of humor in hectic evenings.

He texted her. *Sorry to interrupt. Just wanted to make sure you're okay.*

No answer.

Ten minutes passed. Still no answer.

*Don't get paranoid.* She'd probably turned the ringer off and was so immersed in her essay that she hadn't noticed his text.

Wrestling his apprehension, he texted again. Why was he so unsettled? Sabrina had never caused the type of trouble that would prevent Megan from answering her phone, and homework had previously consumed her to the point that she hadn't noticed messages. Not answering a text promptly wasn't abnormal for her.

But that initial message about radio silence was.

On a night when she knew he was worried about her.

He called. No answer.

Of course no answer. If she had been paying attention to her phone, she'd have noticed his texts.

He attempted to dissect his edginess. Did he think Sabrina had locked Megan in a closet, sent Trevor a phony text so he wouldn't expect to hear from her, then disguised herself as Megan so she could go break Trevor's windshield and puncture his tires?

He called again. Three unanswered texts and now two unanswered calls. While Megan's voice mail message played, Trevor lowered the phone from his ear and studied her picture on the screen. Her face was flushed, her blue eyes radiant, her sweaty hair slipping from the improvised bun she'd held in place with a pen from his backpack. She'd laughed, bewildered, when she'd seen he'd chosen this unkempt hiking shot as her contact picture, but it was his favorite. She glowed with joy, so beautiful it awed him.

Without leaving another voice message, he hung up. If he was being obnoxious and overprotective, so be it. It was senseless to keep sitting here too distracted to pay attention to his work, obsessively checking his phone to make sure the volume was on. He logged out of his computer, grabbed his keys and coat, and exited his office.

One of the application processors was walking along the hallway, carrying a bag of Skittles and a folder. "Good evening, Trev."

"Emma."

"Bailing out already? You'll miss the late-night pizza. And Gabriel's making his traditional crunch-time guess-what-mystery-food-I-added-this-time smoothies."

"Save me a glass of it. I'll be back."

"I was afraid you were quitting for good after that shouting we heard this afternoon. What happened?"

Trevor didn't want to have this conversation, but he didn't want Emma curious about why he was acting brusque and hurried. "A father was angry that I wouldn't override a rejection and admit his son." He took a step toward the door.

"What's the story?" she asked.

"He said the kid is Einstein; the low grades are because he doesn't like irrelevant busywork. I told him according to his transcript, he apparently thought all of high school was irrelevant busywork and he wasn't ready for the demands of Britt. The dad seemed to think that committing to an early decision plan meant the kid would definitely get admitted."

"That was one of mine, wasn't it? Transcript looked like the D key got stuck and the essays were *so* his parents' work?"

"Yep."

"Good grief. I'm sorry you got yelled at."

"See you in a while." Ditching his goal of not causing talk in the office, he headed for the door so fast he was almost running.

Megan's car was parked in her customary place at the curb, and her apartment lights shone. He stepped out of his truck into the winter-evening silence, beginning to feel sheepish. She'd told him how busy she'd be, yet he'd panicked when she'd gone an hour without checking her phone. Why did he think a prankster who'd tried to avoid direct conflict would take a three-week hiatus and then seek out direct conflict by coming here when Megan was obviously home?

Megan would be gracious about the paranoid way he'd come to thump on her door, but would she privately think his behavior was overbearing and clumsy? The useless act of defender who draws his sword only to nick his own hand and swing the blade in the wrong direction?

Should he leave without interrupting her? *Not a chance.* He'd rather make a clown of himself than return to campus still worried and unable to concentrate on his work. He needed to verify that she was safe.

He knocked on her door.

No footsteps. No answer.

With brute force, he shoved logic past inflated fear. *She's studying in her bedroom and didn't hear you knock.*

He rang the doorbell and waited. No response.

Could she be in the shower? Maybe she'd decided a hot shower on a frigid night would reenergize her. But she didn't customarily break for more than a few minutes when she had a lot of work to do—unless he bribed her with chocolate fondue. She liked to focus and finish.

Trevor pulled out his phone. He'd try calling again.

Through the door, he heard Tchaikovsky's *Romeo and Juliet Overture* begin to play—the selection that Rachel the Ringtone Ninja had downloaded onto Megan's phone for his calls.

The call went to voice mail.

If she'd recently turned her ringer back on, she would have checked to see if she'd missed calls and would have at least texted a brief, *Sorry, forgot to turn the volume up. Essay is going great.*

Logic and anxiety meshed: something was off. Trevor searched through the keys on his ring, found the new key, and unlocked the knob and dead bolt.

He opened the door. "Megan?"

Her computer was open on the kitchen table, and her backpack leaned against the leg of a chair. Her phone lay next to the computer.

No gush of water running through pipes. She wasn't in the shower.

"Megan?" He loosened his tie and undid his top button so air could get between his collar and his perspiring neck. Alert for any noises, he walked cautiously toward the back of the apartment.

Megan's bedroom door was open, and the overhead light was on. The bedside lamp lay on the floor, the shade bent and the ceramic base cracked. The clock radio hung by its cord, dangling over the side of the nightstand.

"*Meg!*" Moving so speedily his eyes and limbs got out of sync, he bumped into her bookshelf and slammed his shin into the bedframe as he checked the rest of the small bedroom. There was no further evidence of what had happened to Megan.

The bathroom—nothing out of place. The utility room.

Ice split his heart. Crumpled on the floor, motionless, her hair soaked with blood—

It was Adrianne.

Grabbing his phone from his pocket, Trevor sprang toward her. His right hand called 911 while his left hand probed her throat and felt a faint pulse. Was she breathing? He leaned close; a feeble breath, scarcely perceptible, touched his cheek.

Drops of blood dotted the stairs that led to the bulkhead doors. The bolt had already been unlocked: Trevor threw the doors open.

"Megan!" He leaped up the stairs and into the backyard. "*Meg—*" He was yelling into the ear of the emergency operator. "There's been an attack. A woman is seriously injured, head injury. Send an ambulance and police to—" His thoughts jammed. "On . . . Strafford Street . . . number . . . hang on." He tapped the screen to look up Megan's address and heard the operator say, "Forty-three, sir?"

"Forty-three B," Trevor said. "The basement apartment."

Blood had frozen onto the sidewalk. A trail through the snow had been scraped and mixed—to camouflage footprints, blood, other evidence? No sign of Megan, but a single set of footprints led from the side of the house to the biggest patch of disturbed snow.

"One woman injured, one missing," he said to the operator.

"Missing, sir?"

"Megan O'Connor is missing. She should be here. There were signs of a fight in her bedroom. She's missing." Terror tore Trevor's self-possession to scraps. "Get the police out here now!"

"Help is coming, sir. Stay on the line."

Staying on the sidewalk so he wouldn't mar any footprints, Trevor followed their trail. Someone had walked . . . run . . . walked—the pattern of the marks changed—from the sidewalk at the front of the house. No prints led to the street; the person had come from inside the house . . . No, it didn't prove that; someone could have come from the street but walked along the sidewalk until they'd veered into the snow near the house.

He couldn't process information, couldn't analyze any of this, couldn't fix Adrianne, couldn't find Megan.

Couldn't find Megan.

\* \* \*

At first, Megan had shivered in her long-sleeved shirt and wool cardigan, but the struggle to break the tape warmed her up. The muscles in her arms and shoulders burned, and swelling bruises heated her wrists.

Her captor had brought her inside this new location and dropped her on a bed, locked her in, and left. He hadn't explained anything or threatened her again. This room was cold but not freezing like the room where she'd woken up. No strong smells like the ammonia scent in her first cell, just a hint of cedar on the pillowcase.

Who was the male kidnapper? Bryce? His voice reminded her of Kristen's unidentifiable whisper during Rachel's kidnapping. When the female kidnapper in Megan's apartment had ordered the man to keep Megan quiet, she hadn't disguised her voice with a whisper, but Megan hadn't recognized it.

Whether they'd kidnapped her for ransom, for revenge, out of hate, or out of sick obsession, she was certain they didn't intend to scare her with a few hours of imprisonment and release her unharmed. They'd taken tremendous risks with tremendous consequences if things went wrong for them: this wasn't a hoax or a prank.

A few seconds of contorting and wrenching against the tape, a few seconds of rest, over and over. Sweat drenched her body.

*You can do this.* She pulled at the tape, gasping as the pain in her shoulders intensified to agony. *Fight harder.*

\* \* \*

"Mr. Drake." A hand rested on Trevor's shoulder. Detective Powell. "Sir, would you please come with me? This is an active crime scene, and you need to get out of the way."

Trevor nodded. He'd been standing near the wall in Megan's kitchen, gazing vacantly at the refrigerator where Megan had hung a few snapshots of the two of them and pictures of Rachel, Larissa, and other friends. He'd kept his hands in his pockets. He couldn't risk smearing any fingerprints the attacker might have left. He'd made enough of a wreck of the evidence already, touching the bulkhead doors, stomping on bloodstained stairs.

Adrianne had been alive when the paramedics had driven her away in the ambulance, but would she live much longer? If she did survive, would she be able to function?

Was Megan injured? Was she dead? If the attacker had murdered her, wouldn't she—he?— have left her body with Adrianne's? Had the blood on the stairs to the bulkhead and on the sidewalk been Megan's or Adrianne's?

He'd made a horrific mistake in agreeing with Megan's assumption that the prankster was finished. Had Adrianne been a target because she'd told the police about Sabrina? Or collateral damage because she'd been in the apartment when the kidnapper had come for Megan? If he weren't an incompetent clod, maybe he'd have something to contribute besides ignorance and questions.

This might not even be related to the harassment. It could be a kidnapping for ransom. By linking Megan with the Drake clan, he might have made her—and Adrianne—targets.

He needed to talk to his parents. He hadn't called them yet. He shrank from echoing the call he'd made three years ago to tell them Rachel was gone and he'd failed to protect her

He needed to get out on the streets, search Britteridge and adjacent towns, talk to everyone he could, learn if anyone had seen—

"Sir, come with me." Powell grasped his arm and escorted him toward the front door. Had Powell told him where they were headed?

Trevor hadn't been listening. His footsteps thumped too hard against the ground, as though he couldn't remember how high to lift his feet for normal walking.

"Would you mind sitting with me in my car for a few minutes?" Powell said. "I need to ask you some questions."

Trevor nodded. Powell guided him to a blue Crown Victoria parked amidst patrol cars, opened the passenger door, and gestured for Trevor to get in. Trevor's effort to sit down was as clumsy as his footsteps. He nearly whacked his head on the doorframe; Powell's hand deftly redirected him.

Powell slid into the driver's seat, started the engine, and switched the heat to high. "We'll do everything possible to locate Megan. Officers are going door to door, checking if anyone saw or heard anything."

Saw or heard anything like Megan being dragged away or her screaming for help while Trevor, oblivious, skimmed through student transcripts.

Powell opened his notebook. "Tell me what happened tonight. What brought you here?"

Trevor wanted to smash Powell's dashboard. Megan's life was in jeopardy, and all he could do was sit and explain how he hadn't arrived in time to help her.

"Mr. Drake," Powell said. "I know this is difficult, but the more information you can give me, the better for Megan. Had you arranged to visit Megan tonight?"

Trying to speak rationally, he explained. Considering how many times Powell interrupted to ask him to elaborate, clarify, or repeat, his report was about one level above rambling nonsense.

"I believe only you and Megan had keys to the new locks?" Powell said.

"Yes." Realization and anger rattled Trevor. "You think Megan did this." He didn't want tact tonight; if Powell suspected Megan, he'd better say it candidly. "You think she and Adrianne argued—"

"I am not assuming anything," Powell said. "I'm collecting information."

"Megan would *not* have attacked Adrianne. If you waste time blaming this on Megan while she's in danger—"

"We're doing everything we can to find her."

Trevor steadied himself. "I need to call my parents. If this is a ransom situation, like with Rachel, the demand might go directly to them. They need to be prepared."

"Yes. Could you do that now, please?"

*Yes. I'll tell them another member of the family has been kidnapped. Another family friend is dying.*

"If it's easier, I can make the call," Powell said. "I know this is excruciating for you."

Trevor shook his head and pulled out his phone.

# Chapter 24

BRYCE SQUINTED. CRAZY BLACK NIGHT . . . Couldn't see at all . . . Why was he sitting up? Must have conked out on the couch watching TV . . . No . . . The TV was off . . .

His head tipped backward. Cold upholstery under his neck. Smelled like cloves and ginger. The air freshener he'd found in the closet where his mom kept cleaning supplies. He'd hung it in his car.

His car . . . How . . . ? He lifted his head again.

Light blazed into his eyes. He pinched his eyelids shut.

"Welcome back from la-la land." Jessica's voice.

Through his eyelids, he saw the light dim. Warily, he peeked. She'd lowered a flashlight and now held it between the two front seats, resting it on the center console.

Between the front seats. He was in the backseat. Shifting, he tried to stretch his cramped arms, but they stayed squashed behind his back. She'd tied his hands.

"What . . . is . . . going on?" he muttered. Jessica was all dark. Dark mask covering her face. Dark coat. It was hard to see her at all. Maybe she wasn't here. He wasn't here. Weird nightmare.

"You feeling okay?" she asked.

"What are you . . . doing to me?"

"You kidnapped Megan O'Connor tonight," Jessica said. "Wow, Bryce. You must be addicted to orange jumpsuits."

Kidnapped? Huh? He hadn't kidnapped Megan. "Why'd you tie my hands? Let me loose. What are you doing?"

"I'll explain what you did. You went to Megan's apartment, tackled her, drugged her, tied her up, and brought her to what you thought was a safe place."

He swallowed. Dry mouth. Did Jessica have any more of that soda, the blood orange?

No. He'd asked her. She'd only brought two bottles. "Where are we?"

"Doesn't matter."

"What's . . . up with the mask? Not like I don't know it's you."

"I'm cold."

Eating. Drinking. The kitchen at his house. Sick . . . woozy . . . What happened after . . . ? Standing up . . . falling back into his chair . . . Jessica . . . He couldn't remember . . . "You doped me. That food. What did you slip me?"

"I didn't give you anything. It was your stuff. You took it yourself."

Took it himself . . . ? He wouldn't . . . He blinked, sharpening his vision. "I . . . didn't even have anything in the house."

"The police won't believe that. Want to know what you did next?"

"You've lost your mind."

"Once you grabbed Megan, you panicked and hid her as soon as you could. Left your fingerprints everywhere. Embarrassing. That's basic criminal technique, Bryce. Keep your gloves on."

Gloves. He flexed his fingers. Was he wearing gloves? No.

"Once you calmed down, you took her to a more secure spot," Jessica continued. "This time, you were smart enough not to leave fingerprints."

He flexed his fingers again, rechecking. No gloves.

"Here's how it goes," she said. "I have proof you kidnapped Megan."

His brain pulsed with a headache, swelling against his skull, squeezing his thoughts. Shrinking. Swelling, squeezing his thoughts. Shrinking. Swelling.

"Bryce! You with me?"

"Huh?"

"I have proof you kidnapped Megan."

He wouldn't kidnap Megan. He wouldn't kidnap anybody. Why was Jessica acting crazy? "I didn't."

"I have proof."

Bryce groaned. This was a practical joke. Or a game.

"But the police won't find that proof unless something leads them to the first place you locked her up," Jessica said. "The place where you left fingerprints and . . . other evidence."

"What trip are you on?" Bryce wiggled his shoulders. "Untie me. I'm not playing along, and doping me was not cool."

"This isn't a game. We need to hurry, so pay attention."

Circles in the mask exposed her eyes and mouth, but it was too dark for him to see if her eyes were stony or had that devil-cute twinkle. "What do you want?"

"Something you won't miss at all. You give it to me and the police won't find the evidence to convict you."

"Jess, this isn't fun. It's psycho. Cut my hands loose and drive me home, or I'll leave on my own and tell the cops you kidnapped me."

"You don't want to go to the cops. Sweetie, *you kidnapped Megan O'Connor.* I know you don't remember. That's because you have no idea what you did for the last few hours. But I have proof."

Proof? Comprehension stayed buried; a foot of snow had settled on his brain. Had he done something to Megan while he was drugged? *No, chump. Jessica thinks this is funny. Way to let her talk you into going out with her.*

"I'm leaving." Bryce rotated his body so his tied hands could reach the door handle. If he convinced her he would walk out, she'd end the game rather than risk legal trouble. He tugged the handle. The door was locked.

He tried again. Locked. The child safety locks. That button on the dashboard.

"The evidence that you kidnapped Megan would make this a no-brainer for a jury," Jessica said.

He slouched, shoulders hitting the seat, spine tilted so he didn't mash his prickling hands. "How gullible do—"

She tipped the flashlight so the beam caught him in the eyes again. He turned his head, and she lowered the beam.

"This is for real." The last drop of humor in her voice froze. "If I wanted to set up an awesome practical joke, I wouldn't waste it on the loser who dumped me because his Mommy said I was trash. I wouldn't waste it on a stuck-up ex-con who's so superior he doesn't even want me in his house. You think I asked you to go to a concert because you're my only hope of a friend? I set you up. Framed you, and it was genius."

"I don't understand . . . Jess, you're losing your—"

"If you don't give me what I want, I'll send you back to prison. Watching you get locked up until you're eighty would be the most fun I've ever had with you."

"You . . . kidnapped Megan? Made it look like I did it?"

"Glad I don't have to repeat myself again."

Stupefied, Bryce couldn't prod his groggy brain into suggesting a way to stop this. "Are you wanting to set a record for dumb? The Drakes won't pay another ransom. Not for Megan or anyone."

"I didn't say anything about a ransom from the Drakes. I don't want a ransom."

"You . . . don't want a ransom? Why'd you take her, then? Just to frame me?" *Prison.* A sentence for kidnapping. How long would that be? A decade? Two or three?

"I want something from you," Jessica said. "Something you'll be glad to get rid of."

Wooziness from panic magnified the wooziness remaining from the drug. "What do you want?"

"Your mom's stuff. Antiques. Collectibles."

"*What?* You want . . . old furniture and clocks and Charlie Chaplin figurines?"

"Easy, right? You won't miss any of it. You always groused about how silly it was to spend big money on old junk."

"You're blackmailing me for Mom's antiques."

"Yes."

He closed his eyes, cushioned his head on the back of the seat, and tried to concentrate. "Why the antiques? I don't get it."

"If you start withdrawing wads of cash, the police might notice—in fact, withdraw too much, and the bank has to report it to the government. But no one will notice or care if your mom's antiques disappear a few at a time and get sold."

The antiques. How familiar was Jessica with his mother's collection? He remembered babbling to her about the value of some of his mother's treasures and the cash he could get if he sold them. He'd babbled about it a *lot*, whenever he was broke and the cravings were chewing him up. He'd definitely griped about the gold and gemstone jewelry his mother had inherited from her great-grandma and stowed in a safe deposit box so Bryce couldn't steal it. He'd complained about that Wedgewood china set that was worth like 10K. And some pieces of her furniture were worth six figures.

"You think you can take everything?" he asked.

"Not everything. When my net profit hits half a million, I'll disappear, and we'll never see each other again. This won't hurt you at all. You don't care about the antiques, and you have enough money to buy whatever you want anyway."

Half a million. He didn't know the details of all of his mother's collection, but he knew everything combined was worth at least double that. "What will you do"—he wanted to sound intimidating but ran out of air and croaked the rest of the question—"to Megan?"

"Nothing," Jessica said. "Catch and release."

"You'll let her go."

"Yes."

"Like . . . Kristen O'Connor was planning to let Rachel go. Before things went wrong, and she shot her."

"We're not shooting Megan."

"Yeah, sure. Because everything will work out for you. Like when I sneaked into an 'empty' house to steal a bunch of cash that was supposed to be under the mattress." Fooled by a scheming old lady; fooled by Jessica. Furious at himself, Bryce said hoarsely, "I thought it would be easy, but I got *no* money, my mother got *murdered*, and I got locked up. Something will go wrong. I know that. This will be a disaster."

"Don't flip out." Jessica moved her serial-killer face back a little. "Megan already escaped or she *thinks* it was an escape. You're a dud kidnapper and didn't keep her secure enough. She slipped away."

"She already escaped?"

"Yes. That's the whole reason we kept her at two different locations. The first place has the evidence against you, and Megan has no idea where it is. The second is where she escaped from, so that's the place she'll take the police. No evidence there."

"The . . . first place is the place with my fingerprints."

"Right. As long as you cooperate with me, I'll make sure the cops don't get information that leads them to the evidence against you. You don't mention me to the cops. I don't mention you to the cops. If they ever bring up my name, don't tell them I came to your house after the time I brought you cookies."

"Someone probably saw—"

"No one saw. I parked far away and was in disguise walking to your house. Once the whole town quits freaking out, I'll visit you every few weeks to take what I want of your mother's antiques. The police will never figure out who kidnapped Megan. They'll give up and move on to new cases. We'll all be happy."

"What did you make me do while I was doped?"

"Incriminate yourself."

"The cops will come after me no matter what. They've hounded me already about Megan. Wait. Are *you* the person who's been harassing her? Sabrina Erickson? That picture didn't look like you."

"What picture? Who's Sabrina?"

"Never mind." Maybe she was lying, but probably not. Why would Jessica care about harassing Megan unless she could get money out of it?

"Yeah, the cops will ask you questions," Jessica said. "But they won't be able to prove anything. Tell them you went to the Crew Socks concert tonight."

"That's no alibi. I can't prove I was there."

"The police can't prove you weren't. You remember what Socks concerts are like. They're a zoo. I heard them play last month. It'll be totally believable that no one noticed you." She tossed a folded piece of paper onto the seat next to him. "There's info about the Crew Socks and the bar where they're performing, to refresh your memory."

"You are insane. We're both doomed."

"As long as the police don't have evidence against you, they can't arrest you, even if you are an ex-con, a druggie, and a thief who almost killed an old guy because he messed with you."

"I'll tell them you framed—"

"Won't help you. Why would *I* go after Megan? I have no connection to her. I don't even have a current connection to *you*. It's been like eight years since we dated." She stuck her face between the front seats. The ski mask looked so chilling that Bryce had a ferocious urge to yell for help. He kept his mouth shut. Drawing attention from neighbors, if there were neighbors close by, would make this worse.

"I know you don't really care what Megan did," she said. "But like you said, the cops have already hounded you. They think you hate her. If they get evidence against you, they'll wolf it down—and no, I wouldn't be stupid enough to give them the evidence myself. They'll find it in a way that doesn't link to me."

"If you're stupid enough to do this, you're stupid enough to give yourself away." *Good effort. Now try an insult that's true.* Jessica had a knack for getting away with mischief.

"Go ahead and gamble the rest of your life on the chance that I'll foul something up," she said. "By the way, I have a strong alibi for tonight."

Bryce imagined reporting this conversation to Powell. "My ex-girlfriend drugged me and made me do stuff—no clue what—and she kidnapped Megan and framed me and said if I didn't give her my mother's antiques, she'd send me to prison."

Sure. He'd sound more coherent if he told Powell about that dream where he'd been hired to operate a Ferris wheel, but frogs kept hopping onto the control panel, and a pair of Mormon missionaries offered to translate their croaks.

"You couldn't do this alone," he said. "Who's working with you?"

Bordered by the black ski mask, her smile went eerie. "A guy who thought he could use me for his dirty work, then throw me away. Like you threw me away. Now he obeys my orders, or I'll destroy him. If you don't cooperate, I'll destroy you."

If he rammed his foot between the seats and knocked the wind out of her—

The flashlight scorched his eyes. "Lean back and keep your distance."

Bryce didn't move.

"If you pick a fight with me, here's what happens," she said. "We knock you out and leave you for the cops, with Megan's hair stuck to your coat and your fingerprints all over her cell. You tell them lunatic lies, they check my alibi, apologize to me, and lock you up."

"I'll tell them to test my blood," Bryce said. "It will prove you drugged me."

"Oh, I forgot to explain that. They'll find the syringe you used with your fingerprints on it. You won't be able to convince anyone you didn't give the stuff to yourself. They'll think you got yourself so doped you couldn't even stop Megan from climbing out the window."

"What did LA do to you? You weren't like this before."

"Back when I was putting up with being used and betrayed?"

"I never did anything to—"

"It's my turn. I'm controlling things now." Her mouth made a quiet, sticky sound that reminded him of someone speaking too close to a microphone. She licked her lips. "There is one issue. Megan's landlady interrupted when you were taking Megan. You . . . couldn't let her call the cops."

The words smashed into his ears, smashed into his brain, rocketed through the rest of his body. "You *killed* someone?"

Jessica's whispery voice ruptured, and a shrill yell escaped. "I said I attacked her, not killed her! I—you—hit her on the head and knocked her out. An assault committed in the middle of another felony. You've done that before."

*Done that before.* Grime shadowed his vision, coated his brain, dirtied his hands. "Is she . . . going to be okay?"

"I don't know."

"I never thought you would—"

"*Do we have a deal?*"

"Whatever," he mumbled. "Come to the house; take what you want."

"I will," Jessica said. "But we have to be smart how we work this. Remember, if you say anything to the cops about me, they'll find enough evidence against you to convince any jury, but they'll find *nothing* to back up your wild story about me. Your goal is to keep me safe. Clear?"

Bryce gave a weary nod of surrender.

* * *

Relieved to hear Jessica opening the door that led from the garage to the house, Noah scurried away from the peephole Jessica had drilled into the door of the bedroom where they'd imprisoned Megan. He met Jessica in the kitchen. "What did Bryce say?"

Jessica peeled her mask up to her hairline. "He's scared. He'll cooperate."

"You didn't mention me, right?"

"I told you I wouldn't. No point in telling him anything we don't have to. He'll never guess you'd have the guts to take risks."

Noah had stopped caring that Jessica thought he was a coward. He didn't even have the urge to mock her, though he could. In the light of the camping lantern, he'd seen her hand trembling when she'd pulled up her mask, and her face was so bleached out that she looked sick. She was frightened too, but who cared? He only wanted to get out of here.

"Why'd you wear your mask?" he asked. "You aren't hiding your identity from him."

Jessica ignored his question. "You kept an eye on Megan?"

"I did my job." Standing at the peephole and monitoring Megan in the glow from a night-light had been a better assignment than Jessica's task of talking to Bryce. "What if she breaks free before we want her to? She's thrashing around."

"Do you see her making progress? She's just bruising herself. She won't get free until I help her." Jessica ran her gloved thumb over the scratches on her face and neck. Noah had watched her cleaning under Megan's fingernails while Megan was unconscious. She'd better have dug out every atom of incriminating DNA.

"Did you . . . tell him . . . everything?" Noah asked. "About . . . the problem?"

"Yes." Jessica lowered her gaze and hooked the zipper of her coat. It seemed senseless to fasten it; she was planning to change into Bryce's coat in a moment.

"How did he react?"

"It made him even more scared of the cops. But he was getting worked up about Megan, worrying we were going to kill her, so I told him she'd already escaped. I figured that would calm him down. We don't want him to lose it completely. Let's get him home so I can set up her jailbreak."

"Right," he said, relieved Jessica hadn't changed her mind about the plan to free Megan. She'd sworn all along that they were letting her go, but after she'd grabbed that snowy rock from the border of a planting bed and slammed it into Adrianne's skull—

*Forget about it. There's no way to fix what happened.* After they took Bryce home, Jessica would drop Noah at his condo, return here, cut the tape on Megan's wrists, and give her food, pretending she'd bind her hands again once she'd eaten. Megan would be intelligent enough to ignore the food and hunt for ways to escape. It wouldn't take her long to climb out the window, but with her ankles shackled, it would take her a while to shuffle through the trees and find help. Before she could talk to the police, Jessica would have time to return the car she'd stolen for tonight and to arrive home.

Both of them would be home safe before the police started investigating Megan's abduction. Noah would be cocooned in the quilt

his mother had sewn when he was in preschool, finished with this re-
pugnant plan of Jessica's, knowing he never had to speak to her again.

Knowing he'd helped her carry Adrianne's body.

"I'm thinking you should come back here with me and stay
until Megan gets away," Jessica said. "It's smarter if we both—"

He restrained himself from shouting, but moved so close to
Jessica that his angry whisper struck her in the face. "*No!* You said
once we dropped Bryce off, I was done. You said you didn't need
muscle to set up the escape. You can't change your terms now."

"I can do whatever I want."

"Go ahead and threaten to turn me in; you won't do it now.
Not when you almost have your money. I'm done."

"*Whatever.* I'd rather finish alone than deal with your tantrums."
She picked up the lantern. "I blindfolded Bryce so his evil eye won't
boil your brains. And he'll stay out of sight. I ordered him to lie on
the seat."

Wishing he didn't have to get near his now-lucid cousin at all,
Noah trailed Jessica into the garage. She snatched Bryce's hat from
the front seat of the car, pulled it over her own hat, and swapped her
coat for Bryce's. She'd wear his gear and drive his car. It would have
been more logical to cast Noah as Bryce, but she'd assigned him to
the stolen car, saying if he chauffeured Bryce, he'd be so agitated
he'd run red lights and get pulled over. He hadn't objected. He'd
rather play a lowlife car thief than sit in the same car with Bryce,
wondering if Gail's ghost was next to her son, sobbing over what
Noah had done to him.

As he followed Jessica's car away from the house on Britteridge
Pond Road, Noah anticipated feeling calmer, but his anxiety shifted
to new fears. Would Bryce make trouble and cause Jessica to crash?
What if a hair had slipped from under Noah's hat and fallen in
Megan's cell and the crime-scene investigators found it? What if
Megan *did* break that duct tape and escape before she was supposed
to so Jessica didn't have time to get home before the police began
hunting for kidnappers? What if the owners of the house where
Megan was imprisoned cut short their snowbird months in Florida

and showed up tonight at the same time Jessica did, and Jessica panicked and grabbed a knife or a hammer—

*They won't come home. They spend every winter in Florida and don't come back until April. Jessica is positive of that.*

Noah parked at the curb when he was still out of sight of Bryce's house, while Jessica drove Bryce home. It was fortunate that Bryce—unlike Gail—actually parked in the garage so Jessica wouldn't have to release him in the open.

Shivering in this car that got cold the instant he turned the engine off and stunk like rancid hamburgers, Noah imagined Gail's blue Accord in her driveway. Even after Charlie had died and the garage was no longer his workshop, she hadn't parked there. She chose to scrape snow off her car rather than drive filthy, wet tires over what had been Charlie's spotless work area. Honoring Charlie's memory.

He'd tried to honor Gail's memory, but instead he'd betrayed her son. Now he'd allow a woman she'd loathed to steal and sell the antiques she'd adored.

Jessica had offered to give him a small cut of the money. "I'm a fair boss. I don't expect my flunkies to work for free." He'd refused. He'd rather carry a pocket full of sulfuric acid than money from Gail's stolen antiques.

A few minutes later, Jessica hurried toward the car, wearing her own thrift-store parka and hat. Noah heaved himself over the gearshift and flopped in the passenger seat. He didn't want to drive a stolen car any longer than he had to.

"All good," she whispered as she slipped into the driver's seat and shut the door.

*All good.* Nothing had been good since he'd knocked on Jessica's door two months ago. *All done* was as positive as things could get. Jessica would return the car tonight. The owners, friends of friends of her stepfather's, were out of town. They'd never know she'd slinked through a window, swiped the keys they'd left on the dresser, and borrowed their car to use in a kidnapping.

The snowbird owners of Megan's prison *would* find out kidnappers had broken into their house—they'd get a call from the police tonight. After Noah was safe.

"Listen." Jessica drove toward his neighborhood. "If the police come to you, you have to keep your cool no matter what they say."

"I will."

"If they ask what you were doing this evening, do you know exactly what you'll tell them?"

"Yes. I picked a couple of movies on TV tonight, ones I've already seen, and refreshed my memory of the plots. What about your face? It's swollen where she punched you, and what if someone asks how you got clawed? Cat attack?"

"I'll add it to my alibi and say my friend did it. We got drunk and got in a fight. If I pay him a bonus, he'll go along with that. Besides, the police won't come to me. It won't be a problem. This worked out. We're even. I won't contact you again. Don't ever mention my name to anyone, and I won't mention yours."

"Yeah, I got it."

Jessica stopped the car a quarter of a mile from Noah's condo. "Don't forget to dump all your outer clothes."

"Don't forget to leave me the sign when everything is done."

"I won't forget. You think I want you so worried you start acting like you have brain parasites?"

Noah stepped out of the car. Even with his aching foot, he was tempted to run from Jessica, but he kept his pace normal, trying not to limp. In five minutes, he was through the back door of his condo. He hadn't seen anyone on the street or lights in neighbors' apartments. No one had noticed him.

No longer needing to hide his injury, he limped into the kitchen and took a garbage bag from under the sink. Staring at the closed window blinds rather than looking at what he was doing, he removed his gloves, hat, and the coat with the folded ski mask in the pocket. The dark clothes would camouflage blood, but he still didn't want to risk seeing areas where the fabric appeared different—darker or with a stiffer texture.

Not wanting to risk smelling anything either, he forced the air out of his lungs while he stuffed the clothes into the garbage bag, exhaling for so long that he got lightheaded. He moved toward a kitchen chair but changed his mind and sat on the floor instead. If there was any blood on his pants, he didn't want even a molecule of it on his furniture.

He removed the boot from his injured foot and eased his sock off. The top of his foot was deformed by swelling, red and purple, creased with the pattern of his boot.

He curled his toes; his foot burned. He couldn't ask a doctor to X-ray it, so he'd have to wrap it and hope it healed on its own. He removed his other boot and sock and shoved the footwear into the bag.

Tomorrow, as soon as he could blend in with people leaving for early commutes, he'd find a random Dumpster and throw away the bag. There was no danger in hiding it here overnight. Even if the police came to question him, they wouldn't have evidence for a warrant, so they couldn't search his place. It was safer to wait than to go out at eleven at night to chuck a bag into a commercial trash bin. If someone saw him, then heard about the kidnapping, they'd tell the cops about the creeper at the Dumpster the night Megan and Adrianne—

Noah rested his head on his bent knees, but the possibility of blood on his pants made him whip his head back. He needed to cram the rest of his clothes into the bag and take a long shower. Shower all night.

Shower the rest of his life.

# Chapter 25

THE DRONE OF CAR ENGINES stopped in front of his house. Bryce went immobile, thumb hooked inside the sock he'd been about to remove. Too soon for the police . . . right? He'd only been home for maybe fifteen minutes.

He crept to his bedroom window, pushed the closed blinds a few millimeters away from the frame, and used one eyeball to peek through the gap.

A patrol car and a dark sedan.

Bryce cursed Jessica. Had the police been spying on his house, waiting for him? He wasn't ready to face them.

*How could you get more ready?* He'd read the info Jessica had given him, and he'd already been familiar with the Crew Socks, so he could answer questions about the concert. It was a useless alibi, not provable, but it wasn't supposed to prove anything. What was supposed to save his neck was a *lack* of evidence that he'd taken Megan. They couldn't arrest him just because he couldn't prove he hadn't.

*Sucker. I'm a total sucker.*

The doorbell rang. He didn't have to answer it, but hiding was futile.

His shambling gait, bumping into the stair railing, and missing the last step so he almost fell would have made great silent-movie slapstick. Megan's landlady . . . Powell had mentioned her before, but her name . . . Andrea. Allison. Debbie. Diane. Adrianne. Adrianne Mullins. Had Jessica attacked her, or had she bullied her sidekick into doing it?

He tried to black out repulsive memories of an elderly man falling down the stairs, the thump of his head and limbs as he'd tumbled, the blood on his face as he'd lain unconscious.

"An assault committed in the middle of another felony. You've done that before." If Jessica shared whatever evidence she'd created to frame him, he could never convince Powell, or even one juror, that he hadn't hurt Adrianne.

He plodded toward the door. *Don't look scared. Look annoyed.*

Which meant what? Raise his eyebrows? Lower them? Scowl and slap himself so his face was red instead of pale? Forget faking it. The cops could identify bad acting.

Bryce opened the door. Powell and Mendoza.

"Hello, Mr. Ludlum," Powell said. "We apologize for disturbing you late at night."

"Why are you back here?" Bryce snapped. "I could sue you for harassment."

"We have a few questions for you concerning a new and critical matter. May we come in?"

"What kind of questions?"

"Have you been home all evening, sir?" Powell asked.

If Powell had had a sidekick monitoring the house, he already knew Bryce had been gone. Nice try hoping for a flagrant lie that would crack Bryce's credibility. It wouldn't take much to crack the flaking, decomposing credibility of an ex-con.

"I just got home," Bryce said. "But I haven't been drinking or anything." He glanced at the patrol car at the curb. The officers hadn't exited their car yet. Backup in case Bryce wigged out.

"Where have you been tonight?" Powell asked.

"Why is it your business?"

"Would you mind telling me?"

"I don't care. I went to a concert in Lawrence. Didn't drink though. Just ginger ale. I haven't done anything wrong."

Frigid wind gusted through the doorway. Bryce grimaced.

"May we come in?" Powell repeated.

"Fine." Bryce stalked into the living room, letting the cops close the door behind themselves. Powell and Mendoza followed him and sat down. Neither man removed his coat.

"Were you with anyone tonight?" Powell asked. "Friends?"

"Yeah. Friends. The whole town wants to hang out with me. Next time, I'm renting a bus so I can fit everyone who—"

"Were you with anyone?" Powell repeated mildly.

"No. I went alone."

"What concert did you attend?"

"The Crew Socks. At Aisling's."

"Hey, I went to a few of their concerts in high school," Mendoza said. "Their drummer, the beanpole guy who moves his arms at light speed, he's incredible."

"Yeah, Kersey Carr," Bryce said. "He wasn't there though. His wife just had a baby. Sub was decent but not as brilliant as Carr." Good thing Jessica had been thorough on that info sheet, or Bryce would have demolished his alibi.

"What time did you arrive?" Powell asked.

"About . . . I don't know. Eight? Concert started at eight thirty."

"Can anyone confirm your presence there?"

"Uh . . . I doubt it. It was crowded. I didn't talk to anyone except to order a drink. No way would the bartender remember me; it was a zoo. I didn't have any alcohol. Check my breath if you want."

"We have a serious situation," Powell said. "Adrianne Mullins, the property manager who lives in the same building with Megan O'Connor, was attacked tonight. She's unconscious and in critical condition. Megan is missing."

"What?" Bryce's surprise was partly faked, but all his dismay was real. Adrianne was in critical condition. And Jessica had claimed Megan had escaped, but now Powell was telling him Megan was missing. Had Jessica lied? Was Megan still a prisoner?"

"Were you anywhere in the vicinity of Megan's apartment tonight?" Powell asked.

"I don't even know where she lives. I told you, I was in Lawrence. I had nothing to do with whatever happened at Megan's place." He thought of the Styrofoam containers of food and the bottles of soda Jessica had brought. If he could show Powell the containers and Powell could test them, that might be proof against Jessica. But he'd checked as soon as he'd arrived home, and the containers weren't in his inside or outside trash cans. Jessica had taken them with her.

"Bryce," Powell said. "If you know anything, please tell me. Consequences will be much less severe if you voluntarily come clean and Megan comes home safely."

Bryce wanted to scream curses and kick over the stained glass lamp next to him—one fewer treasure for Jessica. What if Megan was trapped like Rachel had been? What if Jessica—

He couldn't tell Powell the truth. Couldn't risk it. Powell wouldn't believe his story about a treacherous ex-girlfriend, and it wouldn't help Megan anyway; he had no idea where Jessica had imprisoned her. He wasn't trading the rest of his life for a lost cause, and he was overreacting anyway. Megan probably had escaped but hadn't found a phone yet.

"I don't know anything," Bryce said.

* * *

The instant Noah closed the car door, Jessica drove away from the curb. *Good riddance.* No more dealing with that worm.

Hours of wearing latex gloves under leather gloves had made her hands so sweaty and itchy she wanted to tear her gloves off and drive barehanded. So what if she got prints on the steering wheel? Before she returned the car, she'd wipe everything she'd touched.

*Don't do it. Don't risk it. Fate will trick you into missing something.*

Awesome and horrible. Flawless and total wreck. That summed up tonight.

At least it was better than the rest of her life, which was *all* wreck.

She drew a huge breath, but the greasy onion-and-ketchup smell of the car made her wish she'd grand-theft-autoed any other vehicle. She opened her window an inch.

That nosy twit. Jessica had only wanted to knock Adrianne out and leave her tied up in Megan's apartment so Adrianne couldn't call the police until they were done. She'd had no idea she was striking hard enough to crush bone. With that dented skull, Adrianne must be dead by now.

Total accident. Not Jessica's fault.

Most of the scheme *had* worked. Bryce had acted like she'd predicted. He wasn't stubborn enough to risk prison for life so he could hang on to an inlaid Hepplewhite table or an . . . ugh, what was the name of that blown-glass vase that was worth several thousand, the purple one on the mantel? She'd researched it and hounded Noah to give her all the details he remembered about Gail's collection—he knew a lot—but tonight she was too wired to remember most of what she'd learned. It didn't matter. She'd wait until everything quieted down, then go to Bryce's, take pictures of everything interesting, and claim a few pieces to get her started.

The antiques as payment was a genius idea. She could get rich without large, suspicious payments passing between Bryce and her. No dicey ransom drops or marked money or FBI agents. This operation should have worked out with no problems. Why did sleek plans always end up with stains and knots?

Big knots.

*Loser, loser, loser, worthless, trashy girl, why did you let him provoke you?* While arguing with Noah in that abandoned house, she'd been too traumatized by the issue with Adrianne to realize what a disastrous mistake that conversation had been. She'd lost control and raised her voice—her own, undisguised voice, like she had in Megan's apartment. Noah had lost control and raised his voice, and his loud insult had made it clear she'd known Gail.

"No wonder Gail despised you! She looked past that Barbie-doll face and saw you were rotten!"

*Sloppy. Loser.* At the time, she'd only been edgy about the noise in a house that should be deserted but hadn't thought about Megan overhearing. She'd assumed Megan was unconscious in her cell upstairs.

But had she been awake when they'd gone to her about . . . twenty minutes later? The timing of the conversation should have occurred during a safe window of time, according to what Shane had told her, but drugs weren't exact. Megan was in good shape. Could her body have broken the drug down more quickly? What if she had been conscious or even half conscious? Even if the argument had seemed like a dream, she might remember it and repeat it to the cops.

What if the police researched Gail's and Bryce's pasts? "Barbie-doll face" implied pretty and young. A pretty, young woman whom Gail had hated. Whenever Jessica had griped to anyone about Gail, they'd been puzzled; everyone except Jessica seemed to see Gail as a jolly, loving, down-to-earth woman. There couldn't be many people she'd openly hated. What if the police learned about Bryce and Jessica and Gail's attitude toward her?

Jessica poked the lump on her cheekbone. Even through two layers of gloves, she could feel how swollen it was. That wimp Noah was much bigger than Megan. Why hadn't he controlled her? What were his muscles made of? Mashed bananas?

Megan would tell the police she'd clawed and punched a light-skinned female—a light-skinned blonde female; she might have seen Jessica's hair when she'd almost ripped her mask off. The police would assume the hair was real; why would Sabrina wear a wig under a ski mask? Jessica could hurry and dye her hair brown or black, but she was blonde in her driver's license photo and in the picture on the cutesy schedule board her boss had posted in the back of the donut shop. If the cops started investigating her, they might question her coworkers. "When did Jessica Barnett dye her hair?" "She was blonde at work yesterday, officer. And she looks like someone beat her up."

Makeup could camouflage the injuries, but it wouldn't make them invisible to anyone standing close to her. She'd examined her face in the bathroom mirror at the house where Megan was a prisoner, and the scratches were deep, bloodied tracks in the skin. It would take makeup as thick as drywall spackle to cover them, and then it would be plain she was covering something. Only a bag over her head would hide the swelling. She knew from experience it would be puffy for a while.

She rolled up her window, but her irregular shivers worsened. One at a time, she took her hands off the steering wheel and flexed and stretched her arms, trying to relax her muscles. If Megan gave the police information that spawned interest in Jessica and they tracked her down and saw her lumpy cheekbone and the heavy makeup covering her face and neck—

Good thing Noah didn't know Shane wouldn't actually agree to claim he'd injured her in a squabble. Punching a woman in the face and clawing her like a girl in a cat fight? Bribing Shane to appear that pathetic would cost more money than she'd ever make, no matter how many antiques she sold or hit songs she recorded.

Even if Shane agreed to say they'd fought, his testimony wouldn't be enough. She'd thought she was overprepared, paying him off to say she was with him since she didn't think the police would actually question her—and on the shred of a chance that they did, she figured they'd just ask for information about Bryce. But if they interrogated her as a suspect, they'd scrutinize her alibi. Shane had no criminal record, but he'd have one if he weren't so lucky. The police might have him on their suspicious-citizen roster, and they might not believe anything he told them. If they offered him a reward, he'd sell her out. If they threatened him with arrest, he'd sell her out.

If Megan never talked to the police, the police would have no grounds for treating Jessica as a serious suspect.

Noah was a calamity, whining that he didn't want anyone to get hurt but botching things so Jessica had to fix his mistakes. He'd been so loopy with guilt over Adrianne that she hadn't dared tell him what his other mistakes meant for Megan. To settle him down, she'd have had to stab him in the heart.

Hurrah for reverse psychology. She'd worried that instead of cooperating with their plan to take him home after they'd finished with Bryce, he'd want to return and verify that Megan had escaped. If he'd had any urge to keep an eye on her, her feigning that she wanted him to come back had wiped it out. He didn't suspect the consequences of his idiocy and wouldn't find out until it was too late for him to give her grief.

Tonight, when she drove past his condo en route to the freeway, she'd signal that things had gone well. By the time he learned that "well" meant Megan *hadn't* escaped so she wasn't a danger, he'd feel distant from it, since he hadn't been there and it was over. Self-preservation would keep him from freaking out. He'd blame it all on Jessica and soothe himself with the chant that he was innocent and she was scum. At this point, she didn't care.

And for Bryce, this would be another potent reason to keep his mouth shut.

*Take care of Megan, return the car, put the keys back on the dresser. Walk home, don't get noticed, gather all the kidnapping clothes and other junk, hide them until you can dump them after work tomorrow.*

Her headache was a whole-head ache, eyes, cheeks, and jaw included. Next time, she'd bring pain relievers as part of her gear.

*Next time.* Never again. No need for it. She would not waste everything she'd done tonight. She'd make this work; she'd get the money she needed.

She'd succeed.

# Chapter 26

OUT OF BREATH, MEGAN FLOPPED her legs to the bed and rested her tied hands on her stomach. She must have ripped every muscle in her upper body, and no human shoulder was meant to stretch like she'd stretched hers. Divine assistance must have held her joints together while she'd fought to get her hands in front of her.

Her exhausted limbs felt useless. Jellyfish tentacles that needed water to float them. A jellyfish on the beach.

*Concentrate. You're trying to escape, not write a poem.*

Rallying, she lifted her hands to her face. Her fingertips were partly deadened; she ended up scratching her forehead and cheek as she pulled the blindfold down.

She scanned her prison. It was a spacious bedroom, weakly lit by a night-light plugged into an outlet near a window. A tall something—a dresser, covered with a sheet—stood against the wall to her left. Sheets covered all the furniture. The blinds on the window were closed, but moonlight showed around the edges.

She burrowed her fingernails under the edge of the duct tape gag and tore it loose. The tape stuck to her fingers; she had an intense wrangle with it, attempting to toss it to the floor. She stuck it to the sheet covering the bed.

Squinting at her wrists, she mused over how to break tight, multiple layers of duct tape. She'd heard there was a way to do it, but she had no idea what it was.

*A-plus on preparing yourself. Great foresight on not earning a black belt in karate or studying kickboxing or anything that might have helped you tonight.*

She drew her knees up. For a few seconds, she probed and yanked at the shackles around her ankles, but it was hopeless. The good news—fantastic news—was that she wasn't chained to anything; Rachel had been tethered to a metal ring on the floor.

Praying, she jerked her wrists against the tape. Trevor had broken free of duct tape once after Kristen had drugged him and tied him up. How? Technique or strength? Both?

*Think it through.* She examined the tape and tried to twist her crossed wrists. They were already so battered that pulling against the tape made her queasy with pain. How could she tear it? She tugged one hand up and one hand down. Why hadn't she set aside the Melville and Shakespeare and browsed survivalist websites?

Something sharp. She sat up, rested her feet on the floor and gingerly stood, praying the floor wouldn't creak and she wouldn't pass out.

No creaking. No dizziness.

She waited, listening. A couple of times, she'd heard footsteps outside the door, but nothing in a while. Either she had a silent guard, or her captors were in another part of the house.

She shuffled to the dresser and lifted the sheet draped over it. The edges of the dresser were rounded, blunt. Not helpful.

She pivoted to what looked like a desk and removed its sheet. More rounded edges. Books between bookends. She tapped one of the bookends. Smooth wood.

Something cube-shaped, shorter than the books, sat on the left side of the desk. She explored it with her hands. Chilly stone. A sculpture. Relief carvings on the front, sides, and back, with right angles at the corners where the stone hadn't been polished. This might work. She picked up the sculpture.

On the floor, with her legs out straight, Megan pinned the sculpture between her knees with an edge pointing upward and scraped the tape against it.

After several minutes of sawing, she stretched one pinky to probe the condition of the tape. Rough. Damaged.

Whispering another prayer, Megan continued rubbing the tape against the stone, her wrists increasingly hot from friction. Every few seconds, she'd pause and try to wrench her hands apart. How long until her captors barged in?

When the tape snapped at last, tears of gratitude flowed down her face. She peeled the tape off her wrists and stuck it to the floor.

Arms scorched and legs shaking, she drew herself to her feet. What could she use to unlock the shackles? She opened desk drawers, seeking a paperclip or anything else thin enough to stick in a lock. Pencils, paper, folders, sticky notes. Even if she could find a paper clip, she had no idea how to pick a lock.

Time to leave. Being restricted to slow walking was less dangerous than lingering here, fumbling ignorantly with the leg irons and hoping the kidnappers wouldn't interrupt her.

She didn't dare exit through the door to the hallway. The window? She shuffled to the window and lifted one corner of the curtains.

First floor. Thank heavens. Undisturbed snow frosted the ground between the trees, and to the left, down a steep slope, was a flat area, gray on the perimeter, reflecting moonlight in the center. Britteridge Pond, partially thawed.

Britteridge Pond Road. This was one of the beautiful houses built on the hill above the pond, like the house where Rachel had been held prisoner. Coincidence? A link to the first kidnapping? Or convenience. The houses had enormous lots and were located back from the road, isolated by trees. Private.

Did she know anyone who lived on Britteridge Pond Road? This was the polar opposite of student-style housing.

She slid the curtains apart and evaluated the window. A basic latch—lift it to release it. Steeling herself, afraid she'd hear the blare of an alarm, she flipped the latch up.

No alarm. Megan felt foolish for cringing. How could they risk an active security system? The last thing they wanted was for a security company to send the police.

She tried to lift the window, but her hands were so fatigued it only shifted a little and squeaked. She tried again and pulled too hard. The window swished upward and bumped against its upper limit. She winced.

No audible reaction from outside her room.

Side clips secured the screen. She released them and manipulated the screen until she freed it. She set it on the floor against the wall.

Gripping the side of the window frame to stabilize herself, she sat on the windowsill. The ground was a few feet below her, so jumping should have been simple, but with her ankles chained, she hoped she didn't lose her balance and splat stomach down in the snow. She rotated her feet so they dangled over the sill, then she scooted off.

The crunch of her feet breaking through icy snow panicked her. Her kidnappers must have heard . . . Was there anything nearby she could use as a weapon—

*You think you can defend yourself by throwing ice balls? Just go.* She shuffled toward the trees at the side of the yard, iced-over snow gouging at her ankles and loose snow slipping inside her canvas shoes. She needed to find somewhere with a phone.

Hiding among the trees made her feel a fraction less terrified, though she wished there were more evergreens and fewer bare branches. Her restricted steps were painfully slow as she followed the direction of a long, ploughed driveway toward the road. Not daring to go out onto the road—how could she know if a car driving past carried the kidnappers?—she remained among the trees and turned in the direction of town, shivering in her sweater.

\* \* \*

Sore and exhausted but too jittery to go to bed, Bryce paced the house, glancing frenetically from antique to antique, predicting what Jessica would steal first, fighting the most savage craving he'd had since before prison. He needed a fix, needed anything that would ease the misery and terror inside him. *Don't. You leave and go seek it out and Powell will follow you. Don't. For your mother's sake, don't.*

What was happening to Megan? Had Jessica let her escape? Would Powell call and tell him when they'd found her? Why would he? Should he call Powell and ask? Or call Trevor?

*Why would Jessica kill her? It won't get her more money. Why would she tell you Megan escaped if she didn't? She told you about . . . about Adrianne.*

He picked up a Dresden figurine of a man and woman dancing and hurled it to the floor. Porcelain shattered and skittered across the hardwood. There was a few hundred dollars, or whatever the figurine was worth, that Jessica wouldn't get.

He pulled his phone out of his pocket. He could call Trevor. Trevor wouldn't be surprised that the police had questioned Bryce, and asking for an update on Megan wouldn't look suspicious . . . any more suspicious than not asking.

He found Trevor's contact info and smacked his finger against the screen.

"Bryce." Trevor answered instantly. "What's going on?"

The desperation—anticipation?—in Trevor's voice answered Bryce's question before he asked it. Megan was still missing, and Trevor hoped he'd called to confess and hand her over. Alive.

His saliva felt thick as mud, and his tongue kept sticking in it. "The . . . police were here. Questioning me. I swear I . . . had nothing to do with whatever happened to Megan." He licked his lips as if that would make him more articulate. "Is she still . . . missing?"

Trevor's tone went heavy. "Yes."

Bryce paced into the kitchen. "No leads?"

"No."

He filled a glass with water. Why did he feel so horrible? He hadn't kidnapped Megan. Guilt burner stuck on high. Malfunctioning, drawing all the fuel from the line.

He gulped water. *Say something nice. What comforting stuff would Trevor say?* "Man, I'm sorry. Are you okay?"

"No."

"Are you . . . with your parents?"

"No. Driving around."

"Driving around?"

"Yeah, being productive. Staring at houses, staring at cars, staring at anyone outside. Driving past the houses of anyone who might have any trace of animosity toward Megan or might dislike my family or hate identical twins or college admissions directors or admissions decisions or rich entrepreneurs, tuition fees, rusty cars, dirty trucks, or Megan's leather coat. I drove past your place twice."

"Waste of your time." It surprised him Trevor could ramble. "I don't hate anything on your list."

"If you have any information, *please* share it."

Trevor's plea lit a weird flicker of memory: Bryce's dad telling stories of the Salem witch trials and the man who got executed via boulders on his chest. Bryce rested a hand on his sternum and took a breath to stretch out his rib cage. The pressure remained.

What if he told Trevor the truth?

*Yeah, do it. Awesome idea.* Bryce didn't even know what evidence Jessica had created besides forcing him to leave fingerprints. Had he done other things he didn't remember?

Nobody would believe he was innocent. Trevor already didn't.

"Bryce?" The intensity in Trevor's voice reappeared. Bryce's hesitation made Trevor think he knew something.

"Sorry." The word smeared itself on Bryce's tongue. "I don't know anything. Hang in there." Without waiting for Trevor to answer, he hung up and shoved his phone in his pocket.

*You hate me enough to destroy me, Jess?* He snatched the glass of water and swallowed a gulp so big it hurt all the way to his stomach. Yeah, she hated him, but at least she wanted money more than she wanted to destroy him.

Who was the sap who'd helped her? Sounded like Jessica was blackmailing him too.

Bryce slumped into a kitchen chair and scanned the clean surface of the table. No crumbs from the garlic bread. No smear of marinara sauce where he'd dropped that noodle. Jessica had not only collected the garbage so he couldn't send it to the police lab, but she'd also wiped the table.

Had she been plotting this since before she'd visited him that first time? Or had this been a spiteful plan B, created after he'd ignored her hints that she needed money and made it clear he didn't want her in his life?

How had she come up with the warped idea of using Megan O'Connor against him? After she'd moved back from California, she must have heard gossip that Megan was in Britteridge and figured Bryce hated the twin of the woman who'd killed his mother, so that was a motive for Bryce to—

No. Not right. She'd said she knew he didn't care about Megan, just that the police would think he hated her. It didn't matter. He wasn't sure if he hated her or not, and yeah, Powell thought he—

Hold on. Why would Jessica say she knew he didn't care? *Knew?* The word glinted in his mind. He'd never talked about Megan to her. Did she assume he was too laid-back to carry a grudge, or, like Noah thought, too self-centered to—

Noah.

*Noah* as a kidnapper? Yeaaaaah. Noah in his creased trousers and starched shirt, using a disassembled Montblanc pen to pick the lock on Megan's apartment, commanding her to tie herself up because he didn't like the sticky feel of duct tape, and warning her not to drip any blood on his car upholstery.

Besides, Noah had always despised Jessica. He wouldn't even talk to her now, let alone do anything she could blackmail him for. Anonymous hate mail was Noah's limit, and even if Jessica somehow had an informant who'd slipped her info about Noah's poison pen, that wasn't enough to make Noah her lackey. If Noah *was* guilty of more serious harassment of Megan, yeah, maybe Jessica could blackmail him with the threat of telling the cops and getting him arrested. He'd be terrified of getting his name in the paper and of his father—

*Give it up. You think Noah was involved in pranking Megan? The guy chose the same Halloween costume every year, and anyone with identical Scooby-Doo costumes in size tiny to size teenager isn't the brains guiding Sabrina. And what woman could he coax into playing the role of—*

Bryce bowed his head until his forehead hit the table. He stayed there, eyes shut.

What woman.

He'd talked to Noah about Jessica when Noah had visited him and found that plate of cookies on his porch. He'd mentioned that she was living in Massachusetts again, that she needed money. He'd sarcastically suggested Noah hire her.

Noah had fired back that the only thing he'd hire Jessica for was car theft.

Megan's good luck had enraged Noah. Had the conversation given him the idea of hiring Jessica to harass her? Noah: sitting in an executive chair, ordering his minion to cause mayhem so he didn't have to sweat in his button-down shirt.

Those sneaky, ingenious hoaxes didn't seem like things Noah could create, but Jessica could. Could she mimic Megan's voice? In high school, he'd heard her imitate different accents, mocking people. If she'd wanted to learn to imitate the voice of a specific person, he didn't doubt she could do it. Maybe she'd even done voice work in LA, part of whatever acting she'd been involved in. He'd asked her about LA, but she hadn't told him much.

The antiques. Noah had always been fascinated by Gail's antiques, and Gail had enjoyed talking about them. Noah knew a lot of details about her collection, far more than Bryce did. Had it been his idea to take the antiques instead of cash?

*Sheesh. No.* Gail had detested Jessica. Noah would never let her touch any of Gail's property. He wouldn't kidnap Megan. He wouldn't . . . not the attack on Adrianne Mullins either; he wasn't violent. He wouldn't even want Bryce back in prison. Bryce's record mortified Noah; he wouldn't risk splatting his cousin's name into the news again.

He wouldn't want to take any of those risks. But under blackmail?

"A guy who thought he could use me for his dirty work, then throw me away. Now he obeys my orders, or I'll destroy him."

Noah hated Megan. He'd wanted her punished. He knew Jessica was smart, wily, creative, and not worried about what was or wasn't legal. None of Noah's friends would have those qualities; he wouldn't associate with people like that.

Bryce turned his head and rested one cheek against the table. He'd lied, flatly *lied* to Powell when Powell had asked if he knew of anyone with a grudge against Megan. Had he protected the guy who'd then helped Jessica frame him?

*If Noah is guilty, what difference does it make? You're still stuck. Fight Jessica and she'll send you to prison.*

He started to sit up. Weary, he let his head fall back to the table. His cheekbone bonked hard against the wood. A bruise. Nice. Who cared?

This whole theory about Noah was crazy. Sort of.

Bryce would be trapped keeping Jessica's secret while she leeched away the items his mother had treasured. He'd be protecting the people who'd hurt Adrianne Mullins, always wondering if his own cousin was involved, the guy who had judged Bryce for his idiot choices.

Would Jessica honestly let Megan go?

Head still on the table, Bryce held his phone on its side next to his eyes and checked the time. Nearly midnight. Noah usually went to bed early.

Was stress keeping him awake tonight?

Bryce tried to sit up straight and slumped against the back of his chair instead. If Noah answered the phone, Bryce could ask if he'd heard about the kidnapping and assess Noah's reaction. Any odd statements? Any agitation?

Excellent plan. He had all the patience he needed to subtly test Noah and listen for any flubs. His brain was so sharp and concentration so focused he could calculate Noah's guilt by counting how often he took a breath while he claimed he hadn't heard anything about Megan because he'd been preoccupied making split-pea soup and scrubbing his furnace filter.

Patience and concentration and subtlety. Yeah, those were gone.

Powell couldn't be listening. He couldn't have enough evidence for a warrant yet. Bryce tapped the phone to call Noah.

It rang twice. "What is it?" Noah answered tersely. "It's the middle of the night."

"Hey." Bryce straightened his back and clamped his hand on the edge of the table. "What did Jessica threaten to do if you didn't help her kidnap Megan O'Connor?"

# Chapter 27

LAST TIME JESSICA HAD OPENED this garage door, she'd admired how quiet it was, but now the same soft growl seemed so loud she wished she'd muffled the motor in sound-absorbing foam. She parked in the garage and tapped the remote to close the door, grimacing again at the noise she was generating on this dead-silent street.

*Stop being so skittish.* No neighbors would hear anything. The houses were too far apart, and this wasn't the only house in this posh area that was empty in winter months. Jessica knew the scoop on Britteridge Pond Road; her mother's boyfriend between Jessica's dad and stepdad had made a living taking care of luxury homes like this while the residents spent months snorkeling in Key West or Aruba.

The cops wouldn't be searching for Megan yet. They wouldn't learn she'd disappeared until Trevor tried to contact her in the morning, and he wouldn't call the police the instant she didn't answer her phone. It would take him a while to figure out something was seriously wrong, maybe until Megan started missing classes. Jessica had plenty of time. She'd take care of Megan, go home, and stay away from Britteridge until her face healed. It would take weeks for the scratches to disappear completely, but once they'd mostly healed, light makeup would hide them, and she could start collecting Gail's antiques. She'd better not have permanent scars.

*That dimwit Megan.* If she hadn't fought like a demented chimpanzee, no one would have been hurt, not more than a bruise.

Too bad Jessica didn't have a smooth escape plan like she'd bragged to Noah. She'd gambled she wouldn't need one, and setting it up would have been too hard, like, impossibly hard. Counterfeit ID, new social security number—she could figure out how to get those, but she didn't have the money to pay for black market services, or money to live on. If she fled now, she'd end up helpless in an ugly underworld, controlled and used. Or she'd get arrested before she left the state.

No thanks, to both of those choices.

She opened her car door. The garage was dark; she'd unscrewed the bulb attached to the door opener. She flicked on her flashlight and walked toward the coil of rope she'd noticed when she'd staked out the house. It hung on a hook on the wall next to looped extension cords and garden tools on pegs. She slipped her folding knife from her pocket and sawed off a couple of feet of rope. In one corner was a stack of bricks, probably leftovers from a home-improvement project. She closed her knife, slid it into her pocket, and walked toward the bricks.

She wouldn't lose control like she had with Adrianne. She would hit Megan only hard enough to knock her out. No blood. She'd be unconscious before the blow even stung. While she was oblivious, Jessica would strangle her—after covering her face with a sheet so Jessica wouldn't have to watch her suffocate. She didn't want that image in her head. Already she shuddered at her mental slideshow of Adrianne.

She entered the house and tried to hurry toward Megan's cell. Her pace lagged. Riding a bicycle up a steep hill, fighting to force the pedals in another rotation. *Do it, or you've lost your whole future. Loser forever.*

She reached the bedroom she'd secured by reversing the handle so the lock was on the outside. Under her gloves, sweat boiled with trapped heat. She balanced the flashlight on top of the brick and rope in her left hand and unlocked the door.

She wouldn't need her flashlight in the room. The night-light was enough; she didn't want extra illumination in there. She stored the flashlight in her pocket and opened the door.

The bed was empty.

Jessica leaped into the room. Megan must be on the floor on the other side of the bed.

She wasn't there. Jessica snatched her flashlight and swept the beam across the carpet. A wad of duct tape, the blindfold, and a cube-shaped stone carving.

Bitter air drifted through a screenless window.

\* \* \*

Enough snow had slithered into Megan's tennis shoes and melted that her shoes and socks were soaked and her ankles numb to the shackles encircling them. Her trail would be easy for her captors to follow, but with her limited pace, taking extra steps to create a convoluted trail to throw them off would result in her getting nowhere. At any moment, they could discover she was missing, and with a flashlight and long strides, they'd catch up to her. All she'd be able to do is watch them come while she inched in the opposite direction like a frostbitten snail and grabbed for a branch or a rock in a futile attempt to defend herself.

The house had been so quiet. Had they left her and gone somewhere else, like to drop a ransom demand where the Drakes would find it? *Please let them be gone for hours.*

One foot slipped on a branch, and she fell to her hands and knees. She'd fallen many times; whenever she stumbled at all, the chain linking her ankles tripped her. The moonlight on the snow was bright enough that she could mostly avoid walking into trees but not bright enough to guide her around bumps on the ground. How long until she reached the next house? The houses on the hill above the pond were built far apart, but she must have crossed enough ground to hit another driveway soon.

What if she met her captors on that driveway? If they saw she was gone and saw the direction of her prints, they'd know where she was heading for help. Where else would she go but to the nearest house?

Frustrated that she couldn't think of a better plan, maddened by her sluggish pace, hating the telltale snow, and wishing March actually meant it was springtime, she kept trudging past trees. Her teeth chattered, and she pulled her hands into the sleeves of her sweater. She'd heard a couple of cars pass but still didn't dare go out on the road.

Finally the ground leveled, and between the trees, she saw a dark, treeless strip that had to be a driveway. She hauled her shackled feet forward and stopped behind a broad tree trunk near the edge of the driveway. She scanned the driveway, but couldn't see anything except black silhouettes of trees and the contrast of snow against the borders of the asphalt. At least she didn't hear footsteps or see flashlights or headlights.

Deciding to take the chance, she stepped into deeper snow, probably thrown from the driveway by a snowblower. Unable to lift one foot at a time above the pile of snow, she got stuck. Using her shins as a snowplow, she tried to push through, but the snow was too compact.

Fighting off the urge to sob—her chattering teeth and hoarse breathing were enough of an "I'm right here!" for the kidnappers—she lowered herself to her hands and knees, freed her chained feet from the snow, and crawled toward the driveway.

On the cleared asphalt, she tried to stand. Her legs quivered, and she kept tripping herself with the shackles, falling forward or backward. *You're panicking. Calm down.* For a few seconds, she stopped struggling, kept her icy hands shielded under her arms, and took control of her breathing. *Okay. You can do this. Get up. You're not crawling to the house.*

In small, painstaking motions, she stood, balanced, then shuffled toward a house she couldn't yet see; the driveway must be curved. *Stay steady. Small steps.*

She passed the curve in the driveway and saw the dim shape of a house. Dark. Completely dark. No one was home.

*Thaw your brain. Of course the house is dark. How late is it?* It could be three in the morning; she had no idea how long she'd been unconscious. Anyone in the house would be asleep. She'd ring the doorbell until they either let her in or called the police on her. Desperate not to get intercepted this close to rescue and warmth, she was tempted to walk faster but kept her gait slow and even. *Be patient. Don't knock yourself over. You'll get there.*

Lights ignited. Megan jerked, staggered, and almost sprawled to the driveway again. *Motion-activated lights. You got close enough to the house to trigger them.* She plodded up the porch stairs and pressed a numb finger against the doorbell. Chimes rang inside the house.

*Please hurry.* Cringing at the visibility of standing on a lighted porch, she rang repeatedly, determined to jolt every member of the household out of bed. She checked over her shoulder. Still only darkness, but with her eyes now adjusted to light, she'd be less able to spot the kidnappers.

She kept ringing. No lights flicked on inside the house. No voices. With her fusillade of chimes, there was only one reason she wouldn't have provoked a response: no one was home. Gone on vacation?

Should she break a window and go inside anyway? Maybe they had a landline she could use—

A security system. Megan took an ungainly step back and surveyed the front windows. In the corner of one window was a red and white sticker with a security company logo. Thank heavens. If she broke a window, sensors would alert the company, and they'd send the police.

And an alarm would go off in the house. If the kidnappers were anywhere in the area, they'd hear the blaring. Blaring alarm, blazing lights. If they were close, they might gamble that they could capture her before the police arrived.

*Risk it.* She was dressed in a sweater and jeans, with her ankles chained, her body shaking, and her hands and feet already numb. Attempting to walk to the next house with no idea how far the hike would be was risking hypothermia and frostbite. Breaking a window was her best option.

Quickly she evaluated the objects on the wraparound porch, searching for something mobile and heavy that could break a window.

The planter near the steps was a massive urn, too heavy to lift. On a table between two rocking chairs was a pot of silk flowers. No, that was a basket of flowers, light and useless.

A snow shovel leaned against one of the porch pillars. She shuffled over and clumsily picked it up. It wasn't an ideal battering ram, not as weighty as she wanted, but it had a metal blade, and at least she could swing it. She shuffled to the window. Rallying every trace of strength, she raised the shovel and slammed it into the window.

Glass shattered with a crash so loud it startled Megan, even though she'd caused it. She waited for the wail of an alarm.

Nothing.

Was there a delay to give the homeowner time to shut off the system in case the trigger had been an error? She wanted to hide, but stepping off the porch and driveway meant footprints in the snow. The kidnappers could follow her no matter where she went. She lifted the shovel, aimed to the right of the hole she'd created and bashed the window until large chunks of glass fell out. Through the opening, she pawed at the curtains to slide them out of the way so she could see into the house and search for lights flashing or a control panel on the wall.

Darkness. The silhouettes of furniture.

Maybe there was no alarm—just a phony sticker to deter thieves. *Don't panic. Get inside and see if there's a phone.* If the homeowners pressed charges for vandalism and breaking and entering, she'd thank the judge, accept her sentence, and celebrate that she was alive.

Climbing through the window would mean grating her shivering body over a rim of broken glass. That was only a workable plan if her goal was blood loss. She needed to open the window. She stuffed deadened fingers into her mouth and warmed them until they were stinging. Mindful not to slash her arm, she reached through the broken window and groped for the latch.

\* \* \*

Each second of Noah's silence kicked Bryce. A closed mouth from Noah? Not anger and harsh questions about what substances Bryce was shooting into his body? Noah was involved. His own cousin. His family.

"What are you talking about?" Noah finally spoke, his volume hushed. He didn't want to be overheard, and Bryce doubted it was because he cared about disturbing sleeping neighbors. "Are you high?"

"No." Bryce wrestled his fury. "But I was drugged up earlier this evening. What did Jessica slip me? How'd she do it?"

Another silence. Noah was wondering if Bryce was guessing or if Jessica had told. "You're doing drugs with Jessica again? You bozo."

Bryce pulled his sweaty phone away from his face, wiped the screen on his shirt, then lifted it back to his ear. "You are low, cousin. Mom treated you like my brother, and you set me up."

"You're out of your mind." Noah's whisper trembled. "I don't know anything about whatever happened to Megan. She got kidnapped? Are the police accusing you?"

"They'd be accusing *you*," Bryce said, "if I hadn't lied for you a couple of weeks ago."

"Lied?"

"I told Detective Powell you don't have a grudge against Megan. Didn't tell him that you hate her and don't think anything good should happen in her life. Didn't tell him you have a history of sending hate mail like the letter that started all this harassment. Or that you hired Jessica to play the role of Sabrina Erickson."

Another pause. Bryce imagined Noah scanning his mental teleprompter, frantically searching for what he'd say if he weren't guilty. "I never did any of that. I never sent letters to anyone."

"Mom knew. You told her about a letter your dad got, and you faked that you didn't know where it came from, but she knew you'd done it. I heard her talking to my dad about it."

"It's not true."

Delivering the words as believably as he could, he said, "I'll let Powell worry about proof."

"What kind of an idiot are you?"

"Nationally ranked." *Not a big enough idiot to buy revenge when Jessica's selling it at life-in-prison prices, but a big enough idiot to scare you into thinking I'd do it.*

"You're using again," Noah said. "You got involved with Jessica, and she lured you back into the sewer. You flunked a drug test at work, didn't you? You got fired."

Good thing Noah wasn't in the room, or Bryce would have socked him in the mouth. "Where's Megan? Jessica said you were letting her escape, but she's still missing. Is she alive?"

"Why would I kidnap Megan? I don't need money. I have an excellent job. I'm doing fine. Never screwed up my life or did time."

"Fine. Just wanted to let you know what info I'll be taking to Powell."

"What is your deal? Why would you try to cause trouble for me?"

"Why would you try to cause it for me? I'm a cruddy ex-con, so you think it's okay to frame me? What about Adrianne Mullins? Who smashed her head in—you or Jessica? Did you use the same hammer Kristen used on Mom?"

Noah didn't answer. Bryce watched the microwave clock and listened to Noah's panicky breathing. A full minute passed. Longer.

"If Jessica told you I was involved, she was lying." From the way Noah hissed the words, he must be covering his phone in spit. "Are you recording this? You think I'll confess something?"

"I don't care if you confess. That's Powell's deal. I'm just warning you I'm not playing your game. I'm telling the cops everything Jessica told me."

"You're lying!"

"You wish you were sure of that, don't you?"

"The bluff's not working."

"I'm not cooperating with—" Bryce's brain sucked the phony threat in, analyzed it, fed it, sent it surging through his bloodstream.

He could tell Powell the truth.

*Risk going to prison for life?* It was an outlandish story, and Jessica had an alibi. Powell wouldn't believe Bryce; he'd suspected him all along. Powell didn't even believe Bryce when Bryce made sense.

*So go Noah's route and let Jessica blackmail you. Go Mom's route. Protect kidnappers and killers.*

Gail had sacrificed her integrity to try to keep Bryce out of prison. Good thing he didn't have any integrity to begin with. Not much to sacrifice there.

Right?

Was he still like that?

Did he think if he paid off Jessica that this would have a smiley-face ending? Like when his mother had buckled to Kristen's blackmail, thinking if she gave Kristen what she wanted, no one would get hurt? Two dead, two injured. *Smiley face.*

Adrianne Mullins was critically injured. Megan was a prisoner, maybe in mortal danger, maybe already dead.

Could he ignore that? Not even try to help her?

He couldn't help her. Why risk prison? Her problems were her problems. He didn't owe her his freedom.

"Yeah, you're lying." Noah broke the silence in a weird, giddy voice. "Don't act so stupid. Go to bed."

"I'm calling Powell," Bryce said. "Dead serious."

"You're crazy!" Back to panic. Sheesh, did the guy know how obviously he was giving himself away?

"Yeah, I'm crazy," Bryce said. "But I'm calling."

"What'd you do tonight? You hurt someone? This Adrianne woman you're talking about? Or Megan? Now you're blaming me?"

"Where is Megan?"

"You tell me. If you call the police and lie about me, they'll know you're trying to hide what you did. They'll find evidence against you. Solid evidence."

"Hey, weird. You're quoting Jessica. Big coincidence."

"You'll end up in prison. For life. I'm serious. You don't want to call them while your mind is fried like this. Go to bed and sleep off whatever you took."

"You tell me what I took. What did Jessica slip me?"

"Listen. To. Me." His words were more gasps than speech. Meltdown.

"I'm listening," Bryce said. "Where's Megan? Is Jessica really releasing her?"

"The police will *find evidence*. They'll arrest you. You'll get convicted of kidnapping. Murder. You want a life sentence?"

"No." Bryce gazed out the kitchen window at tree branches illuminated by the lights his mother had installed when she'd busted him sitting in the backyard on a summer night, shooting up. "But I'm still not playing Jessica's game. Let's see how foolproof of a job you did framing me."

He hung up and reached into his pocket for the business card Powell had given him tonight. *Noah's right. You're crazy. Don't do this. Do it.*

His phone vibrated—Noah calling back. He rejected the call and stared at Powell's number. The Drakes would think he was guilty. After how kind they'd been to him, even giving him a job, they'd think he'd kidnapped their son's fiancée. He should talk to them first—

*You can't take the time. Grab every mangled scrap of character you can find, and call Powell.*

Another call from Noah. He rejected it.

He threw the card on the table. He didn't have enough scraps of integrity to get him to choose prison over cooperation.

*Don't make Mom's mistakes.*

He picked up the card. He threw it down. He picked it up and ripped it in half. He aligned the pieces so he could read the number. He tore each piece in half and mixed them up.

*Enjoy your smiley-face ending, coward.*

He snatched his phone and texted Trevor as fast as he could: *My ex Jessica Barnett took Megan. She's trying to frame me. Looks like Noah helped her. I just talked to him and told him I was calling the cops. I swear I wasn't involved. I'll tell Powell everything I know.*

He hit send and assembled the fragments of Powell's card.

# Chapter 2 8

"HE WON'T DO IT. HE won't do it." Noah chanted the words as he tried three times to call Bryce back. Voice mail. Had Jessica lied about concealing his name from Bryce? She wouldn't provoke Bryce with information that would make him angrier. Bryce was making assumptions, thinking everything had started with that letter.

That lazy weakling wouldn't risk himself. Right now, he was chugging a beer and smirking at how he'd scared Noah, trying to make himself feel better after getting owned by Jessica.

Bryce wouldn't call the police.

What if he did?

*Not happening. If he were going to fight this, he'd have told Jessica to her face. Not waited.*

Told Jessica to her face that he was going to turn her in? While his hands were tied behind him, he was woozy, and didn't know what weapons Jessica had?

*If the police come here, act baffled, tell them you have no idea what Bryce is talking about and thought he was stoned when he called. He has no evidence.*

Evidence. The clothes that might be stained with Adrianne's blood. He'd concealed the bag in the back of his bedroom closet.

*Relax.* Even if Bryce called, his whacko accusations wouldn't give the cops enough for a warrant. They couldn't search Noah's condo.

Noah opened a kitchen cupboard and swiped a bottle of ibuprofen. His head ached, heartburn scorched his throat, and every time he moved his swollen foot, it hurt like Megan's heel had smashed it again.

The injuries from Megan. Those scratches on Jessica's face.

If Bryce talked, the cops would have to confront Jessica, even if they assumed Bryce was lying. They'd go to her apartment, find she wasn't home, though her car was there, and wait for her. She'd get caught by surprise, arriving in the middle of the night, her face bruised and clawed. Wearing the clothes she'd worn when she'd struck Adrianne. There must be blood on her, though he hadn't seen it on the dark fabric.

A suspicious arrival home—walking home on a winter night. She'd prepped her alibi-friend to say he'd picked her up for their movie night and taken her home afterward, but if the police saw her walking, she couldn't use that story. She could claim she'd had to walk home because they'd fought, but she wouldn't have time to alert her friend to the new story.

An injured face. Bryce's testimony. Megan's testimony. No matter what her sleazy friend claimed, it wouldn't be enough to avert the issuing of a warrant. They'd search her place.

What would they find? The recordings Jessica had made of his conversations with her? The note he'd left at the donut shop, informing her he wanted to meet concerning a job? Cash he'd given her and envelopes with his fingerprints on them? The wigs she'd worn while dressing up as Megan and Sabrina?

He fumbled with the cap on the medication bottle, unable to line the notches up so he could snap the lid off. Forget it; it wasn't strong enough to help much anyway. He slung the bottle back into the cupboard, bowling over all the bottles near it.

He had to warn Jessica. Had she finished arranging Megan's escape and verifying that she was gone? He'd checked for the signal right before Bryce had called, but she could have come in the past few minutes. He limp-galloped into his bedroom. Leaving the lights off so he could see out the window, he took his binoculars from the windowsill and studied the streetlight on the other side of the lawn behind the condos. The resolution was fuzzy; he must have bumped the binoculars out of focus. He fumbled to adjust the lenses, so frustrated with his inept fingers that if his foot hadn't been injured, he would have sprinted outside to check in person.

The image cleared. Rapidly he scanned the streetlight up and down. If Megan was free and everything had gone well, Jessica would have left a piece of orange duct tape at head height. If there was trouble and Noah needed to meet her at the abandoned house to figure out what to do next, the square would be at knee height. No tape meant she hadn't come yet.

No tape. Wheezing a sigh of relief, he closed the blinds and limped to the closet. If she was at the house on Britteridge Pond Road, he had time to warn her. As fast as he could, he dressed in a sweatshirt and jeans and loosely laced his running shoes. From the kitchen drawer, he grabbed a roll of masking tape—he didn't have any duct tape—and a marker. On the tape, he scribbled *Need to talk. Important.* He'd stick the message on the light pole where Jessica would see it. If she was en route to the light pole while he was en route to Britteridge Pond Road, she'd get his message and they'd rendezvous at that mildewed, abandoned house.

After that he'd ditch the bag of contaminated clothes. Given Bryce's threats, he didn't dare keep them here any longer.

* * *

The porch lights had switched off automatically, and with no lights inside or outside, the house was so black Megan nearly flipped a light switch. She stopped herself. The porch light had been enough of a beacon; now that it was off, she didn't want new light showing through the windows. If the kidnappers followed her footprints, she was doomed anyway, but the fewer ways she flagged them down from a distance, the better. She opened curtains instead and hoped moonlight would be enough to let her search for a phone.

Shivering, feeling around furniture, Megan plodded through the house. No phone on the desk in the study at the back of the house. On the wall in the kitchen, the moonlight through the kitchen window revealed a phone jack on the wall—with no phone plugged in. As a last resort, she trekked up the stairs and checked each bedroom. No phones. They must only use cell phones.

The house was chilly but far warmer than outside. Megan's hands and feet prickled, and the stinging in her warming ankles made her wince with each step. The shackles must be scraping her skin off. The prospect of another excruciating slog through the snow made her want to slump to the floor, empty a dresser drawer on top of herself, and hope that if the kidnappers searched the house, she could pass for part of a messy room.

*See if there's a coat and gloves here you can borrow and move on before you get caught. Get to a place where you can call for—*

The computer in the office. Why hadn't she immediately thought to use it? She'd message and e-mail Trevor, Rachel, Sandra, Michael, Adrianne, and anyone else she could think of until she got a response.

Did anyone know she was missing? She and Trevor usually swapped a few texts on evenings when they weren't together. If he'd contacted her and she hadn't answered, would he be concerned? Pre-Sabrina, he would have chalked her lack of a reply up to homework. Post-Sabrina, he must know she wouldn't overlook his messages. *Please let him have called the police, and let him be monitoring his phone now for any contact from me.*

Megan breathed deeply, preparing for the pain in her feet and ankles, and stepped haltingly down the stairs.

To her right, light flashed in the living room. She whirled, gouging metal into her ankles and bumping into the wall. Someone had triggered the porch lights.

Soft thuds. One set of feet walking up the porch stairs. Brighter, white light shone through the window she'd shattered, then moved away. A flashlight. No red and blue lights, no car noises, no voices.

Pressing both icy hands over her mouth, Megan frantically considered her options. If she hid in a closet, she'd get cornered there; if she fled, she'd die on the back porch when the kidnapper caught her hobbling away. Or she could die in the kitchen, ineffectually wielding a knife while staggering on half-frozen, chained feet.

*Get to that computer. Barricade yourself in the study.* Megan slid her feet along the floor, thinking that would make walking quieter, but her tennis shoes squeaked against the hardwood. Lifting her feet, she straggled toward the study.

Double doors led into the study, but one door stood ajar; the other was already secured. She stepped inside, eased the door shut, and fingered the doorknob until she found the lock. It was a flimsy indoor lock that could be sprung with a bobby pin, but it would give her a few minutes. Or a few seconds. At least the doors felt solid.

The crunch of shoes against shards of glass came from the living room. Had only one of the kidnappers pursued her, or was one inside and one guarding the outside? Megan shuffled to the computer and fumbled until she found the power button.

The cooling fan and hard drive hummed so noisily she felt she'd shouted her location, but even silence wouldn't prevent the kidnapper from noticing the locked door. In the light from the monitor, she inspected the room for something she could shove against the door to block it. The desk chair was on wheels. The bookcase was a built-in behemoth covering a whole wall.

The tread of footsteps faded; the kidnapper must have turned toward the kitchen, not the study. Grateful for extra time, Megan reached for the computer mouse.

The welcome screen offered several icons for different users. She clicked on the first one. It asked for a password.

*Please no.* Panicking, she clicked all the usernames. All password-protected. Was there a way to bypass this screen, to use the computer without accessing a particular account? She hit multiple function keys and clicked futilely all over the screen.

Should she climb out the window and go for help at her laborious pace, promptly getting herself intercepted, or did she stay in this room and fight to hold off a siege until—

*Until they get bored and go home? It won't work. Get out.*

Megan tottered to the window. Moonlight outlined leafless trees against a slope down to the pond. A steep slope. Even though she was on the first floor, there was a significant drop here between the window and the angled ground. Too far to jump.

The last of Megan's already-cracked hopes broke away, tearing so much of her composure with them that she almost opened the window and screamed, even though screaming would immediately draw the kidnappers to her. Unless a wolf or a rabbit brought a rescue party, nobody could reach her before the kidnappers shot her.

Megan retreated from the window. She'd entombed herself in a room with only one exit, and she couldn't access the computer.

She grabbed the edge of the desk, bent her knees, and pushed the massive desk toward the double doors. The desk didn't move.

Footsteps.

Planting her burning feet against the floor to keep the flat soles of her tennis shoes from slipping, she shoved again. The desk lifted a smidgeon, then thumped back into place. The opposite edge was snagging in the deep carpet.

Louder footsteps. The doorknob rattled.

Megan stumbled to the other side of the desk, groped to find a handhold, and pulled.

Her hands slipped off the polished wood, and she tumbled to the carpet.

# Chapter 29

A SPASM IN HIS NECK pierced Noah every time he glanced behind him, but he kept checking to reassure himself that any headlights he saw in his rearview mirror weren't from a police car. At night it was difficult to tell what vehicles were behind him, and after checking so frequently that he nearly ran a stop sign, he forced himself to keep his eyes on the road. If he saw flashing red and blue lights in his mirrors, *then* he'd look back.

*Take it easy. Cut the paranoia.* Even if Bryce ratted on Jessica and Noah, which was a long shot, he'd be calling the cops right now, and there would be a delay before they talked to Noah. They wouldn't instantly trust an ex-con, recovering addict—undoubtedly current addict. They'd escort Bryce to the police department, interrogate him, and see if his accusations were credible, which they weren't. They'd think he'd panicked after what he did to Megan and Adrianne and wanted to blame someone else, but his drug-scorched synapses couldn't invent a rational story.

"Good luck, bozo," Noah whispered. If Bryce got incarcerated again, that was his choice and his fault. As long as Noah could warn Jessica, she'd be ready if the cops did come to her. She'd destroy incriminating evidence and inform her alibi-friend of the changes to his story.

Wishing he could hose his esophagus and stomach with antacids, Noah swore softly, then escalated to a yell, cursing Jessica. A police car approached, heading in the other direction. Noah closed his mouth, his vocal cords as raw as his stomach. *Stay calm. He'll drive right past you. Won't care or notice.*

The patrol car passed him. Noah continued toward Britteridge Pond Road. He was paranoid. He had to be paranoid, had to stay paranoid, had to be suspicious of everything.

He turned onto the driveway of the house, where he hoped Megan was still working to escape. He'd make sure Jessica didn't go back on her promise to free Megan, but if Bryce agitated things, it would be safer if Megan couldn't talk to the police until after Jessica had finished with damage control and cleanup. Unable to open the garage without a remote, he parked in the driveway and hurried to peek through the diamond-shaped garage windows to see if Jessica's stolen car was there.

Too dark to see. He shone his phone flashlight through the glass. *Yes.* The car was here.

His ski mask. He'd left it in the trunk in the bag of contaminated clothing. Could he touch it again, cover his face with fabric that could be stained with blood, risk inhaling traces of it?

He didn't need the mask. He wouldn't see Megan, only Jessica, and he'd put on his regular hat to catch any hair.

*Get the ski mask. Don't take risks. You should be wearing it right now.*

He popped the trunk. Holding his breath in case the lack of air circulation in the bag had magnified the odor of blood, he fished the hat out and tied the bag shut again.

Softly, he shut the trunk. As he limped toward the front door, he flapped the mask in the cold air, trying to scent it with snow and evergreens.

On the porch, he stretched the mask over his face and pressed the door lever. To his surprise, it moved. He'd expected Jessica to leave it locked.

He yanked his naked hand back. *Gloves.* He extracted his regular gloves from his coat pockets, put them on, and used the front of his sweatshirt to wipe his prints from the lever. He'd get a glass-cleaning wipe from his car and do a detailed job of cleaning the lever before he left.

Holding one fist ready to strike if Jessica panicked and attacked him, he sidled into the house and closed the door.

No sound. No glimmer from Jessica's flashlight or the camping lantern. Using his phone flashlight so he could avoid colliding with furniture, he walked toward the kitchen.

The light from his phone didn't illuminate enough of the darkness to make him confident Jessica wasn't hiding in a corner, recognizing it was him but concluding he was a liability she needed to get rid of. Hunching his shoulders and fighting the impulse to cross his arms over his head to shield his skull, he twisted, sweeping the light around the kitchen. "Where are you?" he whispered, putting as much volume into the question as he could without making his voice recognizable.

Jessica didn't answer. This situation was insane: driving around Britteridge at midnight, parking his own car in this driveway, wearing his own coat and shoes into a crime scene. He had to warn Jessica immediately and get out of here.

Was she skulking outside Megan's cell? Bruised foot throbbing, Noah headed out of the kitchen. He shone the light in front of him, behind him, in front again, monitoring both directions as he limped, wishing he'd brought his high-power flashlight and tempted to switch on the overhead lights even though Jessica had wanted to minimize the light visible through the windows of a house where the owners were gone.

The hallway leading to the ground-floor bedroom was a deserted, shadowy corridor. "Where are you?" he whispered again, stepping closer to Megan's cell. The door was open.

He inched forward and directed his phone light through the doorway.

The adrenaline already zapping his nerves surged to a higher voltage. The room was empty, and the window open. How long had Megan been gone? Long enough to reach help and send the police here? If Megan was gone, so was Jessica; she'd planned to leave as soon as Megan escaped. The car . . . ? Maybe the battery had died, so she'd called her alibi-friend for a ride? Not good. Jessica had wanted to avoid calling or texting him when she was supposedly with him in person.

Too scared to pamper the pain in his foot, Noah tried to race out the front door, but his gait became a stagger. He slowed. No sirens or lights or engines. He had time to get away from here, and Jessica's friend would chauffeur her past the light pole to leave her sign. She'd see his note; they'd rendezvous and solve this catastrophe.

He groaned, abhorring the fact that he had to be on the streets in his own car, even after Megan might have reached the police. The police would start paying attention to every vehicle, running plates and making notes. Why hadn't Jessica listened when he'd told her over and over that this scheme was too dangerous? Why had he ever hired her? Was there any alchemy that could vaporize the past few months so he could redo them without contacting her at all?

At his car, Noah stripped off his mask and scrabbled inside his coat pockets, searching for his keys. Had he put them in his jeans? No. Wait, he hadn't locked the car, hadn't wanted to make it beep and blink the headlights. Had he left his keys in—

Snow crunched. He spun toward the trees bordering the driveway. A murky shape sprinted toward him. Not Jessica—too big.

He yanked his car door open, but a foot slammed it shut again. "So Bryce told the truth. Is this where you and Jessica Barnett are holding Megan?"

The police. No. Noah squinted in the moonlight. *Trevor Drake?* Bryce had told Trevor?

The mad rhythm of his heart fired pain down his sternum and into his shoulders. His heart would stop before Trevor could fracture his ribs and jaw. Could he get away and lock himself in the house?

Impossible. Trevor stood close to him; if Noah moved, he'd attack. How had Trevor tracked him? Noah hadn't noticed anyone following him, but he'd been worried about the flashing lights of police cars, not every car on the road.

*Bluff. Act irritated.* "What nonsense did Bryce tell you?"

Trevor switched a flashlight on. He didn't shine it straight into Noah's eyes but held the beam high enough to illuminate his face.

Noah contracted his jaw along with every other muscle he could stiffen. Was he pale? A dizzy, headachy prickling ringed his eyes.

"He told me you and Jessica Barnett kidnapped Megan and were framing him for it," Trevor said.

"*What?* The guy's lost it. You're *following* me? You've lost it too."

"I was in your neighborhood. I've been driving around town, watching for anything unusual. I looked up your address an hour or so ago and drove by your place a couple of times. I'd just gone back there, thinking of knocking on the door this time."

Trevor had suspected he was involved even before Bryce had blabbed. "Stalking's illegal, Drake. I could call the police. Ugly press might tarnish your dad's sterling reputation."

"I'll take the chance."

"Why were you stopping by my place? What do you want?"

"To find out whether you know anything, which you do. Where's Megan?"

"You're insane."

"Bryce warned you he was talking to the police. You reacted by driving here at midnight." Trevor aimed the flashlight at the mask Noah clutched. "You put on a ski mask, entered a dark house, and took care of something without turning on any lights."

Noah hoped his dark gloves against his dark coat would camouflage his trembling hands. Trevor must have parked his truck on the side of the road and walked down the long driveway. While Noah hunted for Jessica, Trevor had crept around outside the house, doing recon.

*Invent an explanation. You're a lot more credible than Bryce.* "Bryce called me, babbling about Megan being kidnapped. I thought he was hallucinating, back on drugs. I asked him what he was taking, and he yelled that he'd blame it on me, the police would think I did it, me and Jennifer Barnett. I mean Jessica."

"Did you call the police?"

"Because I thought he was high? I wouldn't turn my cousin in. I told him I wanted to help him, and he gave me this address. He said to come in disguise, that his enemies might see me. I wore the mask to humor him."

"Is he here?"

Reading Trevor's uncannily even tone was impossible. Did he believe Noah? *Why wouldn't he? Bryce is the crook; you're the good guy.* "No. The house is empty. I was hoping I could drive him home so he could sleep off whatever he took. Is Megan actually missing? I thought he was flashing back to what happened to your sister."

"She's missing."

"I'm sorry. I didn't know. I didn't think he'd . . . I know he hates her, but I don't believe he'd . . . You're sure she's missing? That she didn't lose her phone or go somewhere?"

"She's *missing*. Another woman has been attacked and is dying."

"You're kidding! That's terrible. Who?"

"Adrianne Mullins. Megan's apartment manager. If Bryce was involved, do you have any idea where he'd take Megan?"

"No idea at all," Noah said, feeling less like an earthquake was vibrating the ground. Trevor was taking him seriously. "Do you want to look inside here? The door's unlocked." He waved toward the house. "I didn't see anybody, but I only glanced around. I didn't check closets or anything. If Bryce gave me this address, that's got to mean something. Maybe he . . . hid her?" While Trevor sprinted inside to search, Noah could drive away.

"What happened to your foot?" Trevor asked. "You were limping."

"I slipped on the ice. Twisted it." Was that the purr of a car? Out of the corner of his eye, Noah checked for a flicker of headlights between trees. Had Megan already sent the cops? *No, fool. The cops would tell bigshot Trevor Drake if she was free.* Was it Jessica's friend coming to pick her up? Jessica must be hiding outside.

"Bryce won't answer my calls," Noah said. "I'm going to his house to see if he's there. No telling what that nitwit will do if he's in this serious of trouble." That was a strong excuse for not accompanying Trevor to search the house. "He was having a breakdown on the phone. I need to help him, try to calm him down."

Engine noises buzzed louder, and headlights moved along the driveway toward them. *Don't come to the house!* If Trevor saw Jessica's friend—

It was a patrol car. Two patrol cars, with light bars dark. "Work it out with the police," Trevor said.

* * *

Megan flipped on the overhead lights. There was no point in hiding in the dark now; the kidnappers knew where she was. She unplugged the power strip from the floor outlet under the desk, dragged the computer tower away from the desk, and lifted the printer and monitor to the floor so the desk wouldn't snag on cords or bear extra weight. She swept everything else off the desk—books, pictures, a plant, a lamp—and sat on the floor on the far side of the desk. With both feet braced against the desk, she used her legs to shove as hard as she could.

The motion moved Megan backward more than it moved the desk forward, but the desk did move two or three inches.

Quiet clicks came from the doorknob. The kidnapper was picking the lock. Praying, Megan shoved again. The desk moved more smoothly this time, sliding maybe a foot. She relaxed her muscles for an instant, then pushed again. More progress. The desk was nearing the door, but it was off center, completely blocking the door on the right, but leaving the door on the left clear. Megan crawled to the back of the desk so she could shove it sideways to barricade both doors. She shoved, but the desk stuck in the carpet again, tipped slightly, and thudded back into the same spot.

The door on the right crashed into the desk and bounced back, slamming itself shut. Igniting every sliver of energy she had, Megan shoved. The first door opened again, slowly, and something clicked near the ceiling. The latch holding the second door shut.

The muscles in her legs felt like they were scorching and ripping. She kept shoving. The desk moved a few inches, barely overlapping the second door.

The second door swung open, and the edge caught the corner of the desk. Desperate to block the door more completely, Megan tried to scoot the desk farther, but her muscles jiggled in spasms, and the shackles sawed deeper into her ankles. Panting, she dropped her legs to the carpet. At least neither door would open wide enough for even a small person to wedge through.

Wanting to give her legs a few seconds to recover, she rolled to her stomach and skimmed the bookshelves and wall decorations behind her, searching for a weapon. If the kidnapper had a gun, she was dead no matter what, but she'd fight with whatever she could grab.

Books . . . paintings . . . knickknacks . . . no. Megan army-crawled to the closet, rose tremulously onto her knees, and pulled the door open. Two boxes of printer paper.

A crash vibrated the walls, knocking over books on the shelves. Megan looked back and saw the door on the left slam into the edge of the desk. The side of the door was dented and splintering. If the kidnapper could pulverize the edge of the door by pounding it against the desk, the door would clear the desk and open.

Frantically, Megan turned back to the closet. Next to the extra paper sat a canister vacuum with a stretchy hose and a long metal wand. Exhaling hard to keep herself from screaming in pain, Megan clutched the closet doorknob and heaved herself to her feet. Her legs were so feeble that she knew she couldn't shove that humongous desk any farther.

Savage bangs of the door against the desk jarred a painting from the wall. She could press herself against the door, straining to hold it shut and keep it intact longer, but she didn't dare. Pushing on it would make it clear where she stood, an impossible-to-miss target for a bullet through the wood.

She disconnected the metal wand from the vacuum hose and hobbled to the left of the splintering door. The carpet brush on the end of the wand was unwieldy; she wrenched it off and extended the metal wand to full length. The instant the kidnapper entered, before he spotted her, she'd swing the metal pole at his head. She had to knock him out or at least daze him enough to give her a second chance to strike.

The door crashed against the desk again, but instead of rebounding, it stuck. Afraid her clammy hands would slide on the metal wand, Megan wanted to dry her palms on her jeans but didn't dare remove either hand from her weapon.

A crunch. A scrape. The door dragged partway along the edge of the desk and stalled. Megan tried to adjust her stance to make herself as stable as possible, but the shackles didn't give much leeway. If the kidnapper pushed her, she'd fall; she couldn't avoid that. She had to strike first.

The partly open door stayed motionless, wedged against the desk. In the lull, Megan wished she could turn out the lights, hide, even jump out the window and risk broken bones.

Something struck the door with an earsplitting thud. The door popped clear of the desk and clattered against the wall.

Ready to swing, Megan braced herself, but the kidnapper didn't enter. He suspected she was ready for him; he wasn't blundering inside without assessing the situation. If she couldn't surprise him, she didn't have a chance.

Jumping with both feet at once to avoid tripping herself, she landed in the open doorway and rammed the vacuum wand forward at chest level. It struck the kidnapper, but not as hard as Megan had planned; he had retreated a little. He gasped and wobbled but didn't fall. Megan inched forward and targeted his ski-mask-covered head—no, *her* head; the hallway lights were on, and the kidnapper was obviously the smaller of the two.

The kidnapper ducked, and the wand struck the wall. Megan swung again and hit the kidnapper's arm. She raised the wand higher and drove it downward; the kidnapper leaped aside, and the wand smacked her shoulder, a fierce blow but useless at incapacitating her. The kidnapper swore and attempted to snatch the wand out of Megan's hands. Megan jabbed it into the woman's stomach; she grunted and hunched forward. As Megan raised her arms to slam the wand against the kidnapper's skull, the kidnapper threw herself toward Megan's knees. Megan tried to leap out of her way, but the shackles tripped her. As she fell, the kidnapper bashed into her, hurtling her into the wall.

Stupefied by the impact, shoulders and head pressed against the wall and legs squashed under the kidnapper, Megan struggled to focus blurry thoughts. *Take a breath . . . Take a breath . . . You're as strong as she is; throw her off of you. Find the vacuum wand.*

Megan writhed; the kidnapper shifted positions to mash Megan's legs harder into the floor. Megan inhaled croakily. *Breathe, breathe. Clear your head. You can't fight if you're dizzy.*

Metal clicked. A folding knife, the blade now locked into position.

Before the kidnapper could aim the blade toward her, Megan flung her upper body forward and grabbed the kidnapper's hand with both her hands. A stormy current of dizziness confused her brain. Was she tipping sideways, sinking back, collapsing toward the blade of the knife? She couldn't see . . . fuzziness . . . blackness . . . fuzziness . . . Both hands locked around the kidnapper's hand, a leather glove, the bony tension of a fist holding a knife. *Push her hand away from you. Push it back. Don't pass out. You can't pass out.*

Her eyes began to focus, but her arms trembled. Exhaustion, bruised muscles, stamina gone . . . *Push the knife back.*

The kidnapper's free hand pounded Megan's right elbow, punching it inward, hyperextending the joint. Megan screamed. The kidnapper seized Megan's right wrist, gouged her fingers into the flesh, and wrenched outward, breaking Megan's grip on her knife hand. Megan struggled to free her wrist from the kidnapper's grasp, but pain melted muscles and ligaments; her arm wilted, nearly paralyzed. *Scream again. Draw a big breath, and scream louder. Keep screaming.*

*Won't help . . . Who can hear you? Scream anyway.*

She screamed. Her left hand pushed the kidnapper's knife back—a fatigued, nondominant hand against the kidnapper's strength. She struggled to move her legs enough to jostle the kidnapper so she'd have trouble controlling the knife. Futile battle . . . Kristen and her knife . . . Not Kristen . . . Her eyesight blurring, the kidnapper looming over her, upright, giant . . . No . . . the kidnapper was sitting, pinning Megan to the ground, gripping her right wrist, pulling against her weakening left hand—

A shriek. The kidnapper's hands tore loose, and she swooped upward, her weight lifting from Megan's legs.

Megan stretched her hand toward the vacuum wand but didn't make a quaking effort to stand. At this point, she was more stable on the ground.

An object clunked next to her feet. The knife. The kidnapper skated backward, kicking and thrashing.

Trevor was dragging her.

Relief engulfed Megan, but confusion brought a haze she couldn't disperse. How could Trevor have found her? Was she escaping into fantasy and imagining him while the knife punctured her heart?

Trevor pressed the kidnapper to her knees and bent her arms behind her. She screeched something about Megan causing this, messing things up, her accusation splattered with insults. Trevor dipped his head to her ear level and said, "If you want any of your bones intact, close your mouth."

The kidnapper rotated her face toward Trevor's and went quiet. Did she recognize him, or was the lethal fury in his face sufficient to shut her up?

Trevor focused on Megan, the anger in his face changing to anxiety. "Are you okay? The police are right behind me. I'm so sorry, Meg. I should have been faster, should have known you were in trouble. I shouldn't have left you at all."

He definitely talked like real-life Trevor, blaming himself for not being able to predict all danger and protect her from it. She hadn't whacked her head hard enough to create *this* long of a hallucination. Using her less injured arm, she pushed herself up so she was sitting, at least tentatively. "I'm fine," she croaked. Heels against the floor, she scooted back so she could steady herself against the wall.

Distantly, she heard footsteps on the porch and a yell. "Police!" Footsteps crunched as the officers crossed the broken glass in the living room. Why hadn't she or the kidnapper heard Trevor enter?

Because Megan had been screaming, had felt impelled to scream, even when she didn't think it would help. Her cries had obscured his steps, letting him sneak up on the kidnapper. *"Thank you."* The prayer brushed Megan's chapped lips.

"We're in the hallway!" Trevor shouted. With one hand, he kept the kidnapper's arms pinned while he tore off her ski mask. She was young. Short blonde hair. Bloodied scratches scored her cheek, and a bruise bulged on one cheekbone. Megan had no idea who she was.

"This is Jessica Barnett," Trevor said as two officers approached. "I haven't searched her. I don't know if she's armed."

Jessica Barnett. Megan had heard her name before but couldn't remember the context.

Two more officers entered the hallway. "I don't think anyone else is in the house," Megan rasped. "There were two kidnappers. The other is male and tall, but I haven't seen him here. This isn't where they were holding me. That was the next house, the one in that direction." She lifted her hand. Disoriented, she couldn't decide which way to point.

"We know where the house is," Trevor said. "I followed your footprints here." He waited until two officers flanked Jessica before he released her. Another officer moved carefully past the splintered door to search the study; the last headed toward the kitchen.

Trevor knelt next to Megan. She tilted toward him, crumpling into his arms.

"I . . . think I owe the homeowners a lot of repair money," she said.

Trevor placed his hand on her cheek, his fingers light. "Are you sure you're all right?"

"Yes." She would have lifted her head and kissed him, but she'd depleted all her strength. Slack against him, her head on his shoulder, she closed her eyes.

"I love you," he said.

"Love you too." With Trevor's arms shielding her, she rested.

# Chapter 30

*Five Months Later*

A TENDRIL OF HAIR WAFTED across Megan's face and clung to her lipstick. She pivoted so the summer evening breeze could nudge the hair loose. Letting nature do the job was safer than touching her hair or her makeup and getting reprimanded by Rachel, who was walking toward her. If Rachel hadn't been watching, Megan might have yielded to the urge to once again finger the loops and miniature white roses of her up-do.

"I thought you two might need refueling." Rachel offered glasses of punch.

"Thanks." Megan took one of the glasses; Trevor took the other. "You did a beautiful job, Rach. Thank you for everything."

"Loved every minute of it. I *so* adore your dress. It's perfect for you. That lace!"

Megan lifted the overskirt away from the white satin beneath to highlight the pattern of the lace. "Thank you."

"I've already recommended your dress designer to, like, a dozen other clients. I should take your mom to lunch to thank her for finding him for me. Oops, that garland is coming loose." Rachel hurried toward the garland of lavender roses, greenery, and white lights that decorated the railing of the Drakes' two-tiered patio.

"I'm disappointed she let that segment of garland droop three microns lower than the rest of it," Trevor said as Rachel adjusted the already flawless garland. "Let's demand our money back."

Megan laughed and handed her glass to the teenage girl who came to retrieve it. Despite Rachel's wedding-planner friend who was here supervising things so Rachel could be with her family, Rachel got restless whenever she tried to stand and chat. She kept swishing off to consult with the caterers or give unneeded instructions to the group of Drake cousins clearing glasses and plates off tables. Megan had tried several times to tell her to relax but had finally given up. Rachel obviously relished ensuring there were no glitches tonight.

A friend of Trevor's approached. While the two men reminisced about high school robotics competitions, Megan's thoughts meandered to the garland Rachel had tinkered with.

She couldn't care less if the garland came unwound or soiled dishes sat too long on a table. The glitch she had worried about hadn't happened. She looked at Pamela, standing near Sandra and Michael, smiling and talking with an elderly man wearing a Red Sox tie. Throughout the day, her mother had been gracious. No complaints about not being able to witness the temple sealing, no snippy remarks about how you'd think the Drakes would have provided a sit-down, lobster-and-filet-mignon dinner for their guests instead of a buffet in their backyard, no drama to elbow herself into the spotlight.

Over the spring and summer, the precipitous, rocky trail she and Pamela had staggered up in the weeks before and after her kidnapping began to even out. With dogged effort, with professional guidance, with each of them respecting that the other didn't want their relationship to fall apart, they made progress. The path remained steep, but it was smoother and marked clearly. Megan hadn't felt this comfortable with her mother since childhood. There were occasional episodes of skidding backward, but even when Pamela backslid, she tried not to criticize Trevor. "I'm glad you found a good man, dear. Your father would adore him."

Was her father here tonight? He must be. She wished she could see him. *I love you, Dad.*

A woman approached. Trevor was still laughing with his friend about a malfunctioning robot with a winking blue eye, so Megan made a solo turn toward the new guest.

Adrianne walked with a cautious gait, steadying herself with a cane. She stopped in front of Megan and smiled. "Congratulations."

"Thank you." Megan embraced her. "You look fantastic." Adrianne wore a coral-colored wrap dress, and her short blonde hair, growing back after her injuries and the multiple surgeries she'd undergone throughout the winter, looked so classy that Megan wondered if she would decide to keep it short.

"Aren't I supposed to be complimenting the bride, not the bride complimenting me?" Adrianne asked.

"I didn't know there were rules about that. Don't tell Rachel I blew it."

Adrianne laughed. "You look gorgeous," she said. She glanced at Trevor. "I'm happy for both of you."

"Thank you. How are you doing?"

"Very well." Adrianne tapped her cane against the patio. "I'm still having trouble with balance, obviously, but I'm thankful I've progressed to where a cane is enough. My doctor thinks I'll get to where I don't even need the cane."

"That's great news."

"I suspect he's astounded that I'm alive, let alone making this much progress. I've started working again, doing bookkeeping for my parents. They're patient bosses. I still have memory and focus issues, but it's rejuvenating to be more active."

"That's wonderful. Will you eventually go back to property management?"

"I doubt it. It wasn't my favorite job even before I met Sabrina. So you two decided to stay in Britteridge? I heard you were talking about moving."

"We talked about it," Megan said. "A lot of discussion and prayer."

"Wondering if it would be emotionally easier to go somewhere else? Fresh start?"

"Yes. But we decided we don't want to leave. We love it here, and Trevor loves his job. He thrives on bringing new students to Britt, helping them succeed, helping Britt grow—he's as dedicated to that place as his father is. I want to graduate here, and we enjoy being near his family."

Adrianne glanced behind her, probably checking to see if other guests were waiting to talk to Megan. None were; it was late in the reception, and rush hour had ended. "And Noah Sahlberg is in prison, and Jessica Barnett is locked up, waiting for her trial, so they aren't a danger," Adrianne said quietly. "But I shouldn't bring that up on your wedding day."

Megan touched Adrianne's arm. "If you can talk about it, so can I."

"I have no problem talking about it. It happened; I'm dealing with it. I'm just glad the police and the courts are making progress sorting out the truth." Adrianne gestured toward the table where Bryce sat, picking a strawberry off his plate with a toothpick and talking to Trevor's older brother, Evan. "It could have been a catastrophe for him."

"Yes." Megan watched Bryce laughing and spearing a piece of shrimp. He'd been willing to get crushed by Jessica's set-up, if that was the cost of refusing to yield to blackmail.

If that was the cost of warning Trevor in time to save Megan's life.

Bryce's gaze shifted in Megan's direction. He glanced from her to Adrianne, leaned toward Evan and spoke, then rose to his feet.

"We got caught gawking," Adrianne remarked as Bryce headed in their direction. "Good. I'm interested to meet him. How's he doing?"

"Very well. He started taking classes at Britt this summer. He works grounds crew there."

"What does he want to study?"

"Landscape architecture, ultimately. He's focusing on GE right now."

Bryce reached them. "Hey." He held out his hand and smiled. "You're Adrianne Mullins. I'm Bryce Ludlum."

Adrianne switched her cane to her left hand and shook Bryce's hand. "I recognized you," she said. "Same way you recognized me, I guess."

"Yeah, wow, fame is awesome, right? I always stare at the candy when I go through checkout lines so I won't risk seeing myself on a tabloid cover."

Adrianne smiled. "By the time I was well enough to go through checkout lines, the tabloids were bored with me, thank goodness."

"Too bad you missed experiencing your fifteen minutes of fame," Bryce said. "If you want a substitute for the fun you missed, get food poisoning and then slam your hand in a door."

"Thanks for the tip."

"Are you doing all right?" Bryce asked. "Man, I feel like I should apologize for . . . uh, I guess . . . knowing Jessica?"

Adrianne raised her eyebrows.

"Uh . . . for being connected to her and connected to the Drakes so she followed the connection to you?"

"Really?" Adrianne said. "Jessica Barnett tried to use you to get rich, and when I endangered her scheme, she clonked me. None of it's your fault."

Larissa approached, holding hands with her boyfriend, Edmond. Megan couldn't remember his last name; his first name stuck in her brain because it reminded her of *The Count of Monte Cristo*. Adrianne started to step past Megan to make room for new guests but saw it was her sister and stayed in place.

"Is Jessica going to cause trouble for you at her trial?" Adrianne asked Bryce. Larissa released Edmond's hand and advanced so she was shoulder to shoulder with Adrianne, plainly wanting to hear Bryce's answer.

"I'm not worried," Bryce said. "Besides Noah's testimony that they faked the evidence against me, there's a lot of physical evidence that she and Noah were the ones responsible. They didn't have time to get rid of anything before they were arrested, so the police have the, uh, bloodstained clothes they found in Noah's car and in the car Jessica stole. Also, the trash from that dinner where Jessica drugged me, with the drug residue in the bottle."

"I read about that," Larissa said excitedly. "She melted a tiny hole in the bottom of a soda bottle, injected the drug, and resealed it."

He grimaced. "Yeah. And they found a bunch of evidence that she and Noah were behind the harassment of Megan from the beginning. Jessica was using the evidence to blackmail Noah, but now it's evidence against both of them. Dumb guy, thinking he could hire her and control her. He knew Jessica; he should have known she'd eat him alive."

"I'm surprised she decided to go to trial." Megan glided her fingertips over the cream and lavender roses in her bouquet, simultaneously appreciating how beautiful the flowers were and picturing a masked kidnapper with a knife in her hand. Rachel would frown on this discussion, worrying it would tarnish Megan's wedding day, but the memories made Megan *more* grateful to be here. She made eye contact with Bryce, and he smiled—a rueful but tranquil smile.

"Yeah, Noah was a lot smarter to plea bargain," Bryce said. "I figure Jessica will try to convince a jury that the whole shebang was Noah's baby, he's the one who attacked Adrianne, and she got fooled and bullied into helping him."

"She can't spin the fact that she got caught trying to—" Larissa paused and adjusted her mosaic hair clip to catch blonde hairs that had slipped loose.

"Kill me," Megan finished.

"Too bad she's dragging it out," Adrianne said. "Bryce, this is my sister, Larissa, and her friend Edmond Beckford."

"Bryce Ludlum." Bryce shook hands. "Nice to meet you."

"Nice to meet you," Larissa said. "I'd apologize for eavesdropping on your conversation, but come on, how am I supposed to pretend I'm not hungry for the scoop?"

Bryce grinned. "No problem. We're used to being notorious."

Trevor's robotics friend walked away, and Trevor turned to Megan's group. He hugged Adrianne, then Larissa. "Thanks for coming."

Sandra caught sight of the Mullins women and stretched out her arms to them. "Adrianne, Larissa, it's wonderful to see you."

As Bryce stepped back and the Mullinses and Edmond moved toward Sandra, Trevor faced Megan. He enclosed her in his arms and kissed her, a soft, light kiss, but one that continued for so long that Rachel finally poked him and whispered, "For heaven's sake, Trevor!"

Trevor released Megan and stepped back for a moment, then leaned forward again and kissed her cheek, left eyebrow, and forehead. Evan's toddler daughter ran up, screeching with giggles and clutching a rose she must have pilfered from a centerpiece. She tried to hide from her father by wrapping herself in Megan's lacy skirt. Chuckling, Evan apologized and retrieved her.

Trevor's arms circled Megan again. "How are you?"

"Happy." She wanted to elaborate, but it would take countless words to explain her joy, her peace, the strength she saw in his eyes and felt in herself. "Happy," she repeated.

"I know the feeling," he said.

"Grateful," Megan added. "I'm grateful."

Trevor's grasp tightened. He stood immobile, holding her, memories and anxiety revealed in his taut grip.

"Very grateful," Megan said quietly.

His arms loosened, relaxing into a gentle embrace, and his lips pressed tender kisses along her cheek and ear. "I know that feeling too," he whispered.

# About the Author

STEPHANIE BLACK HAS LOVED BOOKS since she was old enough to grab the pages and has enjoyed creating make-believe adventures since she and her sisters were inventing long Barbie games filled with intrigue and danger or running around, pretending to be detectives. She is a four-time Whitney Award winner for Best Mystery/Suspense Novel and a Whitney Award finalist for Best Speculative Novel.

Stephanie was born in Utah and has lived in various places, including Arkansas, Arizona, Massachusetts, and Limerick, Ireland. She currently lives in northern California, plays the violin in a community symphony but never practices enough, and enjoys spending time with her husband, Brian, and their family. She is a fan of dark chocolate, homemade chocolate chip cookies, and putting chocolate chips in banana bread.

Stephanie enjoys hearing from readers. You can contact her via e-mail at info@covenant-lds.com or by mail care of Covenant Communications, 920 E. State Rd., Ste. F, P.O. Box 416, American Fork, UT 84003-0416. Visit her website at www.stephanieblack. net and her author Facebook page at www.facebook.com/ stephanieblackauthor.